D0067935

The
Greatest
Cowboy Stories
Ever Told

Also from The Lyons Press

The Greatest Adventure Stories Ever Told
The Greatest Baseball Stories Ever Told
The Greatest Boxing Stories Ever Told
The Greatest Cat Stories Ever Told
The Greatest Climbing Stories Ever Told
The Greatest Disaster Stories Ever Told
The Greatest Dog Stories Ever Told
The Greatest Escape Stories Ever Told
The Greatest Exploration Stories Ever Told
The Greatest Fishing Stories Ever Told
The Greatest Flying Stories Ever Told
The Greatest Football Stories Ever Told
The Greatest Gambling Stories Ever Told
The Greatest Horse Stories Ever Told
The Greatest Hunting Stories Ever Told
The Greatest Golf Stories Ever Told
The Greatest Romance Stories Ever Told
The Greatest Sailing Stories Ever Told
The Greatest Search and Rescue Stories Ever Told
The Greatest Survival Stories Ever Told
The Greatest Treasure-Hunting Stories Ever Told
The Greatest War Stories Ever Told

The Greatest Cowboy Stories Ever Told

Incredible Tales of the Western Frontier

EDITED BY
STEPHEN BRENNAN

THE LYONS PRESS
Guilford, Connecticut
An imprint of Rowman & Littlefield

Copyright © 2005 by Stephen Brennan

ALL RIGHTS RESERVED. No part of this book may be reproduced or transmitted in any form by any means, electronic or mechanical, including photocopying and recording, or by any information storage and retrieval system, except as may be expressly permitted in writing from the publisher.

The Lyons Press is an imprint of Rowman & Littlefield.

Distributed by NATIONAL BOOK NETWORK

ISBN-10: 1-59228-904-5
ISBN-13: 978-1-59228-904-2

The Library of Congress has previously cataloged an earlier (hardcover) edition.

To Andy

I always rode better'n you,

but you always shot straighter.

Ingram 1045 12117 1378178

Contents

"Ya-hoo!"

Hey, look there, the Cowboy's come to town. The long drive is over and he's been paid off and is looking for a little recreation. Did he check his Colt with the Sheriff? Not likely. But he did see to his horse. Come on now, let's get the children off the street and lock up the women-folk; he's wearing his best new store-bought hat. Did I mention he's got a thirst on him and something a little wild in his eye? Best stay indoors. Damnation! Who in the world does he think he is? Or rather, who is he really? And why has he such a grip on our imaginations?

Native peoples the world over tell stories of a time, early on in their histories, when first they settled their home lands. They call it the *dream-time.* It was said to be a time of great change, when whole peoples moved from place to place and every new thing was named. For Americans, the settling of the West was our dream-time. In that era, that seems not so long past, but is in reality a whole world ago, America grew to become what she is now. This vast migration, with all its attendant suffering and bloodshed and hope, indeed fixed new borders, and named new places, but it also settled so much more than just new territories. In this great epic struggle we also settled on an idea about ourselves, who we are as a people and what it means to be an individual American. This idealization of ourselves finds expression in the stories we tell of that time and those places. It is in a large part of our national mythology, and like any mythology, it is peopled with heros. They were the discoverers, the pioneer settlers, the miners and gamblers and lawmen and horse soldiers, and they were the cowboys.

Especially the cowboy. Of all of them, he is the one we most admire. This may be considered strange because a cowboy is only an ordinary man, doing dangerous, mostly ill-paid work, far from home—if he has any place he can call home. A horse, saddle and sidearms are all he owns. He lives a rough, roof-less existence, on a diet of beans and beef and coffee and tobacco (when he can get the makings.) He's a man without a lot of prospects or he'd be doing something else. His best friend is his horse. What's to admire? Yet he is the one with whom we most identify. And in that sense at least, he is us. Why is this?

Clearly, any attempt to decode the Cowboy Mystique is bound to be ham-handedly simplistic, but we can understand a little of our fascination by comparing our idea of the Cowboy with our idea of ourselves. He's a strong man: look at he life he leads, out in all weathers. He's got no family? We take it as a sign of his independence. He's a free man. Me too. He certainly skilled with his hands, and honest, to a point. Aren't we all? He lives a life full of adventure. We wish. He's a brave man, willing and able to stand up for himself—the equalizer on his hip shows that. He's peaceable enough, but best don't mess with him, don't cross the line. There's always something a little shaded, a little dark-sided, about a cowboy—something he's hiding. Does he have a secret? Don't we all? On balance, he's a good man. And so we all reckon ourselves to be.

From the beginning advertisers and other promoters of various kinds, have understood our attraction to this common man who is also the mythic hero of our national dream-time. Poor old Tex has been used to sell everything from cigarettes to aftershave, cars, clothes, whatever you like, so long as you project a little of that rugged-American-individual mojo. Even politicians try to employ his image in their cause. Now, real cowboys, on the whole, do not run for office. But pols have always tried to glom a little of the Cowboy luster. Presidents ape his choice in headgear, and some even his rolling walk.

Authors too, fast cottoned on to the idea of the Cowboy story as our story. But since they are themselves the shapers, the fashioners of the legend, it's more complicated. There's more give and take. The first cowboy stories were of the penny-dreadful variety. Written by hacks, they were pulp romances of the lives of noted western heros and villains. These largely invented tales, dressed up as true biographies, flooded the East *and* the West. Often a ranch-hand would get get one as a promotion with his tin of Bull Durham; and this might inspire his own literary effort. Pretty soon there were any number of real cowboys writing Cowboy Stories—Charley Siringo, Andy Adams, and Eugene Rhodes come to mind. At the same time there was an explosion of magazine and newspaper articles by people like Mark Twain and Frederic Remington and William Macleod Raine, all feeding a national hunger for participation, albeit at a remove, in our great national adventure. Crossbreed all this with the strain of (newly matured) outdoor adventure novels by people like Stevenson, Conrad and Crane and by the turn of the century Andy Adams, Owen Wister, Emerson Hough and Zane Grey had invented what we now call the classic Western.

And that was just the beginning. What followed was the popularization in novels, movies, radio and television of more than a new cultural and literary genre; it also created a new American icon, and a distinctly American type. When we look in his eyes we see ourselves.

The Golden Age of the Cowboy, or what has been called the Kingdom of Cattle, lasted, more or less, from the close of the Civil War to the turn of the century. Barbed wire and the iron horse put paid to the free range and the long trail drive just as the coming of the law obviated the need for the rough chivalry of the Code of the West. Except in our imaginations, where we may be said to be most truly ourselves.

Stephen Brennan
New York, 2004

The
Greatest
Cowboy Stories
Ever Told

Life in the Cattle Country

BY FREDERIC REMINGTON

The popular Western novelist Emerson Hough is said to have considered Frederic Remington *the* pictorial arbiter of American West, griping ruefully that if Remington was to insist that out West horses were five-legged, most folks would believe it.

Indeed Remington is so well remembered as the immensely prolific, critically acclaimed painter/sculptor of the old West, that we forget what a really fine writer he was. Though he considered himself to be first an artist, it's worth noting that despite his popular and critical acclaim as painter and sculptor, Remington was never fully accepted by the fine arts establishment. Instead literature claimed him for its own, and in his lifetime he was considered to share the stage equally with giants like Twain, Irving, Longfellow and Cooper.

In his short career he wrote 111 stories and articles for the best magazines of the day: *Century, Harper's Weekly, Harper's Monthly, Outing, Cosmopolitan,* and *Collier's.* His writing style is colorful, but clear and direct, in the manner of a dispatch, without any gee-gaws or fancy capers. One critic called it "a sculptor's prose, terse with its bones showing."

"Life in the Cattle Country" was first published in November of 1899, in *Collier's* magazine.

★   ★   ★   ★   ★

The "cattle country" of the West comprises the semi-arid belt lying between the Rocky Mountains and the arable lands of the Missouri and Mississippi Rivers, and extending from Mexico to British America. The name has been given it not because there are more cattle there than elsewhere, but because the land in its present condition is fit for little or nothing but stock raising. One who for the first time traverses the territory known abroad for its cattle, naturally expects to find the broad plains dotted with browsing herds standing knee-deep in

1

lush pasturage; but, in fact, if he travels in the summer season, he sees the brown earth showing through a sparse covering of herbage equally brown, while he may go many miles before he comes upon a straggling bunch of gaunt, long-horned steers picking gingerly at the dry vegetation. In the humid farming regions, where corn and tame grasses can be grown for feeding, the amount of land necessary for the support of a cow is small; but upon the great plains, which lie desolate and practically dead for half the year, the conservative stockman finds it necessary to allow twenty or thirty acres for each head of his herd. No grain is raised there, and none is fed save in great emergency; the only food for the cattle is the wild grass native to the plains. This grass makes its growth in the spring; and when the rains of spring cease it is cured where it stands by the glowing sunlight. This natural hay is scant at the best, and gives little promise to the unpracticed eye; but it is in fact very nutritious, and range cattle will thrive and fatten upon it. Every aspect of the plains suggests the necessity for avoiding the danger of overstocking; the allowance of twenty-five acres for each animal is not extravagant.

For a long time the cattle country of the Northwest was a mere stretch of wild land, wholly unbroken by fences; then the herds ranged freely under semi-occasional oversight from their owners. In that time the "cow-boy" of song and story was in his element. A gradual change has come over that old-time freedom; for where once the land was the property of the Federal government, and open to all who chose to make legitimate use of it, of late years the owners of the herds—the "cattle kings"—have acquired title to their lands, and the individual ranch has taken the place of Nature's range. Railway lines have multiplied; and with individual ownership of land has come the wire fence to mark the bounds of each man's possessions. To the wire fence more than to any other cause is due the passing of the traditional "cow-boy." Of course the fencing of the ranges is not yet universal; but every year sees a nearer approach to that end.

In former time the "round-up" was of much more importance than it is to-day; for with nothing to hinder, the cattle belonging to many owners would mix and mingle intimately, and the process of rounding up was the only method of separating them and establishing ownership. It is altogether likely the people of the next generation will see nothing of this picturesque and interesting activity.

In the cattle lands of the North, the work of rounding up begins so soon as spring is well established. During the winter the herds have been suffered to range freely, and in hard winters will often be found to have drifted far from home. The spring round-up in Nebraska and Dakota begins late in April or in May, and has for its purpose the assembling of the herds which belong to the several ranches of a neighborhood, the separation of each man's cattle from the mass, the branding of calves, etc., and the return of each herd to its own range, where the beef animals are to be put in condition for market, pending the summer and fall round-up. Cattle growers' associations have been formed in the Western States, and when the season opens each association designates the times when the several ranges within its jurisdiction shall round up their cattle, and these times are sought to be arranged that when the first round-up is completed, say in District No. 1, District No. 2, which lies adjoining, will take up the work where No. 1 left off, and No. 3 will follow No. 2 in like manner; and in this way the round-up in the entire State consists not so much of a broken series of drives as of one long drive, with the result that practically every head of stock is discovered, identified and claimed by its owner.

Once the date is fixed for the round-up in a given district, the semi-quiescence of the winter gives instant place to hurry, bustle and strenuous activity. The "cow-ponies" which are to be ridden by the men have been upon the range through the winter, and these must be gathered up and put in condition for riding—often a task of no small difficulty, for after their winter's freedom they are not infrequently so wild as to require to be broken anew to the saddle. But, as Kipling is so fond of saying, that is another story.

The "riders" of the round-up—the men upon whom devolves the actual labor of handling the cattle—rely very greatly upon their saddle ponies. These must necessarily be trained to the work which they are to perform, and know not only the ways of men, but also the more erratic ways of the light-headed steers and cows. Ponies untrained to their duties would make endless trouble, to say nothing of greatly endangering the lives of the men. Each rider takes with him upon the round-up his own "string," consisting of ten or a dozen ponies, which are to be used in turn, so as to insure having a fresh, strong animal in instant readiness for the emergencies which are always arising, but which can never be foretold. Cow-ponies are seldom entirely trustworthy in the matter of habits and temper; but they are stout-hearted, sure-footed little beasts, who know how to keep faith in the crises of driving and "cutting out."

Besides the personal equipment of each man, the ranch sends with the party a general outfit, the principal item of which is a strong and heavy four-horse wagon, carrying bedding, food, cooking utensils, etc., and with this wagon is the man in the hollow of whose skilful hand lies the comfort and welfare of every man on the round-up—that is to say, the camp cook. Nowhere is a good cook more appreciated than in those waste places of the West. The bill of fare for the party on round-up duty is not of very great variety; the inevitable beans, salt pork, canned goods, bread and coffee make the sum total of what the men may expect to eat.

It is of great importance that this food should be well and palatably cooked; and quite independent of his abstract skill, it is always possible for the genius presiding over frying-pan and coffee-pot to make life endurable for men situated as these are. Each ranch which takes part in the round-up sends such an outfit with the men who are delegated to represent it and look after its interests, so that when the camp is pitched upon the plains it presents a very bustling and business-like appearance.

The round-up is under the direct charge of one man, known as the captain, who is sometimes selected by the association at the time of appointing the meeting, and is sometimes chosen by the ranchmen themselves when the party assembles for its work. For the time being the authority of the captain is as nearly absolute as one man's authority can be over American citizens. Violations of his orders are punishable in most cases by the assessment of arbitrary fines; but recourse is not often had to this penalty, for as a rule the men know what is expected of them, and take keen pride in doing their work well. The captain has a lieutenant chosen from the representatives of each ranch taking part in the round-up. Thus officered the force of men is ready for its work.

At the appointed time the delegates from the several ranches come straggling to the place of meeting. There is usually some delay in beginning the work, and while the captain and his aids are planning the details, the riders are wont to engage in a variety of activities, some serious, some designed for amusement—breaking unruly ponies, racing, trading, card-playing, and whatever occurs by way of passing the time. This is all put aside, however, when work actually begins; for the round-up is earnest.

With the opening of spring, when the snows have disappeared from the plains, the cattle will naturally have sought the grazing lands in the neighborhood of the water-courses; therefore, as a rule, the line travelled by the round-up lies along the valley of a small stream, extending back so far as may be necessary upon either hand.

The men are awakened in the morning long before daylight. They have probably slept on the ground, rolled in blankets and with saddles or boots for pillows. Toilets are hurriedly made, for tardiness is not tolerated. The camp breakfast is gulped down in the dark, and every man must be instantly ready to mount when the summons comes. A force of twenty or thirty men is chosen for the day's riding, and this force is divided into two parties, one of which is to cover the territory to the right and the other to the left of the line of the riders' march. For the most part, the land which borders the streams of the far Northwest is broken, rocky and ragged, and to ride a horse over it is certainly not a pleasure trip, to say nothing of the necessity for looking out sharply for straggling bunches of cattle, gathering them up and driving them forward; for range cattle are wild as deer and perverse as swine.

So soon as possible the night's camp is struck and the wagons move forward for five miles or so, where the riders are to assemble after the morning's work. The two parties of riders then strike off in opposite directions, those in each party gradually drawing further and further apart, until the dozen men form a line ten or fifteen miles in length, extending from the site of the night's camp back to the foothills bordering the stream; and then this line, with its members a mile or so apart, moves forward in the direction of the new camp, searching every nook and cranny among the rocks and hills for wandering bunches of grazing cattle. These must be assembled and driven to camp. The man on the inner end of the line keeps close to the stream, riding straight forward, while he at the other end will have to ride for perhaps thirty or forty miles, making a long circling sweep to the hills and then back to the stream. This ride is hard and often perilous, for the land is much broken and cut up by ravines and precipitous "buttes." The half-wild cattle will climb everywhere, and wherever they go the ponies must follow. It may be that in the course of the morning's drive the riders will gather many hundreds or perhaps thousands of cattle; or it is possible that no more than a score or two will be found. At any rate, the drive is carried forward with the intention of reaching camp about midday. Dinner is eaten with a ravenous appetite, but with scant ceremony, and there is no allowance of time for an after-dinner nap, for the herd gathered in the morning must be sorted over and the animals given to their several owners. This is the most trying work of the round-up. It requires clean, strong courage to ride a pony of uncertain temper into the heart of a herd of several hundred or thousand wild cattle which are wrought up, as these are, to a pitch of high nervous excitement; but there is no other recourse.

Each ranch has its individual mark or brand, which is put upon its animals—sometimes a letter or combination of letters, and sometimes a geometrical figure.

The brands are protected by State law, somewhat after the fashion of a copyright, and each is the absolute property of the ranch which uses it. The ranches are commonly known among the cattlemen of the neighborhood by the name of the brand which they use—as "Circle-Bar Ranch," "Lazy L Ranch," etc. A lazy L is an L lying upon its side. In the work of "cutting out," a delegate from a ranch rides into the herd gathered in the morning, singles out one at a time those cattle bearing his ranch's brand, and slowly urges them to the edge of the mass, where they are taken in charge by other riders and kept together in a bunch. Great vigilance is necessary in holding out these separated bunches, for they are constantly striving to return to the main herd. The ponies used in cutting out must be the best, thoroughly broken to the work, and wise as serpents; for in case of some maddened cow or steer forming a sudden disposition to charge, the life of the rider often depends upon the willingness and cool adroitness of his pony in getting out of the way.

Once the herd is apportioned to its owners, there remains the labor of branding. Calves with their mothers are easily identified; but there will always be found some mature animals which have escaped the branding-iron in former round-ups, and which are known as mavericks. It may be imagined that the burning of a brand upon the shoulder, flank or side of a lusty two-year-old bull is fraught with considerable excitement. To do this, it is first necessary that the animal be "roped," or lariated, and thrown down. The skill of men trained to handle the rope is really admirable, and it may be remarked in passing that an expert roper is always in demand. The wildly excited steer or bull will be in full flight over the prairie, diving, dodging, plunging this way and that to escape from the inevitable noose swinging over the head of the shrill-yelling rider in pursuit. The greatest skill lies in throwing the noose so that it will settle upon the ground in such wise as to catch the fore or hind legs of the galloping beast; this is the pride of the adept roper. To throw the noose over the head or horns is a trick held in slight esteem. When the noose has settled to its place, the rider gives to his pony a well-understood signal, and the willing beast settles himself for the shock to come when the captive brings up at the end of the taut rope. The pony goes back upon his haunches, the man takes a few turns with the rope around the high horn of his saddle; then with a jerk and a jar the helpless victim throws a furious summersault, and after that there is nothing for it but to submit to fate. A second rider throws his lariat over the other pair of struggling legs, and with the brute thus pinioned the hot branding-iron is set against his side. Where the iron has touched, the hair may grow no more; or if it grows, it will be so discolored as to leave the brand easily recognizable. When the ropes are loosed the fun is fast; for the infuriated animal seeks vengeance, and will charge blindly at any moving thing with sight. The branding of calves is not child's play, but it is tame as compared with the work upon grown animals.

The work of branding concludes the most serious business of the day, save that the herd requires constant watching throughout the twenty-four hours. When night has fallen and the herd has lain down, riders are detailed to circle continually about to guard against the ever-present danger of a stampede. In the night, cattle will take fright upon very slight alarm, and often quite causelessly. One or two will rise bellowing, and in an instant the entire herd is upon its feet, crazed with fright and desiring nothing but flight. To break a stampede, it is necessary to head off the leaders and turn them back into the herd. If the onward rush can be checked and the herd induced to move around in a circle, the present danger is past; but it is impossible to foretell when another break will occur. The rider who deliberately goes in front of a stampeding herd in the pitchy darkness of a prairie night, thoughtless of everything save his duty, must be a man of fine fibre. And indeed I must say at the last that the "cow-punchers" as a class, maligned and traduced as they have been, possess a quality of sturdy, sterling manhood which would be to the credit of men in any walk of life. The honor of the average "puncher" abides with him continually. He will not lie; he will not steal. He keeps faith with his friends; toward his enemies he bears himself like a man. He has his vices—as who has not?—but I like to speak softly of them when set against his unassailable virtues. I wish that the manhood of the cow-boy might come more into fashion further East.

The Trouble Man

BY EUGENE MANLOVE RHODES

Born in 1869 and raised on the plains of Kansas and Nebraska, in 1881, Eugene Rhodes and his family up-staked and moved to New Mexico. It was the year Pat Garrett nailed Billy the Kid; Gene was twelve. For the next twenty-five years he worked as a cowboy, ranch hand, horse-breaker, miner, schoolteacher, blacksmith, homesteader, carpenter and rancher. Finally, after losing his spread to drought, he moved east and began to write.

All his life a compulsive, protean reader, at first Rhodes had little success as a writer. His literary lights were Stevenson, Conrad, Kipling and Crane; but the popular appetite just then, the shout in the street, was for cowboy stories like Wister's western romance, *The Virginian*. Rhodes' work is different, it lacks any appeal to melodrama or to the broad brush of caricature. Instead, in his tales we hear the voice of a man who actually was there, and knows what he's talking about. His descriptions of the land are evocative, but understated, without a hint of purple in them. It is this careful deployment of detail, judicious layering of character, and gently eccentric diologue (an idiom, really, all its own) that make Rhodes's tales at once humorous and gripping. One critic has called him "a conscious and deliberate stylist, an anomaly in his genre." Another considers his stories "the only body of fiction devoted to the cattle kingdom which is both true to it and written by an artist in prose." He has been called the de Maupassant of the Western/Cowboy genre.

★　★　★　★　★

i

Billy Beebe did not understand. There was no disguising the unpalatable fact: Rainbow treated him kindly. It galled him. Ballinger, his junior in Rainbow, was theme for ridicule and biting jest, target for contumely and abuse; while his own best efforts were met with grave, unfailing courtesy.

Yet the boys liked him; Billy was sure of that. And so far as the actual work was concerned, he was at least as good a roper and brand reader as Ballinger, quicker in action, a much better rider.

In irrelevant and extraneous matters—brains, principle, training, acquirements—Billy was conscious of unchallenged advantage. He was from Ohio, eligible to the Presidency, of family, rich, a college man; yet he had abandoned laudable moss-gathering, to become a rolling, bounding, riotous stone. He could not help feeling that it was rather noble of him. And then to be indulgently sheltered as an honored guest, how beloved soever! It hurt.

Not for himself alone was Billy grieved. Men paired on Rainbow. "One stick makes a poor fire"—so their word went. Billy sat at the feet of John Wesley Pringle—wrinkled, wind-brown Gamaliel. Ballinger was the disciple of Jeff Bransford, gay, willful, questionable man. Billy did not like him. His light banter, lapsing unexpectedly from broad Doric to irreproachable New English, carried in solution audacious, glancing disrespect of convention, established institutions, authorities, axioms, "accepted theories of irregular verbs"—too elusive for disproof, too intolerably subversive to be ignored. That Ballinger, his shadow, was accepted man of action, while Billy was still an outsider, was, in some sense, a reflection on Pringle. Vicarious jealousy was added to the pangs of wounded self-love.

Billy was having ample time for reflection now, riding with Pringle up the Long Range to the Block roundup. Through the slow, dreamy days they threaded the mazed ridges and cañons falling eastward to the Pecos from Guadalupe, Sacramento and White Mountain. They drove their string of thirteen horses each; tough circlers, wise cutting-hoses, sedate night horses and patient old Steamboat, who, in the performance of pack duty, dropped his proper designation to be injuriously known as "the Wagon."

Their way lay through the heart of the Lincoln County War country—on winding trails, by glade and pine-clad mesa; by clear streams, bell-tinkling, beginning, with youth's eager haste, their journey to the far-off sea; by Seven Rivers, Bluewater, the Feliz, Penasco and Silver Spring.

Leisurely they rode, with shady halt at midday—leisurely, for an empire was to be worked. It would be months before they crossed the divide at Nogal, "threw in" with Bransford and Ballinger, now representing Rainbow with the Bar W, and drove home together down the west side.

While Billy pondered his problem Pringle sang or whistled tirelessly—old tunes of amazing variety, ranging from Nancy Lee and Auld Robin Gray to La Paloma Azul or the Nogal Waltz. But ever, by ranch house or brook or pass, he paused to tell of deeds there befallen in the years of old war, deeds violent and bloody, yet half redeemed by hardihood and unflinching courage.

Pringle's voice was low and unemphatic; his eyes were ever on the long horizon. Trojan nor Tyrian he favored, but as he told the Homeric tale of Buckshot Roberts, while they splashed through the broken waters of Ruidoso and held their winding way through the cutoff of Cedar Creek, Billy began dimly to understand.

Between him and Rainbow the difference was in kind, not in degree. The shadow of old names lay heavy on the land; these resolute ghosts yet shaped the acts of men. For Rainbow the Roman *virtus* was still the one virtue. Whenever these old names had been spoken, Billy remembered, men had listened. Horseshoers had listened at their shoeing; cardplayers had listened while the game went on; by campfires other speakers had ceased their talk to listen without comment. Not ill-doers, these listeners, but quiet men, kindly, generous; yet the tales to which they gave this tribute were too often of ill deeds. As if they asked not "Was this well done?" but rather "Was this done indeed—so that no man could have done more?" Were the deed good or evil, so it were done utterly it commanded admiration—therefore, imitation.

Something of all this he got into words. Pringle nodded gravely. "You've got it sized up, my son," he said. "Rainbow ain't strictly up to date and still holds to them elder ethics, like Norval on the Grampian Hills, William Dhu Tell, and the rest of them neck-or-nothing boys. This Mr. Rolando, that Eusebio sings about, give our sentiments to a T-Y-ty. He was scrappy and always blowin' his own horn, but, by jings, he delivered the goods as per invoice and could take a major league lickin' with no whimperin'. This Rolando he don't hold forth about gate money or individual percentages. 'Get results for your team,' he says. 'Don't flinch, don't foul, hit the line hard, here goes nothin!'

"That's a purty fair code. And it's all the one we got. Pioneerin' is troublesome—pioneer is all the same word as pawn, and you throw away a pawn to gain a point. When we drive in a wild bunch, when we top off the boundin' bronco, it may look easy, but it's always a close thing. Even when we win we nearly lose; when we lose we nearly win. And that forms the stay-with-it-Bill-you're doin'-well habit. See?

"So, we mostly size a fellow up by his abilities as a trouble man. Any kind of trouble—not necessarily the fightin' kind. If he goes the route, if he sets no limit, if he's enlisted for the war—why, you naturally depend on him.

"Now, take you and Jeff. Most ways you've got the edge on him. But you hold by rules and formulas and laws. There's things you must do or mustn't do—because somebody told you so. You go into a project with a mental reservation not to do anything indecorous or improper; also, to stop when you've taken a decent lickin'. But Jeff don't aim to stop while he can wiggle; and he makes up new rules as he goes along, to fit the situation. Naturally, when you get in a tight place you waste time rememberin' what the authorities prescribe as the neat thing. Now, Jeff consults only his own self, and he's mostly unanimous. Mebbe so you both do the same thing, mebbe not. But Jeff does it first. You're a good boy, Billy, but there's only one way to find out if you're a square peg or a round one."

"How's that?" demanded Billy, laughing, but half vexed.

"Get in the hole," said Pringle.

ii

"Aw, stay all night! What's the matter with you fellows? I haven't seen a soul for a week. Everybody's gone to the round-up."

Wes' shook his head: "Can't do it, Jimmy. Got to go out to good grass. You're all eat out here."

"I'll side you," said Jimmy decisively. "I got a lot of stored-up talk I've got to get out of my system. I know a bully place to make camp. Box cañon to hobble your horses in, good grass, and a little tank of water in the rocks for cookin'. Bring along your little old Wagon, and I'll tie on a hunk of venison to feed your faces with. Get there by dark."

"How come you didn't go to the work your black self?" asked Wes', as Beebe tossed his rope on the Wagon and led him up.

Jimmy's twinkling eyes lit up his beardless face. "They left me here to play shinny-on-your-own-side," he explained.

"Shinny?" echoed Billy.

"With the Three Rivers sheep," said Jimmy. "I'm to keep them from crossing the mountain."

"Oh, I see. You've got an agreement that the east side is for cattle and the west side for sheep."

Jimmy's face puckered. "Agreement? H'm yes, leastways, I'm agreed. I didn't ask them, but they've got the general idea. When I ketch 'em over here I drive them back. As I don't ever follow 'em beyond the summit they ought to savvy my the'ries by this time."

Pringle opened the gate. "Let's mosey along—they've got enough water. Which way, kid?"

"Left-hand trail," said Jimmy, falling in behind.

"But why don't you come to an understanding with them and fix on a dividing line?" insisted Beebe.

Jimmy lolled sidewise in his saddle, cocking an impish eye at his inquisitor. "Reckon ye don't have no sheep down Rainbow way? Thought not. Right there's the point exactly. They have a dividing line. They carry it with 'em wherever they go. For the cattle won't graze where sheep have been. Sheep pertects their own range, but we've got to look after ours or they'd drive us out. But the understanding's all right, all right. They don't speak no English, and I don't know no *paisano* talk, but I've fixed up a signal code they savvy as well's if they was all college aluminums."

"Oh, yes—sign talk," said Billy. "I've heard of that." Wes' turned his head aside.

"We-ell, not exactly. Sound talk'd be nearer. One shot means 'Git!' two means 'Hurry up!' and three—"

"But you've no right to do that," protested Billy warmly. "They've got just as much right here as your cattle, haven't they?"

"Surest thing they have—if they can make it stick," agreed Jimmy cordially. "And we've got just as much right to keep 'em off if we can. And we can. There ain't really no right to it. It's Uncle Sam's land we both graze on, and Unkie is some busy with conversation on natural resources, and keepin' republics up in South America and down in Asia, and selectin' texts for coins and infernal revenue stamps, and upbuildin' Pittsburgh, and keepin' up the price of wool, and fightin' all the time to keep the laws from bein' better'n the Constitution, like a Bawston puncher trimmin' a growin' colt's foot down to fit last year's shoes. Shucks! *He* ain't got no time to look after us. We just got to do our own regulatin' or git out."

"How would you like it yourself?" demanded Billy.

Jimmy's eyes flashed. "If my brain was to leak out and I subsequent took to sheep-herdin', I'd like to see any dern puncher drive me out," he declared belligerently.

"Then you can't complain if—"

"He don't," interrupted Pringle. "None of us complain—nary a murmur. If the sheep men want to go they go, an' a little shootin' up the contagious vicinity don't hurt 'em none. It's all over oncet the noise stops. Besides, I think they mostly sorter enjoy it. Sheepherdin' is might dull business, and a little excitement is mighty welcome. It gives 'em something to look forward to. But if they feel hostile they always get the first shot for keeps. That's a mighty big percentage in their favor, and the reports on file with the War Department shows that they generally get the best of it. Don't you worry none, my son. This ain't no new thing. It's been goin' on ever since Abraham's outfit and the L O T boys got to scrappin' on the Jordan range, and then some before that. After Abraham took to the hill country, I remember, somebody jumped one of his wells and two of Isaac's. It's been like that, in the shortgrass countries ever since. Human nature's not changed much. By jings! There they be now!"

Through the twilight the winding trail climbed the side of a long ridge. To their left was a deep, impassable cañon; beyond that a parallel ridge; and from beyond that ridge came the throbbing, drumming clamor of a sheep herd.

"The son of a gun!" said Jimmy. "He means to camp in our box cañon. I'll show him!" He spurred by the grazing horses and clattered on in the lead, striking fire from the stony trail.

On the shoulder of the further ridge heaved a gray fog, spreading, rolling slowly down the hillside. The bleating, the sound of myriad trampling feet, the multiplication of bewildering echoes, swelled to a steady, unchanging, ubiquitous tumult. A dog suddenly topped the ridge; another; then a Mexican herder bearing a long rifle. With one glance at Jimmy beyond the blackshadowed gulf he began turning the herd back, shouting to the dogs. They ran in obedient haste to aid, sending the stragglers scurrying after the main bunch.

Jimmy reined up, black and gigantic against the skyline. He drew his gun. Once, twice, thrice, he shot. The fire streamed out against the growing dark. The bullets, striking the rocks, whined spitefully. The echoes took up the sound and sent it crashing to and fro. The sheep rushed huddling together, panic-stricken. Herder and dogs urged them on. The herder threw up a hand and shouted.

"That boy's shootin' mighty close to that *paisano*," muttered Pringle. "He orter quit now. Reckon he's showin' off a leetle." He raised his voice in warning. "Hi! you Jimmy!" he called. "He's a-goin'! Let him be!"

"*Vamos! Hi-i!*" shrilled Jimmy gayly. He fired again. The Mexican clapped his hand to his leg with an angry scream. With the one movement he sank to his knees, his long rifle fell to a level, cuddled to his shoulder, spitting fire. Jimmy's hand flew up; his gun dropped; he clutched at the saddle-horn, missed it, fell heavily to the ground. The Mexican dropped out of sight behind the ridge. It had been but a scant minute since he first appeared. The dogs followed with the remaining sheep. The ridge was bare. The dark fell fast.

Jimmy lay on his face. Pringle turned him over and opened his shirt.

He was quite dead.

iii

From Malagra to Willow Spring, the next available water, is the longest jump on the Bar W range. Working the "Long Lane" fenced by Malpais and White Mountain is easy enough. But after cutting out and branding there was the long wait for the slow day herd, the tedious holding to water from insufficient troughs. It was late when the day's "cut" was thrown in with the herd, sunset when the bobtail had caught their night horses and relieved the weary day herders.

The bobtail moves the herd to the bed ground—some distance from camp, to avoid mutual annoyance and alarm—and holds it while night horses are caught and supper eaten. A thankless job, missing the nightly joking and banter over the day's work. Then the first guard comes on and the bobtail goes, famished, to supper. It breakfasts by starlight, relieves the last guard, and holds cattle while breakfast is eaten, beds rolled and horses caught, turning them over to the day herders at sunup.

Bransford and Ballinger were two of the five bobtailers, hungry, tired, dusty and cross. With persuasive, soothing song they trotted around the restless cattle, with hasty, envious glances for the merry groups around the chuck wagon. The horse herd was coming in; four of the boys were butchering a yearling; beds were being dragged out and unrolled. Shouts of laughter arose; they were baiting the victim of some mishap by making public an exaggerated version of his discomfiture.

Turning his back on the camp, Jeff Bransford became aware of a man riding a big white horse down the old military road from Nogal way. The horse was trotting, but wearily; passing the herd he whinnied greeting, again wearily.

The cattle were slow to settle down. Jeff made several circlings before he had time for another campward glance. The horse herd was grazing off, and the boys were saddling and staking their night horses; but the stranger's hose, still saddled, was tied to a soapweed.

Jeff sniffed. "Oh, Solomon was sapient and Solomon was wise!" he crooned, keeping time with old Summersault's steady fox-trot. "And Solomon was marvelously wide between the eyes!" He sniffed again, his nose wrinkled, one eyebrow arched, one corner of his mouth pulled down; he twisted his mustache and looked sharply down his nose for consultation, pursing his lips. "H'm! That's funny!" he said aloud. "That horse is some tired. Why don't he turn him loose? Bransford, you old fool, sit up and take notice! 'Eternal vigilance is the price of liberty.' "

He had been a tired and a hungry man. He put his weariness by as a garment, keyed up the slackened strings, and rode on with every faculty on the alert. It is to be feared that Jeff's conscience was not altogether void of offense toward his fellows.

A yearling pushed tentatively from the herd. Jeff let her go, fell in after her and circled her back to the bunch behind Clay Cooper. Not by chance. Clay was from beyond the divide.

"Know the new man, Clay?" Jeff asked casually, as he fell back to preserve the proper interval.

Clay turned his head. "Sure. Clem Littlefield, Bonita man."

When the first guard came at last Jeff was on the farther side and so the last to go in. A dim horseman overtook him and waved a sweeping arm in dismissal.

"We've got 'em! Light a rag, you hungry man!"

Jeff turned back slowly, so meeting all the relieving guard and noting that Squatty Robinson, of the V V, was not of them, Ollie Jackson taking his place.

He rode thoughtfully into camp. Staking his horse in the starlight he observed a significant fact. Squatty had not staked his regular night horse, but Alizan, his favorite. He made a swift investigation and found that not a man from the east had caught his usual night horse. Clay Cooper's horse was not staked, but tied short to a mesquit, with the bridle still on.

Pete Johnson, the foreman, was just leaving the fire for bed. Beyond the fire the east-side men were gathered, speaking in subdued voices. Ballinger, with loaded plate, sat down near them. The talking ceased. It started again at once. This time their voices rose clear and distinct in customary badinage.

"Why, this is face up," thought Jeff. "Trouble. Trouble from beyond the divide. They're going to hike shortly. They've told Pete that much, anyhow. Serious trouble—for they've kept it from the rest of them. Is it to my address? Likely. Old Wes' and Beebe are over there somewhere. If I had three guesses the first two'd be that them Rainbow chasers was in a tight."

He stumbled into the firelight, carrying his bridle, which he dropped by the wagon wheel. "This day's sure flown by like a week," he grumbled, fumbling around for cup and plate. "My stomach was just askin' was my throat cut."

As he bent over to spear a steak the tail of his eye took in the group beyond and intercepted a warning glance from Squatty to the stranger. There was an almost imperceptible thrusting motion of Squatty's chin and lips; a motion which included Jeff and the unconscious Ballinger. It was enough. Surmise, suspicion flamed to certainty. "My third guess," reflected Jeff sagely, "is just like the other two. Mr. John Wesley Pringle has been doing a running high jump or some such stunt, and has plumb neglected to come down."

He seated himself cross-legged and fell upon his supper vigorously, bandying quips and quirks with the bobtail as they ate. At last he jumped up, dropped his dishes clattering in the dishpan, and drew a long breath.

"I don't feel a bit hungry," he announced plaintively. "Gee! I'm glad I don't have to stand guard. I do hate to work between meals."

He shouldered his roll of bedding. "Good-by, old world—I'm going home!" he said, and melted into the darkness. Leo following, they unrolled their bed. But as Leo began pulling off his boots Jeff stopped him.

"Close that aperture in your face and keep it that way," he admonished guardedly. "You and me has got to do a ghost dance. Project around and help me find them Three Rivers men."

The Three Rivers men, Crosby and Os Hyde, were sound asleep. Awakened, they were disposed to peevish remonstrance.

"Keep quiet!" said Jeff, "Al, you slip on your boots and go tell Pete you and Os is goin' to Carrizo and that you'll be back in time to stand your guard. Tell him out loud. Then you come back here and you and Os crawl into our bed. I'll show him where it is while you're gone. You use our night horses. Me and Leo want to take yours."

"If there's anything else don't stand on ceremony," said Crosby. "Don't you want my toothbrush?"

"You hurry up," responded Jeff. "D'ye think I'm doin' this for fun? We're It. We got to prove an alibi."

"Oh!" said Al.

A few minutes later, the Three Rivers men disappeared under the tarp of the Rainbow bed, while the Rainbow men, on Three Rivers horses, rode silently out of camp, avoiding the firelit circle.

Once over the ridge, well out of sight and hearing from camp, Jeff turned up the draw to the right and circled back toward the Nogal road on a long trot.

"Beautiful night," observed Leo after an interval. "I just love to ride. How far is it to the asylum?"

"Leo," said Jeff, "you're a good boy—a mighty good boy. But I don't believe you'd notice it if the sun didn't go down till after dark." He explained the situation. "Now, I'm going to leave you to hold the horses just this side of the Nogal road, while I go on afoot and eavesdrop. Them fellows'll be makin' big medicine when they come along here. I'll lay down by the road and get a line on their play. Don't you let them horses nicker."

Leo waited an interminable time before he heard the eastside men coming from camp. They passed by, talking, as Jeff had prophesied. After another small eternity Jeff joined him.

"I didn't get all the details, he reported. "But it seems that the Parsons City people has got it framed up to hang a sheepman some. Wes' is dead set against it—I didn't make out why. So there's a deadlock and we've got the casting vote. Call up your reserves, old man. We're due to ride around Nogal and beat that bunch to the divide."

It was midnight by the clock in the sky when they stood on Nogal divide. The air was chill. Clouds gathered blackly around Capitan, Nogal Peak and White Mountain. There was steady, low muttering of thunder; the far lightnings flashed pale and green and rose.

"Hustle along to Lincoln, Leo," commanded Jeff, "and tell the sheriff they state, positive, that the hangin' takes place prompt after breakfast. Tell him to bring a posse—and a couple of battleships if he's got 'em handy. Meantime, I'll go over and try what the gentle art of persuasion can do. So long! If I don't come back the mule's yours."

He turned up the right-hand road.

iv

"Well?" said Pringle.

"Light up!" said Uncle Pete. "Nobody's goin' to shoot at ye from the dark. We don't do business that way. When we come we'll come in daylight, down the big middle of the road. Light up. I ain't got no gun. I come over for one last try to make you see reason. I knowed thar weren't use talkin' to you when you was fightin' mad. That's why I got the boys to put it off till mawnin'. And I wanted to send to Angus and Salado and the Bar W for Jimmy's friends. He ain't got no kinnery here. They've come. They all see it the same way. Chavez killed Jimmy, and they're goin' to hang him. And, since they've come, there's too many of us for you to fight."

Wes' lit the candle. "Set down. Talk all you want, but talk low and don't wake Billy," he said as the flame flared up.

That he did not want Billy waked up, that there was not even a passing glance to verify Uncle Pete's statement as to being unarmed, was, considering Uncle Pete's errand and his own position, a complete and voluminous commentary on the men and ethics of that time and place.

Pete Burleson carefully arranged his frame on a bench, and glanced around.

On his cot Billy tossed and moaned. His fevered sleep was tortured by a phantasmagoria of broken and hurried dreams, repeating with monstrous exaggeration the crowded hours of the past day. The brain-stunning shock and horror of sudden, bloody, death, the rude litter, the night-long journey with their awful burden, the doubtful aisles of pine with star 'galazies' wheeling beyond, the gaunt, bare hill above, the steep zigzag to the sleeping town, the flaming wrath of violent men—in his dream they came and went. Again, hasty messengers flashed across the haggard dawn; again, he shared the pursuit and capture of the sheep-herder. Sudden clash of unyielding wills; black anger; wild voices for swift death, quickly backed by wild, strong hands; Pringle's cool and steady defiance; his own hot, resolute protest; the prisoner's unflinching fatalism; the hard-won respite—all these and more—the lights, the swaying crowd, fierce faces black and bitter with inarticulate wrath—jumbled confusedly in shifting, unsequenced combinations leading ever to some incredible, unguessed catastrophe.

Beside him, peacefully asleep, lay the manslayer, so lately snatched from death, unconscious of the chain that bound him, oblivious of the menace of the coming day.

"He takes it pretty hard," observed Uncle Pete, nodding at Billy.

"Yes. He's never seen any sorrow. But he don't weaken one mite. I tried every way I could think of to get him out of here. Told him to sidle off down to Lincoln after the sheriff. But he was dead on to me."

"Yes? Well, he wouldn't 'a' got far, anyway," said Uncle Pete dryly. "We're watching every move. Still, it's pity he didn't try. We'd 'a' got him without hurtin' him, and he'd 'a' been out o' this."

Wes' made no answer. Uncle Pete stroked his grizzled beard reflectively. He filled his pipe with cut plug and puffed deliberately.

"Now, look here," he said slowly: "Mr. Procopio Chavez killed Jimmy, and Mr. Procopio Chavez is going to hang. It wa'n't no weakenin' or doubt on my part that made me call the boys off yesterday evenin'. He's got to hang. I just wanted to keep you fellers from gettin' killed. There might 'a' been some sense in your fighting then, but there ain't now. There's too many of us."

"Me and Billy see the whole thing," said Wes', unmoved. "It was too bad Jimmy got killed, but he was certainly mighty brash. The sheep-herder was goin' peaceable, but Jimmy kept shootin', and shootin' close. When that splinter of rock hit the Mexican man he thought he was shot, and he turned loose. Reckon it hurt him like sin. There's a black-and-blue spot on his leg big as the palm of your hand. You'd 'a' done the same as he did.

"I ain't much enthusiastic about sheep-herders. In fact, I jerked my gun at the time; but I was way down the trail and he was out o' sight before I could shoot. Thinkin' it over careful, I don't see where this Mexican's got any hangin' comin'. You know, just as well as I do, no court's goin' to hang him on the testimony me and Billy's got to give in."

"I do," said Uncle Pete. "That's exactly why we're goin' to hang him ourselves. If we let him go it's just encouragin' the *pastores* to kill up some more of the boys. So we'll just stretch his neck. This is the last friendly warnin', my son. If you stick your fingers between the anvil and the hammer you'll get 'em pinched. 'Tain't any of your business, anyway. This ain't Rainbow. This is the White Mountain and we're strictly home rulers. And, moresoever, that war talk you made yesterday made the boys plumb sore."

"That war talk goes as she lays," said Pringle steadily. "No hangin' till after the shootin'. That goes."

"Now, now—what's the use?" remonstrated Uncle Pete. "Ye'll just get yourself hurted and 'twon't do the greaser any good. You might mebbe so stand us off in a good, thick 'dobe house, but not in this old shanty. If you want to swell up and be stubborn about it, it just means a grave apiece for you all and likely for some few of us."

"It don't make no difference to me," said Pringle, "if it means digin' a grave in a hole in the cellar under the bottomless pit. I'm goin' to make my word good and do what I think's right."

"So am I, by Jupiter! Mr. Also Ran Pringle, it is a privilege to have known you!" Billy, half awake, covered Uncle Pete with a gun held in a steady hand. "Let's keep him here for a hostage and shoot him if they attempt to carry out their lynching," he suggested.

"We can't Billy. Put it down," said Pringle mildly. "He's here under flag of truce."

"I was tryin' to save your derned fool hides," said Uncle Pete benignantly.

"Well—'tain't no use. We're just talkin' round and round in a circle, Uncle Pete. Turn your wolf loose when you get ready. As I said before, I don't noways dote on sheepmen, but I seen this, and I've got to see that this poor devil gets a square deal. I got to!"

Uncle Pete sighed. "It's a pity!" he said; "a great pity! Well, we're comin' quiet and peaceful. If there's any shootin' done you all have got to fire the first shot. We'll have the last one."

"Did you ever stop to think that the Rainbow men may not like this?" inquired Pringle. "If they're anyways dissatisfied they're liable to come up here and scratch your eyes out one by one."

"Jesso. That's why you're goin' to fire the first shot," explained Uncle Pete patiently. "Only for that—and likewise because it would be a sorter mean trick to do—we could get up on the hill and smoke you out with rifles at long range, out o' reach of your six-shooters. You all might get away, but the sheepherder's chained fast and we could shoot him to kingdom come, shack and all, in five minutes. But you've had fair warnin' and you'll get an even break. If you want to begin trouble it's your own lookout. That squares us with Rainbow."

"And you expect them to believe you?" demanded Billy.

"Believe us? Sure! Why shouldn't they!" said Uncle Pete simply. "Of course they'll believe us. It'll be so." He stood up and regarded them wistfully. "There don't seem to be any use o' sayin' any more, so I'll go. I hope there ain't no hard feelin's?"

"Not a bit!" said Pringle; but Billy threw his head back and laughed angrily. "Come, I like that! By Jove, if that isn't nerve for you! To wake a man up and announce that you're coming presently to kill him, and then expect to part the best of friends!"

"Ain't I doin' the friendly part?" demanded Uncle Pete stiffly. He was both nettled and hurt. "If I hadn't thought well of you fellers and done all I could for you, you'd 'a' been dead and done forgot about it by now. I give you all credit for doin' what you think is right, and you might do as much for me."

"Great Caesar's ghost! Do you want us to wish you good luck?" said Billy, exasperated almost to tears. "Have it your own way, by all means—you gentle-hearted old assassin! For my part, I'm going to do my level best to shoot you right between the eyes, but there won't be any hard feeling about it. I'll just be dong what I think is right—a duty I owe to the world. Say! I should think a gentleman of your sportsmanlike instincts would send over a gun for our prisoner. Twenty to one is big odds."

"Twenty to one is a purty good reason why you could surrender without no disgrace," rejoined Uncle Pete earnestly. "You can't make nothin' by fightin', cause you lose your point, anyway. And then, a majority of twenty to one—ain't that a good proof that you're wrong?"

"Now, Billy, you can't get around that. That's your own argument," cried Pringle, delighted. "You've stuck to it right along that you Republicans was dead right because you always get seven votes to our six. *Nux vomica*, you know."

Uncle Pete rose with some haste. "Here's where I go. I never could talk politics without gettin' mad," he said.

"Billy, you're certainly making good. You're a square peg. All the same, I wish," said Wes' Pringle plaintively, as Uncle Pete crunched heavily through the gravel, "that I could hear my favorite tune now."

Billy stared at him. "Does your mind hurt your head?" he asked solicitously.

"No, no—I'm not joking. It would do me good if I could only hear him sing it."

"Hear who sing what?"

"Why, hear Jeff Bransford sing The Little Eohippus—right now. Jeff's got the knack of doing the wrong thing at the right time. Hark! What's that?"

It was a firm footstep at the door, a serene voice low chanting:
"There was once a little animal
No bigger than a fox,
And on five toes he scampered—"
"Good Lord!" said Billy. "It's the man himself."

Questionable Bransford stepped through the half-open door, closed it and set his back to it.

"That's my cue! Who was it said eavesdroppers never heard good of themselves?"

V

He was smiling, his step was light, his tones were cheerful, ringing. His eyes had looked on evil and terrible things. In this desperate pass they wrinkled to pleasant, sunny warmth. He was unhurried, collected, confident. Billy found himself wondering how he had found this man loud, arbitrary, distasteful.

Welcome, question, answer; daybreak paled the ineffectual candle. The Mexican still slept.

"I crawled around the opposition camp like a snake in the grass," said Jeff. "There's two things I observed there that's mightily in our favor. The first thing is, there's no whisky goin'. And the reason for that is the second thing—our one best big chance. Mister Burleson won't let 'em. Fact! Pretty much the entire population of the Pecos and tributary streams had arrived. Them that I know are mostly bad actors, and the ones I don't know looked real horrid to me; but your Uncle Pete is the bell mare. 'No booze!' he says, liftin' one finger; and that settled it. I reckon that when Uncle Simon Peter says 'Thumbs up!' those digits'll be elevated accordingly. If I can get him to see the gate the rest will only need a little gentle persuasion."

"I see you persuading them now," said Billy. "This is a plain case of the irresistible force and the immovable body."

"You will," said Jeff confidently. "You don't know what a jollier I am when I get down to it. Watch me! I'll show you a regular triumph of mind over matter."

"They're coming now," announced Wes' placidly. "Two by two, like the animals out o' the ark. I'm glad of it. I never was good at waitin'. Mr. Bransford will now oblige with his monologue entitled 'Givin' a bull the stop signal with a red flag.' Ladies will kindly remove their hats."

It was a grim and silent cavalcade. Uncle Pete rode at the head. As they turned the corner Jeff walked briskly down the path, hopped lightly on the fence, seated himself on the gatepost and waved an amiable hand.

"Stop, look, and listen!" said this cheerful apparition.

The procession stopped. A murmur, originating from the Bar W contingent, ran down the ranks. Uncle Pete reined up and demanded of him with marked disfavor: "Who in merry hell are you?"

Jeff's teeth flashed white under his brown moustache. "I'm Ali Baba," he said, and paused expectantly. But the allusion was wasted on Uncle Pete. Seeing that no introduction was forthcoming, Jeff went on:

"I've been laboring with my friends inside, and I've got a proposition to make. As I told Pringle just now, I don't see any sense of us gettin' killed, and killin' a lot of you won't bring us alive again. We'd put up a pretty fight—a very pretty fight. But you'd lay us out sooner or later. So what's the use?"

"I'm mighty glad to see some one with a leetle old horse-sense," said Uncle Pete. "Your friends is dead game sports all right, but they got mighty little judgment. If they'd only been a few of us I wouldn't 'a' blamed 'em a mite for not givin' up. But we got too much odds of 'em."

"This conversation is taking an unexpected turn," said Jeff, making his eyes round. "I ain't named giving up that I remember of. What I want to do is to rig up a compromise."

"If there's any halfway place between a hung Mexican and a live one," said Uncle Pete, "mebbe we can. And if not, not. This ain't no time for triflin', young fellow."

"Oh, shucks! I can think of half a dozen compromises," said Jeff blandly. "We might play seven-up and not count any turned-up jacks. But I was thinking of something different. I realize that you outnumber us, so I'll meet you a good deal more than half way. First, I want to show you something about my gun. Don't anybody shoot, 'cause I ain't going to. Hope I may die if I do!"

"You will if you do. Don't worry about that," said Uncle Pete. "And maybe so, anyhow. You're delayin' the game."

Jeff took this for permission. "Everybody please watch and see there is no deception."

Holding the gun, muzzle up, so all could see, he deliberately extracted all the cartridges but one. The audience exchanged puzzled looks.

Jeff twirled the cylinder and returned the gun to its scabbard. "Now!" he said, sparkling with enthusiasm. "You all see that I've only got one cartridge. I'm in no position to fight. If there's any fighting I'm already dead. What happens to me has no bearing on the discussion. I'm out of it.

"I realize that there's no use trying to intimidate you fellows. Any of you would take a big chance with odds against you, and here the odds is for you. So, as far as I'm concerned, I substitute a certainty for chance. I don't want to kill up a lot of rank strangers—or friends, either. There's nothing in it.

"Neither can I go back on old Wes' and Billy. So I take a half-way course. Just to manifest my entire disapproval, if any one makes a move to go through that gate I'll use my one shot—and it won't be on the man goin' through the gate, either. Nor yet on you, Uncle Pete. You're the leader. So, if you want to give the word, go it! I'm not going to shoot you. Nor I ain't going to shoot any of the Bar W push. They're free to start the ball rolling."

Uncle Pete, thus deprived of the initiatory power, looked helplessly around the Bar W push for confirmation. They nodded in concert. "He'll do whatever he says," said Clay Cooper.

"Thanks," said Jeff pleasantly, "for this unsolicited testimonial. Now, boys, there's no dare about this. Just cause and effect. All of you are plumb safe to make a break—but one. To show you that there's nothing personal about it, no dislike or anything like that, I'll tell you how I picked that one. I started at some place near both ends or the middle and counted backward, or forward, sayin' to myself, 'Intra, mintra, cutra, corn, apple seed and brier thorn,' and when I got to 'thorn' that man was stuck. That's all. Them's the rules.'"

That part of Uncle Pete's face visible between beard and hat was purple through the brown. He glared at Jeff, opened his mouth, shut it tightly, and breathed heavily through his nose. He looked at his horse's ears, he looked at the low sun, he looked at the distant hills; his gaze wondered disconsolately back to the twinkling indomitable eyes of the man on the gatepost. Uncle Pete sighed deeply.

"That's good! I'll just about make the wagon by noon," he remarked gently. He took his quirt from his saddle-horn. "Young man," he said gravely, flicking his horse's flank, "any time you're out of a job come over and see me." He waved his hand, nodded, and was gone.

Clay Cooper spurred up and took his place, his black eyes snapping. "I like a damned fool," he hissed; "but you suit me too well!"

The forty followed; some pausing for quip or jest, some in frowning silence. But each, as he passed that bright, audacious figure, touched his hat in salute to a gallant foe.

Squatty Robinson was the last. He rode close up and whispered confidentially:

"I want you should do me a favor, Jeff. Just throw down on me and take my gun away. I don't want to go back to camp with any such tale as this."

"You see, Billy," explained Jeff, "you mustn't dare the denizens— never! They dare. They're uncultured; their lives ain't noways valuable to society and they know it. If you notice, I took pains not to dare anybody. Quite otherhow. I merely stated annoyin' consequences to some other fellow, attractive as I could, but impersonal. Just like I'd tell you: 'Billy, I wouldn't set the oil can on the fire—it might boil over.'

"Now, if I'd said: 'Uncle Pete, if anybody makes a break I'll shoot your eye out, anyhow,' there'd 'a' been only one dignified course open to him. Him and me would now be dear Alphonsing each other about payin' the ferryman.

"Spose I'd made oration to shoot the first man through the gate. Every man Jack would have come 'a-snuffin'—each one tryin' to be first. The way I put it up to 'em, to be first wasn't no graceful act—playin' safe at some one else's expense—and then they seen that some one else wouldn't be gettin' an equitable vibration. That's all there was to it. If there wasn't any first there couldn't conveniently be any second, so they went home. B-r-r! I'm sleepy. Let's go by-by. Wake that dern lazy Mexican up and make him keep watch till the sheriff comes!"

Sugar

BY TOM MCGUANE

The work of cowboying today seems almost an anachronism. It's little practiced anymore, and if you aren't actually a cowboy yourself, the very idea is all mixed up with the memories of John Wayne/Ford westerns, Billy the Kid, and a lot of half-remembered advertisements for the Marlborough Man. How delicious it is then to read a memoir by a man who is himself a cowboy and one of the most potent writers of our time.

Tom McGuane's novels include: *The Sporting Club* (1969), *The Bushwacked Piano* (1971), *Ninety-Two in the Shade* (1973), *Panama* (1978), *Nobody's Angel* (1981), *Something To Be Desired* (1984), *Keep the Change* (1989), and *Nothing But Blue Skies* (1992).

"Sugar" was first published by The Lyons Press in a collection of McGuane stories entitled *Some Horses*.

★ ★ ★ ★ ★

Years ago, I took a twelve-year-old broodmare that I owned to a cutting-horse clinic in Livingston, Montana. She was out of shape, and I didn't know what to expect. But I knew that she had once been a cutting horse. When my turn came, I rode her into the herd of cattle that milled at the end of the arena.

All I had to do was cut one cow from the herd. But each one I tried slipped past me.

Already the mare had begun to change beneath me. I felt her heightened alertness, a flow of new energy. The reins with which I guided her required a lighter and lighter touch. Finally, only one cow stood in front of us. The mare's attention was riveted, and I no longer needed the reins at all.

When the cow tried to get back to the herd, I knew I would ride cutting horses for the rest of my life. With liquid quickness, the mare countered every move that the cow made. Riding her on a slack rein gave me a sense of controlled free fall. Centered between the ears of my horse as if in

2 5

BARIGHT PUBLIC LIBRARY
5555 S. 77th St.
Ralston, NE 68127

the sights of a rifle, the cow faked and dodged. Much of the time I didn't know where I was or where the cow was, and I was certainly no help to the horse. But by the time I picked up the reins to stop, I was addicted to the thrilling shared movement of cutting, sometimes close to violence, which was well beyond what the human body could ever discover on its own.

In ranch work, the cutting horse is used to sort out unproductive cows from the herd, to separate bulls, to replace heifers, and to bring out sick or injured cattle for treatment. The herd instinct of cattle is tremendously strong, and to drive out an individual cow and hold her against this tidal force, a horse must act with knowledge, physical skill, and precision. Otherwise, the cow escapes and returns to a thoroughly upset herd.

The day of the cutting horse as a common ranch tool is waning, and the training and use of cutting horses has become largely a sporting proposition. To deny this would be like claiming your old bird dog was just another food-gathering device you maintained to keep your kitchen humming. Still, there is beauty and grace in the cutting horse, as well as a connection to a world older than we are. Amazingly, cutting horses can be found in all states except Alaska, and competitions sanctioned by the National Cutting Horse Association are held in forty-four states.

As a sport, cutting has a low entry level. Anyone who is reasonably comfortable riding can get on a cutting horse, hang on tight to the saddle horn, and feel the satisfaction and excitement of sitting astride a trained cow horse. But the journey to competence can be very long, and the frustration can be extreme. You must learn to ride in a way that does not drag at the motion of a horse. The body language between you and the horse must be bright and clear. A polished cutter sits in the middle of the saddle, holding the saddle horn but not pushing on it, never slinging his weight or dropping a shoulder into the turns. This quiet, eye-of-the-storm riding style is not easily achieved on the back of a sudden-moving, half-ton athlete. But to violate this style is to take the horse's mind off his work and increase his vulnerability to the movements of the cow.

Cutting begins and ends with horses—the minds, bodies, and souls of horses. You have to have a deep love of horses to endure the training. If you don't sense a kind of magic watching a horse take two steps or put his nose underwater or switch flies, there's no real point. Cow-horse people sometimes can't tell their horses from themselves. You either learn to look at the world through the eyes of a horse or you quit cutting.

I bought a bay filly named Sugar O Lynn in Alabama, and she was broken to ride by a good hand there and sent to my ranch in McLeod, Montana, in the spring of 1988, at the age of two. I wanted to train her myself. My wife, Laurie, and I compete in Montana on our mature or "open" cutting horses, usually six years or older. Competing on young horses, which are comparatively inexperienced and volatile, is quite different, and we had never done it successfully. Laurie had her own filly, April, wisely entrusted to Sam Shepard, a talented trainer in Hartford, Alabama.

I began to ride Sugar out in the country and tried to get her to be quiet and serious. She was good-hearted but wound fairly tight, would jump back from water and strange shapes. You wanted to have a deep seat on her if you were taking her on a long ride by yourself.

I started her in cattle work, and she came right along, though she worried about cows and sometimes kicked at them when I rode her in the herd. By fall, I could guide her to sort a cow from the herd and then drop the reins for a few turns and let Sugar work on her own. It surprised me how she faced the unknown with confidence.

That winter I had work that took me out of the state and later out of the country. I sent Sugar to Tom Campbell, a good cowboy in Brady, Montana, and he gave her back to me in the spring of 1990 much improved. I rode her through the summer and fall and used up every cow in our valley trying to teach Sugar to run, stop, and turn correctly.

Next we sorted the ranch's calves off their mothers, and I schooled Sugar on them. At first their speed frightened her, and she worked wide-eyed, with her head practically in my lap. Eventually she settled down and tried to understand the rapid little animals, but they often beat her. When we sold the calves in October, Sugar and I worked the mothers. This was like going back to kindergarten for her, and she handled these cattle almost nonchalantly. Her big dark eyes sparkled with pleasure.

By this time, we could move quietly in the herd and sort out an individual cow. Sugar would run, stop, and turn intensely to hold the cow, but without continuing guidance from the reins she would soon get lost. Cows would head-fake her or press her back and run into the herd.

In cutting-horse competition, the reins cannot be used after a cow is cut. To hold the cow away from the herd, the horse must work on a slack rein. I wanted to enter Sugar in the most prestigious of all cutting-horse events: the NCHA Futurity, an annual competition in Fort Worth for three-year-old horses that have never been shown before. The futurity was just a couple of months away and it was starting to snow. Hard as it was for me to admit, Sugar was still not a contest horse, any more than I was a real horse trainer.

I called my friend Buster Welch. If anyone could put my program on track, Buster could. I realized that he might not want another horse to ride, and even if he did, he might not like mine. Buster had had open-heart surgery two years earlier. When I called, he was ranching fifty thousand acres in addition to getting cutting horses ready for himself, his wife, and about a half dozen friends who, like me, wanted to get something done at the futurity.

I was fortunate that he took Sugar on. I knew what kind of cutting horses Buster liked, because he had told me. He liked them "steeped in background, never crippled, and never had their hearts broke." I had ridden Sugar plenty in her short life, and I hoped he would find that she qualified. I sent her down to Texas.

I gave Sugar about a week to get a good look at those snappy West Texas cattle while Buster worked with her. Then I called Buster. His thoughts were composed. "Tom, I believe you held onto the reins too long," he said. "If you ride two-handed too long, a horse will stay a bronc all his life. When Sugar got here, I thought she couldn't outrun a fat man, but I guess she was only tired. I've shortened up her stride and quickened her moves wherever I could. You had a beautiful stop on her, but they really don't pay you to stop in Fort Worth."

He paused and let me take all this in. "She's got all the speed that is required," he continued, "and she is not going to quit us. You never gave her more than she wanted or could understand."

I wondered if I had given her enough to understand. Then Buster added, "But if they call from Fort Worth and want to put the futurity back a month, say yes."

I headed for Sweetwater by way of Abilene, Texas, to meet Buster and practice before heading for Fort Worth. The futurity has various divisions, but the principal ones are the non-professional class and the open, which is primarily for trainers. I was getting ready for the non-pro, and I had bitten off all I could chew.

I flew into Abilene at night and tried to rent a car that I could drop off in Fort Worth. Not everyone wanted me to do that. It was late and the small airport was quiet. I found one agency with a car that could be left in Fort Worth, but its plates were expired. "Expired back in October," said the pleasant woman, biting a wide mint patty. "Sittin' out there since then."

I went to another counter. I didn't see anyone. I looked around, and then something behind the counter caught my attention. The agent, a woman around thirty, was sleep on the floor. I noticed her shoes neatly arranged on the counter, which was, I suppose, a way of telling customers she had turned in. She sensed my presence and stood up, rubbing the sleep from her eyes. "I got to catch a nap whenever I can," she said. "Some folks prod me awake with their foot. Ain't that cold?"

After being assured that I could leave the car in Fort Worth, I asked her to direct me to Sweetwater, and she told me the way to Highway 20. "Go forty-five miles and be sure not to blink," she said.

"Are you going back to sleep?" I asked.

"I'm up now," she said.

The next morning I wandered around Sweetwater, admired its pleasant neighborhoods and numerous churches. The streets had cast-iron manhole covers that said DO NOT MOLEST, a useful general remark. I stopped in a café for breakfast, and when my waffles came, they were embossed with the map of Texas.

These waffles take us to Texas the pride, which is not fixing to die. The so-called chauvinism of Texas, which I find to be a hearty pride of heritage, is a booming and immodest thing. It brings grand rejuvenating powers to its citizens. Texas is an oasis of undamaged egos, a place where Birkenstocks, oat bran, foreign films, and Saabs spontaneously catch fire and then smolder grimly in an alien climate.

I gave Buster a call. I wanted to find out when he was coming to town with the horses to practice in the Nolan County Coliseum. "You better come out here and help me," he said a over his truck radio. "If you-all want me to come to Sweetwater tomorrow and help you, you've got to help me today."

I missed a turn heading out to Buster's place and pulled into a ranch yard to ask for directions. It turned out to be a large breeding kennel for Chihuahuas, and when I got out of my car, they swarmed toward me at ankle height, driving me back inside. I decided I had better find my own way.

Buster's ranch is in the middle of some of the prettiest land I've ever seen in Texas, winding caliche roads, deeply cut red-banked riverbeds, country that looked pink and green in a certain light. I complimented Buster on his property. "It's outdoors," he said, "all of it."

We loaded three-year-old bulls and carried them around the ranch in a stock trailer, vaccinating them and dropping them off wherever Buster wanted. Between times, Buster issued commands over the truck radio and speculated about our horses, for whom we all had such high hopes. Of his own stallion, Peppy Olé, Buster said, "God has decided to give Buster Welch one more good horse."

Meanwhile, Laurie and April had gone to Ardmore, Oklahoma, to practice for the futurity. I had no idea if Laurie was gaining an advantage or falling behind me, because things occur in Oklahoma that are clothed in secrecy. We had wished each other luck, knowing that many of the sorest issues of the age lay in the outcome of our competition. If, for example, Laurie won the futurity and I fell off my horse, nothing anyone could say would help me. If I won and Laurie fell off her horse, some of the things that have caused the pots and pans to fly around our house in the last few years would be with us again.

The next morning, early, Buster and I were in the coliseum along with fifty young cutting horses, their riders, and plenty of crossbred cattle. I rode Sugar around for a while; it was good to be on her familiar back again. Then I joined Buster as he watched his son Greg work a horse he had trained, a quick, attentive stud, perfectly prepared.

In a cutting-horse competition, judges evaluate the performances of horses and riders as if they were working on an open range. A herd of about sixty cattle is brought into an arena and settled along the back fence. Two mounted herd holders are stationed on either side of the herd, and a pair of mounted turn-back riders are in front, prepared to keep the cattle that have been cut focused on returning to the herd. The mounted cutter enters the herd and selects a cow to drive out. He then must control the cow until he releases her and cuts another. He has two and a half minutes to cut either two or three cattle. The rider is awarded points based on how cleanly he makes each cut, how well he controls the cow afterward, and how difficult the cow is to handle.

A cutting horse not only has to be quicker than the cow but also has to have the strategic sense to deal with the cow's bold first moves. The rider, through weight shifts and other body signals (such as leg pressure and touches of the spurs), can tell the horse what he thinks the cow will do. The rider must also react without interference to moves the horse devises on his own. The shared signals constitute the elusive "feel" of cutting.

As Greg schooled his horse, Buster explained things to me. "Pick up that cow, go with it," he said. "Shadow that cow. Don't get in a race. If you get in a race, let the cow win. And when you're cutting a cow, stalk it. That will tell your horse what you are up to."

Then a trainer named Gary Bellenfant worked a mare on three different hard-running cows without ever having to raise the rein to make an adjustment. Buster remarked that we might just as well be trying to make violins. It took thousands of hours, no matter how smart and talented you were, to train a cutting horse. The horse had to see so many cattle, and he had to grow up and experience the world enough for new places not to terrify him and prevent him from doing his work. These cutting horses were, after all, excitable young animals being asked to do and understand a lot.

Buster's wife, Sheila, worked her horse cleanly, quietly. "Next time I get on her will be at Fort Worth," she said afterward. She was back on her the next day. In the uninterfering style of riding that Buster advocates, Sheila excels from long practice and tutelage and her own competitive spirit.

During my week in Sweetwater I took long hikes in the mesquite-dotted hills, watched fifty horses work a day, rode Sugar, and felt how far she'd come under Buster's saddle, and by the end of the week I was close to chewing wood. I was amazed at the ability of some seasoned cutters to go into a state of suspended animation for days on end in the coliseum's bleachers. On Thanksgiving there was a general retreat to the cavelike twilight of motel rooms for football games. I decided a change of cuisine was in order and deserted Whataburger for McDonald's, where I spent part of Thanksgiving evening listening to a spirited debate between two old farmers about Jack Ruby.

It was time to head for Fort Worth. I drove east through country given over mainly to cotton, with large cotton wagons that gleaned the bolls from windrows in the field. There was a beautiful big sun out, and soft, indefinite clouds. The hours on the highway isolated my hopes for the futurity and then twisted them into baseless fears: I can't get my horse into the coliseum because I can't find the gate; I ride Sugar around Fort Worth in a traffic jam, unable to reach an off-ramp; my chaps blow over my face while I'm trying to cut cattle, and I can't find the herd in the deafening laughter. Various bursts of demoralizing nonsense.

Laurie arrived in Fort Worth from Oklahoma, and we went to a pleasant Italian restaurant on Camp Bowie Boulevard called Sardine's, where she described every good horse she had seen in Ardmore, and I described every good horse I had seen in Sweetwater.

"How's your horse?" I asked.

"Solid. How's yours?"

"Hotter than a two-dollar pistol. Did you have any problems?"

"Did you?"

"Let's just enjoy our meal," I said. She seemed to be regarding me, twirling her pasta fork in the air and sizing me up. Cutting is a sport for the whole family.

Laurie was assigned to ride on November 26, the first day of the futurity. The day before, Will Rogers coliseum was surrounded by horse trucks and trailers with license plates from across the nation. I walked in and looked around the coliseum's spacious interior, a venerable place to cutters. The bleachers were empty, the judges' boxes untenanted. I sat down close to the rail and remembered a night thirteen years earlier, when Buster had won the futurity on Little Peppy: I had never seen anything like it in my life, the mercurial speed of that young stallion, his impact on a coliseum filled with people who had nothing on their minds but a love of cutting horses. It would seem like a privilege to ride my young mare onto that sand—win, lose, or draw.

Laurie had a nice controlled run that assured her of a slot in the second go-round. I couldn't help but notice how quietly she cut her cows and how lightly she sat on her quick little horse. I wouldn't work until the next day, so I watched and tried to make myself memorize individual cattle in the herd.

Heather Stiles had a fine run on a horse Buster had trained. Heather, a high school senior, has grown up on the one-and-a-quarter-million-acre King Ranch in South Texas, where her father is in charge of the cattle. She is a natural rider and a remarkably serious individual. I would have been quite pleased if Heather had won the non-pro class and its $35,454 first prize. I even had generous thoughts about Laurie getting to the finals or even winning. So many horses were making their way through the go-rounds, 165 in non-pro alone, that no one really cared what happened to you until you did enough to suggest that it would be a shame if you failed.

Nevertheless, there was a feeling of intense scrutiny; and indeed the five judges, sequestered in their towers, clipboards on their knees, were looking at the riders very closely.

Sometimes it helped just to walk around and visit with people. I watched a few runs with Ned Huntt, a cutter from Maryland who has ridden all his life. He is in the landscaping business. He lost an arm in his late teens and, unable to hold the saddle horn, he rides as we all should, by sheer balance. He was watching the clock, waiting for his turn. Ned and I talked about the difficulty of controlling all the variables in cutting competition, like your place in the draw, the mood of your horse, the freshness of your cattle, and the quality of the herd holders and turn-back riders. Ned thought these variables were the most daunting aspect of the sport, the thing that took the pleasure out of it for some cutters.

I watched a few runs with Spencer Harden, who trains his own horses in Millsap, Texas, though he's a non-professional. Last year he won the open class, an extremely rare occurrence for a non-pro.

I walked around and ran into L.H. Wood standing in line to buy a cup of coffee. He trains border collies, and I have one of his dogs, Ella H., a useful ranch dog and gifted beggar of table scraps. He shows horses trained by his son Kobie and has been a frequent futurity finalist. He didn't look as nervous as I felt. He backed up to wall and made his hat rise on his head as if by magic while he inflated his cheeks.

The alarm went off the morning of my first go-round. The shower in the residential hotel had no hot water, and I woke up too fast. As I tried to get a quick snack for breakfast, the toaster caught fire. I headed for the coliseum. Matt Lopez, a Sioux cowboy who works for Buster, was riding Sugar around. I took Sugar from Matt and joined the competitors loping in a circle to warm up. Matt said, "Good luck."

Suddenly my name was called, and I was riding toward the herd. Behind me, I heard a woman's voice say, "Load the wagon and don't mind the mules!" Was she talking to me?

As we passed the judges, Sugar craned around and had a good look at them. She was filled with suspicion. Apparently, my horse was confident. Once we were in the herd, I felt better. We rode around and moved some cattle out in front of us. One particular black cow looked fresh, head up and not out of breath. She stood and let us cut her. The rest of the herd moved quietly away and behind us.

I put my reining hand down. The cow realized she was alone. She made a hard run to the right, spun, and went the other way. I felt that first magical hard break that a cutting horse makes with a cow, the hindquarters sinking into the stop so that the floor of the arena seems to rise sharply around you, and suddenly you're going the other way. It is an exhilarating movement, akin to flight.

Sugar handled this cow correctly, with good hard stops, staying right with her, nose to nose. Then we cut a wild motley-faced cow that nearly sent us home. I could feel Sugar get a bit lost as the pace picked up. The cow didn't respect anything Sugar did, and Sugar's confidence was eroding. She became unsure of the correct way to do things and desperate as she tried to beat the cow to the stops. She became much harder to ride.

We made the second go-round by the skin of our teeth. I was going to have to make up a lot of ground if I hoped to reach the semifinals. And I knew Sugar was rattled.

Larry Mahan, in a tweed coat and cardigan sweater, arrived to watch the competition. A six-time world-champion rodeo cowboy, he's now a good non-professional cutting-horse rider. Mahan took on this sport with becoming modesty, given his credentials in rodeo. When riding broncs or bulls, he says, "You sublimate everything in order to react to what happens; you just kind of gas it for eight seconds. You get to where you even divorce yourself from that guy out there making the ride. But with cutting horses, you have to find a harmony with the horse. You have to reflect that horse's energy, and he has to reflect yours. You have to be sharp. You have to react. But the thing you have to have is the feel."

And the feel could come from anywhere—your attitude, the demeanor of the animal, the smell of the sweat on the horse's shoulders, the look in his eye, the electric suddenness of his moves. You could never be sure who had that feel. It might well be somebody's grandmother.

A young Californian, Phil Rapp, riding a horse he had trained, won the first go-round with a run that suggested he and his horse could go the entire distance. A curious thing happens in cutting: if your start is wobbly, you begin to shift your attention to horses and riders who seem more deserving of success. The hope of virtue being rewarded is part of the atmosphere.

In the second go-round, on November 29, Laurie had another nice run. Her horse was so intense, so locked down in her stops, that people cheered. Laurie was headed for the semis. With a better-than-average run, I could join her there, and we could compete in an atmosphere of good sportsmanship, our entry fees won back and our earlier scores erased, a clean slate. As I rode Sugar around, warming up amid a stream of galloping horses, I listened to the announcer and began to feel comfortable. A little positive thinking was coming into my consciousness.

And then I was walking toward the herd. It was now or never. Heather Stiles had been eliminated when she was nearly run over by a black cow with a red ear tag, and I was trying to follow the cow's progress in the herd to be sure I didn't cut her. As I watched the cattle melt away in front of me until one was isolated, I dropped my hand. I waited for that decisive move that mirrors the first break of the cow, but it never came. Sugar jumped sharply to my right, toward the wrong cow.

It was over.

I walked across the warm-up pen. Another cutter was already working. At least at an event this big you get to have your defeat to yourself. When I climbed into the bleachers, I looked back at Sugar tied to the rail, one back foot tipped up, asleep. She had had her whole life ahead of her. I knew, absolutely, that she was a good horse.

Suddenly, though, I was a pedestrian, a cheerleader. By the time the semifinals rolled around the next night, I was accustomed to my new role, even looking forward to it. But Laurie overrode her horse trying to hold a tough cow and went off the end—the horse never stopped, and the cow cut back to the herd behind her. Laurie was eliminated, and soon we would be homeward bound.

I sat for while in the bleachers. Time was certainly not flying. I ran into Ian Tyson, a singer-songwriter friend from Alberta. The previous year he had reached the futurity finals, before, as he put it, being hammered by gum-chewing California girls with ice water in their veins. It was nice to hear a lighter view of something you have spent so long trying to do and failed at. "Well, Ian, what are you working on?" I asked.

Ian thought for a moment and, seeming to focus on something in a faraway but pleasant place, smiled and said, "I'm working on a reggae about magpies."

I felt better already.

Laurie and I stayed to watch the finals the next night. Sheila Welch and a number of other people we knew were among the twenty remaining riders. Phil Rapp did not make the finals on his great young mare. Heather Stiles looked depressed. We saw a couple of real heartbreakers as good horses and riders got beaten by treacherous cows.

Spencer Harden again did brilliantly, finishing second in the non-pro division. Matt Gaines, a college student from Stephenville, Texas, and a lifelong cutter, won. When I spoke to him later, I got the feeling he would never quite believe he had won. Matt talked about his heroes, including his father, who had helped him train his horse. I could see Matt had little chance of escaping his dream of understanding these horses and the open-range skills they celebrated.

I remembered the previous year's weekend cuttings, through a summer's endless golden progress, the ten o'clock sundowns when I walked Sugar through the cottonwood shadows to cool her down. Listening to this young champion, it all came back, that search for something in a horse and in myself.

The Kid

BY WALTER NOBLE BURNS

Nearly a half century after Pat Garrett shot Billy the Kid, Walter Noble Burns published *The Saga of Billy the Kid,* from which this excerpt is taken. This book was by no means the first treatment of the Billy story, or the last. There have been dozens of books and at least fifty films on the subject. In the Kid's own time the public knew something of this outlaw cowboy through articles in the various police gazettes and dime novels. These tales were highly colored, romanticized, sensational adventures, the best known of them was *The Authentic Life of Billy the Kid* by Pat Garrett. In 1903 Walter Wood penned a hit Broadway show (a melodrama really) portraying the Kid as a good man forced by circumstance to kill and kill again. At that time this was a controversial point of view. The outlaw west was still too fresh in people's memories and much of the public had little use for a homicidal maniac said to have killed twenty-one men, one for each of his twenty-one years.

By the mid-1920s, when Walter Noble Burns turned his hand to Billy's story, enough time had passed, he felt, to get a first true fix on the legend of America's outlaw-cowboy-hero. Burns was just the man for this job, an author and newspaperman, he was a master polemicist who had made a hugely successful career out of the business of shaping the public's perception of events and personalities. Though Burns himself was not a westerner and knew cattle only through the medium of a steak at Delmonico's restaurant, he was able to use Garrett's book, and much of the other cowboy literature of the time to write a best seller that was indeed to fix the Kid in our imagination for generations.

The legend of Billy the Kid was the perfect subject for his, if not yellow, then slightly jaundiced (but very potent) brand of journalism. But let's forgive Burns. In his milieu he was something of an outlaw himself; and something of a cowboy too—in the pejorative sense of the word. We know him best as the master-manipulator, the driven, unscrupulous newspaper editor of Ben Hecht's *The Front Page.*

3 5

★ ★ ★ ★ ★

Billy the Kid's legend in New Mexico seems destined to a mellow and genial immortality like that which gilds the misdeeds and exaggerates the virtues of such ancient rogues as Robin Hood, Claude Duval, Dick Turpin, and Fra Diavolo. From the tales you hear of him everywhere, you might be tempted to fancy him the best-loved hero in the state's history. His crimes are forgotten or condoned, while his loyalty, his gay courage, his superman adventures are treasured in affectionate memory. Men speak of him with admiration; women extol his gallantry and lament his fate. A rude balladry in Spanish and English has grown up about him, and in every *placeta* in New Mexico, Mexican girls sing to their guitars songs of Billy the Kid. A halo has been clapped upon his scapegrace brow. The boy who never grew old has become a sort of symbol of frontier knight-errantry, a figure of eternal youth riding for ever through a purple glamour of romance.

Gray-beard skald at boar's-head feast when the foaming goblets of mead went round the board in the gaunt hall of vikings never sang to his wild harp saga more thrilling than the story of Billy the Kid. A boy is its hero: a boy when the tale begin, a boy when it ends; a boy born to battle and vendetta, to hatred and murder, to tragic victory and tragic defeat, and who took it all with a smile.

Fate set a stage. Out of nowhere into the drama stepped this unknown boy. Opposite him played Death. It was a drama of Death and the Boy. Death dogged his trail relentlessly. It was for ever clutching at him with skeleton hands. It lay in ambush for him. It edged him to the gallows' stairs. By bullets, conflagration, stratagems, every lethal trick, it sought to compass his destruction. But the boy was not to be trapped. He escaped by apparent miracles; he was saved as if by necromancy. He laughed at Death. Death was a joke. He waved Death a jaunty good-bye and was off to new adventures. But again the inexorable circle closed. Now life seemed sweet. It beckoned to love and happiness. A golden vista opened before him. He set his foot upon the sunlit road. Perhaps for a moment the boy dreamed this drama was destined to a happy ending. But no. Fate prompted from the wings. The moment of climax was at hand. The boy had had his hour. It was Death's turn. And so the curtain.

Billy the Kid was the Southwest's most famous desperado and its last great outlaw. He died when he was twenty-one years old and was credited with having killed twenty-one men—a man for every year of his life. Few careers in pioneer annals have been more colourful; certain of his exploits rank among the classic adventures of the West. He lived at a transitional period of New Mexican history. His life closed the past; his death opened the present. His destructive and seemingly futile career served a constructive purpose: it drove home the lesson that New Mexico's prosperity could be built only upon a basis of stability and peace. After him came the great change for which he involuntarily had cleared the way. Law and order came in on the flash and smoke of the six-shooter that with one bullet put an end to the outlaw and to outlawry.

That a boy in a brief life-span of twenty-one years should have attained his sinister preëminence on a lawless and turbulent frontier would seem proof of a unique and extraordinary personality. He was born for his career. The mental and physical equipment that gave his genius for depopulation effectiveness and background and enabled him to survive in a tumultuous time of plots and murders was a birthright rather than an accomplishment. He had the desperado complex which, to endure for any appreciable time in his environment, combined necessarily a peculiarly intricate and enigmatic psychology with a dextrous trigger-finger.

Billy the Kid doubtless would fare badly under the microscope of psychoanalysis. Weighed in the delicate balance of psychiatry, he would be dropped, neatly labelled, into some category of split personality and abnormal psychosis. The desperado complex, of which he was an exemplar, may perhaps be defined as frozen egoism plus recklessness and minus mercy. It its less aggravated forms it is not uncommon. There are desperadoes of business, the pulpit, the drawing room. The business man who plots the ruin of his rival; the minister who consigns to eternal damnation all who disbelieve in his personal creed; the love pirate, who robs another woman of her husband; the speed-mad automobilist who disregards life and limb, are all desperado types. The lynching mob is a composite desperado. Among killers there are good and bad desperadoes; both equally deadly, one killing lawlessly and the other to uphold the law. Wild Bill won his reputation as an officer of the law, killing many men to establish peace. The good "bad man" had a definite place in the development of the West.

But in fairness to Billy the Kid he must be judged by the standards of his place and time. The part of New Mexico in which he passed his life was the most murderous spot in the West. The Lincoln County war, which was his background, was a culture-bed of many kinds and degrees of desperadoes. There were the embryo desperado whose record remained negligible because of lack of excuse or occasion for murder; the would-be desperado who loved melodrama and felt called upon, as an artist, to shed a few drops of blood to maintain the prestige of his melodrama; and the desperado of genuine spirit but mediocre craftsmanship whose climb toward the heights was halted abruptly by some other man an eighth of a second quicker on the trigger. All these men were as ruthless and desperate as Billy the Kid, but they lacked the afflatus that made him the finished master.

They were journeymen mechanics laboriously carving notches on the handles of their guns. He was a genius painting his name in flaming colours with a six-shooter across the sky of the Southwest.

With his tragic record in mind, one might be pardoned for visualizing Billy the Kid as an inhuman monster revelling in blood. But this conception would do him injustice. He was a boy of bright, alert mind, generous, not unkindly, of quick sympathies. The steadfast loyalty of his friendships was proverbial. Among his friends he was scrupulously honest. Moroseness and sullenness were foreign to him. He was cheerful, hopeful, talkative, given to laughter. He was not addicted to swagger or braggadocio. He was quiet, unassuming, courteous. He was a great favourite with women, and in his attitude toward them he lived up to the best traditions of the frontier.

But hidden away somewhere among these pleasant human qualities was a hiatus in his character—a sub-zero vacuum—devoid of all human emotions. He was upon occasion the personification of merciless, remorseless deadliness. He placed no value on human life, least of all upon his own. He killed a man as nonchalantly as he smoked a cigarette. Murder did not appeal to Billy the Kid as tragedy; it was merely a physical process of pressing a trigger. If it seemed to him necessary to kill a man, he killed him and got the matter over with as neatly and with as little fuss as possible. In his murders, he observed no rules of etiquette and was bound by no punctilios of honour. As long as he killed a man he wanted to kill, it made no difference to him how he killed him. He fought fair and shot it out face to face if the occasion demanded but under other circumstances he did not scruple at assassination. He put a bullet through a man's heart as coolly as he perforated a tin can set upon a fence post. He had no remorse. No memories haunted him.

His courage was beyond question. It was a static courage that remained the same under all circumstances, a noon or at three o'clock in the morning. There are yellow spots in the stories of many of the West's most famous desperadoes. We are told that in certain desperate crises with the odds against them, they weakened and were no braver than they might have been when, for instance, the other man got the drop on them and they looked suddenly into the blackness of forty-four calibre death. But no tale has come down that Billy the Kid ever showed the "yellow streak." Every hour in his desperate life was the zero hour, and he was never afraid to die. "One chance in a million" was one of his favourite phrases, and more than once he took that chance with the debonair courage of a cavalier. Even those who hated him and the men who hunted him to his death admitted his absolute fearlessness.

But courage alone would not have stamped him as extraordinary in the Southwest where courage is a tradition. The quality that distin-

guished his courage from that of other brave men lay in a nerveless imper-
turbability. Nothing excited him. He had nerve but no nerves. He retained
a cool, unruffled poise in the most thrilling crises. With death seemingly
inevitable, his face remained calm; his steady hands gave no hint of quickened pulses; no unusual flash in his eyes—and eyes are accounted the Judas
Iscariots of the soul—betrayed his emotions or his plans.

The secrets of Billy the Kid's greatness as a desperado—and by
connoisseurs in such matters he was rated as an approach to the ideal desperado type—lay in a marvellous coordination between mind and body.
He not only had the will but the skill to kill. Daring, coolness, and quick-
thinking would not have served unless they had been combined with
physical quickness and a marksmanship which enabled him to pink a man
neatly between the eyes with a bullet at, say, thirty paces. He was not pitted
against six-shooter amateurs but against experienced fighters adept themselves in the handling of weapons. The men he killed would have killed
him if he had not been their master in a swifter deadliness. In times of danger, his mind was not only calm but singularly clear and nimble, watching
like a hawk for an advantage and seizing it with incredible celerity. He was
able to translate an impulse into action with the suave rapidity of a flash of
light. While certain other men were a fair match for him in target practice,
no man in the Southwest, it is said, could equal him in the lightning-like
quickness with which he could draw a six-shooter from its holster and
with the same movement fire with deadly accuracy. It may be remarked
incidentally that shooting at a target is one thing and shooting at a man
who happens to be blazing away at you is something entirely different; and
Billy the Kid did both kinds of shooting equally well.

His appearance was not unprepossessing. He had youth, health,
good nature, and a smile—a combination which usually results in a certain
sort of good looks. His face was long and colourless except for the deep
tan with which it had been tinted by sun, wind, and weather, and was of an
asymmetry that was not unattractive. His hair was light brown, worn usually rather long and inclined to waviness. His eyes were gray, clear and
steady. His upper front teeth were large and slightly prominent, and to an
extent disfigured the expression of a well-formed mouth. His hands and
feet were remarkably small. He was five feet eight inches tall, slender and
well proportioned. He was unusually strong for his inches, having for a
small man quite powerful arms and shoulders. He weighed, in condition,
one hundred and forty pounds. When out on the range, he was as rough-
looking as any other cowboy. In towns, among the quality-folk of the
frontier, he dressed neatly and took not a little care in making himself per-
sonable. Many persons, especially women, thought him handsome. He was
a great beau at fandangos and was considered a good dancer.

He had an air of easy, unstudied, devil-may-care insuociance which gave no hint of his dynamic energy. His movements were ordinarily deliberate and unhurried. But there was a certain element of calculation in everything he did. Like a billiardist who "plays position," he figured on what he might possibly have to do next. This foresightedness and fore-handedness even in inconsequential matters provided him with a sort of subconscious mail armour. He was forearmed even when not forewarned; for ever on guard.

Like all the noted killers of the West, Billy the Kid was of the blond type. Wild Bill Hickok, Ben Thompson, King Fisher, Henry Plum-mer, Clay Allison, Wyatt Earp, Doc Holliday, Frank and Jesse James, the Youngers, the Daltons—the list of others is long—were all blond. There was not a pair of brown eyes among them. It was the gray and blue eye that flashed death in the days when the six-shooter ruled the frontier. This blondness of desperadoes is a curious fact, contrary to popular imagination and the traditions of art and the stage. The theatre immemorially has por-trayed its unpleasant characters as black-haired and black-eyed. The popu-lar mind associates swarthiness with villainy. Blue eyes and golden hair are, in the artistic cannon, a sort of heavenly hall mark. No artist has yet been so daring as to paint a winged cherub with raven tresses, and a search of the world's canvases would discover no brown-eyed angel. It may be remarked further, as a matter of incidental interest, that the West's bad men were never heavy, stolid, lowering brutes. Most of them were good-looking, some remarkably so. Wild Bill Hickok, beau ideal of desperadoes, was con-sidered the handsomest man of his day on the frontier, and with his blue eyes and yellow hair falling on his shoulders, he moved through his life of tragedies with something of the beauty of a Greek god. So much for fact versus fancy. Cold deadliness in Western history seems to have run to frosty colouring in eyes, hair, and complexion.

Though it is possible that the record of twenty-one killings attrib-uted to Billy the Kid is exaggerated, there is strong reason to believe it true. He was remarkably precocious in homicide; he is said to have killed his first man when he was only twelve years old. He is supposed to have killed about twelve men before he appeared in Lincoln County. This early phase of his life is vague. From the outbreak of the Lincoln County war, his career is easily traceable and clearly authentic.

It is impossible now to name twenty-one men that he killed, though, if Indians be included, it is not difficult to cast up the ghastly total. It may be that in his record were secret murders of which only he himself knew. There are rife in New Mexico many unauthenticated stories in which the names of his victims are not given. One tale credits him with having killed five Mexicans in camp near Seven Rivers. Another has it that a number of the twenty or more unmarked graves on the banks of the Pecos at the site of John Chisum's old Bosque Grande ranch contain the dust of men the Kid sent to their long sleep.

The Kid himself claimed to have killed twenty-one. He made this statement unequivocally a number of times to a number of men and he was never regarded as a braggart or a liar.

"I have killed twenty-one men and I want to make it twenty-three before I die," he said a little before his death to Pete Maxwell at Fort Sumner. "If I live long enough to kill Pat Garrett and Barney Mason, I'll be satisfied."

Sheriff Pat Garrett, who for several years was the Kid's close friend—and who killed him—placed the Kid's record at eleven. John W. Poe, who was with Garrett at the Kid's death, accepted the Kid's own statement. In a letter written to me shortly before his death in 1923, Poe said:

Billy the Kid had killed more men than any man I ever knew or heard of during my fifty years in the Southwest. I cannot name the twenty-one men he killed; nor can any man alive to-day. I doubt if there ever was a man who could name them all except the Kid himself. He was the only man who knew exactly. He said he had killed twenty-one and I believe him.

Poe, who succeeded Pat Garrett as sheriff of Lincoln County and was at the time of his death president of the Citizens National Bank of Roswell, was a veteran man-hunter and knew the criminal element of the Southwest as few men did. If Poe, with his first-hand knowledge of the Kid, had faith in the Kid's own statement, it would seem fair grounds for presumption that the statement is true.

So the matter stands. With most of the actors in the old drama now dead and gone, it is safe to say the tragic conundrum of how many men fell before Billy the Kid's six-shooters will never be definitely answered. Certainly the list was long. And it is worth remembering that the Kid was only a boy when he died and, however his record is itemized, each item is a grave.

To realize the bizarre quality of Billy the Kid's character try to fancy yourself in his place. Suppose, if you please, that under stress of circumstances you had killed several men. Assume that you felt justified in these homicides. Very well. Would an easy conscience bring you peace of mind? No. If you did not regret the killings, you would regret profoundly the necessity for them. The thought of blood on your soul would for ever haunt you. Your spirit would be shaken and shadowed by remorse.

But that would not be all. The relatives and friends of those you had killed would hate you. They would hound you everywhere with their hatred. They would dog your footsteps and lie in wait to take your life. They would watch with jungle eyes for an opportunity for revenge.

Nor would this fill the cup of your misery. You would have achieved the sinister reputation of a fighter and a killer. Men who had no cause of quarrel against you, to whom your killings had meant nothing, would look upon you as they might upon a dangerous beast, a menace to society, a being outside the pale of human sympathy and law. The pack would be ready at any time to fall upon you without mercy and tear you to pieces. You would approach every rock and tree with caution lest some hidden foe fire upon you. You would not dare sleep in the same bed twice. You would suspect every man of treachery. When you sat at meat, you would feel that Death sat across the table with hollow eyes fixed upon you. Any minute you might expect a bullet or the plunge of a knife driven by unutterable hatred. Fear would walk hand in hand with you and lie down with you at night. You could not smile; peace and happiness would be denied you; there would be no zest, no joy for you this side of the grave. In your despair, you would welcome death as an escape from the hopeless hell of your hunted, haunted life.

But Billy the Kid was not of the stuff of ordinary men. There must have been in him a remarkable capacity for forgetfulness; he might seem to have drunk every morning a nepenthe that drowned in oblivion all his yesterdays. For him there was no past. He lived in the present from minute to minute, yet he lived happily. He killed without emotion and he accepted the consequences of his killings without emotion. His murders were strong liquor that left no headache. Surrounded by enemies who would have killed him with joy, breathing an atmosphere of bitter hatred, in danger of violent death every moment, he went his way through life without remorse, unracked by nerves or memories, gay, light-hearted, fearless, always smiling.

If you would learn in what affectionate regard the people of New Mexico cherish the memory of Billy the Kid to-day, you have but to journey in leisurely fashion through the Billy the Kid country. Every one will have a story to tell you of his courage, generosity, loyalty, light-heartedness, engaging boyishness. More than likely you yourself will fall under the spell of these kindly tales and, before you are aware, find yourself warming with romantic sympathy to the idealized picture of heroic and adventurous youth.

Sit, for instance, on one of the benches under the shade trees in the old square at Santa Fé where the wagon caravans used to end their long journey across the plains. Here the rich and poor of this ancient capital of the land of mañana and sunshine come every day to while away an hour and smoke and talk politics. Mention Billy the Kid to some leisurely burgher. Instantly his face will light up; he will cease his tirade against graft and corruption in high places and go off into interminable anecdotes. Yes, Billy the Kid lived here in Santa Fé when he was a boy. Many a time when he was an outlaw with a price on his head, he rode into town and danced all night at the dance hall over on Gallisteo Street. The house is still there; the pink adobe with the blue door and window shutters. Did the police attempt to arrest him? Not much. Those blue-coated fellows valued their hides. Why, that boy wasn't afraid of the devil. Say, once over at Anton Chico . . .

Or drop into some little adobe home in Puerta de Luna. Or in Santa Rosa. Or on the Hondo. Or anywhere between the Ratons and Seven Rivers. Perhaps the Mexican housewife will serve you with frijoles and tortillas and coffee with goat's milk. If you are wise in the ways of Mexicans, you will tear off a fragment of tortilla and, cupping it between your fingers, use it as a spoon to eat your frijoles that are red with chili pepper and swimming in soup rich with fat bacon grease. But between mouthfuls of these beans of the gods—and you will be ready to swear they are that, else you are no connoiseur in beans—don't forget to make some casual reference to Billy the Kid. Then watch the face of your hostess. At mention of the magic name, she will smile softly and dream-light will come into her eyes.

"Billee the Keed? Ah, you have hear of heem? He was one gran' boy, señor. All Mexican pepul his friend. You nevair hear a Mexican say one word against Billee the Keed. Everybody love that boy. He was so kind-hearted, so generous, so brave. And so 'andsome. *Nombre de Dios!* Every leetle señorita was crazy about heem. They all try to catch that Billee the Keed for their sweetheart. Ah, many a pretty *muchacha* cry her eyes out when he is keel; and when she count her beads at Mass, she add a prayer for good measure for his soul to rest in peace. Poor Billee the Keed! He was good boy—*muy valiente, muy caballero.*"

Or ask Frank Coe about him. You will find him a white-haired old man now on his fruit ranch in Ruidoso Cañon. He fought in the Lincoln County war by the Kid's side and as he tells his story you may sit in a rocking chair under the cottonwoods while the Ruidoso River sings its pleasant tune just back of the rambling, one-story adobe ranch house.

"Billy the Kid," says Coe, "lived with me for a while soon after he came to Lincoln County in the fall of 1877. Just a little before he went to work for Tunstall on the Feliz. No, he didn't work for me. Just lived with me. Riding the chuck line. Didn't have anywhere else special to stay just then. He did a lot of hunting that winter. Billy was a great hunter, and the hills hereabouts were full of wild turkey, deer, and cinnamon bear. Billy could hit a bear's eye so far away I could hardly see the bear.

"He was only eighteen years old, as nice-looking a young fellow as you'd care to meet, and certainly mighty pleasant company. Many a night he and I have sat up before a pine-knot fire swapping yarns. Yes, he had killed quite a few men even then, but it didn't seem to weigh on him. None at all. Ghosts, I reckon, never bothered Billy. He was about as cheerful a little hombre as I ever ran across. Not the grim, sullen kind; but full of talk, and it seemed to me he was laughing half his time.

"You never saw such shooting as that lad could do. Not a dead shot. I've heard about these dead shots but I never happened to meet one. Billy was the best shot with a six-shooter I ever saw, but he missed sometimes. Jesse Evans, who fought on the Murphy side, used to brag that he was as good a shot as the Kid, but I never thought so, and I knew Jesse and have seen him shoot. Jesse, by the way, used to say, too that he wasn't afraid of Billy the Kid. Which was just another one of his brags. He was scared to death of the Kid, and once when they met in Lincoln, Billy made him take water and made him like it. Billy used to do a whole lot of practice shooting around the ranch, and had the barn peppered full of holes. I have heard people say they have seen him empty his shooter at a hat tossed about twenty feet into the air and hit it six times before it struck the ground. I won't say he couldn't do it, but I never saw him do it. One of his favourite stunts was to shoot at snowbirds sitting on fence posts along the road as he rode by with his horse at a gallop. Sometimes he would kill a half-a-dozen birds one after the other; and then he would miss a few. His average was about one in three. And I'd say that was mighty good shooting.

"Billy had had a little schooling, and he could read and write as well as anybody else around here. I never saw him reading any books, but he was a great hand to read newspapers whenever he could get hold of any. He absorbed a lot of education from his newspaper reading. He didn't talk like a backwoodsman. I don't suppose he knew much about the rules of grammar, but he didn't make the common, glaring mistakes of ignorant people. His speech was that of an intelligent and fairly well-educated man. He had a clean mind; his conversation was never coarse or vulgar; and while most of the men with whom he associated swore like pirates, he rarely used an oath.

"He was a free-hearted, generous boy. He'd give a friend the shirt off his back. His money came easy when it came; but sometimes it didn't come. He was a gambler and, like all gamblers, his life was chicken one day and feathers the next, a pocketful of money to-day and broke to-morrow. Monte was his favourite game; he banked the game or bucked it, depending on his finances. He was as slick a dealer as ever threw a card, and as a player, he was shrewd, usually lucky, and bet 'em high—the limit on every turn. While he stayed with me, he broke a Mexican monte bank every little while down the cañon at San Patricio. If he happened to lose, he'd take it like a good gambler and, like as not, crack a joke and walk away whistling with his hands rammed in his empty pockets. Losing his money never made him mad. To tell the truth, I never saw Billy the Kid mad in my life, and I knew him several years.

"Think what you please, the Kid had a lot of principle. He was about as honest a fellow as I ever knew outside of some loose notions about rustling cattle. This was stealing, of course, but I don't believe it struck him exactly that way. It didn't seem to have any personal element in it. There were the cattle running loose on the plains without any owner in sight or sign of ownership, except the brands, seeming like part of the landscape. Billy, being in his fashion a sort of potentate ruling a large portion of the landscape with his six-shooter, felt, I suppose, like he had a sort of proprietary claim on those cattle, and it didn't seem to him like robbery— not exactly—to run them off and cash in on them at the nearest market. That's at least one way of figuring it out. But as for other lowdown kinds of theft like sticking up a lonely traveller on the highway, or burglarizing a house, or picking pockets, he was just as much above that sort of thing as you or me. I'd have trusted him with the last dollar I had in the world. One thing is certain, he never stole a cent in his life from a friend."

The history of Billy the Kid already has been clouded by legend. Less than fifty years after his death, it is not always easy to differentiate fact from myth. Historians have been afraid of him, as if this boy of six-shooter deadliness might fatally injure their reputations if they set themselves seriously to write of a career of such dime-novel luridness. As a consequence, history has neglected him. Fantastic details have been added as the tales have been told and retold. He is already in process of evolving into the hero of a Southwestern Niebelungenlied. Such a mass of stories has grown about him that it seems safe to predict that in spite of anything history can do to rescue the facts of his life, he is destined eventually to be transformed by popular legend into the Robin Hood of New Mexico—a heroic out-law endowed with every noble quality fighting the battle of the common people against the tyranny of wealth and power.

Innumerable stories in which Billy the Kid figures as a semi-mythical hero are to be picked up throughout New Mexico. They are told at every camp fire on the range; they enliven the winter evenings in every Mexican home. There is doubtless a grain of truth in every one, but the troubadour touch is upon them all. You will not find them in books, and their chief interest perhaps lies in the fact that they are examples of oral legend kept alive in memory and passed on by the story-tellers of one generation to the story-tellers of the next in Homeric succession. They are folklore in the making. As each narrative adds a bit of drama here an a picturesque detail there, one wonders what form these legends will assume as time goes by, and in what heroic proportions Billy the Kid will appear in fireside fairy tales a hundred years or so from now.

A Mexican Plug

In the 1860's, a young Sam Clemens (Mark Twain) accompanied his
brother west to the Nevada badlands. The brother had been appointed
Secretary of the Territory, and Sam was to serve as secretary to his brother.
It soon transpired that the position of secretary to the Secretary was an un-
paid office, so Sam was on his own. Thus began what he describes as "several years of variegated vagabondizing," the fruit of which was the book
Roughing It, from which this story is taken. It is a tenderfoot story, and one
of the best in our literature.

    The Tenderfoot is a stock character in cowboy lore. He's the fel-
low, probably newly come from the East, who can't rope or shoot or ride.
He doesn't measure up, he doesn't know the deal. He's not to be depended
on, and he's a little dangerous to be around, not because of any malice, or
flaw in his character, but simply because he's so inept. "Mister, I wouldn't
set that coal-oil on the stove. It ain't judicious." What he is though, is aw-
fully funny and he serves as an object lesson and warning to others. Generally this species of tale is told on someone else, but not with Mark Twain,
not in this story. He takes it on himself, makes himself the butt, and what
might have been the tale of a joke played on some "turnip" who doesn't
know his horseflesh, becomes a deeply humorous, so funny you about cry,
saga of one man's troubles. In the end Sam is able to flog his genuine Mexican Plug off on some other innocent newcomer. No one stays a tenderfoot long.

★   ★   ★   ★   ★

I resolved to have a horse to ride. I had never seen such wild, free, mag-
nificent horsemanship outside of a circus as these picturesquely-clad
Mexicans, Californians and Mexicanized Americans displayed in Carson streets every day. How they rode! Leaning just gently forward out
of the perpendicular, easy and nonchalant, with broad slouch-hat brim

blown square up in front, and long *riata* swinging above the head, they swept through the town like the wind! The next minute they were only a sailing puff of dust on the far desert. If they trotted, they sat up gallantly and gracefully, and seemed part of the horse; did not go jiggering up and down after the silly Miss-Nancy fashion of the riding-schools. I had quickly learned to tell a horse from a cow, and was full of anxiety to learn more. I was resolved to buy a horse.

While the thought was rankling in my mind, the auctioneer came skurrying through the plaza on a black beast that had as many humps and corners on him as a dromedary, and was necessarily uncomely; but he was "going, going, at twenty-two!—a horse, saddle and bridle at twenty-two dollars, gentlemen!" and I could hardly resist.

A man whom I did not know (he turned out to be the auctioneer's brother) noticed the wistful look in my eye, and observed that that was a very remarkable horse to be going at such a price; and added that the saddle alone was worth the money. It was a Spanish saddle, with ponderous *tapidaros*, and furnished with the ungainly sole-leather covering with the unspellable name. I said I had half a notion to bid. Then this keen-eyed person appeared to me to be "taking my measure"; but I dismissed the suspicion when he spoke, for his manner was full of guileless candor and truthfulness. Said he:

"I know that horse—know him well. You are a stranger, I take it, and so you might think he was an American horse, but I assure you he is not. He is nothing of the kind; but—excuse my speaking in a low voice, other people being near—he is, without the shadow of a doubt, a Genuine Mexican Plug!"

I did not know what a Genuine Mexican Plug was, but there was something about this man's way of saying it, that made me swear inwardly that I would own a Genuine Mexican Plug, or die.

"Has he any other—er—advantages?" I inquired, suppressing what eagerness I could.

He hooked his forefinger in the pocket of my army-shirt, led me to one side, and breathed in my ear impressively these words:

"He can out-buck anything in America!"

"Going, going, going—at *twenty*-four dollars and a half, gen—"

"Twenty-seven!" I shouted in a frenzy.

"And sold!" said the auctioneer, and passed over the Genuine Mexican Plug to me.

I could scarcely contain my exultation. I paid the money, and put the animal in a neighboring livery-stable to dine and rest himself.

In the afternoon I brought the creature into the plaza, and certain citizens held him by the head, and others by the tail, while I mounted him.

As soon as they let go, he placed all his feet in a bunch together, lowered his back, and then suddenly arched it upward, and shot me straight into the air a matter of three or four feet! I came as straight down again, lit in the saddle, went instantly up again, came down almost on the high pommel, shot up again, and came down on the horse's neck—all in the space of three or four seconds. Then he rose and stood almost straight up on his hind feet, and I, clasping his lean neck desperately, slid back into the saddle, and held on. He came down, and immediately hoisted his heels into the air, delivering a vicious kick at the sky, and stood on his forefeet. And then down he came once more, and began the original exercise of shooting me straight up again. The third time I went up I heard a stranger say:

"Oh, *don't* he buck, though!"

While I was up, somebody struck the horse a sounding thwack with a leathern strap, and when I arrived again the Genuine Mexican Plug was not there. A Californian youth chased him up and caught him, and asked if he might have a ride. I granted him that luxury. He mounted the Genuine, got lifted into the air once, but sent his spurs home as he descended, and the horse darted away like a telegram. He soared over three fences like a bird, and disappeared down the road toward the Washoe Valley.

I sat down on a stone, with a sigh, and by a natural impulse one of my hands sought my forehead, and the other the base of my stomach. I believe I never appreciated, till then, the poverty of the human machinery—for I still needed a hand or two to place elsewhere. Pen cannot describe how I was jolted up. Imagination cannot conceive how disjointed I was—how internally, externally and universally I was unsettled, mixed up and ruptured. There was a sympathetic crowd around me, though.

One elderly-looking comforter said:

"Stranger, you've been taken in. Everybody in this camp knows that horse. Any child, any Injun, could have told you that he'd buck; he is the very worst devil to buck on the continent of America. You hear *me.* I'm Curry. *Old* Curry. Old *Abe* Curry. And moreover, he is a simon-pure, out-and-out genuine d—d Mexican plug, and an uncommon mean one at that, too. Why, you turnip, if you had laid low and kept dark, there's chances to buy an *American* horse for mighty little more than you paid for that bloody old foreign relic."

I gave no sign; but I made up my mind that if the auctioneer's brother's funeral took place while I was in the Territory I would postpone all other recreations and attend it.

After a gallop of sixteen miles the Californian youth and the Genuine Mexican Plug came tearing into town again, shedding foam-flakes like the spume-spray that drives before a typhoon, and, with one final skip over a wheelbarrow and a Chinaman, cast anchor in front of the "ranch."

Such panting and blowing! Such spreading and contracting of the red equine nostrils, and glaring of the wild equine eye! But was the imperial beast subjugated? Indeed he was not. His lordship the Speaker of the House thought he was, and mounted him to go down to the Capitol; but the first dash the creature made was over a pile of telegraph poles half as high as a church; and his time to the Capitol—one mile and three quarters—remains unbeaten to this day. But then he took an advantage—he left out the mile, and only did the three quarters. That is to say, he made a straight cut across lots, preferring fences and ditches to a crooked road; and when the Speaker got to the Capitol he said he had been in the air so much he felt as if he had made the trip on a comet.

In the evening the Speaker came home afoot for exercise, and got the Genuine towed back behind a quartz wagon. The next day I loaned the animal to the Clerk of the House to go down to the Dana silver mine, six miles, and *he* walked back for exercise, and got the horse towed. Everybody I loaned him to always walked back; they never could get enough exercise any other way. Still, I continued to loan him to anybody who was willing to borrow him, my idea being to get him crippled, and throw him on the borrower's hands, or killed, and make the borrower pay for him, but somehow nothing ever happened to him. He took chances that no other horse ever took and survived, but he always came out safe. It was his daily habit to try experiments that had always before been considered impossible, but he always got through. Sometimes he miscalculated a little, and did not get his rider through intact, but *he* always got through himself. Of course I had tried to sell him; but that was a stretch of simplicity which met with little sympathy. The auctioneer stormed up and down the streets for four days, dispersing the populace, interrupting business, and destroying children, and never got a bid—at least never any but the eighteen-dollar one he hired a notoriously substanceless bummer to make. The people only smiled pleasantly, and restrained their desire to buy, if they had any. Then the auctioneer brought in his bill, and I withdrew the horse from the market. We tried to trade him off at private vendue next, offering him at a sacrifice for second-hand tombstones, old iron, temperance tracts—any kind of property. But holders were stiff, and we retired from the market again. I never tried to ride the horse any more. Walking was good enough exercise for a man like me, that had nothing the matter with him except ruptures, internal injuries, and such things. Finally I tried to *give* him away. But it was a failure. Parties said earthquakes were handy enough on the Pacific coast—they did not wish to own one. As a last resort I offered him to the Governor for the use of the "Brigade." His face lit up eagerly at first, but toned down again, and he said the thing would be too palpable.

Just then the livery stable man brought in his bill for six weeks' keeping—stall-room for the horse, fifteen dollars; hay for the horse, two hundred and fifty! The Genuine Mexican Plug had eaten a ton of the article, and the man said he would have eaten a hundred if he had let him.

I will remark here, in all seriousness, that the regular price of hay during that year and a part of the next was really two hundred and fifty dollars a ton. During a part of the previous year it had sold at five hundred a ton, in gold, and during the winter before that there was such scarcity of the article that in several instances small quantities had brought eight hundred dollars a ton in coin! The consequence might be guessed without my telling it; people turned their stock loose to starve, and before the spring arrived Carson and Eagle valleys were almost literally carpeted with their carcases! Any old settler there will verify these statements.

I managed to pay the livery bill, and that same day I gave the Genuine Mexican Plug to a passing Arkansas emigrant whom fortune delivered into my hand. If this ever meets his eye, he will doubtless remember the donation.

Now whoever has had the luck to ride a real Mexican plug will recognize the animal depicted in this chapter, and hardly consider him exaggerated—but the uninitiated will feel justified in regarding his portrait as a fancy sketch, perhaps.

Jack Hildreth Among the Indians

BY KARL MAY

Here is a European cowboy tale, and a tenderfoot story, with a difference. You might even call it: *The Tenderfoot's Answer* or *The Revenge of the Tenderfoot.* In this story, young Jack Hildreth leaves his middle class home in Germany and betakes himself out west to "the mountian region of New Mexico." You'd think this would make him Grade A prime tenderfoot. But the thing about Jack is that he does everything better than everyone else around him. In any company, he is the natural leader. He's stronger, quicker, ropes and rides better, shoots straighter and is more judicious than everyone he meets up with. He's even modest about it.

Karl May is one of the most popular novelists of all time. Though only a little known in the United States, he is still, after more than a century, widely read in Europe and around the world. In his own day he was a blockbuster best-seller with more copies of his over sixty books in print than any of his contemporaries, in any language. He was said to be Albert Schweitzer's favorite novelist.

This selection is from *Winnetou, The Apache Knight,* and was first published in 1893.

★ ★ ★ ★ ★

Toward the Setting Sun

It is not necessary to say much about myself. First of all because there is not very much to tell of a young fellow of twenty-three, and then because I hope what I have done and seen will be more interesting than I am, for, between you and me, I often find Jack Hildreth a dull kind of person, especially on a rainy day when I have to sit in the house alone with him.

When I was born three other children has preceded me in the world, and my father's dreamy blue eyes saw no way of providing suitably for this superfluous fourth youngster. And then my uncle John came forward and said: "Name the boy after me, and I'll be responsible for his future." Now Uncle John was rich and unmarried, and though my father could never get his mind down to anything more practical than deciphering cuneiform inscriptions, even he saw that this changed the unflattering prospects of his latest-born into unusually smiling ones.

So I became Jack Hildreth secundus, and my uncle nobly fulfilled his part of the contract. He kept me under his own eye, gave me a horse before my legs were long enough to bestride him, nevertheless expecting me to sit him fast, punished me well if I was quarrelsome or domineering with other boys, yet punished me no less surely if when a quarrel was forced upon me, I showed the white feather or failed to do my best to whip my enemy.

"Fear God, but fear no man. Never lie, or sneak, or truckle for favor. Never betray a trust. Never be cruel to man or beast. Never inflict pain deliberately, but never be afraid to meet it if you must. Be kind, be honest, be daring. Be a man, and you will be a gentleman." This was my uncle's simple code; and as I get older, and see more of life, I am inclined to think there is none better.

My uncle sent me to the Jesuit college, and I went through as well as I could, because he trusted me to do so. I did not set the college world afire, but I stood fairly in my classes, and was first in athletics, and my old soldier uncle cared for that with ill-concealed pride.

When I left the student's life, and began to look about on real life and wonder where to take hold of it, I was so restless and overflowing with health and strength that I could not settle down to anything, and the fever for life on the plains came upon me. I longed to be off to the wild and woolly West—the wilder and woollier the better—before I assumed the shackles of civilization forever.

"Go if you choose, Jack," my uncle said. "Men are a better study than books, after you've been grounded in the latter. Begin the study in the primer of an aboriginal race, if you like; indeed it may be the best. There's plenty of time to decide on your future, for, as you're to be my heir, there's no pressing need of beginning labor."

My uncle had the necessary influence to get me appointed as an engineer with a party which was to survey for a railroad among the mountains of New Mexico and Arizona—a position I was competent to fill, as I had chosen civil engineering as my future profession, and had studied it thoroughly.

I scarcely realised that I was going till I found myself in St. Louis, where I was to meet the scouts of the party, who would take me with them to join the surveyors at the scene of our labors. On the night after my arrival I invited the senior scout, Sam Hawkins, to sup with me, in order that I might make his acquaintance before starting in the morning.

I do not know whether the Wild West Show was unconsciously in my mind, but when Mr. Hawkins appeared at the appointed time I certainly felt disappointed to see him clad in ordinary clothes and not in the picturesque costume of Buffalo Bill, till I reflected that in St. Louis even a famous Indian scout might condescend to look like every-day mortals.

"So you're the young tenderfoot; glad to make your acquaintance, sir," he said, and held out his hand, smiling at me from an extraordinary face covered with a bushy beard of many moons' growth and shadowed by a large nose a trifle awry, above which twinkled a pair of sharp little eyes.

My guest surprised me not a little, after I had responded to his greeting, by hanging his hat on the gas-fixture, and following it with his hair.

"Don't be shocked," he said calmly, seeing, I suppose, that this was unexpected. "You will excuse me, I hope, for the Pawnees have taken my natural locks. It was a mighty queer feeling, but fortunately I was able to stand it. I went to Tacoma and bought myself a new scalp, and it cost me a roll of good dollars. It doesn't matter; the new hair is more convenient than the old, especially on a warm day, for I never could hang my own wig up like that."

He had a way of laughing inwardly, and his shoulders shook as he spoke, though he made no sound.

"Can you shoot?" asked my queer companion suddenly.

"Fairly," I said, not so much, I am afraid, because I was modest as because I wanted to have the fun of letting him find out that I was a crack marksman.

"And ride?"

"If I have to."

"If you have to! Not as well as you shoot, then?"

"Pshaw! what is riding? The mounting is all that is hard; you can hang on somehow if once you're up."

He looked at me to see whether I was joking or in earnest; but I looked innocent, so he said: "There's where you make a mistake. What you should have said is that mounting is hard because you have to do that yourself, while the horse attends to your getting off again."

"The horse won't see to it in my case," I said with confidence— born of the fact that my kind uncle had accustomed me to clinging to high-strung beasts before I had lost my milk-teeth.

"A kicking broncho is something to try the nettle of a tenderfoot," remarked Hawkins dryly.

I suppose you know what a tenderfoot is. He is one who speaks good English, and wears gloves as if he were used to them. He also has a prejudice in favor of nice handkerchiefs and well-kept finger-nails; he may know a good deal about history, but he is liable to mistake turkey-tracks for bear-prints, and, though he has learned astronomy, he could never find his way by the stars. The tenderfoot sticks his bowie-knife into his belt in such a manner that it runs into his thigh when he bends; and when he builds a fire on the prairie he makes it so big that it flames as high as a tree, yet feels surprised that the Indians notice it. But many a tenderfoot is a daring, strong-bodied and strong-hearted fellow; and though there was no doubt that I was a tenderfoot fast enough, I hoped to convince Sam Hawkins that I had some qualities requisite for success on the plains.

By the time our supper was over there was a very good understanding established between me and the queer little man to whose faithful love I was to owe so much. He was an eccentric fellow, with a pretence of crustiness covering his big, true heart; but it was not hard to read him by the law of contraries, and our mutual liking dated from that night of meeting.

We set out in the early dawn of the following morning, accompanied by the other two scouts, Dick Stone and Will Parker, whom I then saw for the first time, and whom I learned to value only less than Sam as the truest of good comrades. Our journey was as direct and speedy as we could make it to the mountain region of New Mexico, near the Apache Indian reservation, and I was welcomed by my fellow-workers with a cordiality that gave rise to hopes of pleasant relations with them which were never realised. The party consisted of the head engineer, Bancroft, and three men under him. With them were twelve men intended to serve as our protectors, a sort of standing army, and for whom, as hardworking pioneers, I, a new-comer, had considerable respect until I discovered that they were men of the lowest moral standards.

Although I had entered the service only for experience, I was in earnest and did my duty conscientiously; but I soon found out that my colleagues were genuine adventurers, only after money, and caring nothing for their work except as a means of getting it.

Bancroft was the most dishonest of all. He loved his bottle too well and got private supplies for it from Santa Fe, and worked harder with the brandy-flask than with his surveying instruments. Riggs, Marcy, and Wheeler, the three surveyors, emulated Bancroft in this unprofitable pursuit; and as I never touched a drop of liquor, I naturally was the laborer, while the rest alternated between drinking and sleeping off the effects.

It goes without saying that under such circumstances our work did not progress rapidly, and at the end of the glorious autumn and three months of labor we found ourselves with our task still unaccomplished, while the section with which ours was to connect was almost completed. Besides our workmen being such as they were, we had to work in a region infested with Comanches, Kiowas, and Apaches, who objected to a road through their territory, and we had to be constantly on our guard, which made our progress still slower.

Personally my lot was not a bed of roses, for the men disliked me, and called me "tenderfoot" ten times a day, and took a special delight in thwarting my will, especially Rattler, the leader of our so-called guard, and as big a rascal as ever went unhanged. I durst not speak to them in an authoritative manner, but had to manage them as a wise woman manages a tyrannical husband without his perceiving it.

But I had allies in Sam Hawkins and his two companion scouts, Dick Stone and Will Parker. They were friendly to me, and held off from the others, in whom Sam Hawkins especially managed to inspire respect in spite of his droll peculiarities. There was an alliance formed between us silently, which I can best describe as a sort of feudal relation; he had taken me under his protection like a man who did not need to ask if he were understood. I was the "tenderfoot," and he the experienced frontiersman whose words and deeds had to be infallible to me. As often as he had time and opportunity he gave me practical and theoretical instruction in everything necessary to know and do in the Wild West; and though I graduated from the high school later, so to speak, with Winneotu as master, Sam Hawkins was my elementary teacher.

He made me expert with a lasso, and let me practise with that useful weapon on his own little person and his horse. When I had reached the point of catching them at every throw he was delighted, and cried out: "Good, my young sir! That's fine. But don't be set up with this praise. A teacher must encourage his stupid scholars when they make a little progress. I have taught lots of young frontiersmen, and they all learned much easier and understood me far quicker than you have, but perhaps it's possible that after eight years or so you may not be called a tenderfoot. You can comfort yourself with the thought that sometimes a stupid man gets on as well as or even a little better than a clever one."

He said this as if in sober earnest, and I received it in the same way, knowing well how differently he meant it. We met at a distance from the camp, where we could not be observed. Sam Hawkins would have it so; and when I asked why, he said: "For mercy's sake, hide yourself, sir. You are so awkward that I should be ashamed to have these fellows see you, so that's why I keep you in the shade—that's the only reason; take it to heart."

The consequence was that none of the company suspected that I had any skill in weapons, or special muscular strength—an ignorance that I was glad to foster.

One day I gave Rattler an order; it was some trifling thing, too small for me to remember now, and he would have been willing to carry it out had not his mood been rather uglier than usual.

"Do it yourself," he growled. "You impudent greenhorn, I'll show you I'm as good as you are any day."

"You're drunk," I said, looking him over and turning away.

"I'm drunk, am I?" he replied, glad of a chance to get at me, whom he hated.

"Very drunk, or I'd knock you down," I answered.

Rattler was a big, brawny fellow, and he stepped up in front of me, rolling up his sleeves. "Who, me? Knock me down? Well, I guess not, you blower, you kid, you greenhorn—"

He said no more. I hit him square in the face, and he dropped like an ox. Fearing mischief from Rattler's followers, and realising that now or never was my authority to be established, I drew my pistol, crying: "If one of you puts his hand to a weapon I'll shoot him on the spot." No one stirred. "Take your friend away, and let him sober up, and when he comes to his senses he may be more respectful," I remarked.

As the men obeyed me, Wheeler, the surveyor, whom I thought the best of the lot, stepped from the others and came up to me. "That was a great blow," he said. "Let me congratulate you. I never saw such strength. They'll call you Shatterhand out here."

This seemed to suit little Sam exactly. He threw up his hat, shouting joyously: "Shatterhand! Good! A tenderfoot, and already won a name, and what a name! Shatterhand; Old Shatterhand. It's like Old Firehand, who is a frontiersman as strong as a bear. I tell you, boy, it's great, and you're christened for good and all in the Wild West."

And so I found myself in a new and strange life, and beginning it with a new name, which became as familiar and as dear to me as my own.

My First Buffalo

Three days after the little disciplining I had given Rattler, Mr. White, the head engineer of the next section, rode over to us to report that their work was finished, and to inquire what our prospects were for making speedy connection. When he set out on his return he invited Sam Hawkins and me to accompany him part of the way through the valley.

We found him a very agreeable companion; and when we came to the point where we were to turn back we shook hands cordially, leaving him with regret. "There's one thing I want to warn you of," Mr. White said in parting. "Look out for redskins."

"Have you seen them?" Sam asked.

"Not them, but their tracks. Now is the time when the wild mustangs and the buffaloes go southward, and the Indians follow in the chase. The Kiowas are all right, for we arranged with them for the road, but the Apaches and Comanches know nothing of it, and we don't dare let them see us. We have finished our part, and are ready to leave this region; hurry up with yours, and do likewise. Remember there's danger, and good-by."

Sam looked gravely after his retreating form, and pointed to a footprint near the spring where we had paused for parting. "He's quite right to warn us of Indians," he said.

"Do you mean this footprint was made by an Indian?"

"Yes, an Indian's moccasin. How does that make you feel?"

"Not at all."

"You must feel or think something."

"What should I think except that an Indian has been here?"

"Not afraid?"

"Not a bit."

"Oh," cried Sam, "you're living up to your name of Shatterhand; but I tell you that Indians are not so easy to shatter; you don't know them."

"But I hope to understand them. They must be like other men, enemies to their enemies, friends to their friends; and as I mean to treat them well, I don't see why I should fear them."

"You'll find out," said Sam, "or you'll be a greenhorn for eternity. You may treat the Indians as you like, and it won't turn out as you expect, for the results don't depend on your will. You'll learn by experience, and I only hope the experience won't cost you your life."

This was not cheering, and for some time we rode through the pleasant autumn air in silence.

Suddenly Sam reined up his horse, and looked ahead earnestly through half-closed lids. "By George," he cried excitedly, "there they are! Actually there they are, the very first ones."

"What?" I asked. I saw at some distance ahead of us perhaps eighteen or twenty dark forms moving slowly.

"What!" repeated Sam, bouncing up and down in his saddle. "I'd be ashamed to ask such a question; you are indeed a precious greenhorn. Can't you guess, my learned sir, what those things are before your eyes there?"

"I should take them for deer if I didn't know there were none about here; and though those animals look so small from here, I should say they were larger than deer."

"Deer in this locality! That's a good one! But your other guess is not so bad; they certainly are larger than deer."

"O Sam, they surely can't be buffaloes?"

"They surely can. Bisons they are, genuine bisons beginning their travels, and the first I have seen. You see Mr. White was right: buffaloes and Indians. We saw only a footprint of the red men, but the buffaloes are there before our eyes in all their strength. What do you say about it?"

"We must go up to them."

"Sure."

"And study them."

"Study them? Really study them?" he asked glancing at me side-wise in surprise.

"Yes; I never saw a buffalo, and I'd like to watch them."

I felt the interest of a naturalist, which was perfectly incomprehensible to little Sam. He rubbed his hands together, saying: "Watch them, only watch them! Like a child putting his eye to a rabbit's hole to see the little bunnies! O you young tenderfoot, what I must put up with in you! I don't want to watch them or study them, I tell you, but hunt them. They mean meat—meat, do you understand? and such meat! A buffalo-steak is more glorious than ambrosia, or ambrosiana, or whatever you call the stuff the old Greeks fed their gods with. I must have a buffalo if it costs me my life. The wind is towards us; that's good. The sun's on the left, towards the valley, but it's shady on the right, and if we keep in the shade the animals won't see us. Come on."

He looked to see if his gun, "Liddy," as he called it, was all right, and I hastily overhauled my own weapon. Seeing this, Sam held up his horse and asked: "Do you want to take a hand in this?"

"Of course."

"Well, you let that thing alone if you don't want to be trampled to jelly in the next ten minutes. A buffalo isn't a canary bird for a man to take on his finger and let it sing."

"But I will —"

"Be silent, and obey me," he interrupted in a tone he had never used before. "I won't have your life on my conscience, and you would ride into the jaws of certain death. You can do what you please at other times, but now I'll stand no opposition."

Had there not been such a good understanding between us I would have given him a forcible answer; but as it was, I rode after him in the shadow of the hills without speaking, and after a while Sam said in his usual manner: "There are twenty head, as I reckon. Once a thousand or more browsed over the plains. I have seen early herds numbering a thousand and upward. They were the Indians' food, but the white men have taken it from them. The redskin hunted to live, and only killed what he needed. But the white man has ravaged countless herds, like a robber who for very lust of blood keeps on slaying when he is well supplied. It won't be long before there are no buffaloes, and a little longer and there'll be no Indians, God help them! And it's just the same with the herds of horses. There used to be herds of a thousand mustangs, and even more. Now a man is lucky if he sees two together."

We had come within four hundred feet of the buffaloes unobserved, and Hawkins reined in his horse. In the van of the herd was an old bull whose enormous bulk I studied with wonder. He was certainly six feet high and ten long; I did not then know how to estimate the weight of a buffalo, but I should now say that he must have weighed sixteen hundred pounds—an astounding mass of flesh and bone.

"That's the leader, whispered Sam, "the most experienced of the whole crowd. Whoever tackles him had better make his will first. I will take the young cow right back of him. The best place to shoot is behind the shoulder-blade into the heart; indeed it's the only sure place except the eyes, and none but a madman would go up to a buffalo and shoot into his eyes. You stay here, and hide yourself and your horse in the thicket. When they see me they'll run past here; but don't you quit your place unless I come back or call you."

He waited until I had hidden between two bushes, and then rode slowly forward. It seemed to me this took great courage. I had often read how buffaloes were hunted, and knew all about it; but there is a great difference between a printed page and the real thing. To-day I had seen buffaloes for the first time in my life; and though at first I only wished to study them, as I watched Sam I felt an irresistible longing to join in the sport. He was going to shoot a young cow. Pshaw! that, I thought, required no courage; a true man would choose the strongest bull.

My horse was very restless; he, too, had never seen buffaloes before, and he pawed the ground, frightened and so anxious to run that I could scarcely hold him. Would it not be better to let him go, and attack the old bull myself? I debated this question inwardly, divided between desire to go and regard for Sam's command, meantime watching his every movement.

He had approached within a hundred feet of the buffaloes, when he spurred his horse and galloped into the herd, past the mighty bull, up to the cow which he had selected. She pricked up her ears, and started to run. I saw Sam shoot. She staggered, and her head dropped, but I did not know whether or not she fell, for my eyes were chained to another spot.

The great bull, which had been lying down, was getting up, and turned toward Sam Hawkins. What a mighty beast! The thick head with the enormous skull, the broad forehead with its short, strong horns, the neck and breast covered with the coarse mane, made a picture of the greatest possible strength. Yes, it was a marvellous creature, but the sight of him aroused a longing to measure human strength with this power of the plains. Should I or should I not? I could not decide, nor was I sure that my roan would take me towards him; but just then my frightened horse sprang forth from our cover, and I resolved to try, and spurred him towards the bull. He heard me coming, and turned to meet me, lowering his head to receive horse and rider on his horns. I heard Sam cry out something with all his might, but had no time even to glance at him. It was impossible to shoot the buffalo, for in the first place he was not in the right position, and in the second place my horse would not obey me, but for very fear ran straight towards the threatening horns. The buffalo braced his hind legs to toss us, and raised his head with a mighty bellow. Exerting all my strength, I turned my horse a little, and he leaped over the bull, while the horns grazed my leg.

My course lay directly towards a mire in which the buffalo had been sleeping. I saw this, and fortunately drew my feet from the stirrups; my horse slipped and we both fell.

How it all happened so quickly is incomprehensible to me now, but the next moment I stood upright beside the morass, my gun still in my hand. The buffalo turned on the horse, which had also risen quickly, and came on him in ungainly leaps, and this brought his flank under my fire. I took aim. One more bound and the buffalo would reach my horse. I pulled the trigger; he stopped, whether from fear or because he was hit I did not know, but I fired again, two shots in rapid succession. He slowly raised his head, froze my blood with a last awful roar, swayed from side and side and fell where he stood.

I might have rejoiced over this narrow escape, but I had something else to attend to. I saw Sam Hawkins galloping for dear life across the valley, followed by a steer not much smaller than my bull had been.

When the bison is aroused his speed is as great as that of a horse; he never gives up his object, and shows a courage and perseverance one would not have expected of him. So this steer was pressing the rider hard, and in order to escape him Sam had to make many turns, which so wearied his horse that he could not hold out as long as the buffalo, and it was quite time that help arrived.

I did not stop to see whether or not my bull was dead. I quickly reloaded both chambers of my gun, and ran across the grass towards Sam. He saw me, and turned his horse in my direction. This was a great mistake, for it brought the horse's side towards the steer behind him. I saw him lower his horns, and in an instant horse and rider were tossed in the air, and fell to the ground with a dreadful thud. Sam cried for help as well as he could. I was a good hundred and fifty feet away, but I dared not delay, though the shot would have been surer at shorter range. I aimed at the steer's left shoulder-blade and fired. The buffalo raised his head as if listening, turned slowly, then ran at me with all his might. Luckily for me, his moment of hesitation had given me time to reload, and therefore I was ready for him by the time the beast had made thirty paces towards me. He could no longer run; his steps became slow, but with deep-hanging head and protruding, bloodshot eyes he came nearer and nearer to me, like some awful, unavoidable fate. I knelt down and brought my gun into position. This movement made the buffalo halt and raise his head a little to see me better, thus bringing his eyes just in range of both barrels. I sent one shot into the right, and another into the left eye; a quick shudder went through his body, and the beast fell dead.

Springing to my feet, I rushed toward Sam; but it was not necessary, for I saw him approaching.

"Hallo!" I cried, "are you alive?"

"Very much so, only my left hip pains me, or the right; I'm sure I can't tell which."

"And your horse?"

"Done for; he's still alive, but he's torn past help. We'll have to shoot him to put him out of his misery, poor fellow. Is the buffalo dead?"

I was not able to answer this question positively, so we made sure that there was no life in my former foe, and Hawkins said: "He treated me pretty badly, this old brute; a cow would have been gentler, but I suppose you can't expect such an old soldier to be lady-like. Let us go to my poor horse."

We found him in a pitiable condition, torn so that his entrails protruded, and groaning with agony. Sam loaded, and gave the poor creature the shot that ended his suffering, and then he removed the saddle and bridle, saying: "I'll be my own horse, and put these on my back."

"Where will you get another horse?" I asked.

"That's the least of my trouble; I'll find one unless I'm mistaken."

"A mustang?"

"Yes. The buffaloes are here; they've begun travelling southward, and soon we'll see the mustangs, I'm sure of that."

"May I go with you when you catch one?"

"Sure; you'll have to learn to do it. I wonder if that old bull is dead; such Mathusalas are wonderfully tough."

But the beast was dead, as we found on investigation; and as he lay there I realized more fully what a monster he was. Sam looked him over, shook his head, and said: "It is perfectly incredible. Do you know what you are?"

"What?"

"The most reckless man on earth."

"I've never been accused of recklessness before."

"Well, now you know that 'reckless' is the word for you. I forbade you meddling with a buffalo or leaving your hiding-place; but if you were going to disobey me, why didn't you shoot a cow?"

"Because this was more knightly."

"Knightly! Great Scott! This tenderfoot wants to play knight!" He laughed till he had to take hold of the bushes for support, and when he got his breath he cried: "The true frontiersman does what is most expedient, not what's more knightly."

"And I did that, too."

"How do you make that out?"

"That big bull has much more flesh on him than a cow."

Sam looked at me mockingly. "Much more flesh!" he cried. "And this youngster shot a bull for his flesh! Why, boy, this old stager had surely eighteen or twenty years on his head, and his flesh is as hard as leather, while the cow's flesh is fine and tender. All this shows again what a greenhorn you are. Now go get your horse, and we'll load him with all the meat he can carry."

In spite of Sam's mocking me, that night as I stood unobserved in the door of the tent where he and Stone and Parker sat by their fire I heard Sam say: "Yes, sir, he's going to be a genuine Westerner; he's born one. And how strong he is! Yesterday he drew our great oxcart alone and single-handed. Now to-day I owe him my life. But we won't let him know what we think of him."

"Why not?" asked Barker.

"It might swell his head," replied Sam. "Many a good fellow has been spoiled by praise. I suppose he'll think I'm an ungrateful old curmudgeon, for I never even thanked him for saving my life. But to-morrow I'll give him a treat; I'll take him to catch a mustang, and, no matter what he thinks, I know how to value him."

I crept away, pleased with what I had heard, and touched by the loving tone of my queer friend's voice as he spoke of me.

Wild Mustangs and Long-Eared Nancy

The next morning as I was going to work Sam came to me, saying: "Put down your instruments; we have something on hand more interesting than surveying."

"What is it?"

"You'll see. Get your horse ready; we're going to ride."

"And how about the work?"

"Nonsense! You've done your share. However, I expect to be back by noon, and then you can measure as much as you will."

After arranging with Bancroft for my absence, we started; and as Sam made a mystery of the object of our expedition, I said nothing to show that I suspected what it was.

We went back of the ravine where we were surveying to a stretch of prairie which Sam had pointed out the day before. It was two good miles broad, and surrounded by woody heights, from which flowed a brook irrigating the plain. We rode to the westerly boundary, where the grass was freshest, and here Sam securely tied his horse—his borrowed horse—and let him graze. As he looked about him an expression of satisfaction shone on his rugged face, like sunshine on rocks. "Dismount, sir," he said, "and tie your horse strong; we'll wait here."

"Why tie him so strongly?" I asked, though I knew well.

"Because you might lose him. I have often seen horses go off with such companions."

"Such companions as what?" I asked.

"Try to guess."

"Mustangs?"

"How did you know?"

"I've read that if domestic horses weren't well tied they'd join the wild ones when a herd came along."

"Confound it! you've read so much a man can't get the best of you."

"Do you want to get the best of me?"

"Of course. But look, the mustangs have been here."

"Are those their tracks?"

"Yes; they went through here yesterday. It was a scouting party. Let me tell you that these beasts are uncommonly sharp. They always send out little advance-parties, which have their officers exactly like soldiers, and the commander is the strongest and most experienced horse. They travel in circular formation, stallions outside, mares next them inside, and the foals in the middle, in order that the males may protect the mares and young. I have already shown you how to catch a mustang with a lasso; do you remember? Would you like to capture one?"

"Certainly I would."

"Well, you'll have a chance before noon to-day."

"Thanks, but I don't intend to catch one."

"The dickens you don't! And why not?"

"Because I don't need a horse."

"But a real frontiersman never asks whether he needs a horse or not."

"Now look here, Sam; only yesterday you were speaking of the brutal way the white men, though they do not need meat, kill the buffaloes in masses, depriving the Indians of their food. We agreed that was a crime against beasts and men."

"Assuredly."

"This is a similar case. I should do wrong to rob one of these glorious fellow of his freedom unless I needed a horse."

"That's well said, young man; bravely said. Any man, any Christian worth calling so, would feel thus; but who said anything about robbing him of his freedom? Just put your education in lasso-throwing to the proof, that's all."

"That's a different thing; I'll do that."

"All right; and I'll use one in earnest, for I do need a horse. I've often told you, and now I'll say again: Sit strong in your saddle, control your horse well when you feel the lasso tighten, and pull; for if you don't you'll be unseated, and the mustang will gallop off, taking your horse and lasso with him. then you'll lose your mount and be, like me, only a common foot soldier."

He was about to give more advice, but stopped suddenly, and pointed to the northern end of the prairie. There stood a horse, one single solitary horse. He walked slowly forward, not stopping to graze, turning his head first to one side, then to the other, snuffing the air as he came.

"Do you see?" whispered Sam. "Didn't I tell you they'd come? That's the scout come on ahead to see if all's safe. He's a wise beast! See how he looks in all directions! He won't discover us, though, for we have the wind towards us."

The mustang broke into a trot, running to the right, then to the left, and finally turned and disappeared as we had seen him come.

"Did you see him?" cried Sam admiringly. "How wise he is! An Indian scout could not have done better."

"That's so; I'm surprised at him."

"Now he's gone back to tell his general the air is pure. How we fooled him! They'll all be here shortly. You ride back to the other end of the prairie, and wait there, while I go towards them and hide in the trees. When they come I'll chase them, and they'll fly in your direction; then you show yourself, and they'll turn back towards me. So we'll drive them back and forth till we've picked out the two best horses, and we'll catch them and choose between them. Do you agree?"

"How can you ask? I know nothing of the art of mustang-catching, of which you are past master, and I've nothing to do but follow your directions."

"All right. I have caught mustangs before to-day, and I hope you're not far wrong in calling me a 'master' of that trade. Now let's take our places."

We turned and rode in opposite directions, he northward, I southward to the spot where we had entered the prairie. I got behind some little trees, made one end of the lasso fast, and coiled the other ready for use. The further end of the prairie was so far off that I could not see the mustangs when they first appeared, but after I had been waiting a quarter of an hour I saw what looked like a dark cloud rapidly increasing in size and advancing in my direction. At first it seemed to be made up of objects about as big as sparrows, then they seemed like cats, dogs, calves, and at last I saw them in their own proportions. They were the mustangs in wild gallop, coming towards me. What a sight these lordly beasts were, with their manes flying about their necks, and their tails streaming like plumes in the wind! There were at least three hundred head, and the earth seemed to tremble beneath the pounding of their hoofs. A white stallion led them, a noble creature that any man might be glad to capture, only no prairie hunter would ride a white horse, for he would be too conspicuous to his enemies.

Now was the time to show myself. I came out, and the startled leader sprang back as though an arrow had pierced him. The herd halted; one loud, eager whinny from the white stallion which plainly meant: Wheel, squadron! and the splendid fellow turned, followed by all his companions, and tore back whence they had come. I followed slowly; there was no hurry, for I knew Sam Hawkins would drive them back to me. I wanted to make sure I was right in which I had seen, for in the brief instant the herd had halted it seemed to me that one of them was not a horse, but a mule. The animal that I thought a mule had been in the front ranks, immediately behind the leader, and so seemed not merely to be tolerated by its companions, but to hold honorable rank among them.

Once again the herd came towards me, and I saw that I was not mistaken, but that a mule really was among them, a mule of a delicate light brown color, with dark back-stripe, and which I thought had the biggest head and the longest ears I had ever seen. Mules are more suitable for rough mountain-riding than horses, are surer-footed, and less likely to fall into abysses—a fact worth consideration. To be sure they are obstinate, and I have known a mule be beaten half to death rather than take another step, not because it was overladen or the way was hard, but simply because it would not. It seemed to me that this mule showed more spirit than the horses, and that its eyes gleamed brighter and more intelligently than theirs, and I resolved to capture it. Evidently it had escaped from its former owner and joined the mustangs.

Now once more Sam turned the herd, and we had approached each other till I could see him. The mustangs could no longer run back and forth; they turned to the side, we following them. The herd had divided, and I saw that the mule was with the more important part, still keeping beside the white horse, and proving itself an unusually strong and swift animal. I pursued this band, and Sam seemed to have the same design.

"Get around them; I left, you right," he shouted.

We spurred our horses, and not only kept up with the mustangs, but rode so swiftly that we headed them off from the woods. They began to scatter to all sides like chickens when a hawk swoops down among them; and as we both chased the white stallion and the mule, Sam cried: "You'll always be a greenhorn. Who else would pick out a white horse?"

I answered him, but his loud laugh drowned my reply, and if he thought I was after the white horse it did not much matter. I left the mule to his tender care, and in a moment he had come so near her that he threw the lasso.

The noose encircled the beast's neck, and now Sam had to hold on as he had directed me to do, and throw himself backward to make the lasso hold when it tautened. This he did, but a moment too late; his horse did not obey on the instant, and was thrown by the force of the jerk. Sam flew through the air, and landed on the ground with a thump. The horse shook himself free, and was up and off in a moment, and the mule with him, since the lasso was fast to the saddle-bow.

I hastened to see if Sam was hurt, and found him standing, much shaken, but not otherwise the worse. He said to me in mournful tones: "There go Dick Stone's chestnut and the mule without saying good-by."

"Are you hurt?"

"No. Jump down and give me your horse."

"What for?"

"To catch them, of course. Hurry up."

"Not much; you might turn another somersault, and then both our horses would be gone to the four winds." With these words I put my horse after the mule and Dick's horse. Already they were in trouble, one pulling one way, the other another, and held together by the lasso, so I could easily come up with them. It never entered my head to use my lasso, but I grabbed the one holding them, wound it around my hand, and felt sure the day was won. I drew the noose tighter and tighter, thus easily controlling the mule, and brought her back, together with the horse, in apparent subjection to where Sam stood.

Then I suddenly pulled the noose taut, when the mule lost her breath and fell to the ground.

"Hold on fast till I have the rascal, and then let go," shouted Sam, springing to the side of the prostrate beast. "Now!" he cried.

I let go the lasso, and the mule instantly jumped up, but not before Sam was on her back. She stood motionless a moment in surprise, then rushed from side to side, then stood first on her hind legs, then on her fore legs, and finally jumped into the air with all four bunched together, and her back arched like a cat's. but still little Sam sat fast.

"Don't get near; she's going to try her last hope and run away, but I'll bring her back tamed," shouted Sam.

He proved to be mistaken, however; she only ran a little way, and then deliberately lay down and rolled. This was too much for Sam's ribs; he had to get out of the saddle. I jumped from my horse, seized the lasso, and wound it around some tough roots near at hand. The mule, finding she had no rider, got up and started to run off; but the roots were strong, the noose drew tight, and again the animal fell. Sam had retired to one side, feeling his legs and ribs, and making a face as if he had eaten sauerkraut and marmalade.

"Let the beast go," he said. "I believe nobody can conquer her."

"Well, I guess not," said I. "No animal whose father was no gentleman, but a donkey, is going to shame me. She's got to mind me. Look out."

I unwound the lasso from the bushes, and stood astride the mule, which at once got up, feeling herself freed. Now it was a question of strength of legs, and in this I far surpassed Sam. If a rider presses his beast's ribs with strong knees it causes intense pain. As the mule began to try to throw me as she had Sam, I caught up the lasso, half hanging on the ground, and fastened it tight behind the noose. This I drew whenever she began any of her tricks, and by this means and pressure of the knees I contrived to keep her on all fours.

It was a bitter struggle, strength against strength. I began to sweat from every pore, but the mule was dripping, and foam fell from her lips in great flakes. Her struggles grew more and more feeble, her heavy breathing became short gasps, till at last she gave in altogether, not willing, but because she was at her last limit, and stood motionless with bulging eyes. I drew long, deep breaths; it seemed to me as if every bone and sinew in my body were broken.

"Heavens! what a man you are!" cried Sam. "You're stronger than the brute! If you could see your face you would be scared; your eyes are staring, your lips are swollen, your cheeks are actually blue."

"I suppose so; that comes of being a tenderfoot who won't be beaten, while his teacher gives in and lets a horse and a mule conquer him."

Sam made a wry face. "Now let up, young fellow. I tell you the best hunter gets whipped some times."

"Very likely. How are your ribs and other little bones?"

"I don't know; I'll have to count 'em to find out. That's a fine beast you have under you there."

"She is indeed. See how patiently she stands; one feels sorry for her. Shall we saddle and bridle her and go back?"

The poor mule stood quiet, trembling in every limb; nor did she try to resist when we put saddle and bridle on her, but obeyed the bit like a well-broken horse. "She's had a master before," said Sam. "I'm going to call her Nancy, for I once had a mule by that name, and it's too much trouble to get used to another. And I'm going to ask you to do me a favor."

"Gladly; what is it?"

"Don't tell at the camp what has happened this morning, for they'd have nine days' sport with me."

"Of course I won't; you're my teacher and friend, so I'll keep your secrets."

His queer face lighted up with pleasure. "Yes, I'm your friend, and if I knew you had a little liking for me, my old heart would be warmed and rejoiced."

I stretched out my hand to him, surprised and touched. "I can easily give you that pleasure, dear Sam," I said. "You may be sure I honestly care for you with real respect and affection."

He shook my hand, looking so delighted that even my young self-sufficiency could perceive how lonely this rough, cranky old frontiersman was, and how great was his yearning for human sympathy.

I fastened Dick Stone's horse with the lasso, and mounting mine, as Sam got on Nancy, we rode away.

"She's been educated, this new Nancy, in a very good school," Sam remarked presently. "I see at every step she is going to be all right, and is regaining the old knowledge which she had forgotten among the mustangs. I hope she has not only temperament but character."

"We've had two good days, Sam," I said.

"Bad ones for me, except in getting Nancy; and bad for you, too, in one way, but mighty honorable."

"Oh, I've done nothing; I came West to get experience. I hope to have a chance at other sport."

"Well, I hope it will come more easily; yesterday your life hung by a hair. You risked too much. Never forget you're a greenhorn tenderfoot. The idea of creeping up to shoot a buffalo in the eye! Did ever any one hear the like? But though hunting buffaloes is dangerous, bear-hunting is far more so."

"Black bear?"

"Nonsense! The grizzly. You've read of him?"

"Yes."

"Well, be glad you don't know him outside of books; and take care you don't for you might have a chance to meet him. He sometimes comes about such places as this, following the rivers even as far as the prairie. I'll tell you more of him another time; here we are at the camp."

"A mule, a mule! Where did you get her, Hawkins?" cried all the men.

"By special delivery from Washington, for a ten-cent stamp. Would you like to see the envelope?" asked Sam, dismounting.

Though they were curious, none asked further questions, for, like the beast he had captured, when Sam wouldn't he wouldn't, and that was the end of it.

A Grizzly and a Meeting

The morning after Sam and I had caught Miss Nancy we moved our camp onward to begin labor on the next section of the road. Hawkins, Stone, and Parker did not help in this, for Sam was anxious to experiment further with Nancy's education, and the other two accompanied him to the prairie, where they had sufficient room to carry out this purpose. We surveyors transferred our instruments ourselves, helped by one of Rattler's men, while Rattler himself loafed around doing nothing.

We came to the spot where I had killed the two buffaloes, and to my surprise I saw that the body of the old bull was gone, leaving a broad trail of crushed grass that led to the adjoining thicket.

"I thought you had made sure both bulls were dead," Rattler exclaimed. "The big one must have had some life in him."

"Think so?" I asked.

"Of course, unless you think a dead buffalo can take himself off."

"Must he have taken himself off? Perhaps it was done for him."

"Yes, but who did it?"

"Possibly Indians, we saw an Indian's footprint over yonder."

"You don't say! How well a greenhorn can explain things!" sneered Rattler. "If it was done by Indians, where do you think they came from? Dropped from the skies? Because if they came from anywhere else we'd see their tracks. No, there was life in that buffalo, and he crawled into the thicket, where he must have died. I'm going to look for him."

He started off, followed by his men. He may have expected me to go, too, but it was far from my thoughts, for I did not like the way he had spoken. I wanted to work, and did not care a button what had become of the old bull. So I went back to my employment, and had only just taken up the measuring-rod, when a cry of horror rang from the thicket, two, three shots echoed, and then I heard Rattler cry: "Up the tree, quick! up the tree, or you're lost! he can't climb."

Who could not climb? One of Rattler's men burst out of the thicket, writhing like one in mortal agony.

"What is it? What's happened?" I shouted.

"A bear, a tremendous grizzly bear!" he gasped, as I ran up to him.

And within the thicket an agonised voice cried: "Help, help! He's got me!" in the tone of a man who saw the jaws of death yawning before him.

Evidently the man was in extreme danger, and must be helped quickly, but how? I had left my gun in the tent, for in working it hindered me; nor was this an oversight, since we surveyors had the frontiersmen purposely to guard us at our work. If I went to the tent to get the gun, the bear would have torn the man to shreds before I could get back; I must go to him as I was with a knife and two revolvers stuck in my belt, and what were these against a grizzly bear?

The grizzly is a near relation of the extinct cave-bear, and really belongs more to primeval days than to the present. It grows to a great size, and its strength is such that it can easily carry off a deer, a colt, or a young buffalo cow in its jaws. The Indians hold the killing of a grizzly a brilliant feat, because of its absolute fearlessness and inexhaustible endurance.

So it was to meet such a foe that I sprang into the thicket. The trail led further within, where the trees began, and where the bear had dragged the buffalo. It was a dreadful moment. Behind me I could hear the voices of the engineers; before me were the frontiersmen screaming, and between them and me, in indescribable agony, was their companion whom the bear had seized.

I pushed further in, and heard the voice of the bear; for, though this mighty beast differs from others of the bear family in not growling, when in pain or anger it utters something like a loud, harsh breathing and grunting.

And now I was on the scene. Before me lay the torn body of the buffalo, to right and left were the men, who were comparatively safe, having taken to the trees, which a grizzly bear seldom has been known to climb, if ever. One of the men had tried to get up a tree like the others, but had been overtaken by the bear. He hung by both arms hooked to the lowest limb, while the grizzly reached up and held him fast with its fore paws around the lower part of his body.

The man was almost dead; his case was hopeless. I could not help him, and no one could have blamed me if I had gone away and saved myself. But the desperation of the moment seemed to impel me onward. I snatched up a discarded gun, only to find it already emptied. Taking it by the muzzle I sprang over the buffalo, and dealt the bear a blow on the skull with all my might. The gun shattered like glass in my hand; even a blow with a battle-axe would have no effect on such a skull but I had the satisfaction of distracting the grizzly's attention from its victim.

It turned its head toward me, not quickly, like a wild beast of the feline or canine family, but slowly, as if wondering at my stupidity. It seemed to measure me with its little eyes, decided between going at me or sticking to its victim; and to this slight hesitation I owe my life, for in that instant the only possible way to save myself came to me. I drew a revolver, sprang directly at the bear, and shot it, once, twice, thrice, straight in the eyes, as I had the buffalo.

Of course this was rapidly done, and at once I jumped to one side, and stood still with my knife drawn. Had I remained where I was, my life would have paid for my rashness, for the blinded beast turned quickly from the tree, and threw itself on the spot where I had stood a moment before. I was not there, and the bear sought mine with angry mutterings and heavy breathing. It wheeled around like a mad thing, hugged itself, rose on its hind legs, reaching and springing all around to find me, but fortunately I was out of reach. Its sense of smell would have guided it to me, but it was mad with rage and pain, and this prevented its instinct from serving it.

At last it turned its attention more to its misfortune than to him who had caused it. It sat down, and with sobs and gnashing of teeth laid its fore paws over its eyes. I was sorry that necessity for saving human life was causing the big fellow such pain, and, with pity for it, as well as desire for my own safety, tried to make it short. Quietly I stood beside it and stabbed it twice between the ribs. Instantly it grabbed for me, but once more I sprang out of the way. I had not pierced its heart, and it began seeking me with redoubled fury. This continued for fully ten minutes. It had lost a great deal of blood, and evidently was dying; it sat down again to mourn its poor lost eyes. This gave me a chance for two rapidly repeated knife-thrusts, and this time I aimed better; it sank forward, as again I sprang aloof, made a feeble step to one side, then back, tried to rise, but had not sufficient strength, swayed back and forth in trying to get on its feet, and then stretched out and was still.

"Thank God!" cried Rattler from his tree, "the beast is dead. That was a close call we had."

"I don't see that it was a close call for you," I replied. "You took good care of your own safety. Now you can come down."

"Not yet; you make sure it's truly dead."

"It is dead."

"You don't know; you haven't an idea how tough such a creature is. Go examine it."

"If you doubt me, examine it yourself; you're an experienced frontiersman, and I'm a tenderfoot, you know."

So saying I turned to his comrade, who still hung on the tree in an awful plight. His face was torn, and his wide-open eyes were glassy, the flesh was stripped from the bones of his legs, and he was partly disembowelled. I conquered the horror of the sight enough to say: "Let go, my poor fellow; I will take you down." He did not answer, or show any sign of having heard me, and I called his comrades to help me. Only after I had made sure the bear was dead would the courageous gang come down from their trees, when we gently removed the wounded man. This required strength to accomplish, for his arms had wound tightly around the tree, and stiffened there: he was dead.

This horrible end did not seem to affect his companions in the least, for they turned from him to the bear, and their leader said: "Now things are reversed; the bear meant to eat us, but we will eat it. Quick, you fellows, take its pelt, and let us get at the paws and steak."

He drew his knife and knelt down to carry out his words, but I checked him. "It would have been more fitting if you had used your knife when it was alive. Now it's too late; don't give yourself the trouble."

"What!" he cried. "Do you mean to hinder me?"

"Most emphatically I do, Mr. Rattler."

"By what right?"

"By the most indisputable right. I killed that bear."

"That's not so. Maybe you think a greenhorn can kill a grizzly with a knife! As soon as we saw it we shot it."

"And immediately got up a tree! Yes, that's very true."

"You bet it's true, and our shots killed it, not the two little needle-pricks of your knife. The bear is ours, and we'll do with it what we like. Understand?"

He started to work again, but I said coolly: "Stop this minute, Rattler. I'll teach you to respect my words; do you understand?" And as he bent forward to stick the knife into the bear's hide I put both arms around his hips and, raising him, threw him against the next tree so hard that it cracked. I was too angry just then to care whether he or the tree broke, and as he flew across the space I drew my second and unused revolver, to be ready for the next move.

He got up, looked at me with eyes blazing with rage, drew his knife, and cried: "You shall pay or this. You knocked me down once before; I'll see it doesn't happen a third time." He made a step towards me, but I covered him with my pistol, saying: "One step more and you'll have a bullet in your head. Drop that knife. When I say 'three' I'll shoot you if you still hold it. Now: One, two —" He held the knife tight, and I should have shot him, not in the head, but in the hand, for he had to learn to respect me; but luckily I did not get so far for at this moment a loud voice cried: "Men, are you mad? What reason have the whites to tear out one another's eyes? Stop!"

We looked in the direction whence the voice came, and saw a man appearing from behind the trees. He was small, thin, and hunch-backed, clad and armed like a red man. One could not tell whether he was an Indian or a white; his sharp-cut features indicated the former, while the tint of his face, although sunburned, was that of a white man. He was bare-headed, and his dark hair hung to his shoulders. He wore leather trousers, a hunting-shirt of the same material, and moccasins, and was armed with a knife and gun. His eyes shone with unusual intelligence, and there was nothing ridiculous in his deformity. Indeed, none but stupid and brutal men ever laugh at bodily defects; but Rattler was of this class, for as soon as he looked at the new-comer he cried:

"Hallo! What kind of a freak comes here? Do such queer things grow in the big West?"

The stranger looked at him calmly, and answered quietly: "Thank God that your limbs are sound. It is by the heart and soul that men are judged, and I should not fear a comparison with you in those respects."

He made a gesture of contempt, and turned to me, saying: "You are strong, young sir; it is not every one can send a man flying through the air as you did just now; it was wonderful to see." Then touching the grizzly with his foot, he added: "And this is the game we wanted, but we came too late. We discovered its tracks yesterday, and followed over hill and dale, through thick and thin, only to find the work done when we came up with it."

"You speak in the plural; you are not alone?" I asked.

"No; I have two companions with me. But before I tell you who they are, will you introduce yourselves? You know one cannot be too cautious here, where we meet more bad men than good ones." He glanced significantly at Rattler and his followers, but instantly added in a friendly tone: "However, one can tell a gentleman that can be trusted. I heard the last part of your discussion, and know pretty well where I stand."

"We are surveyors, sir," I explained. "We are locating a railroad to go through here."

"Surveyors! Have you purchased the right to build your road?"

His face became stern as he asked the question, for which he seemed to have some reason; so I replied: "I have occupied myself with my task, and never thought of asking."

"Ah, yes; but you must know where you are. Consider these lands whereon we stand are the property of the Indians; they belong to the Apaches of the Mascaleros tribe. I am sure, if you are sent to survey, the ground is being marked out by the whites for some one else."

"What is that to you?" Rattler cried. "Don't bother yourself with the affairs of others. Any one can see you are a white man."

"I am an Apache, one of the Mascaleros," the stranger said quietly. "I am Kleki-Petrah."

This name in the Apache tongue is equivalent to White Father, and Rattler seemed to have heard it before. He bowed with mock deference, and said: "Ah, Kleki-Petrah, the venerated school-master of the Apaches! It's a pity you are deformed, for it must annoy you to be laughed at by the braves."

"They never do that, sir. Well-bred people are not amused by such things, and the braves are gentlemen. Since I know who you are and why you are here, I will tell you who my companions are, or perhaps you had better meet them."

He called in the Indian tongue, and two extraordinarily interesting figures appeared, and came slowly towards us. They were Indians, father and son, as one could see at the first glance. The elder was a little above medium height, very strongly built. His air was truly noble; his earnest face was of pure Indian type but not so sharp and keen as that of most red men. His eyes had a calm gentle expression, like one much given to contemplation. His head was bare, his hair worn in a knot in which was stuck an eagle's feather, the badge of chieftainship. His dress consisted of moccasins, leather leggings, and hunting-jacket, very simple and unadorned. From his belt, in which a knife was thrust, hung all the appointments necessary to a dweller on the plains. A medicine-charm with sacred inscriptions cut around its face hung from his neck, and in his hand he carried a double-barrelled gun, the handle adorned with silver nails.

The younger man was clad like his father, except that his garments were showier; his leggings were beautifully fringed, and his hunting-shirt was embellished with scarlet needlework. He also wore a medicine-charm around his neck, and a calumet; like his father he was armed with a knife and a double-barrelled gun. He, too, was bareheaded, his hair bound in a knot, but without the feather; it was so long that the end below the knot fell thick and heavy on his shoulders, and many a fine lady might have coveted it. His face was even nobler than his father's, its color a light brown with a touch of bronze. He seemed to be, as I afterwards learned he was, of the same age as myself, and his appearance made as profound an impression on me then, when I saw him first, as his character has left upon me today, after our long friendship.

We looked at one another long and searchingly, and I thought I saw for a moment in his earnest dark eyes a friendly light gleam upon me.

"These are my friends and companions," said Kleki-Petrah, introducing first the father, then the son. "This is Intschu-Tschuna Good Sun, the chief of the Mascaleros, whom all Apaches acknowledge as their head. And here stands his son Winnetou, who already in his youth has accomplished more deeds of renown than any ten old warriors have in all their lives. His name will be known and honored as far as the prairies and Rockies extend."

This sounded like exaggeration, but later I found that he had spoken only the truth.

Rattler laughed insultingly, and said: "So young a fellow, and committed such deeds? I say committed purposely, for every one knows they are only deeds of robbery and cruelty. The red men steal from every one."

This was an outrageous insult, but the Indians acted as though they had not heard it. Stooping down over the bear, Kleki-Petrah admired it, calling Winnetou's attention to its size and strength. "It was killed by a knife and not a bullet," he said as he rose.

Evidently, I thought, he had heard the dispute and wished me to have justice.

"What does a school-master know of bear-hunting?" said Rattler. "When we take the skin off we can see what killed him. I won't be robbed of my rights by a greenhorn."

Then Winnetou bent down, touched the bloody wound, and asked me in good English: "Who stabbed the beast?"

"I did," I replied.

"Why did not my young white brother shoot him?"

"Because I had no gun with me."

"Yet here are guns."

"They are not mine; they were thrown away by these men when they climbed the trees shrieking with terror."

"Ugh! the low cowards and dogs, to fly like tissuepaper! A man should make resistance, for if he has courage he may conquer the strongest brute. My young white brother has such courage."

"My son speaks truly," added the father in as perfect English. "This brave young pale-face is no longer a greenhorn. He who kills a grizzly in this manner is a hero; and he who does it to save those who climb trees deserves thanks, not insults. Let us go to visit the pale-faces that have come into our dominion."

They were but three, and did not know how many we numbered, but that never occurred to them. With slow and dignified strides they went out of the thicket, we following.

Then for the first time Intschu-Tschuna saw the surveying instruments standing as we had left them, and, stopping suddenly, he turned to me, demanding: "What is this? Are the pale-faces measuring the land?"

"Yes," I answered.

"Why?"

"For a railroad."

His eyes lost their calmness, and he asked sternly: "Do you obey these people, and measure with them?"

"Yes."

"And are paid for it?"

"Yes."

He threw a scornful glance upon me, and in a contemptuous tone he said to Kleki-Petrah: "Your teachings sound well, but they do not often agree with what I see. Christians deceive and rob the Indians. Here is a young pale-face with a brave heart, open face, honorable eyes, and when I ask what he does here he tells me he has come to steal our land. The faces of the white men are good and bad, but inside they are all alike."

To be honest, his words filled me with shame. Could I well be proud of my share in this matter—I, a Catholic, who had been taught so early: "Thou shalt not covet thy neighbor's goods"? I blushed for my race and for myself before this fine savage; and before I could rally enough even to try to reply, the head engineer, who had been watching us through a hole in the tent, came forth to meet us, and my thoughts were diverted by what then took place.

The Speech of the Apache Chief

The first question the head engineer asked us as we came up, although he was surprised to see the Indians with us, was what had become of the bear.

Rattler instantly replied: "We've shot him, and we'll have bear-paws for dinner, and bear-steak to-night for supper."

Our three guests looked at me as if to see whether I would let this pass, and I said: "I claim to have stabbed the bear. Here are three witnesses who have corroborated my statement; but we'll wait till Hawkins, Stone, and Parker come, and they will give their opinion, by which we will be guided. Till then the bear must lie untouched."

"Not much will I leave it to the scouts," growled Rattler. "I'll go with my men and cut up the bear, and whoever tries to hinder us will be driven off with a dozen shots in his body."

"Hold on, Mr. Rattler," said I. "I'm not as much afraid of your shots as you were of the bear. You won't drive me up a tree with your threats. I recommend you to bury your dead comrade; I would not leave him lying thus."

"Is some one dead?" asked Bancroft, startled.

"Yes, Rollins," Rattler replied. "The poor fellow had jumped for a tree, like the rest of us, and would have been all right, but this greenhorn came up, excited the bear, and it tore Rollins horribly."

I stood speechless with amazement that he should dare go so far. It was impossible to endure such lying, and in my very presence. I turned on Rattler and demanded: "Do you mean to say Rollins was escaping and I prevented it?"

"Yes," he nodded, drawing his revolver.

"And I say the bear had seized him before I came."

"That's a lie," said Rattler.

"Very well; here's a truth for you," and with these words I knocked his revolver from his hand with my left, and with the right gave him such a blow on the ear that he staggered six or eight feet away, and fell flat on the ground.

He sprang up, drew his knife, and came at me raging like a wild beast. I parried the knife-thrust with my left hand, and with my right laid him senseless at my feet.

"Ugh! ugh!" grunted Intschu-Tschuna, surprised into admiration, which his race rarely betray.

"That was Shatterhand again," said Wheeler, the surveyor.

I kept my eye on Rattler's comrades; they were angry but no one dared attack me, and though they muttered among themselves they did no more.

"You must send Rattler away, Mr. Bancroft," I said. "I have done nothing to him, yet he constantly seeks a quarrel with me. I am afraid he'll make serious trouble in the camp. Send him away, or, if you prefer, I'll go myself."

"Oh, things aren't as bad as that," said Bancroft easily.

"Yes, they are, just as bad as that. Here are his knife and revolver; don't let him have them, for I warn you they'd not be in good hands."

Just as I spoke these words our three scouts joined us, and having heard the story of Rattler's lying claim, and my counter-statement, they set off at once to examine the bear's carcass to settle the dispute. They returned in a short time, and as soon as he was within hailing distance Sam called out: "What idiocy it was to shoot a grizzly and then run! If a man doesn't intend making a fight, then what on earth does he shoot for? Why doesn't he leave the bear in peace? You can't treat grizzlies like poodle-dogs. Poor Rollins paid dear for it though. Now, who killed that bear did you say?

"I did," cried Rattler, who had come to. "I killed him with my gun."

"Well, that agrees; that's all right. The bear was shot."

"Do you hear that, men? Sam Hawkins has decided for me," cried Rattler triumphantly

"Yes, for you," said Sam. "You shot him, and took off the tip of his ear, and such a loss naturally ended the grizzly, ha! ha! ha! If you shot again it went wide of the mark, for there's no other gun-shot on him. But there are four true knife-thrusts, two above the heart and two in it; who gave him those?"

"I did," I said.

"You alone?"

"No one else."

"Then the bear belongs to you. That is, the pelt is yours; the flesh belongs to all, but you have the right to divide it. This is the custom of the West. Have you anything to say, Mr. Rattler?"

Rattler growled something that condemned us to a much warmer climate, and turned sullenly to the wagon where the liquor was stored. I saw him pour down glass after glass, and knew he would drink till he could drink no more.

The Indians had listened to our discussion, and watched us in silent interest; but now, our affairs being settled, the chief, Intschu-Tschuna, turned to the head engineer, saying: "My ear has told me that among these pale-faces you are chief; is this so?"

"Yes," Bancroft replied.

"Then I have something to say to you."

"What is it?"

"You shall hear. But you are standing, and men should sit in conference."

"Will you be our guest?" asked Bancroft.

"No, for it is impossible. How can I be your guest when you are on my lands, in my forests, my valleys, my prairies? Let the white men be seated."

"Tell me what you wish of me," said Bancroft.

"It is not a wish, but a command," answered Intschu-Tschuna proudly.

"We will take no command," responded the head engineer with equal pride.

A look of anger passed over the chief's face, but he controlled himself, and said mildly: "My white brother will answer me one question truthfully. Have you a house?"

"Yes."

"With a garden?"

"Yes."

"If a neighbor would cut a path through that garden would my brother submit to it?"

"No."

"The lands beyond the Rocky Mountains and east of the Missis-sippi belong to the pale-faces. What would they say if the Indians came to build a railroad there?"

"They would drive them away."

"My white brother has answered truly. But the palefaces come here on these lands of ours, and drive away our mustangs and kill our buf-faloes; they seek among us for gold and precious stones, and now they will build a long, long road on which their fire-horses can run. Then more pale-faces will follow this road, and settle among us, and take the little we have left us. What are we to say to this?"

Bancroft was silent.

"Have we fewer rights than they? You call yourselves Christians, and speak of love, yet you say: We can rob and cheat you, but you must be honest with us. Is that love? You say your God is the Good Father of all men, red and white. Is He only our stepfather, and are you His own sons? Did not all the land belong to the red man? It has been taken from us, and what have we instead? Misery, misery, misery. You drive us ever farther and farther back, and press us closer and closer together, and in a little time we shall be suffocated. Why do you do this? Is it because you have not room enough? No, for there is room in your lands still for many, many millions. Each of your tribes can have a whole State, but the red man, the true owner, may not have a place to lay his head. Kleki-Petrah, who sits here before me, has taught me your Holy Book. There it says that the first man had two sons, and one killed the other, and his blood cried to Heaven. How is it with the two brothers, the red and the white? Are you not Cain, and are we not Abel, whose blood cries to Heaven? And when you try to destroy us you vanish us to make no defence. But we will defend ourselves, we will defend ourselves. We have been driven from place to place, ever farther away; now we collide here, where we believed ourselves at rest, but you come to build your railroad. Have we not the same rights you have over your house and garden? If we followed our own laws we should kill you; but we only wish your laws to be fulfilled towards us: are they? No! Your laws have two faces, and you turn them to us as it suits your advantage. Have you asked our permission to build this road?"

"No," said Bancroft. "It was not necessary."

"Have you bought the land, or have we sold it?"

"Not to me."

"Nor to any other. Were you an honest man sent here to build a way for the fire-horse, you would first have asked the man who sent you whether he had a right to do this thing, and made him prove it. But this you have not done. I forbid you to measure further."

These last words were spoken in a tone of most bitter earnest.

I had read much of the red man, but never had found in any book such a speech from an Indian, and I wondered if he owed his fluent English and forcible logic to Kleki-Petrah.

The head engineer found himself in an awkward predicament. If he was honest and sincere he could not gainsay what Intschu-Tschuna had spoken; but there were considerations more weighty with Bancroft than honesty, so the chief had to wait his answer, looking him straight in the eyes.

Seeing that Bancroft was shifting about in his mind for a way out of his difficulty, Intschu-Tschuna rose, saying decidedly: "There is no need of further speech. I have spoken. My will is that you leave here to-day, and go back whence you came. Decide whether you will obey or not. I will now depart with my son Winnetou, and will return at the end of that time which the pale-faces call an hour, when you will give me your answer. If you go, we are brothers; if you stay, it shall be deadly enmity between you and me. I am Intschu-Tschuna, the chief of all the Apaches. I have spoken."

Winnetou followed him as he went out from among us, and they were soon lost to sight down the valley.

Kleki-Petrah remained seated, and Bancroft turned to him and asked his advice. He replied: "Do as you will, sir. I am of the chief's opinion. The red race has been cruelly outraged and robbed. But as a white man I know that the Indian must disappear. If you are an honest man and go to-day, to-morrow another will come to carry on your work. I warn you, however, that the chief is in earnest."

He, too, rose, as if to put an end to further questioning. I went up to him and said: "Sir, will you let me go with you? I promise to do or say nothing that will annoy you. It is only because I feel extraordinary interest in Intschu-Tschuna, and even more in Winnetou."

That he himself was included in this interest I dared not say.

"Yes, come with me a little way," he replied. "I have withdrawn from my race, and must know them no more; but since you have crossed my path, there can be no harm in our meeting, and some good may result from it. We will walk a little together. You seem to me the most intelligent of these men; am I right?"

"I am the youngest, and not clever, and I should be honored if you allowed me to go with you," I answered respectfully.

"Come, then," said Kleki-Petrah kindly, and we walked slowly away from the camp.

An Eleven Hundred Mile Horseback Ride Down the Chisholm Trail

BY CHARLES A. SIRINGO

Generally speaking, cowboy-ing is a part-time job, though highly skilled. It is also a young man's job, what with the danger involved, the long hours, the physical punishment and the poor pay. But if you work hard and save your money and have a little luck you might eventually make yourself into a cattleman with vast herds and money in the bank. Or you might do something else altogether.

Charles Siringo was born in Southwest Texas in 1856, and grew up in the early years of the great cattle boom. He began his working life as a ranch hand and cattle driver. In those days tobacco companies offered inexpensive paperback books as premiums with their products; this may have been what first sparked this young cow-hand's interest in writing. By his late twenties he'd written his first book: *A Texas Cowboy*. Siringo later claimed that it sold nearly a million copies; unlikely, but there you have it. Maybe we should put this down as yet another Texas tall tale. By his early thirties, he was looking to widen his horizons. An acquaintance by the name of Pat Garrett provided him with a reference, and he joined the Pinkerton Detective Agency. For the next twenty-two years Siringo chased cattle rustlers, investigated frauds, and infiltrated and reported on labor organizations and other 'radical' groups. His work took him all over the States and abroad as well. He was a member of that legendary posse that chased Butch Cassidy and the Sundance Kid into South America. His writing style, we can plainly see, owes a good deal to his work as a Pinkerton agent. It is as simple and direct as a report to the Agency home office. His books include: *The Cowboy Detective, A History of Billy the Kid, Bad Men of the West, Riata and Spurs,* and *A Lone Star Cowboy,* from which this story is excerpted.

★ ★ ★ ★ ★

After laying around the home ranch a few weeks Mr. Moore put me in charge of a scouting outfit, to drift over the South Staked Plains, in search of any cattle which might have escaped from the line-riders.

While on this trip I went to church several times.

A colony of Illinois Christians, under the leadership of the Reverend Mr. Cahart, had established the town of Clarendon, on the head of Salt Fork, a tributary of Red River, and there built a white church house among the buffalo and wolves.

Clarendon is still on the map, being the county seat of Donnely county, Texas.

When spring came I was called in from the plains and put in charge of a round-up crew, consisting of a cook and twelve riders.

Our first round-up was on the Goodnight range, at the mouth of Mulberry Creek. Here we had the pleasure of a genuine cattle-queen's presence. Mrs. Goodnight, a noble little woman, a dyed in the wool Texan, whose maiden name was Dyer, attended these roundups with her husband.

Mrs. Goodnight touched a soft spot in my heart by filling me up on several occasions, with juicy berries which she had gathered with her own hands.

At this writing Mr. and Mrs. Charlie Goodnight are still alive, and living in the town of Goodnight, Texas, which has been made famous as the home of the largest herd of buffalo in that state, and possibly the whole United States.

The foundation of this herd of buffalo was started on this round-up in the spring of 1879.

In the round-up at the head of Mulberry Creek was a lone buffalo bull. When ready to turn the round-up cattle loose Mr. Buffalo was roped and thrown, and a cow-bell fastened to his neck. When turned loose he stampeded, and so did the thousands of cattle.

In the round-up the following spring the bell-buffalo was with the cattle, and had with him several female buffalos.

During that summer Mr. Goodnight fenced his summer range on Mulberry Creek, and this small herd of buffalo found themselves enclosed with a strong barbed wire fence.

From what I was told Charlie Goodnight increased this buffalo herd by having cowboys rope young animals to be put inside the Mulberry Creek fenced pasture.

Many years afterwards I rode through this tame herd of buffalos, near the town of Goodnight.

We wound up this spring round-up on the Rocking Chair range, at the mouth of McClellan Creek, where I saw about 50,000 cattle in one bunch—more than I had ever seen before in one band.

Now we returned to the home ranch with about 500 LX cattle, which had drifted away from the range during the winter.

Shortly after our return Mr. Moore had us help him brand some large long-horn steers, late arrivals from South Texas.

We did the branding on the open plains, at Amarillo Lake.

While roping and tying down these wild steers we had great sport in seeing "Center-fire" saddles jerked over sideways from the pony's back, the riders with them.

Mr. Moore had got his cowboy training in California, where they use "center-fire", high horn saddles and riatas, (ropes) which they wrap around the saddle-horn when roping on horseback. The cinchas on these saddles being broad, and in the center of the saddle, which makes it difficult to keep the saddle tight on the pony's back.

Mr. Moore had persuaded many of his cowboys to use these saddles and the long rawhide "riatas"—hence a large order had been sent to California in the early spring. In the order were many silver mounted spurs and Spanish bridle bits. I sent for one of these ten dollar bridle bits, and am still using it to ride with.

I must confess that Moore never got a fall from his "center-fire" saddle, as he had learned his lesson early in life. He was also an expert roper with his 75-foot "riata." He could throw the large loop further and catch his animal oftener than any man in the crowd of about twenty-five riders.

Moore tried his best to persuade me, and such Texas raised cowboys as Jim East, Steve Arnold and Lee Hall, not to tie our 30-foot ropes hard and fast to the saddle horns when roping large steers. He argued that it was too dangerous. No doubt he was right, but we had been trained that way.

Later poor Lee Hall was gored to death by a wild steer, roped down in the Indian Territory. The steer had jerked his mount over backward, and one of his spurs caught in the flank cinch, preventing him from freeing himself until too late to save his life.

The spur which hung in the cinch and caused his death, was one of the fine silver mounted pair which Moore sent to California for.

After his death I fell heir to Lee Hall's spurs and they are used by me to this day, over 40 years later.

In the latter part of June Mr. Moore put me in charge of 800 fat steers for the Chicago market. My outfit consisted of a well filled mess-wagon, a cook and five riders.

We headed for Nickerson, Kansas, on the Arkansas River, across country through No-Mans-Land—now the 30 mile strip of Oklahoma which butts up against New Mexico on the west, and on the north is bordered by Kansas and Colorado, the Texas Panhandle being the south border.

Late in the fall we arrived in Nickerson, Kansas, and turned the steers over to "Deacon" Bates.

Leaving Whiskey-Pete and a Missouri mare, which I had traded for, with a "fool hoe-man," five miles south of town, "Jingle-bob" Joe Hargraves and I started west across country to meet another herd of fat steers.

As the snow had begun to fly it was thought best to turn this herd towards Dodge City, Kansas—hence we being sent to pilot the outfit to Dodge City.

While on this lonely ride I came within an ace of "passing in my checks." We ran out of grub and for supper one night filled up on canned peaches, without anything else to eat with them. All night these juicy peaches held a war-dance in the pit of my stomach, and before daylight I was all in. "Jingle-bob" Joe wanted me to pray, but I told him that I would wait a little longer, in hopes that I might pull through.

Joe Hargraves was not much on the pray himself, but I believe he has a passport to heaven for one kindly act done the winter previous. He was on his way to Dodge City, over the Bascom trail, when he stopped for the night on the Cimarron River, where a short time previous a small store had been established.

The next morning a "fool hoe-man" and his hungry and ragged family drove up in a covered wagon drawn by two skinny ponies. They were half starved and didn't have a cent of money.

"Jingle-bob" Joe asked the store man what he would take for all the goods in his place. He set the price at $150.00, which was accepted. Then the goods were loaded into the "hoeman's" wagon, and he drove off singing "Home, Sweet Home". He was looking for a free home to settle on.

We finally found the steer outfit and turned them towards Dodge City. There the fat steers were put aboard two trains, and I took charge of one train, thus taking my second lesson in cow-punching, with a spiked pole and lantern.

As on the former trip the steers were unloaded across the Mississippi River from Burlington, Iowa, and fed.

In the city of Burlington we punchers were treated royally. None of the candy and ice-cream merchants would take a penny from us. Everything in that line was free.

On arriving in Chicago Mr. Beals met us. Then at the Palmer House Mr. Beals settled up my wage and expense account. With a few hundred dollars in my pocket I started out to see the sights again.

I had told Mr. Beals of my intention to quit his outfit and spend the winter in Southern Texas. He agreed that if I concluded to go back to work for the XL company in the spring, he would arrange for me to boss a herd of steers up the trail. Said he had already contracted with Charlie Word of Goliad, Texas, for two herds to be delivered on the LX Ranch.

A couple of days and nights sight-seeing put me almost "on the bum," financially. Then a train was boarded for Nickerson, Kansas.

Whiskey-Pete and the bay mare were found hog fat. The "fool hoe-man" had shoved corn to them with a scoop shovel.

After purchasing a pack-saddle, and some grub, I had just six dollars in cash left to make my eleven hundred mile journey down the Chisholm trail to the gulf coast of Texas.

Puck was not far off when he wrote: "What fools these mortals be." For here was a fool cowboy starting out to ride eleven hundred miles, just to be in the saddle, and to get a pony back home.

On the way down the trail I kept myself supplied with cash by swapping saddles, pack pony, watches, and running races with Whiskey-Pete, who was hard to beat in a three hundred yard race.

At one place in middle Texas I laid over a couple of days to rest my ponies, and to make a few dollars picking cotton.

One morning I was sent out by the farmer, with a bunch of bare-footed girls, to pick cotton in a field which had already been picked over. These young damsels gave me the "horse-laugh" for my awkwardness in picking the snowy balls of cotton.

When night came I had earned just thirty cents, while the girls had made more than a dollar each. This was my last stunt as a cotton picker.

On Pecan Creek, near Denton, I put up one night at the home of old man Murphy—the father of Jim Murphy, who was a member of the Sam Bass gang of train robbers, and whose name is mentioned in the Sam Bass song, which was a favorite with trail cowboys.

The old Chisholm trail was lined with negroes, headed for Topeka and Emporia, Kansas, to get a free farm and a span of mules from the state government.

Over my pack there was a large buffalo robe, and on my saddle hung a fine silver-mounted Winchester rifle. These attracted the attention of those green cotton-field negroes, who wore me out asking questions about them.

Some of these negroes were afoot, while others drove donkeys and oxen. The shiny black children and half-starved dogs were plentiful. Many of the outfits turned back when I told them of the cold blizzards and deep snow in Kansas.

My eleven hundred mile journey ended at the old Rancho Grande headquarter ranch, after being on the trail one month and twelve days.

The balance of the winter was spent on hunting trips after deer and wild hogs, and visiting friends throughout the county of Matagorda.

Early in the spring I mounted Gotch, a pony traded for, and bidding Whiskey-Pete goodbye, he being left with my chum, Horace Yeamans, we headed for Goliad to meet Charlie Word. He was found near Beeville, thirty miles west of Goliad, putting up a herd of long-horn steers for the LX company. He had received a letter from Mr. David T. Beals telling him to put me in charge of one of the herds.

This first herd was to be bossed "up the trail" by Liash Stevens.

The outfit was up to their ankles in sticky mud, in a large round corral, putting the road-brand on the steers, when I found them. I pitched in and helped, and was soon covered with mud from head to feet. Each steer had to be roped and thrown afoot, which made it a disagreeable job in the cold drizzling rain. And to finish out the days work, after my thirty mile ride from Goliad, I stood guard over the steers until after midnight.

Mr. Word had just purchased a band of "wet" ponies from old Mexico, and I showed my skill in riding some of the wildest ones.

One large iron-grey gelding, which the Mexicans said was a man-killer, broke my cinchas and dumped me and the saddle into the mud. Then he pawed the saddle with his front feet until it was ruined. I had to buy a new saddle to finish breaking this man-killing broncho. But he proved to be a dandy cow pony when tamed.

After the herd had been road-branded and turned over to Mr. Stevens and his crew of trail cowboys, Charlie word asked me to help him get the herd started on the trail.

Our first night out proved a strenuous one. Mr. Stevens had taken a fool notion to arm his cowboys with bulls-eye lanterns, so that they could see the location of each other on dark nights. He had ordered a few extra ones and insisted on me trying one that night, which I did.

About ten o'clock a severe storm came up and we were all in the saddle ready for stampede.

While I was running at break-neck speed, to reach the lead of the herd, my pony went head over heels over a rail fence. The light from the lantern had blinded him, so that he failed to see it in time.

The pony was caught and mounted and the new-fangled bulls-eye lantern was left on the ground.

Strange to relate, this lantern is prized today as a souvenir of by-gone days. It was picked up next day by a young rancher, who, at this writing lives near Kingston, Sierra County, New Mexico.

I finally reached the lead of the herd, and from that time 'till day-light it was one stampede after another.

Daylight found young Glass and me alone with about half the herd of 3700 head. We were jammed into the foot of a lane, down which the cattle had drifted during the last hour of darkness.

This lane was built with five strands of new barbed wire, and was cut off by a cross fence. Here the herd was jammed together so tightly that it was impossible to ride to the rear.

There we had to wait and pray that another stampede wouldn't start while hemmed in on three sides by a high wire fence. A stampede would have, no doubt, sent us to the happy hunting ground.

It required two days hard work to gather up steers lost during the night. They had become mixed up with range cattle.

In that camp the price of bulls-eye lanterns took a tumble. It was almost impossible to give one away.

After the herd was strung out again on the trail I went to Goliad to meet Charlie Word.

Here he made up a crew of twelve riders, a cook and mess-wagon, with five ponies to the rider, and turned them over to me. With this crew I drifted northwesterly to the crooked-street, straggling town of San Antonio,—now one of the leading cities of Texas.

In San Antonio we had all of our ponies shod, as we were going into a rocky country.

When out of San Antonio about fifty miles a bucking broncho "busted" a blood vessel in my bread basket. Being in great misery, and un-able to sit up straight in the saddle, I concluded to ride back to the Alamo City and consult that great German doctor, Herff. The crew were in-structed to lay over until my return.

In San Antonio I made inquiry as to where Doctor Herff could be found.

Riding up to a large, old-fashioned, stone residence I found this noted doctor—more than ninety years of age—hoeing in his garden. He informed me that he had turned his practice over to his son.

I found Dr. Herff, Jr. living in a fine two-story stone mansion. He laid me on a couch and examined the seat of pain. He pronounced a blood vessel stretched out of shape, so that the blood was not flowing through it—hence the great pain.

He told me to go back to camp, and on rising every morning, for a couple of weeks, to drink all the water I could possibly hold, and then, immediately afterwards, to drink that much more. He said this was all the medicine I needed. His charge was fifty cents for the examination and advice.

The next morning after reaching camp I took a half-gallon coffee-pot down to the creek and filling it drank it empty. It seemed impossible to drink any more, but by a great effort the coffee pot was emptied again.

After the first morning it was no trick at all to drink a gallon of water at one siting.

In a few days I was completely cured, and the memory of Doctor Herff and his half-dollar fee will stay with me to the grave.

Now we continued the journey up the Llano River.

On reaching Kimble County we laid over in a new village called Junction City, now the prosperous seat of government of Kimble county, to load up our mess-wagon with grub, etc.

Farther up the river we came to the end of our journey, at the Joe, and Creed Taylor ranches. We established camp on Paint Creek, in a very rough, rocky country.

Charlie Word had bought 2500 head of cattle from Joe Taylor, and it was our duty to gather them from this range.

Mr. Creed Taylor had raised a son, "Buck" who was a reckless, daredevil. He was buried with his boots on—that is, shot and killed.

In the beginning of the '70s, around Quero, in Victoria County, Texas, a bloody feud raged between the Taylor and Sutton gangs.

In one of their bloody battles in the town of Quero, it was reported that nine men were killed.

About thirty-five years later I tried to obtain the truth of this report.

In the little city of Las Cruces, New Mexico, lives one of these noted feudists. He is a highly respected banker and cattle raiser. It is said that he lay in jail, on account of the Taylor-Sutton feud, seven long years before being freed by the higher courts.

About the year 1914 I happened to be in Las Cruces, and concluded to find out the truth about this bloody battle in Quero.

I was stopping at the Park Hotel, owned by the president of the First National Bank of that town. This gentleman had been brought up in the neighborhood of Quero, and believed the story was correct, about nine men being killed in one battle, when the Taylor and Sutton gangs met. This didn't satisfy me, so I told the gentleman that I was going to visit this noted feudist at his bank and find out the truth.

He advised me not to do it, as it would result in me being kicked out of the bank, if I mentioned the subject.

On walking into the feudist's bank, he met me with out-stretched hand, and conducted me to his private desk in the rear.

I introduced myself as an early day Texas cowboy who had worked for "Shangai" Pierce. He knew "Shanghai" well, and had much to say in his favor.

After we had talked about different subjects, I finally said: "Oh, by the way, is it true that there were nine men killed in Quero one night when the Taylor and Sutton crowds met?"

In all my long life I never saw a man change so suddenly from a smiling, good-natured man to a scowling demon. His black eyes shot sparks of fire and he straightened up in his chair, striking the desk with his fist, saying: "You bet it is true, we killed them knee-deep that night!"

Just then three men came into the bank and told him to hurry up, as they were waiting for him.

Here he begged my pardon for having to leave me, but he said he had to go out in the country to look at some cattle.

When he uttered the above expression I felt relieved, for it seemed that he was getting ready to kick me out of the bank.

I met the gentleman many times afterwards, but never alone, so as to renew the subject.

About the same time that the Taylor-Sutton feud was raging, there was another bloody feud being enacted in Jackson and Colorado counties, between the Stafford and Townsend gangs. "Tuck" Townsend was the leader on one side and Bob Stafford on the other.

Bob Stafford was a wealthy cattle owner, of Columbus, on the Colorado river.

Only a few of Bob Stafford's warmest friends knew the secret of how he became crippled in the left hand. It happened thus:

Stafford was riding along the road on a skittish horse. On the ground near by sat a twelve year old German boy eating his noonday lunch. Near by grazed his small band of sheep, which he was herding.

The boy's dog ran out and scared Mr. Stafford's mount. Then he drew his pistol and killed the dog.

Now the boy sprang to his feet, and pulling his powder and ball pistol, opened fire on Stafford, who at once began shooting at the boy. But his horse jumping around made his aim untrue.

Bob Stafford had emptied his pistol, while the boy had only shot twice, and was taking aim for the third shot.

Here Stafford threw up his right hand, which held the pistol, saying: "Don't shoot, I'm empty."

The boy replied: "Alright, load up." Then he squatted down on the ground, and taking his powder horn from his shoulder proceeded to load the two empty chambers of his six-shooter.

Stafford replied, as he rode away: "No, I've got enough!" He was wounded in the left hand from one of the boy's shots.

Later Mr. Stafford rewarded the boy for his cool bravery.

Now, on the Creed and Joe Taylor range, we began gathering 2500 head of wild cattle. It was the hardest job of my life, working from daylight 'till dark, and then standing night-guard half the night.

As a rule bosses don't stand guard at night, excepting when there is danger of a stampede. But in order to keep my crew in a good humor I took my regular turn. The boys were worn out, and were almost on the eve of striking, from having to work twenty-six hours out of every twenty-four, as they expressed it.

Finally we got the herd "broke in," and started "up the trail," but not "up the Chisholm trail," which lay to the eastward about 100 miles.

During that spring of 1880 the Chisholm trail was impassible for large herds, as "fool hoe-men" had squatted all over it, and were turning its hard packed surface into ribbons with plows.

When about fifty miles west of Ft. Worth, Charlie Word, who had come around by rail, drove out in a buggy to see how we were getting along, and to supply me with more expense money.

At Doan's store, on Red River, we found Liash Stevens waiting for us. We swapped herds, as it had been decided to drive the herd I was with up into Wyoming.

I arrived at the LX ranch with 3700 head of steers on the first day of July.

Now part of my crew were paid off, and with the balance, six riders, I took the herd onto the South Staked Plains to fatten the steers.

Shortly afterwards I rode into Tascosa, and saw the great changes which had taken place since my last visit, a year previous.

Now there were three saloons and two dance-halls running full blast. Also the foundation laid for a new Court House.

The county of Oldham, with Tascosa as the County-seat, had been organized, and twelve unorganized counties attached to Oldham County.

My cowboy friend, Cape Willingham, had been appointed sheriff of these thirteen counties.

One of the first things I did after riding into Tascosa was to step into Mr. Turner's restaurant to see his pretty daughter, Miss Victoria Turner. I was not hungry, but to have the pleasure of this pretty miss waiting on me I was ordering all the good things in the restaurant. Just then a gang of cowboys came charging through the main street shooting off pistols.

As this was no uncommon thing for a live cow-town, I didn't even get up from the table.

In a moment Sheriff Willingham came running into the cafe with a double-barrel shot-gun in his hand. He asked me to help him arrest some drunken cow-boys who had just dismounted and gone into Jack Ryan's saloon, near by.

Just as we reached the Ryan saloon these cowboys came out. One of them sprang onto his horse, when the sheriff told him to throw up his hands. Instead of throwing up his hands he drew his pistol. Then Willingham planted a charge of buckshot in his heart, and he tumbled to the ground dead.

The dead cowboy was the one the sheriff was after, as he had seen him empty his pistol at a flock of ducks, which a lady was feeding out of her hand, as she sat in a door-way.

In galloping down the street this cowboy remarked to his companions: "Watch me kill some of those ducks." He killed them alright, and the woman fainted.

These nine cowboys had just arrived "up the trail" with a herd of long-horn cattle, and were headed for the north. For fear they might make a raid on him that night, which they threatened to do, the sheriff had me stay with him till morning.

Thus did Tascosa bury her first man with his boots on, which gave her the reputation of being a genuine cow-town.

From now on Tascosa's "Boot-hill" cemetery began to show new-made graves. The largest killing in one night being six. At that time my cowboy friend, James H. East, now a well-to-do citizen of Douglas, Arizona, was sheriff. He held the office for four terms, and helped to lay many wild and wooly cowboys under the sod, with their boots on.

Before the court house and jail were finished Tascosa had a bad murder case to try. The District Judge, and attorney, came from Mobeta to try the case.

Jack Ryan was foreman of the jury, and the upstairs part of his saloon was selected as the jury room.

When the prisoner's case was finished the jury were locked up over the saloon.

About midnight Jack Ryan and some of the jury men were holding out for murder in the first degree.

About that time Frank James, Ryan's gambling partner, got a ladder and climbed up to the outside window of the jury-room. He then called for Ryan, and told him that there was a big poker game going on in the saloon, and that he needed $300.00.

Jack gave him the money from the bank-roll, which he carried in his pocket, at the same time telling him to keep the game going until he could get down there, and take a hand.

Now Ryan called the jury men together and told them about the big poker game down in the saloon. He said it was necessary for him to be there and help Frank James out—hence he had come to the conclusion that the prisoner was innocent, and had no evil intentions of murdering his victim.

In a few moments Ryan had the few stubborn jury-men on his side, and the prisoner was declared innocent. At least this is the story told to me by men who claimed to know the facts of the case. This added another laurel to Tascosa's brow as a wide-open cow-town.

The following year Tascosa put on city airs by the arrival of a young lawyer by the name of Lucius Dills, who hung out a shingle as Attorney at Law.

During that fall the first election of Oldham County was held and Mr. Dills was elected the first County Judge. He was appointed District Attorney for the whole Panhandle district, comprising twenty-four counties, before his term as judge expired. Then he tore down his shingle as Attorney at Law, and moved to Mobeta, thus Tascosa lost her first lawyer.

In the spring of 1885 Mr. Lucius Dills quit the Panhandle country and moved to Lincoln County, New Mexico, finally setting down in Roswell as editor of the Roswell Record. Here he married the lovely daughter of Judge Frank Lea, Miss Gertrude, and at the present writing has two pretty daughters. He is now Surveyor General for the State of New Mexico, and lives in Santa Fe, where his friends are counted by the hundreds.

Deadwood Dick

BY NAT LOVE

Nat Love was born in a plantation slave cabin in Tennessee in 1854. By his mid-teens he'd already left home and drifted west. This was the time of the great post–Civil War cattle drives, and Love soon found cowboy work on one of them, chasing herds north out of Texas. For the next fifteen or sixteen years he lived the cowboy life he was later to memorialize in *The Life and Adventures of Nat Love,* from which this yarn is excerpted. In 1876 he won the roping and shooting events in a rodeo contest in the Dakota Territory township of Deadwood, where he was acclaimed "Deadwood Dick," an honorific of which he was so immensely proud that he was to use it as the subtitle for his subsequent autobiography.

Now cowboy-ing is a young man's occupation, rarely a life's work, and so it was with Love. By and by the reach of the railroad became so extensive as to make the great cattle drives a thing of the past. Love traded in his cattle pony for an iron horse and spent the rest of his working life as a Pullman Porter.

The publication in 1907 of his *Life and Adventures* made (and still makes) him the most celebrated African American cowboy; though we know that cowboys come in all colors, and that thousands of former slaves made new lives for themselves in the American West. Perhaps the most interesting aspect of the memoir is what it leaves out. From the moment Love heads west he makes no further reference to his color, makes no mention of conflicts or any other incidents of prejudice or of racial bias in his life as a cowboy. He chooses not to tell us. Nat Love is an idealist. Here is a man who is proud of the life he has lived and the work he has done, and *that* is the story he wishes to tell us.

★　★　★　★　★

In the spring of 1876 orders were received at the home ranch for three thousand head of three-year-old steers to be delivered near Deadwood, South Dakota. This being one of the largest orders we had ever received at one time, every man around the ranch was placed on his mettle to execute the order in record time.

Cow boys mounted on swift horses were dispatched to the farthest limits of the ranch with orders to round up and run in all the three-year-olds on the place, and it was not long before the ranch corrals began to fill up with the long horns as they were driven by the several parties of cow boys; as fast as they came in we would cut out, under the bosses' orders such cattle as were to make up our herd.

In the course of three days we had our herd ready for the trail and we made our preparations to start on our long journey north. Our route lay through New Mexico, Colorado and Wyoming, and as we had heard rumors that the Indians were on the war path and were kicking up something of a rumpus in Wyoming, Indian Territory and Kansas, we expected trouble before we again had the pleasure of sitting around our fire at the home ranch. Quite a large party was selected for this trip owing to the size of the herd and the possibility of trouble on the trail from the Indians. We, as usual, were all well armed and had as mounts the best horses our ranch produced, and in taking the trail we were perfectly confident that we could take care of our herd and ourselves through anything we were liable to meet. We had not been on the trail long before we met other outfits, who told us that General Custer was out after the Indians and that a big fight was expected when the Seventh U. S. Cavalry, General Custer's command, met the Crow tribe and other Indians under the leadership of Sitting Bull, Rain-in-the-Face, Old Chief Joseph, and other chiefs of lesser prominence, who had for a long time been terrorizing the settlers of that section and defying the Government.

As we proceeded on our journey it became evident to us that we were only a short distance behind the soldiers. When finally the Indians and soldiers met in the memorable battle or rather massacre in the Little Big Horn Basin on the Little Big Horn River in northern Wyoming, we were only two days behind them, or within 60 miles, but we did not know that at the time or we would have gone to Custer's assistance. We did not know of the fight or the outcome until several days after it was over. It was freely claimed at the time by cattle men who were in a position to know and with whom I talked that if Reno had gone to Custer's aid as he promised to do, Custer would not have lost his entire command and his life.

It was claimed Reno did not obey his orders, however that may be, it was one of the most bloody massacres in the history of this country.

We went on our way to Deadwood with our herd, where we arrived on the 3rd of July, 1876, eight days after the Custer massacre took place.

The Custer Battle was June 25, '76, the battle commenced on Sunday afternoon and lasted about two hours. That was the last of General Custer and his Seventh Cavalry. How I know this so well is because we had orders from one of the Government scouts to go in camp, that if we went any farther North we were liable to be captured by the Indians.

We arrived in Deadwood in good condition without having had any trouble with the Indians on the way up. We turned our cattle over to their new owners at once, then proceeded to take in the town. The next morning, July 4th, the gamblers and mining men made up a purse of $200 for a roping contest between the cow boys that were then in town, and as it was a holiday nearly all the cow boys for miles around were assembled there that day. It did not take long to arrange the details for the contest and contestants, six of them being colored cow boys, including myself. Our trail boss was chosen to pick out the mustangs from a herd of wild horses just off the range, and he picked out twelve of the most wild and vicious horses that he could find.

The conditions of the contest were that each of us who were mounted was to rope, throw, tie, bridle and saddle and mount the particular horse picked for us in the shortest time possible. The man accomplishing the feat in the quickest time to be declared the winner.

It seems to me that the horse chosen for me was the most vicious of the lot. Everything being in readiness, the "45" cracked and we all sprang forward together, each of us making for our particular mustang.

I roped, threw, tied, bridled, saddled and mounted my mustang in exactly nine minutes from the crack of the gun. The time of the next nearest competitor was twelve minutes and thirty seconds. This gave me the record and championship of the West, which I held up to the time I quit the business in 1890, and my record has never been beaten. It is worthy of passing remark that I never had a horse pitch with me so much as that mustang, but I never stopped sticking my spurs in him and using my quirt on his flanks until I proved his master. Right there the assembled crowd named me Deadwood Dick and proclaimed me champion roper of the western cattle country.

The roping contest over, a dispute arose over the shooting question with the result that a contest was arranged for the afternoon, as there happened to be some of the best shots with rifle and revolver in the West present that day. Among them were Stormy Jim, who claimed the championship; Powder Horn Bill, who had the reputation of never missing what he shot at; also White Head, a half breed, who generally hit what he shot at, and many other men who knew how to handle a rifle or 45-colt.

The range was measured off 100 and 250 yards for the rifle and 150 for the Colt 45. At this distance a bulls eye about the size of an apple was put up. Each man was to have 14 shots at each range with the rifle and 12 shots with the Colts 45.

I placed every one of my 14 shots with the rifle in the bulls eye with ease, all shots being made from the hip; but with the 45 Colts I missed it twice, only placing 10 shots in the small circle, Stormy Jim being my nearest competitor, only placing 8 bullets in the bulls eye clear, the rest being quite close, while with the 45 he placed 5 bullets in the charmed circle. This gave me the championship of rifle and revolver shooting as well as the roping contest, and for that day I was the hero of Deadwood, and the purse of $200 which I had won on the roping contest went toward keeping things moving, and they did move, as only a large crowd of cattle men can move things. This lasted for several days when most of the cattle men had to return to their respective ranches, as it was the busy season, accordingly our outfit began to make preparations to return to Arizona.

In the meantime news had reached us of the Custer massacre, and the indignation and sorrow was universal, as General Custer was personally known to a large number of the cattle men of the West. But we could do nothing now, as the Indians were out in such strong force. There was nothing to do but let Uncle Sam revenge the loss of the General and his brave command, but it is safe to say not one of us would have hesitated a moment in taking the trail in pursuit of the blood thirsty red skins had the opportunity offered.

Everything now being in readiness with us we took the trail homeward bound, and left Deadwood in a blaze of glory. On our way home we visited the Custer battle field in the Little Big Horn Basin.

There was ample evidence of the desperate and bloody fight that had taken place a few days before. We arrived home in Arizona, in a short time without further incident, except that on the way back we met and talked with many of the famous Government scouts of that region, among them Buffalo Bill (William F. Cody), Yellow Stone Kelley, and many others of that day, some of whom are now living, while others lost their lives in the line of duty, and a finer or braver body of men never lived than these sccouts of the West. It was my pleasure to meet Buffalo Bill often in the early 70s, and he was as fine a man as one could wish to meet, kind, generous, true and brave.

Buffalo Bill got his name from the fact that in the early days he was engaged in hunting buffalo for their hides and furnishing U. P. Railroad graders with meat, hence the name Buffalo Bill. Buffalo Bill, Yellowstone Kelley, with many others were at this time serving under Gen. C. C. Miles.

The name of Deadwood Dick was given to me by the people of Deadwood, South Dakota, July 4, 1876, after I had proven myself worthy to carry it, and after I had defeated all comers in riding, roping, and shooting, and I have always carried the name with honor since that time.

We arrived at the home ranch again on our return from the trip to Deadwood about the middle of September, it taking us a little over two months to make the return journey, as we stopped in Cheyenne for several days and at other places, where we always found a hearty welcome, especially so on this trip, as the news had preceded us, and I received enough attention to have given me the big head, but my head had constantly refused to get enlarged again ever since the time I sampled the demijohn in the sweet corn patch at home.

Arriving at home, we received a send off from our boss and our comrades of the home ranch, every man of whom on hearing the news turned loose his voice and his artillery in a grand demonstration in my honor.

But they said it was no surprise to them, as they had long known of my ability with the rope, rifle and 45 Colt, but just the same it was gratifying to know I had defeated the best men of the West, and brought the record home to the home ranch in Arizona. After a good rest we proceeded to ride the range again, getting our herds in good condition for the winter now at hand.

★   ★   ★   ★   ★

In the spring of 1877, now fully recovered from the effects of the very serious wounds I had received at the hands of the Indians and feeling my old self again, I joined the boys in their first trip of the season, with a herd of cattle for Dodge City. The trip was uneventful until we reached our destination. This was the first time I had been in Dodge City since I had won the name of "DEADWOOD DICK," and many of the boys, who knew me when I first joined the cow boys there in 1869, were there to greet me now. After our herd had been delivered to their new owners, we started out to properly celebrate the event, and for a space of several days we kept the old town on the jump.

And so when we finally started for home all of us had more or less of the bad whiskey of Dodge City under our belts and were feeling rather spirited and ready for anything.

I probably had more of the bad whiskey of Dodge City than any one and was in consequence feeling very reckless, but we had about exhausted our resources of amusement in the town, and so were looking for trouble on the trail home.

On our way back to Texas, our way led past old Fort Dodge. Seeing the soldiers and the cannon in the fort, a bright idea struck me, but a fool one just the same. It was no less than a desire to rope one of the cannons. It seemed to me that it would be a good thing to rope a cannon and take it back to Texas with us to fight Indians with.

The bad whiskey which I carried under my belt was responsible for the fool idea, and gave me the nerve to attempt to execute the idea. Getting my lariat rope ready I rode to a position just opposite the gate of the fort, which was standing open. Before the gate paced a sentry with his gun on his shoulder and his white gloves showing up clean and white against the dusty grey surroundings. I waited until the sentry had passed the gate, then putting spurs to my horse I dashed straight for and through the gate into the yard. The surprised sentry called halt, but I paid no attention to him. Making for the cannon at full speed my rope left my hand and settled square over the cannon, then turning and putting spurs to my horse I tried to drag the cannon after me, but strain as he might my horse was unable to budge it an inch. In the meantime the surprised sentry at the gate had given the alarm and now I heard the bugle sound, boots and saddles, and glancing around I saw the soldiers mounting to come after me, and finding I could not move the cannon, I rode close up to it and got my lariat off then made for the gate again at full speed. The guard jumped in front of me with his gun up, calling halt, but I went by him like a shot, expecting to hear the crack of his musket, but for some reason he failed to fire on me, and I made for the open prairie with the cavalry in hot pursuit.

My horse could run like a wild deer, but he was no match for the big, strong, fresh horses of the soldiers and they soon had me. Relieving me of my arms they placed me in the guard house where the commanding officer came to see me. He asked me who I was and what I was after at the fort. I told him and then he asked me if I knew anyone in the city. I told him I knew Bat Masterson. He ordered two guards to take me to the city to see Masterson. As soon as Masterson saw me he asked me what the trouble was, and before I could answer, the guards told him I rode into the fort and roped one of the cannons and tried to pull it out. Bat asked me what I wanted with a cannon and what I intended doing with it. I told him I wanted to take it back to Texas with me to fight the Indians with; then they all laughed. Then Bat told them that I was all right, the only trouble being that I had too much bad whiskey under my shirt. They said I would have to set the drinks for the house. They came to $15.00, and when I started to pay for them, Bat said for me to keep my money that he would pay for them himself, which he did. Bat said that I was the only cowboy that he liked, and that his brother Jim also thought very much of me. I was then let go and I joined the boys and we continued on our way home, where we arrived safely on the 1st of June, 1877.

We at once began preparing for the coming big round up. As usual this kept us very busy during the months of July and August, and as we received no more orders for cattle this season, we did not have to take the trail again, but after the round up was over, we were kept busy in range riding, and the general all around work of the big cattle ranch. We had at this time on the ranch upwards of 30,000 head of cattle, our own cattle, not to mention the cattle belonging to the many other interests without the Pan Handle country, and as all these immense herds used the range of the country, in common as there was no fences to divide the ranches, consequently the cattle belonging to the different herds often got mixed up and large numbers of them strayed.

At the round ups it was our duty to cut out and brand the young calves, take a census of our stock, and then after the round up was over we would start out to look for possible strays. Over the range we would ride through canyons and gorges, and every place where it was possible for cattle to stray, as it was important to get them with the main herd before winter set in, as if left out in small bunches there was danger of them perishing in the frequent hard storms of the winter. While range riding or hunting for strays, we always carried with us on our saddle the branding irons of our respective ranches, and whenever we ran across a calf that had not been branded we had to rope the calf, tie it, then a fire was made of buffalo chips, the only fuel besides grass to be found on the prairie.

The irons were heated and the calf was branded with the brand of the finder, no matter who it personally belonged to. It now became the property of the finder. The lost cattle were then driven to the main herd. After they were once gotten together it was our duty to keep them together during the winter and early spring. It was while out hunting strays that I got lost, the first and only time I was ever lost in my life, and for four days I had an experience that few men ever went through and lived, as it was a close pull for me.

I had been out for several days looking for lost cattle and becoming separated from the other boys and being in a part of the country unfamiliar to me. It was stormy when I started out from the home ranch and when I had ridden about a hundred miles from home it began to storm in earnest, rain, hail, sleet, and the clouds seemed to touch the earth and gather in their inpenetrable embrace every thing thereon. For a long time I rode on in the direction of home, but as I could not see fifty yards ahead it was a case of going it blind. After riding for many weary hours through the storm I came across a little log cabin on the Palidore river. I rode up to within one hundred yards of it where I was motioned to stop by an old long haired man who stepped out of the cabin door with a long buffalo gun on his arm. It was with this he had motioned me to stop.

I promptly pulled up and raised my hat, which, according to the custom of the cowboy country, gave him to understand I was a cowboy from the western cow ranges. He then motioned me to come on. Riding up to the cabin he asked me to dismount and we shook hands.

He said, when I saw you coming I said to myself that must be a lost cowboy from some of the western cow ranges. I told him I was lost all right, and I told him who I was and where from. Again we shook hands, he saying as we did so, that we were friends until we met again, and he hoped forever. He then told me to picket out my horse and come in and have some supper, which very welcome invitation I accepted.

His cabin was constructed of rough hewn logs, somewhat after the fashion of a Spanish block house. One part of it was constructed under ground, a sort of dug out, while the upper portion of the cabin was provided with many loop holes, commanding every direction.

He later told me these loop holes had stood him in handy many a time when he had been attacked by Indians, in their efforts to capture him. On entering his cabin I was amazed to see the walls covered with all kinds of skins, horns, and antlers. Buffalo skins in great numbers covered the floor and bed, while the walls were completely hidden behind the skins of every animal of that region, including a large number of rattle snakes skins and many of their rattles.

His bed, which was in one corner of the dug out, was of skins, and to me, weary from my long ride through the storm, seemed to be the most comfortable place on the globe just then. He soon set before me a bountious supper, consisting of buffalo meat and corn dodgers, and seldom before have I enjoyed a meal as I did that one. During supper he told me many of his experiences in the western country. His name was Cater, and he was one of the oldest buffalo hunters in that part of Texas, having hunted and trapped over the wild country ever since the early thirties, and during that time he had many a thrilling adventure with Indians and wild animals.

I stayed with him that night and slept soundly on a comfortable bed he made for me. The next morning he gave me a good breakfast and I prepared to take my departure as the storm had somewhat moderated, and I was anxious to get home, as the boys knowing I was out would be looking for me if I did not show up in a reasonable time.

My kind host told me to go directly northwest and I would strike the Calones flats, a place with which I was perfectly familiar. He said it was about 75 miles from his place. Once there I would have no difficulty in finding my way home. Cater put me up a good lunch to last me on my way, and with many expressions of gratitude to him, I left him with his skins and comfortable, though solitary life. All that day and part of the

night I rode in the direction he told me, until about 11 o'clock when I became so tired I decided to go into camp and give my tired horse a rest and
a chance to eat. Accordingly I dismounted and removed the saddle and
bridle from my horse I hobbled him and turned him loose to graze on the
luxuriant grass, while I, tired out, laid down with my head on my saddle
fully dressed as I was, not even removing my belt containing my 45 pistol
from my waist, laying my Winchester close by. The rain had ceased to fall,
but it was still cloudy and threatening. It was my intention to rest a few
hours then continue on my way; and as I could not see the stars on account of the clouds and as it was important that I keep my direction
northwest in order to strike the Flats, I had carefully taken my direction
before sundown, and now on moving my saddle I placed it on the ground
pointing in the direction I was going when I stopped so that it would enable me to keep my direction when I again started out. I had been laying
there for some time and my horse was quietly grazing about 20 yards off,
when I suddenly heard something squeal. It sounded like a woman's voice.
It frightened my horse and he ran for me. I jumped to my feet with my
Winchester in my hand. This caused my horse to rear and wheel and I
heard his hobbles break with a sharp snap. Then I heard the sound of his
galloping feet going across the Pan Handle plains until the sound was lost
in the distance. Then I slowly began to realize that I was left alone on the
plains on foot, how many miles from home I did not know. Remembering
I had my guns all right, it was my impulse to go in pursuit of my horse as I
thought I could eventually catch him after he had got over his scare, but
when I thought of my 40 pound saddle, and I did not want to leave that, so
saying to myself that is the second saddle I ever owned, the other having
been taken by the Indians when I was captured, and this saddle was part of
the outfit presented to me by the boys, and so tired and as hungry as a
hawk, I shouldered my saddle and started out in the direction I was going
when I went into camp, saying to myself as I did so, if my horse could pack
me and my outfit day and night, I can at least pack my outfit. Keeping my
direction as well as I could I started out over the prairie through the dark,
walking all that night and all the next day without anything to eat or drink
until just about sundown and when I had begun to think I would have to
spend another night on the prairie without food or drink, when I emerged
from a little draw on to a raise on the prairie, then looking over on to a
small flat I saw a large herd of buffalo. These were the first I had seen since
I became lost and the sight of them put renewed life and hope in me as I
was then nearly famished, and when I saw them I knew I had something
to eat.

Off to one side about 20 yards from the main herd and about 150
yards from me was a young calf. Placing my Winchester to my shoulder I

glanced along the shining barrel, but my hands shook so much I lowered it again, not that I was afraid of missing it as I knew I was a dead shot at that distance, but my weakness caused by my long enforced fast and my great thirst made my eyes dim and my hands shake in a way they had never done before, so waiting a few moments I again placed the gun to my shoulder and this time it spoke and the calf dropped where it had stood. Picking up my outfit I went down to where my supper was laying. I took out my jack knife and commenced on one of his hind quarters. I began to skin and eat to my hearts content, but I was so very thirsty. I had heard of people drinking blood to quench their thirst and that gave me an idea, so cutting the calf's throat with my knife I eagerly drank the fresh warm blood.

It tasted very much like warm sweet milk. It quenched my thirst and made me feel strong, when I had eaten all I could, I cut off two large chunks of the meat and tied them to my saddle, then again shouldering the whole thing I started on my way feeling almost as satisfied as if I had my horse with me. I was lost two days, and two nights, after my horse left me and all that time I kept walking packing my 40 pounds saddle and my Winchester and two cattle pistols.

On the second night about daylight the weather became more threatening and I saw in the distance a long column which looked like smoke. It seemed to be coming towards me at the rate of a mile a minute. It did not take it long to reach me, and when it did I struggled on for a few yards but it was no use, tired as I was from packing my heavy outfit for more than 48 hours and my long tramp, I had not the strength to fight against the storm so I had to come alone. When I again came to myself I was covered up head and foot in the snow, in the camp of some of my comrades from the ranch.

It seemed from what I was told afterwards that the boys knowing I was out in the storm and failing to show up, they had started out to look for me, they had gone in camp during the storm and when the blizzard had passed they noticed an object out on the prairie in the snow, with one hand frozen, clenched around my Winchester and the other around the horn of my saddle, and they had hard work to get my hands loose, they picked me up and placed me on one of the horses and took me to camp where they stripped me of my clothes and wrapped me up in the snow, all the skin came off my nose and mouth and my hands and feet had been so badly frozen that the nails came off. After had got thawed out in the mess wagon and took me home in 15 days I was again in the saddle ready for business but I will never forget those few days I was lost and the marks of that storm I will carry with me always.

Justice in the Saddle

Andy Adams is thought by many to be the cowboy writer's Cowboy
Writer and no collection can lay claim to being the greatest cowboy stories without a sampling of his work. It was he, along with Owen Wister
and Emerson Hough, who first shaped the farrango of cowboy lore into
the art-form we call the Western. Though his stories are plainly fiction, the
elements are so rendered together as to make a narrative that very often
reads, feels, like memoir.

"Justice In The Saddle," an excerpt from *The Outlet,* is set in the
time immediately following the Civil War. The four-year conflict had
devastated much of the south-land. In Texas, the cattle business had been
so badly dislocated that hundreds of thousands of beeves roamed free in
the brush, ownerless, free for the rounding up. In those heady days, there
were fortunes to made if you could gather a herd and get it to an *outlet,* a
rail-head, an army fort, or some other market. All this was dangerous and
difficult enough, but once arrived, you faced the very real possibility of
being cheated of your profits by speculators and frauds. It was also common enough at this time for northerners to deal sharply with the former
confederate soldiers, now cowboys up from Texas.

In this story, Don (Colonel) Lovell and his men discover that even
winning at law is not enough, and they're going to have to fight this thing
out, if they want to get justice.

This story is composed of three consecutive chapters (XIII–XV)
and was published in 1905.

★   ★   ★   ★   ★

I t was an hour after the usual time when we bedded down the cattle.
The wagon had overtaken us about sunset, and the cooks' fire piloted
us into a camp fully two miles to the right of the trail. A change of
horses was awaiting us, and after a hasty supper Tupps detailed two

young fellows to visit Ogalalla. It required no urging; I outlined clearly what was expected of their mission, requesting them to return by the way of Flood's wagon, and to receive any orders which my employer might see fit to send. The horse-wrangler was pressed in to stand the guard of one of the absent lads on the second watch, and I agreed to take the other, which fell in the third. The boys had not yet returned when our guard was called, but did so shortly afterward, one of them hunting me up on night-herd.

"Well," said he, turning his horse and circling with me, "we caught onto everything that was adrift. The Rebel and Sponsilier were both in town, in charge of two deputies. Flood and your brother went in with us, and with the lads from the other outfits, including those across the river, there must have been twenty-five of Lovell's men in town. I noticed that Dave and The Rebel were still wearing their six-shooters, while among the boys the arrests were looked upon as quite a joke. The two deputies had all kinds of money, and wouldn't allow no one but themselves to spend a cent. The biggest one of the two—the one who gave you the cigar—would say to my boss: 'Sponsilier, you're a trail foreman from Texas—one of Don Lovell's boss men—but you're under arrest; your cattle are in my possession this very minute. You understand that, don't you? Very well, then; everybody come up and have a drink on the sheriff's office.' That was about the talk in every saloon and dancehall visited. But when we proposed starting back to camp, about midnight, the big deputy said to Flood: 'I want you to tell Colonel Lovell that I hold a warrant for his arrest; urge him not to put me to the trouble of coming out after him. If he had identified himself to me this afternoon, he could have slept on a goose-hair bed to-night instead of out there on the mesa, on the cold ground. His reputation in this town would entitle him to three meals a day, even if he was under arrest. Now, we'll have one more, and tell the damned old rascal that I'll expect him in the morning.'"

We rode out the watch together. On returning to Flood's camp, they had found Don Lovell awake. The old man was pleased with the report, but sent me no special word except to exercise my own judgement. The cattle were tired after their long tramp of the day before, the outfit were saddle weary, and the first rays of the rising sun flooded the mesa before men or animals offered to arise. But the duties of another day commanded us anew, and with the cook calling us, we rose to meet them. I was favorably impressed with Tupps as a segundo, and after breakfast suggested that he graze the cattle over to the North Platte, cross it, and make a permanent camp. This was agreed to, half the men were excused for the day, and after designating, beyond the river, a clump of cottonwoods where the wagon could be found, seven of us turned and rode back for Ogalalla. With picked mounts under us, we avoided the other cattle which could be seen grazing northward, and when fully halfway to town, there before us on the brink of the mesa loomed up the lead of a herd. I soon recognized Jack Splann on the point, and taking a wide circle, dropped in behind him, the column stretching back a mile and coming up the bluffs, forty abreast like an army in loose marching order. I was proud of those "Open A's;" they were my first herd, and though in a hurry to reach town, I turned and rode back with them for fully a mile.

Splann was acting under orders from Flood, who had met him at the ford that morning. If the cattle were in the possession of any deputy sheriff, they had failed to notify Jack, and the latter had already started for the North Platte of his own accord. The "Drooping T" cattle were in the immediate rear under Forrest's segundo, and Splann urged me to accompany him that forenoon, saying: "From what the boys said this morning, Dave and Paul will not be given a hearing until two o'clock this afternoon. I can graze beyond the north ford by that time, and then we'll all go back together. Flood's right behind here with the 'Drooping T's,' and I think it's his intention to go all the way to the river. Drop back and see him."

The boys who were with me never halted, but had ridden on to-wards town. When the second herd began the ascent of the mesa, I left Splann and turned back, waiting on the brink for its arrival. As it would take the lead cattle some time to reach me, I dismounted, resting in the shade of my horse. But my rest was brief, for the clattering hoofs of a cav-alcade of horsemen were approaching, and as I arose, Quince Forrest and Bob Quirk with a dozen or more men dashed up and halted. As their herds were intended for the Crow and Fort Washakie agencies, they would naturally follow up the south side of the North Platte, and an hour or two of grazing would put them in camp. The Buford cattle, as well as Flood's herd, were due to cross this North Fork of the mother Platte within ten miles of Ogalalla, their respective routes thenceforth being north and northeast. Forrest, like myself, was somewhat leary of entering the town, and my brother and the boys passed on shortly, leaving Quince behind. We discussed every possible phase of what might happen in case we were recognized, which was almost certain if Tolleston or the Dodge buyers were encountered. But an overweening hunger to get into Ogalalla was dominant in us, and under the excuse of settling for our sup-plies, after the herd passed, we remounted our horses, Flood joining us, and rode for the hamlet.

There was little external and no moral change in the town. Several new saloons had opened, and in anticipation of the large drive that year, the Dew-Drop-In dance-hall had been enlarged, and employed three shifts of bartenders. A stage had been added with the new addition, and a special importation of ladies had been brought out from Omaha for the season. I use the term *ladies* advisedly, for in my presence one of the proprietors, with marked courtesy, said to an Eastern stranger, "Oh, no, you need no introduction. My wife is the only woman in town; all the balance are ladies." Beyond a shave and a hair-cut, Forrest and I fought shy of public places. But after the supplies were settled for, and some new clothing was secured, we chambered a few drinks and swaggered about with considerable ado. My bill of supplies amounted to one hundred and twenty-six dollars, and when, without a word, I drew a draft for the amount, the proprietor of the outfitting store, as a pelon, made me a present of two fine silk handkerchiefs. Forrest was treated likewise, and having invested ourselves in white shirts, with flaming red ties, we used the new handkerchiefs to otherwise decorate our persons. We had both chosen the brightest colors, and with these knotted about our necks, dangling from pistol-pockets, or protruding from ruffled shirt fronts, our own mothers would scarcely have known us. Jim Flood, whom we met casually on a back street, stopped, and after circling us once, said, "Now if you fellows just keep perfectly sober, your disguise will be complete."

Meanwhile Don Lovell had reported at an early hour to the sheriff's office. The legal profession was represented in Ogalalla by several firms, criminal practice being their specialty; but fortunately Mike Sutton, an attorney of Dodge, had arrived in town the day before on a legal errand for another trail drover. Sutton was a frontier advocate, alike *popular* with the Texas elements and the gambling fraternity, having achieved laurels in his home town as a criminal lawyer. Mike was born on the little green isle beyond the sea, and, gifted with the Celtic wit, was also in logic clear as the tones of a bell, while his insight into human motives was almost superhuman. Lovell had had occasion in other years to rely on Sutton's counsel, and now would listen to no refusal of his services. As it turned out, the lawyer's mission in Ogalalla was so closely in sympathy with Lovell's trouble that they naturally strengthened each other. The highest tribunal of justice in Ogalalla was the county court, the judge of which also ran the stock-yards during the shipping season, and was banker for two monte games at the Lone Star saloon. He enjoyed the reputation of being an honest, fearless jurist, and supported by a growing civic pride, his decisions gave satisfaction. A sense of crude equity governed his rulings, and as one of the citizens remarked, "Whatever the judge said, *went*." It should be remembered that this was in '84, but had a similar trouble occurred five years earlier, it is likely that Judge Colt would have figured in the preliminaries, and the coroner might have been called on to impanel a jury. But the rudiments of civilization were sweeping westward, and Ogalalla was nerved to the importance of the occasion; for that very afternoon a hearing was to be given for the possession of two herds of cattle, valued at over a quarter-million dollars.

The representatives of The Western Supply Company were quartered in the largest hotel in town, but seldom appeared on the streets. They had employed a firm of local attorneys, consisting of an old and a young man, both of whom evidently believed in the justice of their client's cause. All the cattle-hands in Lovell's employ were anxious to get a glimpse of Tolleston, many of them patronizing the bar and table of the same hostelry, but their efforts were futile until the hour arrived for the hearing. They probably have a new court-house in Ogalalla now, but at the date of this chronicle the building which served as a temple of justice was poorly proportioned, its height being entirely out of relation to its width. It was a two-story affair, the lower floor being used for county offices, the upper one as the court-room. A long stairway ran up the outside of the building, landing on a gallery in front, from which the sheriff announced the sitting of the honorable court of Keith County. At home in Texas, lawsuits were so rare that though I was a grown man, the novelty of this one absorbed me. Quite a large crowd had gathered in advance of the hour, and while awaiting the arrival of Judge Mulqueen, a contingent of fifteen men from the two herds in question rode up and halted in front of the court-house. Forrest and I were lying low, not caring to be seen, when the three plaintiffs, the two local attorneys, and Tolleston put in an appearance. The cavalcade had not yet dismounted, and when Dorg Seay caught sight of Tolleston, he stood up in his stirrups and sang out, "Hello there, Archibald! my old college chum, how goes it?"

Judge Mulqueen had evidently dressed for the occasion, for with the exception of the plaintiffs, he was the only man in the court-room who wore a coat. The afternoon was a sultry one; in that first bottom of the Platte there was scarcely a breath of air, and collars wilted limp as rags. Neither map nor chart graced the unplastered walls, the unpainted furniture of the room was sadly in need of repair, while a musty odor permeated the room. Outside the railing the seating capacity of the court-room was rather small, rough, bare planks serving for seats, but the spectators gladly stood along the sides and rear, eager to catch every word, as they silently mopped the sweat which oozed alike from citizen and cattleman. Forrest and I were concealed in the rear, which was packed with Lovell's boys, when the judge walked in and court opened for the hearing. Judge Mulqueen requested counsel on either side to be as brief and direct as possible, both in their pleadings and testimony, adding: "If they reach the stock-yards in time, I may have to load out a train of feeders this evening. We'll bed the cars, anyhow." Turning to the sheriff, he continued: "Frank, if you happen outside, keep an eye up the river; those Lincoln feeders made a deal yesterday for five hundred three-year-olds.—Read your complaint."

The legal document was read with great fervor and energy by the younger of the two local lawyers. In the main it reviewed the situation correctly, every point, however, being made subservient to their object,—the possession of the cattle. The plaintiffs contended that they were the innocent holders of the original contract between the government and The Western Supply company, properly assigned; that they had purchased these two herds in question, had paid earnest-money to the amount of sixty-five thousand dollars on the same, and concluded by petitioning the court for possession. Sutton arose, counseled a moment with Lovell, and borrowing a chew of tobacco from Sponsilier, leisurely addressed the court.

"I shall not trouble your honor by reading our reply in full, but briefly state its contents," said he, in substance. "We admit that the herds in question, which have been correctly described by road brands and ages, are the property of my client. We further admit that the two trail foremen here under arrest as accessories were acting under the orders of their employer, who assumes all responsibility for their acts, and in our pleadings we ask this honorable court to discharge them from further detention. The earnest-money, said to have been paid on these herds, is correct to a cent, and we admit having the amount in our possession. But," and the little advocate's voice rose, rich in its Irish brogue, "we deny any assignment of the original contract. The Western Supply Company is a corporation name, a shield and fence of thieves. The plaintiffs here can claim no assignment, because they themselves constitute the company. It has been decided that a man cannot steal his own money, neither can he assign from himself to himself. We shall prove by a credible witness that The Western Supply Company is but another name for John C. Fields, Oliver Radcliff, and the portly gentleman who was known a year ago as 'Honest' John Griscom, one of his many aliases. If to these names you add a few moneyed confederates, you have The Western Supply Company, one and the same. We shall also prove that for years past these same gentlemen have belonged to a ring, all brokers in government contracts, and frequently finding it necessary to use assumed names, generally that of a corporation."

Scanning the document in his hand, Sutton continued: "Our motive in selling and accepting money on these herds in Dodge demands a word of explanation. The original contract calls for five million pounds of beef on foot to be delivered at Fort Buford. My client is a sub-contractor under that award. There are times, your honor, when it becomes necessary to resort to questionable means to attain an end. This is one of them. Within a week after my client had given bonds for the fulfillment of his contract, he made the discovery that he was dealing with a double-faced set of scoundrels. From that day until the present moment, secret-service men have shadowed every action of the plaintiffs. My client has anticipated their every move. When beeves broke in price from five to seven dollars a head, Honest John, here, made his boasts in Washington City over a champagne supper that he and his associates would clear one hundred thousand dollars on their Buford contract. Let us reason together how this could be done. The Western Supply Company refused, even when offered a bonus, to assign their contract to my client. But they were perfectly willing to transfer it, from themselves as a corporation, to themselves as individuals, even though they had previously given Don Lovell a subcontract for the delivery of the beeves. The original award was made seven months ago, and the depreciation in cattle since is the secret of why the frog eat the cabbage. My client is under the necessity of tendering his cattle on the day of delivery, and proposes to hold this earnest-money to indemnify himself in case of an adverse decision at Fort Buford. It is the only thing he can do, as The Western Supply Company is execution proof, its assets consisting of some stud-horse office furniture and a corporate seal. On the other hand, Don Lovell is rated at half a million, mostly in pasture lands; is a citizen of Medina County, Texas, and if these gentlemen have any grievance, let them go there and sue him. A judgement against my client is good. Now, your honor, you have our side of the question. To be brief, shall these old Wisinsteins come out here from Washington City and dispossess any man of his property? There is but one answer—not in the Republic of Keith."

All three of the plaintiffs took the stand, their testimony supporting the complaint, Lovell's attorney refusing even to cross-examine any one of them. When they rested their case Sutton arose, and scanning the audience for some time, inquired, "Is Jim Reed here?" In response, a tall, one-armed man worked his way from the outer gallery through the crowd and advanced to the rail. I knew Reed by sight only, my middle brother having made several trips with his trail cattle, but he was known to every one by reputation. He had lost an arm in the Confederate service, and was recognized by the gambling fraternity as the gamest man among all trail drovers, while every cowman from the Rio Grande to the Yellowstone knew him as a poker-player. Reed was asked to take the stand, and when questioned if he knew either of the plaintiffs, siad:

"Yes, I know that fat gentleman, and I'm powerful glad to meet up with him again," replied the witness, designating Honest John. "That man is so crooked that he can't sleep in a bed, and it's one of the wonders of this country that he hasn't stretched hemp before this. I made his acquaintance as manager of The Federal Supply Company, and delivered three thousand cows to him at the Washita Indian Agency last fall. In the final settlement, he drew on three different banks, and one draft of twenty-eight thousand

dollars came back, indorsed, *drawee unknown*. I had other herds on the trail
to look after, and it was a month before I found out that the check was
bogus, by which time Honest John had sailed for Europe. There was nothing could be done but put my claim in a judgement and lay for him. But
I've got a grapevine twist on him now, for no sooner did he buy a herd
here last week than Mr. Sutton transferred the judgment to this jurisdiction, and his cattle will be attached this afternoon. I've been on his trail for
nearly a year, but he'll come to me now, and before he can move his beeves
out of this county, the last cent must come, with interest, attorney's fees,
detective bills, and remuneration for my own time and trouble. That's the
reason that I'm so glad to meet him. Judge, I've gone to the trouble and
expense to get his record for the last ten years. He's so snaky he sheds his
name yearly, shifting for a nickname from Honest John to The Quaker.
In '80 he and his associates did business under the name of The Army &
Sutler Supply Company, and I know of two judgments that can be bought
very reasonable against that corporation. His record would convince any
one that he despises to make an honest dollar."

The older of the two attorneys for the plaintiffs asked a few questions, but the replies were so unsatisfactory to their side, that they soon
passed the witness. During the cross-questioning, however, the sheriff had
approached the judge and whispered something to his honor. As there
were no further witnesses to be examined, the local attorneys insisted on
arguing the case, but Judge Mulqueen frowned them down saying:

"This court sees no occasion for any argument in the present case.
You might spout until you were black in the face and it wouldn't change
my opinion any; besides I've got twenty cars to send and a train of cattle to
load out this evening. This court refuses to interfere with the herds in
question, at present the property of and in possession of Don Lovell, who,
together with his men are discharged from custody. If you're in town to-
night, Mr. Reed, drop into the Lone Star. Couple of nice monte games
running there; hundred-dollar limit, and if you feel lucky, there's a nice
bank roll behind them. Adjourn court, Mr. Sheriff."

Turning the Tables

"Keep away from me, you common cow-hands," said Sponsilier, as a group
of us waited for him at the foot of the court-house stairs. But Dave's grav-
ity soon turned to a smile as he continued: "Did you fellows notice The
Rebel and me sitting inside the rail among all the big augers? Paul, was it a
dream, or did we sleep in a bed last night and have a sure-enough pillow
under our heads? My memory is kind of hazy to-day, but I remember the
drinks and the cigars all right, and saying to some one that his luck was too
good to last. And here we are turned out in the cold world again, our fun

all over, and now must go back to those measly cattle. But it's just what I expected."

The crowd dispersed quietly, though the sheriff took the precaution to accompany the plaintiffs and Tolleston back to their hotel. The absence of the two deputies whom we had met the day before was explained by the testimony of the one-armed cowman. When the two drovers came downstairs, they were talking very confidentially together, and on my employer noticing the large number of his men present, he gave orders for them to meet him at once at the White Elephant saloon. Those who had horses at hand mounted and dashed down the street, while the rest of us took it leisurely around to the appointed rendezvous, some three blocks distant. While on the way, I learned from The Rebel that the cattle on which the attachment was to be made that afternoon were then being held well up the North Fork. Sheriff Phillips joined us shortly after we entered the saloon, and informed my employer that the firm of Fields, Radcliff & Co. had declared war. They had even denounced him and the sheriff's office as being in collusion against them, and had dispatched Tolleston with orders to refuse services.

"Let them got on the prod all they want to," said Don Lovell to Reed and the sheriff. "I've got ninety men here, and you fellows are welcome to half of them, even if I have to go out and stand a watch on night-herd myself. Reed, we can't afford to have our business ruined by such a set of scoundrels, and we might as well fight it out here and now. Look at the situation I'm in. A hundred thousand dollars wouldn't indemnify me in having my cattle refused as late as the middle of September at Fort Buford. And believing that I will be turned down, under my contract, so Sutton says, I must tender my beeves on the appointed day of delivery, which will absolve my bondsmen and me from all liability. A man can't trifle with the government—the cattle must be there. Now in my case, Jim, what would you do?"

"That's a hard question, Don. You see we're strangers up in this Northwest country. Now, if it was home in Texas, there would be only one thing to do. Of course I'm no longer handy with a shotgun, but you've got two good arms."

"Well, gentlemen," said the sheriff, "you must excuse me for interrupting, but if my deputies are to take possession of that herd this afternoon, I must saddle and go to the front. If Honest John and associates try to stand up any bluffs on my office, they'll only run on the rope once. I'm much obliged to you, Mr. Lovell, for the assurance of any help I may need, for it's quite likely that I may have to call upon you. If a ring of government speculators can come out here and reuse service, or dictate to my office, then old Keith County is certainly on the verge of decadence. Now,

I'll be all ready to start for the North Fork in fifteen minutes, and I'd admire to have you all go along."

Lovell and Reed both expressed a willingness to accompany the sheriff. Phillips thanked them and nodded to the force behind the mahogany, who dexterously slid the glasses up and down the bar, and politely inquired of the double now confronting them as to their tastes. As this was the third round since entering the place, I was anxious to get away, and summoning Forrest, we started for our horses. We had left them at a barn on a back street, but before reaching the livery, Quince concluded that he needed a few more cartridges. I had ordered a hundred the day before for my own personal use, but they had been sent out with the supplies and were then in camp. My own belt was filled with ammunition, but on Forrest buying fifty, I took an equal number, and after starting out of the store, both turned back and doubled our purchases. On arriving at the stable, whom should I meet but the Wyoming cowman who had left us at Grinnell. During the few minutes in which I was compelled to listen to his troubles, he informed me that on his arrival at Ogalalla, all the surplus cow-hands had been engaged by a man named Tolleston for the Yellowstone country. He had sent to his ranch, however, for an outfit who would arrive that evening, and he expected to start his herd the next morning. But without wasting any words, Forrest and I swung into our saddles, waved a farewell to the wayfaring acquaintance, and rode around to the White Elephant. The sheriff and quite a cavalcade of our boys had already started, and on reaching the street which terminated in the only road leading to the North Ford, we were halted by Flood to await the arrival of he others. Jim Reed and my employer were still behind, and some little time was lost before they came up, sufficient to give the sheriff a full half-mile start. But under the leadership of the two drovers, we shook out our horses, and the advance cavalcade was soon overtaken.

"Well, Mr. Sheriff," said old man Don, as he reined in beside Phillips, "how do you like the looks of this for a posse? I'll vouch that they're all good cow-hands, and if you want to deputize the whole works, why, just work your rabbit's foot. You might leave Reed and me out, but I think there's some forty odd without us. Jim and I are getting a little too old, but we'll hang around and run errands and do the clerking. I'm perfectly willing to waste a week, and remember that we've got the chuck and nearly a thousand saddle horses right over here on the North Fork. You can move your office out to one of my wagons if you wish, and whatever's mine is yours, just so long as Honest John and his friends pay the fiddler. If he and his associates are going to make one hundred thousand dollars on their Buford contract, one thing is certain—I'll lose plenty of money on this year's drive. If he refuses service and you take possession, your office will be perfectly justified in putting a good force of men with the herd. And at ten dollars a day for a man and horse, they'll soon get sick and Reed will get his pay. If I have to hold the sack in the end, I don't want any company."

The location of the beeves was about twelve miles from town and but a short distance above the herds of The Rebel and Bob Quirk. It was nearly four o'clock when we left the hamlet, and by striking a free gait, we covered the intervening distance in less than an hour and a half. The mesa between the two rivers was covered with through cattle, and as we neared the herd in question, we were met by the larger one of the two chief deputies. The under-sheriff was on his way to town, but on sighting his superior among us, he halted and a conference ensured. Sponsilier and Priest made a great ado over the big deputy on meeting, and after a few inquiries were exchanged, the latter turned to Sheriff Phillips and said:

"Well, we served the papers and left the other two boys in temporary possession of the cattle. It's a badly mixed-up affair. The Texas foreman is still in charge, and he seems like a reasonable fellow. The terms of the sale were to be half cash here and the balance at the point of delivery. But the buyers only paid forty thousand down, and the trail boss refuses to start until they make good their agreement. From what I could gather from the foreman, the buyers simply buffaloed the young fellow out of his beeves, and are not hanging back for more favorable terms. He accepted service all right and assured me that our men would be welcome at his wagon until further notice, so I left matters just as I found them. But as I was on the point of leaving, that segundo of the buyers arrived and tried to stir up a little trouble. We all sat down on him rather hard, and as I left he and the Texas foreman were holding quite a big pow-wow."

"That's Tolleston all right," said old man Don, "and you can depend on him stirring up a muss if there's any show. It's a mystery to me how I tolerated that fellow as long as I did. If some of you boys will corner and hold him for me, I'd enjoy reading his title to him in a few plain words. It's due him, and I want to pay everything I owe. What's the programme, Mr. Sheriff?

"The only safe thing to do is to get full possession of the cattle," replied Phillips. "My deputies are all right, but they don't thoroughly understand the situation. Mr. Lovell, if you can lend me ten men, I'll take charge of the herd at once and move them back down the river about seven miles. They're entirely too near the west line of the county to suit me, and once they're in our custody the money will be forthcoming, or the expenses will mount up rapidly. Let's ride."

The under-sheriff turned back with us. A swell of the mesa cut off a view of the herd, but under the leadership of the deputy we rode to its summit, and there before and under us were both camp and cattle. Arriving at the wagon, Phillips very politely informed the Texas foreman that he would have to take full possession of his beeves for a few days, or until the present difficulties were adjusted. The trail boss was a young fellow of possibly thirty, and met the sheriff's demand with several questions, but, on being assured that his employer's equity in the herd would be fully protected without expense, he offered no serious objection. It developed that Reed had some slight acquaintance with the seller of the cattle, and lost no time in informing the trail boss of the record of the parties with whom his employer was dealing. The one-armed drover's language was plain, the foreman knew Reed by reputation, and when Lovell assured the young man that he would be welcome at any of his wagons, and would be perfectly at liberty to see that his herd was properly cared for, he yielded without a word. My sympathies were with the foreman, for he seemed an honest fellow, and deliberately to take his herd from him, to my impulsive reasoning looked like an injustice. But the sheriff and those two old cowmen were determined, and the young fellow probably acted for the best in making a graceful surrender.

Meanwhile the two deputies in charge failed to materialize, and on inquiry they were reported as out at the herd with Tolleston. The foreman accompanied us to the cattle, and while on the way he informed the sheriff that he wished to count the beeves over to him and take a receipt for the same. Phillips hesitated, as he was no cowman, but Reed spoke up and insisted that it was fair and just, saying: "Of course, you'll count the cattle and give him a receipt in numbers, ages, and brands. It's not this young man's fault that his herd must undergo all this trouble, and when he turns them over to an officer of the law he ought to have something to show for it. Any of Lovell's foremen here will count them to a hair for you, and Don and I will witness the receipt, which will make it good among cowmen."

Without loss of time the herd was started east. Tolleston kept well out of reach of my employer, and besought every one to know what this movement meant. But when the trail boss and Jim Flood rode out to a swell of ground ahead, and the point-men began filling the column through between the two foremen, Archie was sagacious enough to know that the count meant something serious. In the mean time Bob Quirk had favored Tolleston with his company, and when the count was nearly half over, my brother quietly informed him that the sheriff was taking possession. Once the atmosphere cleared, Archie grew uneasy and restless, and as the last few hundred beeves were passing the counters, he suddenly concluded to return to Ogalalla. But my brother urged him not to think of going until he had met his former employer, assuring Tolleston that the old man had made inquiry about and was anxious to meet him. The latter, however, could not remember anything of urgent importance between them, and pleaded the lateness of the hour and the necessity of his immediate return to town. The more urgent Bob Quirk became, the more fidgety grew Archie. The last of the cattle were passing the count as Tolleton turned away from my brother's entreaty, and giving his horse the rowel, started off on a gallop. But there was a scattering field of horsemen to pass, and before the parting guest could clear it, a half-dozen ropes circled in the air and deftly settled over his horse's neck and himself, one of which pinioned his arms. The boys were expecting something of this nature, and fully half the men in Lovell's employ galloped up and formed a circle around the captive, now livid with rage. Archie was cursing by both note and rhyme, and had managed to unearth a knife and was trying to cut the lassos which fettered himself and horse, when Dorg Seay rode in and rapped him over the knuckles with a six-shooter, saying, "Don't do that, sweetheart; those ropes cost thirty-five cents apiece."

Fortunately, the knife was knocked from Tolleston's hand and his six-shooter secured, rendering him powerless to inflict injury to any one. The cattle count had ended, and escorted by a cordon of mounted men, both horse and captive were led over to where a contingent had gathered around to hear the result of the count. I was merely a delighted spectator, and as the other men turned from the cattle and met us, Lovell languidly threw one leg over his horse's neck, and, suppressing a smile, greeted his old foreman.

"Hello, Archie," said he; "it's been some little time since last we met. I've been hearing some bad reports about you, and was anxious to meet up and talk matters over. Boys, take those ropes off his horse and give him back his irons; I raised this man and made him the cow-hand he is, and there's nothing so serious between us that we should remain strangers. Now, Archie, I want you to know that you are in the employ of my enemies, who are as big a set of scoundrels as ever missed a halter. You and Flood, here, were the only two men in my employ who knew all the facts in regard to the Buford contract. And just because I wouldn't favor you over a blind horse, you must hunt up the very men who are trying to undermine me on this drive. No wonder they gave you employment, for you're a valuable man to them; but it's at a serious loss,—the loss of your honor. You can't go home to Texas and again be respected among men. This outfit you are with will promise you the earth, but the moment that they're through with you, you won't cut any more figure than a last year's bird's nest. They'll throw you aside like an old boot, and you'll fall so hard that you'll hear the clock tick in China. Now, Archie, it hurts me to see a young fellow like you go wrong, and I'm willing to forgive the past and stretch out a hand to save you. If you'll quit those people, you can have Flood's cattle from here to the Rosebud Agency, or I'll buy you a ticket home and you can help with the fall work at the ranch. You may have a day or two to think this matter over, and whatever you decide on will be final. You have shown little gratitude for the opportunities that I've given you, but we'll break the old slate and start all over with a new one. Now, that's all I wanted to say to you, except to do your own thinking. If you're going back to town, I'll ride a short distance with you."

The two rode away together, but halted within sight for a short conference, after which Lovell returned. The cattle were being drifted east by the deputies and several of our boys, the trail boss having called off his men on an agreement of the count. The herd had tallied out thirty-six hundred and ten head, but in making out the receipt, the fact was developed that there were some six hundred beeves not in the regular road brand. These had been purchased extra from another source, and had been paid for in full by the buyers, the seller of the main herd agreeing to deliver them along with his own. This was fortunate, as it increased the equity of the buyers in the cattle, and more than established a sufficient interest to satisfy the judgment and all expenses.

Darkness was approaching, which hastened our actions. Two men from each outfit present were detailed to hold the cattle that night, and were sent on ahead to Priest's camp to secure their suppers and a change of mounts. The deposed trail boss accepted an invitation to accompany us and spend the night at one of our wagons, and we rode away to overtake the drifting herd. The different outfits one by one dropped out and rode for their camps; but as mine lay east and across the river, the course of the herd was carrying me home. After passing The Rebel's wagon fully a half mile, we rounded in the herd, which soon lay down to rest on the bed-ground. In the gathering twilight, the camp-fires of nearly a dozen trail wagons were gleaming up and down the river, and while we speculated with Sponsilier's boys which one was ours, the guard arrived and took the bedded herd. The two old cowmen and the trail boss had dropped out opposite my brother's camp, leaving something like ten men with the attached beeves; but on being relieved by the first watch, Flood invited Sheriff Phillips and his deputies across the river to spend the night with him.

"Like to, mighty well, but can't do it," replied Phillips. "The sheriff's office is supposed to be in town, and not over on the North Fork, but I'll leave two of these deputies with you. Some of you had better ride in to-morrow, for there may be overtures made looking towards a settlement; and treat those beeves well, so that there can be no charge of damage to the cattle. Good-night, everybody."

Tolleston Butts In

Morning dawned on a scene of pastoral grandeur. The valley of the North Platte was dotted with cattle from hill and plain. The river, well confined within its low banks, divided an unsurveyed domain of green-swarded meadows like a boundary line between vast pastures. The exodus of cattle from Texas to the new Northwest was nearing flood-tide, and from every swell and knoll the solitary figure of the herdsman greeted the rising sun.

Sponsilier and I had agreed to rejoin our own outfits at the first opportunity. We might have exchanged places the evening before, but I had a horse and some ammunition at Dave's camp and was just contentious enough not to give up a single animal from my own mount. On the other hand, Mr. Dave Sponsilier would have traded whole remudas with me; but my love for a good horse was strong, and Fort Buford was many a weary mile distant. Hence there was no surprise shown as Sponsilier rode up to his own wagon that morning in time for breakfast. We were good friends when personal advantages did not conflict, and where our employer's interest were at stake we stood shoulder to shoulder like comrades. Yet Dave gave me a big jolly about being daffy over my horses, well knowing that there is an indescribable nearness between one of our craft and his own mount. But warding off his raillery, just the same and in due time, I cantered away on my own horse.

As I rode up the North Fork towards my outfit, the attached herd was in plain view across the river. Arriving at my own wagon, I saw a mute appeal in every face for permission to go to town, and consent was readily granted to all who had not been excused on a similar errand the day before. The cook and horse-wrangler were included, and the activities of the outfit in saddling and getting away were suggestive of a prairie fire or a stampede. I accompanied them across the river, and then turned upstream to my brother's camp, promising to join them later and make a full day of it. At Bob's wagon they had stretched a fly, and in its shade lounged half a dozen men, while an air of languid indolence pervaded the camp. Without dismounting, I announced myself as on the way to town, and invited any one who wished to accompany me. Lovell and Reed both declined; half of Bob's men had been excused and started an hour before, but my brother assured me that if I would wait until the deposed foreman returned, the latter's company could be counted on. I waited, and in the course of half an hour the trail boss came back from his cattle. During the interim, the two old cowmen reviewed Grant's siege of Vicksburg, both having been participants, but on opposite sides. While the guest was shifting his saddle to a loaned horse, I inquired if there was anything that I could attend to for any one at Ogalalla. Lovell could think of nothing; but as we mounted to start, Reed aroused himself, and coming over, rested the stub of his armless sleeve on my horse's neck, saying:

"You boys might drop into the sheriff's office as you go in and also again as you are starting back. Report the cattle as having spent a quiet night and ask Phillips if he has any word for me."

Turning to the trail boss he continued: "Young man, I would suggest that you hunt up your employer and have him stir things up. The cattle will be well taken care of, but we're just as anxious to turn them back to you as you are to receive them. Tell the seller that it would be well worth his while to see Lovell and myself before going any farther. We can put him in possession of a few facts that may save him time and trouble. I reckon that's about all. Oh, yes, I'll be at this wagon all evening."

My brother rode a short distance with us and introduced the stranger as Hugh Morris. He proved a sociable fellow, had made three trips up the trail as foreman, his first two herds having gone to the Cherokee Strip under contract. By the time we reached Ogalalla, as strong a fraternal level existed between us as though we had known each other for years. Halting for a moment at the sheriff's office, we delivered our messages, after which we left our horses at the same corral with the understanding that we would ride back together. A few drinks were indulged in before parting, then each went to attend to his own errands, but we met frequently during the day. Once my boys were provided with funds, they fell to gambling so eagerly that they required no further thought on my part until evening. Several times during the day I caught glimpses of Tolleston, always on horseback, and once surrounded by quite a cavalcade of horsemen. Morris and I took dinner at the hotel where the trio of government jobbers were stopping. They were in evidence, and amongst the jolliest of the guests, commanding and receiving the best that the hostelry afforded. Sutton was likewise present, but quiet and unpretentious, and I thought there was a false, affected note in the hilarity of the ringsters, and for effect. I was known to two of the trio, but managed to overhear any conversation which was adrift. After dinner and over fragrant cigars, they reared their feet high on an outer gallery, and the inference could be easily drawn that a contract, unless it involved millions, was beneath their notice.

Morris informed me that his employer's suspicions were aroused, and that he had that morning demanded a settlement in full or the immediate release of the herd. They had laughed the matter off as a mere incident that would right itself at the proper time, and flashed as references a list of congressmen, senators, and bankers galore. But Morris's employer had stood firm in his contentions, refusing to be overawed by flattery or empty promises. What would be the result remained to be seen, and the foreman and myself wandered aimlessly around town during the afternoon, meeting other trail bosses, nearly all of whom had heard more or less about the existing trouble. That we had the sympathy of the cattle interests on our side goes without saying, and one of them, known as "the kid-gloved foreman," a man in the employ of Shanghai Pierce, invoked the powers above to witness what would happen if he were in Lovell's boots. This was my first meeting with the picturesque trail boss, though I had heard of him often and found him a trifle boastful but not a bad fellow. He distinguished himself from others on his station on the trail by always wearing white shirts, kid gloves, riding-boots, inlaid spurs, while a heavy silver chain was wound several times round a costly sombrero in lieu of a hatband. We spent an hour or more together, drinking sparingly, and at parting he begged that I would assure my employer that he sympathized with him and was at his command.

The afternoon was waning when I hunted up my outfit and started them for camp. With one or two exceptions, the boys were broke and perfectly willing to go. Morris and I joined them at the livery where they had left their horses, and together we started out of town. Ordering them to ride on to camp, and saying that I expected to return by way of Bob Quirk's wagon, Morris and myself stopped at the court-house. Sheriff Phillips was in his office and recognized us both at a glance. "Well, she's working," said he, "and I'll probably have some word for you late this evening. Yes, one of the local attorneys for your friends came in and we figured everything up. He thought that if this office would throw off a certain percent of its expense, and Reed would knock off the interest, his clients would consent to a settlement. I told him to go right back and tell his people that as long as they thought that way, it would only cost them one hundred and forty dollars every twenty-four hours. The lawyer was back within twenty minutes, bringing a draft, covering every item, and urged me to have it accepted by wire. The bank was closed, but I found the cashier in a poker-game and played his hand while he went over to the depot and sent the message. The operator has orders to send a duplicate of the answer to this office, and the moment I get it, if favorable, I'll send a deputy with the news over to the North Fork. Tell Reed that I think the check's all right this time, but we'll stand pat until we know for a certainty. We'll get an answer by morning sure."

The message was hailed with delight at Bob Quirk's wagon. On nearing the river, Morris rode by way of the herd to ask the deputies in charge to turn the cattle up the river towards his camp. Several of the foreman's men were waiting at my brother's wagon, and on Morris's return he ordered his outfit to meet the beeves the next morning and be in readiness to receive them back. Our foremen were lying around temporary headquarters, and as we were starting for our respective camps for the night, Lovell suggested that we hold our outfits all ready to move out with the herds on an hour's notice. Accordingly the next morning, I refused every one leave of absence, and gave special orders to the cook and horse-wrangler to have things in hand to start on an emergency order. Jim Flood had agreed to wait for me, and we would recross the river together and hear the report from the sheriff's office. Forrest and Sponsilier rode up about the same time we arrived at his wagon, and all four of us set out for headquarters across the North Fork. The sun was several hours high when we reached the wagon, and learned that an officer had arrived during the night with a favorable an-swer, that the cattle had been turned over to Morris without a count, and that the deputies had started for town at daybreak.

"Well, boys," said Lovell, as we came in after picketing our horses, "Reed, here, wins out, but we're just as much at sea as ever. I've looked the situation over from a dozen different viewpoints, and the only thing to do is graze across country and tender our cattle at Fort Buford. It's my nature to look on the bright side of things, and yet I'm old enough to know that justice, in a world so full of injustice, is a rarity. By allowing the earnest-money paid at Dodge to apply, some kind of a compromise might be ef-fected, whereby I could get rid of two of these herds, with three hundred saddle horses thrown back on my hands at the Yellowstone River. I might dispose of the third herd here and give the remuda away, but at a total loss of at least thirty thousand dollars on the Buford cattle. But then there's my bond to The Western Supply Company, and if this herd of Morris's fails to respond on the day of delivery, I know who will have to make good. An Indian uprising, or the enforcement of quarantine against Texas fever, or any one of a dozen things might tie up the herd, and September the 15th come and go and no beef offered on the contract. I've seen outfits start out and never get through with the chuck-wagon, even. Sutton's advice is good; we'll tender the cattle. There is a chance that we'll get turned down, but if we do, I have enough indemnity money in my possession to temper the wind if the day of delivery should prove a chilly one to us. I think you had all better start in the morning."

The old man's review of the situation was a rational one, in which Jim Reed and the rest of us concurred. Several of the foremen, among them myself, were anxious to start at once, but Lovell urged that we kill a beef before starting and divide it up among the six outfits. He also pro-posed to Flood that they go into town during the afternoon and freely an-nounce our departure in the morning, hoping to force any issue that might be smouldering in the enemy's camp. The outlook for an early de-parture was hailed with delight by the older foremen, and we younger and more impulsive ones yielded. The cook had orders to get up something extra for dinner, and we played cards and otherwise lounged around until the midday meal was announced as ready. A horse had been gotten up for Lovell to ride and was on picket, all the relieved men from the attached herd were at Bob's wagon for dinner, and jokes and jollity graced the occasion. But near the middle of the noon repast, some one sighted a mounted man coming at a furious pace for the camp, and shortly the horseman dashed up and inquired for Lovell. We all arose, when the messenger dismounted and handed my employer a letter. Tearing open the missive, the old man read it and turned ashy pale. The message was from Mike Sutton, stating that a fourth member of the ring had arrived during the forenoon, accompanied by a United States marshal from the federal court at Omaha; that the officer was armed with an order of injunctive relief; that he had deputized thirty men whom Tolleston had gathered, and proposed taking possession of the two herds in question that afternoon.

"Like hell they will," said Don Lovell, as he started for his horse. His action was followed by every man present, including the one-armed guest, and within a few minute thirty men swung into saddles, subject to orders. The camps of the two herds at issue were about four and five miles down and across the river, and no doubt Tolleston knew of their location, as they were only a little more than an hour's ride from Ogalalla. There was no time to be lost, and as we hastily gathered around the old man, he said: "Ride for your outfits, boys, and bring along every man you can spare. We'll meet north of the river about midway between Quince's and Tom's camps. Bring all the cartridges you have, and don't spare your horses going or coming."

Priest's wagon was almost on a line with mine, though south of the river. Fortunately I was mounted on one of the best horses in my string, and having the farthest to go, shook the kinks out of him as old Paul and myself tore down the mesa. After passing The Rebel's camp, I held my course as long as the footing was solid, but on encountering the first sand, crossed the river nearly opposite the appointed rendezvous. The North Platte was fordable at any point, flowing but a midsummer stage of water, with numerous wagon crossings, its shallow channel being about one hundred yards wide. I reined in my horse for the first time near the middle of the stream, as the water reached my saddle-skirt; when I came out on the other side, Priest and his boys were not a mile behind me. As I turned down the river, casting a backward glance, squads of horsemen were galloping in from several quarters and joining a larger one which was throwing up clouds of dust like a column of cavalry. In making a cut-off to reach my camp, I crossed a sand dune from which I sighted the marshal's posse less than two miles distant. My boys were gambling among themselves, not a horse under saddle, and did not notice my approach until I dashed up. Three lads were on herd, but the rest, including the wrangler, ran for their mounts on picket, while

Parent and myself ransacked the wagon for ammunition. Fortunately the supply of the latter was abundant, and while saddles were being cinched on horses, the cook and I divided the ammunition and distributed it among the men. The few minutes' rest refreshed my horse, but as we dashed away, the boys yelling like Comanches, the five-mile ride had bested him and he fell slightly behind. As we turned into the open valley, it was a question if we or the marshal would reach the stream first; he had followed an old wood road and would strike the river nearly opposite Forrest's camp. The horses were excited and straining every nerve, and as we neared our crowd the posse halted on the south side and I noticed a conveyance among them in which were seated four men. There was a moment's consultation held, when the posse entered the water and began fording the stream, the vehicle and its occupants remaining on the other side. We had halted in a circle about fifty yards back from the river-bank, and as the first two men came out of the water, Don Lovell rode forward several lengths of his horse, and with his hand motioned to them to halt. The leaders stopped within easy speaking distance, the remainder of the posse halting in groups at their rear, when Lovell demanded the meaning of this demonstration.

An inquiry and answer followed identifying the speakers. "In pursuance of an order from the federal court of this jurisdiction," continued the marshal, "I am vested with authority to take into my custody two herds, numbering nearly seven thousand beeves, now in your possession, and recently sold to Field, Radcliff & Co. for government purposes. I propose to execute my orders peaceably, and any interference on your part will put you and your men in contempt of government authority. If resistance is offered, I can, if necessary, have a company of United States cavalry here from Fort Logan within forty-eight hours to enforce the mandates of the federal court. Now my advice to you would be to turn these cattle over without further controversy."

"And my advice to you," replied Lovell, "is to go back to your federal court and tell that judge that as a citizen of these United States, and one who has borne arms in her defense, I object to having snap judgment rendered against me. If the honorable court which you have the pleasure to represent is willing to dispossess me of my property in favor of a ring of government thieves, and on only hearing one side of the question, then consider me in contempt. I'll gladly go back to Omaha with you, but you can't so much as look at a hoof in my possession. Now call your troops, or take me with you for treating with scorn the orders of your court."

Meanwhile every man on our side had an eye on Archie Tolleston, who had gradually edged forward until his horse stood beside that of the marshal. Before the latter could frame a reply to Lovell's ultimatum, Tolleston said to the federal officer: "Didn't my employers tell you that the old — — — — would defy you without a demonstration of soldiers at your back? Now, the laugh's on you, and —"

"No, it's on you, interrupted a voice at my back, accompanied by a pistol report. My horse jumped forward, followed by a fusillade of shots behind me, when the hireling deputies turned and plunged into the river. Tolleston had wheeled his horse, joining the retreat, and as I brought my six-shooter into action and was in the act of leveling on him, he reeled from the saddle, but clung to the neck of his mount as the animal dashed into the water. I held my fire in the hope that he would right in the saddle and afford me a shot, but he struck a swift current, released his hold, and sunk out of sight. Above the din and excitement of the moment, I heard a voice which I recognized as Reed's, shouting, "Cut loose on that team, boys! Blaze away at those harness horses!" Evidently the team had been burnt by random firing, for they were rearing and plunging, and as I fired my first shot at them, the occupants sprang out of the vehicle and the team ran away. A lull occurred in the shooting to eject shells and refill cylinders, which Lovell took advantage of by ordering back a number of impulsive lads, who were determined to follow up the fleeing deputies.

"Come back here, you rascals, and stop this shooting!" shouted the old man. "Stop it, now, or you'll land me in a federal prison for life! Those horsemen may be deceived. When federal courts can be deluded with sugar coated blandishments, ordinary men ought to be excusable."

Six-shooters were returned to their holsters. Several horses and two men on our side had received slight flesh wounds, as there had been a random return fire. The deputies halted well out of pistol range, covering the retreat of the occupants of the carriage as best they could, but leaving three dead horses in plain view. As we dropped back towards Forrest's wagon, the team in the mean time having been caught, those on foot were picked up and given seats in the conveyance. Meanwhile a remuda of horses and two chuck-wagons were sighted back on the old wood road, but a horseman met and halted them and they turned back for Ogalalla. On reaching our nearest camp, the posse south of the river had started on their return, leaving behind one of their number in the muddy waters of the North Platte.

Late that evening, as we were preparing to leave for our respective camps, Lovell said to the assembled foremen: "Quince will take Reed and me into Ogalalla about midnight. If Sutton advises it, all three of us will go down to Omaha and try and square things. I can't escape a severe fine, but what do I care as long as I have their money to pay it with? The killing of that fool boy worried me more than a dozen fines. It was uncalled for, too, but he would butt in, and you fellows were all itching for the chance to finger a trigger. Now the understanding is that you all start in the morning."

Pecos Bill

BY MODY C. BOATRIGHT

These days, the tallest tales get told around the coffee urn at night, in some truck-stop diner, away out, just west of nowhere. But time was, the great tales got told around the campfire, and in those days or nights, legends were born out of the toil and heartbreak and humor of people's lives. Over and over again semi-mythic figures arose and struggled or adventured in a world wrought of our best and worst imaginings, but in a landscape we knew well. These stories were a kind of therapy, a talking cure, that allowed folk to go to sleep smiling and get up the next day and face their lives. John Henry was a miner, and could he hammer! But he got into a contest with a steam driven machine, and though he beat it, it cost his life. Davey Crockett, the legend not the man, was half-horse, half-alligator, with a smidgen of pole-cat; just what you'd want to be if you spent your life off in the trackless wilds of the American frontier. Mike Fink the riverboatman was a kind of Mississippi Hercules who labored mightily, and did some good, but was just as likely to lose it completely, run amok, and wreak mayhem wherever he went. You see the fruit trees growing wild all over North America? Thank Johnny Appleseed.

Boatright's rendering of the Pecos Bill legend is here composed of three chapters: "The Genesis of Pecos Bill," "Adventures of Pecos Bill," and "The Exodus of Pecos Bill." They first appear in Boatright's *Tall Tales from Texas,* 1934.

★ ★ ★ ★ ★

The Genesis of Pecos Bill

"I suppose," said Lanky, as he sat by the camp-fire with Red and Hank and Joe, now his fast friends, "that the cowboy's life is about the most interesting one there is. I'd like it. Live outdoors, plenty of fresh air to breathe, interesting work—that's the life."

"I ain't kickin'," said Joe. "You see I'm still at it, though I've cussed it as much as anybody in my time, and swore off and quit, too, more than once. But somehow when spring comes, and the grass gits green, and I know the calves is comin', somethin' jest naturally gits under my hide, and I come back to the smell of burnt hair and the creak of saddle-leather."

"Yeah," said Red, "it's jist like a dream I had once. I dreamt I died and went up to a place where there was big pearly gates, and I walked up and knocked on the door, and it come wide open. I went in, and there stood Saint Peter.

"'Come in; welcome to our city,' he says. 'I've been lookin' for you. Go over to the commissary and git you a harp and a pair of wings.'

"'All right,' says I, feelin' mighty lucky to git in.

"As I walked along on the gold sidewalk, I sees a lot of fellers roped and hobbled and hog-tied.

"'What's the matter?' says I; 'Saint Peter, you're not tryin' to buffalo me, are you?'

"'Naw,' he says, 'what makes you think so? Your record ain't nothin' extra good, but you didn't git cut back, did you? Here you are. You're in. Ain't that enough?'

"'Ain't this hell?' I says.

"'Naw,' says Peter, 'this ain't hell a-tall.'

"'Are you shore this ain't hell?' I asks.

"'Naw,' he says, 'this ain't hell. What makes you think it is?'

"'Why,' I says, 'what you got all them fellers roped and tied down for?'

"'Oh,' he says, 'them fellers over there? You see them's cowboys from the Southwest, and I have to keep 'em tied to keep 'em from goin' back. I think maybe they'll git range broke after while so I can turn 'em loose, but it seems like it's takin' a long time.'"

"However," said Joe, "the cow business ain't what it used to be, what with barbed wire, windmills, automobiles and trucks, and the like. They don't want cowhands anymore; what they want is blacksmiths, mechanics, and the like. Still, I reckon it's a good thing, for they couldn't git cowhands if they did want 'em.

"Now, here's Red and Hank. Good boys, both of 'em. And I've leaned 'em a lot about cattle; and they take money at the rodeos, but they ain't like the old cowhands. I don't know jest what it is, but they ain't the same.

"And they ain't but mighty few real cowmen any more. Now, take the big mogul of this outfit. Good feller, always pays wages every month—which is more than some of the old-timers could do. But he ain't no cowman. Sets up all day at a big desk in town—has a secretary, stenographer, and the like. Why, if Pecos Bill had a-done a thing like that, he would of been so ashamed of his self, he would of jest naturally laid down and died."

"Who is this Pecos Bill I've heard you mention?" asked Lanky.

"Who is he? Why, ain't you ever heard of Pecos Bill?"

"Not till I came here."

"Well, well, I reckon you've heard of Sam Houston, and Sam Bass and General Lee and George Washington and Pat Garrett, ain't you?"

"Oh, yes, I've heard a little about them but not anything about Pecos Bill."

"That jest shows that the fellers that make our books don't know what to put in 'em. The idear of leavin' out Pecos Bill."

"But who was Pecos Bill?"

"Who was he? Why he was jest about the most celebrated man in the whole dang cow country."

"What was his real name?"

"So far as I know the only real name he ever had was Pecos Bill. Don't suppose anybody knows what his daddy's name was. You see, in his day it wasn't good manners to ask a feller his name, and besides it wasn't good judgment either. And it ain't been so long. Many a greenhorn bein' ignorant of that little point of good manners has looked down the muzzle of a six-shooter and then died.

"Pecos Bill's daddy didn't say what they called him back in the States, and nobody asked him. They jest called him the Ole Man, for he was old—about seventy some odd when he came to Texas."

"When did he come to Texas?" asked Lanky.

"I couldn't say about that exactly," said Joe. "It must of been right about the time Sam Houston discovered Texas. Anyhow, the Ole Man loaded up all his twelve kids and his Ole Woman and his rifle, and all his other stuff in an oxwagon and lit out hell-bent for Texas as soon as he found out there was sech a place. They say other people that come later didn't have no trouble findin' the way. They jest went by the Indian skeletons that the Ole Man left along his road.

"Well, they finally got to the Sabine River. The Ole Man stops his oxen, old Spot and Buck, he calls 'em, and rounds up all his younguns and has 'em set down and listen while he makes 'em a speech. 'Younguns,' he says, 'that land you see on the other side of the river is Texas, wild and woolly and full of fleas. And if you ain't that way only more so, you ain't no brats of mine.'"

"I'd always heard that Pecos Bill was born in Texas," interrupted Red.

"Jest wait," said Joe. "Jest wait; have I said he wasn't? Them was the other kids.

"As I was about to say, they crossed the river and camped for the night. That was in Texas, savvy. And that night Pecos Bill was born. The next mornin' the Ole Woman put him on a bear's skin and left him to play with his self while she made the corn-pone for breakfast. And right then's when they come dang near losin' Pecos Bill."

"Bears or Indians?" asked Lanky.

"Neither one," said Joe. "Bears and Indians didn't mean nothin' to that old man. He would have et 'em for breakfast. Once later when the Ole Man and the older brats was gone, the Comanches did try to git Bill, but the Ole Woman lit into 'em with the broom-handle and killed forty-nine right on the spot. She never knowed how many she crippled and let git away. No, it wasn't the Indians. It was miskeeters."

"Malaria?" said Lanky.

"You guessed wrong again," said Joe. "This is what happened. The Ole Woman was cookin' corn-pone, and all of a sudden it got dark, and there was the dangest singin' and hummin' you ever heard. Then they see it was a swarm of big black miskeeters; and they was so thick around Bill that you jest couldn't see him.

"The Ole Man felt his way to the wagon and got out his gun. He thought he'd shoot it off in the air and scere them miskeeters away. He pointed the muzzle of the gun toward the sky and pulled the trigger. What he seen then was a little beam of light come through. It was just like bein' in a dark room and lookin' out through a piece of windmill pipe. That was jest for a minute, for right away the hole shet up, and them miskeeters swarmed around Pecos, and the Ole Man seen they was goin' to pack him off if he didn't do somethin' right away.

"Then he happened to recollect that he'd brought his hog-renderin' kettle along; so he fought his way back to the wagon and rolled it out and turned it over the kid. He was scered the lad would git lonesome under there by his self, so he jest slipped the choppin' axe under the edge of the kettle for the chap to play with.

"Well, them danged miskeeters jest buzzed and buzzed around the kettle, tryin' to find a way to git in. D'rec'ly they all backed off, and the Old Man and the Ole Woman thought they'd give up and was goin' way. Then all at once one of them miskeeters comes at that kettle like a bat out of hell. He hit the kettle and rammed his bill clean through it; and he stuck there. Then another one come at the kettle jest like the first one had; and he stuck, too. Then they kept comin', and every one stuck. The Ole Man and the Ole woman and the older brats stood there watchin' them miskeeters ram that kettle. After each one of them varmints (they was too big to be called insects) hit the kettle, there would be a little ring—*ding!* Like that. Purty soon the old folks got on to what was happenin'. Every time a miskeeter would ram his bill through the kettle, Pecos would brad it with the choppin' axe. Well, after while them miskeeters jest naturally lifted that kettle right up and flew off with it. The others thought they had Pecos Bill and follered the kettle off. Of course the Ole Man hated to lose his utensil. He said he didn't know how the Old Woman was going to render up the lard and bear's grease now; but it was worth a hundred kettles to know he had such a smart brat. And from that time the Ole Man would always talk about Bill as a chap of Great Possibilities. He 'lowed that if the brat jest had the proper raisin', he'd make a great man some day. He said he was goin' to try to do his part by him; so he begun givin' him a diet of jerked game with whiskey and onions for breakfast. He lapped it up so well that in three days the Ole Woman weaned him."

"Did the Ole Man settle there on the Sabine?" asked Lanky.

"Naw," said Joe. "He squatted on a little sandy hill on the Trinity somewheres east of where Dallas is now. It was jest an accident that he stopped where he did."

"How was that?" asked Lanky.

"Well," said Joe, "you see, it was like this. They was travelin' west in their customary and habitual manner, which was with the Ole Man and the six oldest kids walkin' alongside Spot and Buck, and the Ole Woman and the seven youngest kids in the wagon. Jest as they was comin' to the foot of a sandy hill, a big rain come up. It rained so hard that the Ole Man couldn't see the wagon, but he stuck close to them trusty oxen of his, and they went right up the hill. When he got to the top, he seen that it had about quit rainin'; and he looked back and seen the wagon still at the bottom of the hill, and there was the brats that had been walkin' with him under it."

"Did the harness break?" asked Lanky.

"Naw, it wasn't that," said Joe. "You see, he was usin' a rawhide lariat for a log-chain, and it had got wet. I reckon you know what rawhide does when it gits wet, don't you, Lanky? It stretches. There ain't no rubber that will stretch like wet rawhide. Well, that's what happened to that lariat. It stretched so that the Ole Man drove his oxen a mile up the hill without movin' the wagon an inch. Not an inch had he moved her, by gar.

"Well, the sun was shinin' now, and it got brighter and brighter, and while the Ole Man was wonderin' what in the dickens to do next, Ole Spot jest dropped down dead from sunstroke. That sort of got next to the Ole Man, for he said that brute had been a real friend to him, and besides he was worth his weight in gold. Still, he 'lowed he'd might as well skin him. So he got out his old Bowie knife and started to work.

"Well, sir, while he was skinnin' Spot, a norther came up, and damn me, if Ole Buck didn't keel over, froze to death.

"So the Ole Man decided he'd jest as well stop there where he was. So he told the Ole Woman to bring up the brats. He throwed the ox yoke over a stump; and the Ole Woman brought up some chuck and some beddin' from the wagon. Then they et supper and tucked the kids into bed. The Ole Man tried to blow out the lantern, but she wouldn't blow. He raised up the globe, and there was the flame froze still as an icicle. He jest broke it off and buried it in the sand and turned in and went to sleep.

"The next mornin' when he woke up, it was clear and the sun was warm. Well, the Ole Woman cooked a bite, and while they was eatin' here come the wagon right up the hill. You see the rawhide was dryin' out. That's the way it does."

"That's what it does, all right," said Red. "Once I knowed a clod-hopper that made his self a rawhide hat. It worked fine till one day he got caught out in the rain. Then the sun come out, and that hat drawed up so he couldn't git it off. And it was drawin' up and mashin' his head somthin' terrible. Lucky for him, it wasn't very far to a tank, and he got off and stood on his head in the water a few minutes and it come right off."

"Well," said Joe, "that's what the rawhide log-chain done. It dried out, and that wagon come right up the hill; and when it got up to where the Ole Man and the Ole Woman was, the Ole Man got his chippin' axe and begun cuttin' down trees to make him a cabin. And that's where he settled."

"Did Pecos Bill grow up there in East Texas?" asked Lanky.

"He left when he was a mere lad," said Joe. "But he lived there a little while. The Ole Man got along fine till his corn give out, because there was plenty of game. But he jest couldn't do without his corn-pone and his corn whiskey. So he cleared a little patch and put it in corn."

"And worked it without his steers?" asked Lanky.

"Why not?" said Joe. "He made him a light Georgie-stock out of wood, and the Ole Woman and one of the bigger kids could pull it fine. He made some harness out of the hide of Old Spot, and he'd hitch 'em and plough all day.

"They used to all go out in the field and leave Pecos Bill in the cabin by his self. One day when Bill was about three years old, the Ole Man was ploughin', and jest as he turned the Ole Woman and the kid he had hitched up with her around to start a new row, the Ole Woman begun yellin' and tryin' to get out of the harness.

"'What's eatin' on you, Ole Woman?' says the Ole Man. 'I never seen you do like this before. Must have a tick in your ear.'

"The Ole Woman yelled that she see a panther go in the cabin where Bill was.

"The Ole Man told her not to git exicted. 'It's a half hour by sun till dinner time yet,' he says, 'and that dang panther needn't expect no help from me nohow. The fool critter ought to of had more sense than to go in there. He'll jest have to make out the best way he can.'

"So they ploughed on till dinner time, and when they come back to the cabin, there was Pecos Bill a-chewin' on a piece of raw panther flank.

"They lived there another year or two before the Ole Man taken a notion to leave."

"I reckon you know how he come to git the idear in his head, don't you, Joe?" said Red.

"I'll bite," said Joe. "Go ahead."

"Why, this ain't no sell," said Red. "I've heard Windy Williams tell it a hundred times.

"One time the Ole Man had the Ole Woman and one of the big kids hitched up to the plough in his customary and habitual manner, jist as Joe has been tellin' about, and all at once here comes piece of paper blowin' across the field. The Ole Woman shied a little bit off to one side; then the kid got to prancin', and then they tore loose and went lickity-split, rearin' and tearin' across that corn patch, draggin' the Ole Man with 'em. The Ole Man stumped his toe on a root, and then they got loose from him and tore up the Georgie-stock. After while they quieted down, and the Ole Man got up and fetched 'em in. Then he went out and picked up the piece of paper where it was hung on a stump. He seen it was an old newspaper. That set him to wonderin'.

"The next mornin' he got his rifle and begun lookin' around. About five miles from his place he found some wagon tracks, and he follered the tracks till he come to a new cabin about fifty miles up the creek. Then he come home and told the Ole Woman and the kids to git ready to leave. He calkilated the country was gittin' too thickly settled for him."

"How did he get away without a team?" asked Lanky.

"Oh, that was easy," said Red. "He sent Pecos Bill out to ketch a couple of mustangs, and in about an hour the lad run 'em down. The Ole Man fixed up the harness he'd been usin' to plough with, and loaded in his stuff and his wife and kids, and pulled out.

"They kept goin' west till finally they come to the Pecos River, which the Ole Man said he'd ford or bust. He got across all right, but as he was drivin' up the bank on the west side, the end-gate come out of the wagon, and Pecos Bill fell out. The Ole Man and the Ole Woman never missed him till they got about thirty miles further on; then they said it wasn't worth while turnin' back. They said they guessed the chap could take kere of his self, and if he couldn't he wasn't worth turnin' back for nohow. So that's how Pecos Bill come to be called Pecos Bill."

"What became of him?" asked Lanky. "What happened to him then?"

"What happened to him then?" said Red. "That would take a long time to tell."

"We'll tell you about that some other time, Lanky," said Joe.

Adventures of Pecos Bill

"How old was Pecos Bill when he was lost on the Pecos River?" Lanky asked Joe on the next night when supper was finished and the four were sitting around the fire smoking.

"I guess he must of been about four year old," said Joe. "Some says he was jest a year old, but that can't be right. The Ole Man made two or three crops down on the Trinity before the country got so thickly settled that he had to leave."

"What became of the family?" asked Lanky.

"That would be hard to answer," said Joe; "hard to answer. I don't suppose there's a soul that knows for certain. There's been tales about 'em bein' et up by wild beasts, but that ain't likely; and there's been tales about 'em bein' killed by the Indians, but that ain't likely neither. Why, them Red-Skins would run like scered jack-rabbits when they seen the Ole Man comin', or the Ole Woman either. Then there's tales about 'em dyin' for water in the desert, which may be so; but more than likely they settled somewhere and lived a happy and peaceful life."

"The chances are," said Red, "that they settled in the Lost Canyon, and their offspring may be livin' there yet for all anybody knows."

"Where is the Lost Canyon?" asked Lanky.

"That's jist what nobody don't know," said Red; "but it's out in the Big Bend Country somewheres, and it opens into the Rio Grande. It gits wide, and there's springs in it, and buffalo a-grazin' on the grass, and it's a fine country."

"How do you know about it?" asked Lanky. "Have you ever been there?"

"Naw," said Red, "but people has. But you never can find it when you're lookin' for it. Them that finds it, finds it accidentally, and then they can't go back. That's jist the place that would of suited Pecos Bill's Ole Man, and the chances are that's where he stopped. Some day I'm goin' to happen on that canyon myself, and if I do, I'll jist stake me out a ranch; that is unless it's inhabited by Pecos Bill's race. If it is, I reckon I'll let 'em have it."

"And what became of Pecos Bill?" asked Lanky.

"Why," said Joe, "he jest growed up with the country. There wasn't nothin' else he could do. He got to runnin' with a bunch of coyotes and took up with 'em. He learned their language and took up all their bad habits. He could set on the ground and howl with the best of 'em, and run down a jack-rabbit jest as quick, too. He used to run ahead of the pack and pull down a forty-eight point buck and bite a hole in his neck before the rest of the coyotes got there. But he always divided with the pack, and that's probably the reason they throwed off on him like they did."

"Did he ever teach anybody else the coyote language?" asked Lanky.

"Jest one old prospector that befriended him once. That was all. You see the old man couldn't find no gold and he went to trappin', and he used the language that Bill had taught him to call up the coyotes and git 'em in his traps. Bill said it was a dirty trick, and he wouldn't teach nobody else how to speak coyote. Bill would of killed the old prospector if it hadn't of been that the old man done him a favor once."

"What did he do?" asked Lanky.

"Why, it was him that found Bill and brought him back to civilization and liquor, which Bill had jest about forgot the taste of."

"How old was Bill at that time?" asked Lanky.

"Oh, I guess he was about ten years old," said Joe. "One day this old prospector comes along and he hears the most terrible racket anybody ever heard of—rocks a-rollin' down the canyon, brush a-poppin', and the awfullest howlin' and squallin' you could imagine; and he looks up the canyon and sees what he first thinks is a cloud comin' up, but purty soon he discovers it's fur a-flyin'.

"Well, he decides to walk up the canyon a piece and investigate, and purty soon he comes on Pecos Bill, who has a big grizzly bear under each arm just mortally squeezin' the stuffin' out of 'em. And while the old prospector stands there a-watchin', Bill tears off a hind leg and begins eatin' on it.

" 'A game scrap, son,' says the old prospector, 'and who be ye?'

" 'Me?' says Bill. 'I'm a varmit.'

" 'Naw, ye ain't a varmit,' says the old prospector; 'you're a human.'

" 'Naw,' says Bill, 'I ain't no human; I'm a varmit.'

" 'How come?' says the prospector.

" 'Don't I go naked?' says Bill.

" 'Shore ye do,' says the old prospector. 'Shore ye're naked. So is the Indians and them critters is part human, anyway. That don't spell nothin'.'

" 'Don't I have fleas?' says Bill.

" 'Shore ye do,' says the old prospector, 'but all Texians has fleas.'

"'Don't I howl?' says Bill.

"'Yeah, ye howl all right,' says the old prospector, 'but nearly all Texians is howlin' most of the time. That don't spell nothin' neither.'

"'Well, jest the same I'm a coyote,' says Bill.

"'Naw, ye ain't a coyote,' says the old prospector. 'A coyote's got a tail, ain't he?'

"'Yeah,' says Bill, 'a coyote's got a tail.'

"'But you ain't got no tail,' says the old prospector. 'Jest feel and see if you have.'

"Bill felt and shore nuff, he didn't have no tail.

"'Well, I'll be danged,' he says. 'I never did notice that before. I guess I ain't a coyote, after all. Show me them humans, and if I like their looks, maybe I'll throw in with 'em.'

"Well, he showed Bill the way to an outfit, and it wasn't long till he was the most famous and noted man in the whole cow country."

"It was him," said Hank, "that invented ropin'. He had a rope that reached from the Rio Grande to the Big Bow, and he shore did swing a mean loop. He used to amuse his self by throwin' a little *Julian*[1] up in the sky and fetchin' down the buzzards and eagles that flew over. He roped everything he ever seen: bears and wolves and panthers, elk and buffalo. The first time he seen a train, he thought it was some kind of varmit, and damn me if he didn't slip a loop over it and dang near wreck the thing.

"One time his ropin' shore did come in handy, for he saved the life of a very dear friend."

"How was that?" asked Lanky.

"Well, Bill had a hoss that he thought the world of, and he had a good reason to, too, for he had raised him from a colt, feedin' him on a special diet of nitroglycerin and barbed wire, which made him very tough and also very ornery when anybody tried to handle him but Bill. The hoss thought the world of Bill, but when anybody else come around, it was all off. He had more ways of pitchin' than Carter had oats. Lots of men tried to ride him, but only one man besides Bill ever mounted that hoss and lived. That's the reason Bill named him Widow-Maker."

"Who was that man?" asked Lanky.

"That was Bill's friend that I was goin' to tell you about Bill savin' his life," said Hank. "You see this feller gits his heart set on ridin' Widow-Maker. Bill tried to talk him out of it, but he wouldn't listen. He said he could ride anything that had hair. It had been his ambition from youth, he said, to find a critter that could make him pull leather. So Bill, seein' the pore feller's heart was about to break, finally told him to go ahead.

[1] A type of loop. Pronounced *hoolián*.

"He gits on Widow-Maker, and that hoss begins to go through his gaits, doin' the end-to-end, the sunfish, and the back-throw; and about that time the rider goes up in the sky. Bill watches him through a spyglass and sees him land on Pike's Peak. No doubt he would of starved to death up there, but Bill roped him by the neck and drug him down, thus savin' his life."

"Yeah," said Red, "Widow-Maker was jist the sort of hoss that suited Bill exactly, For one thing, it saved him a lot of shootin', because he didn't have no trouble keepin' other people off his mount; and as for Bill, he could ride anything that had hair and some things that didn't have. Once, jist for fun, he throwed a surcingle on a streak of lightin' and rode it over Pike's Peak.

"Another time he bet a Stetson hat he could ride a cyclone. He went up on the Kansas line and simply eared that tornado down and got on it. Down he come across Oklahoma and the Panhandle a-settin' on that tornado, a-curlin' his mustache and a-spurrin' it in the withers. Seein' it couldn't throw him, it jist naturally rained out from under him, and that's the way Bill got the only spill he ever had.

"Yeah," continued Red, "I reckon Bill was mighty hard to throw. A smart lad he was, and a playful sort of feller, too. In his spare time he used to amuse his self puttin' thorns on things—bushes and cactuses and the like, and he even stuck horns on the toads so they'd match up with the rest of the country."

"I see he's been at work in this country," said Lanky. "Did he live all his life in Texas?"

"Naw, he didn't," said Joe. "Bill was a good deal like his old man. When he had killed all the Indians and bad men, and the country got all peaceful and quiet, he jest couldn't stand it any longer, and he saddled up his hoss and started west. Out on the New Mexico line he met an old trapper, and they got to talkin', and Bill told him why he was leavin', and said if the old man knowed where there was a tough outfit, he'd be much obliged if he would tell him how to git to it.

"'Ride up the draw about two hundred miles,' says the old traper, 'and you'll find a bunch of buys so tough that they bite nails in two jest for the fun of it.'

"So Bill rides on in a hurry, gittin' somewhat reckless on account of wantin' to git to that outfit and git a look at the bad *hombres* that the old man has told him about. The first thing Bill knowed, his hoss stumps his toe on a mountain and breaks his fool neck rollin' down the side, and so Bill finds his self afoot.

"He takes off his saddle and goes walkin' on, packin' it, till all at once he comes to a big rattlesnake. He was twelve feet long and had fangs like the tushes of a *javelina*; and he rears up and sings at Bill and sticks out his tongue like he was lookin' for a scrap. There wasn't nothin' that Bill wouldn't fight, and he always fought fair; and jest to be shore that rattlesnake had a fair show and couldn't claim he took advantage of him, Bill let him have three bites before he begun. Then he jest naturally lit into that reptile and mortally flailed the stuffin' out of him. Bill was always quick to forgive, though, and let by-gones be by-gones, and when the snake give up, Bill took him up and curled him around his neck, and picked up his saddle and outfit and went on his way.

"As he was goin' along through a canyon, all at once a big mountain lion jumped off of a cliff and spraddled out all over Bill. Bill never got excited. He jest took his time and laid down his saddle and his snake, and then he turned loose on that cougar. Well, sir, the hair flew so it rose up like a cloud and the jack-rabbits and road-runners thought it was sundown. It wasn't long till that cougar had jest all he could stand, and be begun to lick Bill's hand and cry like a kitten.

"Well, Bill jest ears him down and slips his bridle on his head, throws on the saddle and cinches her tight, and mounts the beast. Well, that cat jest tears out across the mountains and canyons with Bill on his back a-spurrin' him in the shoulders and quirtin' him down the flank with the rattlesnake.

"And that's the way Bill rode into the camp of the outfit the old trapper had told him about. When he gits there, he reaches out and cheeks down the cougar and sets him on his haunches and gits down and looks at his saddle.

"There was them tough *hombres* a-settin' around the fire playin' *monte*. There was a pot of coffee and a bucket of beans a-boilin' on the fire, and as Bill hadn't had nothing to eat for several days, he was hungry; so he stuck his hand down in the bucket and grabbed a handful of beans and crammed 'em into his mouth. Then he gabbed the coffee pot and washed 'em down, and wiped his mouth on a prickly-pear. Then he turned to the men and said, 'Who in the hell is boss around here, anyway?'

"'I was,' says a big stout feller about seven feet tall, 'but you are now, stranger.'

"And that was the beginning of Bill's outfit."

"But it was only the beginnin's," said Red; "for it wasn't long after that that he staked out New Mexico and fenced Arizona for a calf-pasture. He built a big ranch-house and had a big yard around it. It was so far from the yard gate to the front door, that he used to keep a string of saddle hosses at stations along the way, for the convenience of visitors. Bill always was a hospitable sort of chap, and when company come, he always tried to persuade them to stay as long as he could git 'em to. Deputy sheriffs and brand inspectors he never would let leave a-tall.

"One time his outfit was so big that he would have his cooks jist dam up a draw to mix the biscuit dough in. They would dump in the flour and the salt and the bakin'-powder and mix it up with teams and fresnoes. You can still see places where the dough was left in the bottom of the draw when they moved on. Alkali lakes they call 'em. That's the bakin'-powder that stayed in the ground.

"One time when there was a big drought and water got scerce on Bill's range, he lit in and dug the Rio Grande and ditched water from the Gulf of Mexico. Old man Windy Williams was water boy on the job, and he said Bill shore drove his men hard for a few days till they got through, and it kept him busy carryin' water."

"I guess it took about all of Bill's time to manage a ranch like that," said Lanky.

"Not all, not all," said Joe. "That was his main vocation and callin', but he found time for a good many other things. He was always goin' in for somethin' else when the cattle business got slack.

"When the S. P. come through, he got a contract furnishin' 'em wood. Bill went down into Mexico and rounded up a bunch of greasers and put 'em to cuttin' wood. He made a contract with 'em that they was to git half the wood they cut. When the time was up, they all had big stacks of cordwood, Mex'can cords, you understand, that they don't know what to do with. So Bill talked it over with 'em and finally agreed to take it off their hands without chargin' 'em a cent. Bill always was liberal.

"He done some of the gradin' on the S. P. too. This time he went out and rounded up ten thousand badgers and put 'em to diggin'. He said they was better laborers than Chinks, because he could learn 'em how to work sooner. Bill had some trouble, however, gittin' 'em to go in a straight line, and that's why the S. P. is so crooked in places.

"He also got a contract fencin' the right-of-way. The first thing that he done was to go out on the line of Texas and New Mexico and buy up all the dry holes old Bob Sanford had made out there tryin' to git water. He pulled 'em up and sawed 'em up into two-foot lengths for post-holes."

"I've heard the Paul Bunyan did that with dry oil-wells," said Lanky.

"Paul Bunyan might of for all I know," said Joe. "But if he did, he learned the trick from Pecos Bill, for this was before oil had been invented.

"However, it cost so much to freight the holes down that Bill give up the plan long before he had used up all of Bob Sanford's wells, and found a cheaper and better way of makin' post-holes."

"What was his new method?" asked Lanky.

"Why, he jest went out and rounded up a big bunch of prairie-dogs, and turned 'em loose where he wanted the fence, and of course every critter of 'em begun diggin' a hole, for it's jest a prairie-dog's nature to dig holes. As soon as a prairie-dog would git down about two feet, Bill would yank him out and stick a post in the hole. Then the fool prairie-dog would go start another one, and Bill would git it. Bill said he found the prairie-dog labor very satisfactory. The only trouble was that sometimes durin' off hours, the badgers that he had gradin' would make a raid on the prairie-dogs, and Bill would have to git up and drive 'em back to their own camp."

"Did Bill have any other occupations?" asked Lanky.

"Well," said Joe, "he used to fight Indians jest for recreation, but he never did make a business of it like some did, huntin' 'em for a dollar a scalp. In fact Bill was not bloodthirsty and cruel, and he never scalped an Indian in his life. He'd just skin 'em and tan their hides."

"That reminds me," said Hank, "of another business he used to carry on as a sort of side-line, and that was huntin' buffalo. You see, it was the hides that was valuable, and Bill thought it was too much of a waste to kill a buffalo jest for the hide; so he'd jest hold the critters and skin 'em alive and then turn 'em aloose to grow a new hide. A profitable business he built up, too, but he jest made one mistake."

"What was that?" asked Lanky.

"One spring he skinned too early, and a norther come up, and all the buffalo took cold and died. Mighty few of 'em left after that."

"Did Bill ever get married?" asked Lanky.

"Oh, yes," said Joe. "He married lots of women in his day, but he never had the real tender affection for any of the rest of 'em that he had for his first wife, Slue-Foot Sue.

"Bill savvied courtin' the ladies all right; yet he never took much stock in petticoats till he met Slue-Foot Sue; but when he saw that gal come ridin' down the Rio Grande on a catfish, it jest got next to him, and he married her right off.

"I say right off—but she made him wait a few days till she could send to San Antonio for a suitable and proper outfit, the principal garment bein' a big steel wire bustle, like all the women wore when they dressed up in them days.

"Well, everything would have gone off fine, but on the very day of the weddin' Sue took a fool notion into her head that she jest had to ride Widow-Maker. For a long time Bill wouldn't hear to it, but finally she begun to cry, and said Bill didn't love her any more. Bill jest couldn't stand to see her cry; so he told her to go ahead but to be keerful.

"Well, she got on that hoss, and he give about two jumps, and she left the saddle. He throwed her so high that she had to duck as she went up to keep from bumpin' her head on the moon. Then she come down, landin' right on that steel bustle, and that made her bounce up jest as high, nearly, as she had went before. Well, she jest kept on bouncin' like that for ten days and nights, and finally Bill had to shoot her to keep her from starvin' to death. It nearly broke his heart. That was the only time Bill had ever been known to shed tears, and he was so tore up that he wouldn't have nothin' to do with a woman for two weeks."

The Exodus of Pecos Bill

Lanky had been sent for, and this was his last night in camp. His face was tanned; he had gained in weight; he had earned money in his own right. He felt that he was now a man.

He and his cronies sat around the fire in silence. Joe and the boys would miss the kid, and he hated to leave. This silence wouldn't do.

"What became of Pecos Bill?" asked Lanky.

"That would be hard to say," said Joe, "hard to say. Everybody knows he's gone, jest like the open range and the longhorn steer; but jest how and where he passed in his checks, I don't suppose anybody will ever find out for certain. A lot of the fellers that knowed him are dead, and a lot of 'em has bad memories—a lot of the old-timers has bad memories—and some of 'em are sech damn liars that you can't go by what they say."

"You've seen Pecos Bill, haven't you, Joe?" said Lanky.

"Well, yes, that is I seen him when I was a young buck. But I never seen him die, and I never could find out jest how he was took off. I've seen some mighty hot arguments on the subject, and I've knowed one or two fellers to die with their boots on after gittin' in a quarrel in jest that way."

"I heard one account a few years ago," said Red, "that may be right. There was a feller in Amarillo named Gabriel Asbury Jackson. He'd worked his self out of a job in Kansas and had come to Texas to buck the cigarette evil. One time he cornered a bunch of us that was too drunk to make a git-away and begun talkin' to us about smokin'.

"'Young men,' he says, 'beware of cigarettes. You think you're smart to smoke a sack of Bull Durham every day, do you? Well, look at Pecos Bill. A stalwart young man he was, tough as nails, a fine specimen. But he got to foolin' with cigarettes. What did they do for him?' he says. 'Why, nothin' at first. But did he quit? No!' he says. 'He puffed away for ninety years, but they finally got him. And they'll git you, every mother's son of you, if you don't leave 'em alone.'"

"That ain't so," said Joe. "That man was jest a liar. Cigarettes never killed Pecos Bill. He was, however, a great smoker, but he never smoked Bull Durham. He made him up a mixture of his own, the principal ingredients bein' Kentucky home-spun, sulphur, and gun-powder. Why, he would have thought he was a sissy if he'd smoked Bull Durham.

"When the matches was scerce Bill used to ride out into a thunderstorm and light his cigarette with a streak of lightnin', and that's no doubt what's back of a tale you hear every once in a while about him bein' struck and kilt. But nobody that knows how Bill throwed a surcingle over a streak of lightnin' and rode it over Pike's Peak will ever believe that story."

"I heard it was liquor that killed pore Bill," said Hank.

"Must of been boot-leg," said Red.

"Naw," said Hank. "You see, Bill bein' brought up as he was from tender youth on whiskey and onions, was still a young man when whiskey lost its kick for him. He got to puttin' nitroglycerin in his drinks. That worked all right for a while, but soon he had to go to wolf-bait; and when that got so it didn't work, he went to fish-hooks. Bill used to say, rather sorrowful-like, that that was the only way he could git an idear from his booze. But after about fifty years the fish-hooks rusted out his interior parts and brought pore Bill to an early grave."

"I don't know who told you that windy," said Joe. "It might have been your own daddy. But it ain't so. It's jest another damn lie concocted by them damn prohibition men."

"I heard another tale," said Red, "which may be right for all I know. I heard that Bill went to Fort Worth one time, and there he seen a Boston man who had jist come to Texas with a mail-order cowboy outfit on; and when Bill seen him, he jist naturally laid down and laughed his self to death."

"That may be so," said Joe, "but I doubt it. I heard one tale about the death of Pecos Bill that I believe is the real correct and true account."

"And what was that?" asked Lanky.

"Well, Bill happened to drift into Cheyenne jest as the first rodeo was bein' put on. Bein' a bit curious to know what it was all about, he went out to the grounds to look the thing over. When he seen the ropers and the riders, he begun to weep; the first tears he's shed since the death of Slue-Foot Sue. Well, finally when a country lawyer jest three years out of Mississippi got up to make a speech and referred to the men on horseback as cowboys, Bill turned white and begun to tremble. And then when the country lawyer went on to talk about 'keepin' inviolate the sacred traditions of the Old West,' Bill jest went out and crawled in a prairie-dog hole and died of solemncholy."

Lanky looked at Red and Hank. They had not missed the point, but they chose to ignore it.

Joe talked on. "After several years," he said, "when all Bill's would-be rivals was sure he was dead, they all begun to try to ruin his reputation and defame his character. They said he was a hot-headed, overbearin' sort of feller. They was too scered to use the word, even after Bill died, but what they meant was that he was a *killer*.

"Now, Pecos Bill did kill lots of men. He never kept no tally his self, and I don't suppose nobody will ever know jest how many he took off. Of course I'm not referrin' to Mex'cans and Indians. Bill didn't count them. But Bill wasn't a bad man, and he hardly ever killed a man without just cause.

"For instance, there was big Ike that he shot for snorin', that Bill's enemies talked up so much. But them that was doin' the talkin would forgit to mention that Bill had been standin' guard over Mexico steers every night for six weeks and was gittin' a bit sleepy.

"Then there was Ris Risbone. Ris was one of these practical jokers, and he ramrodded an outfit that fell in behind Bill's on the trail. Ris had a dozen or so jokes, and when he pulled one, he slapped his knees and laughed and laughed whether anybody else was a-laughin' or not. One day Ris rode up to Bill's chuck-wagon when there wasn't nobody there but the cook, and he was asleep in the shade of the wagon with his head between the wheels. Ris slipped up and gabbed the trace chains and begun rattlin' 'em and yellin' 'Whoa! Whoa!' The pore spick woke up thinkin' that the team was runnin' away, and that he was about to git his pass to Saint Peter. He jumped up and bumped his head on the wagon; then he wakes up and looks around, and there stands Ris slappin' his knees and laughin'. Jest then Bill rides up, but he never said nothin'.

"When the outfits got to Abilene, Bill was in the White Elephant with some of his men, fixin' to take a drink. Jest as Bill was about to drop his fish-hooks in his glass, Ris poked his head in at the winder and yelled, 'Fire! Fire!'—and Bill did.

"In one killin', however, Bill acted a bit hasty, as he admitted his self. One day he called Three-Fingered Ed out of the saloon, sayin' he'd like to speak with him in private. Bill led Ed out into a back alley, and there they stopped.

" 'Say, Ed,' he says, lookin' him right in the eye, 'didn't you say that Mike said I was a hot-headed, over-bearing' sort of feller?'

" 'Naw,' says Ed, 'You mistook me. He never said that.'

" 'Well, doggone,' says Bill, 'ain't that too bad. I've gone and killed an innocent man.'

"Well, Lanky, maybe your pa'll let you come back next fall."

The End

Establishing a Ranch
on the Plains

BY JAMES FRANK DOBIE

James Frank Dobie was an ethnoligist, a novelist, an anthropologist, an his-torian, a storyteller and a critic. His work is wide-ranging in terms of its scope but may generally be said to deal with the life, history and folklore of the American Southwest.

In 1925 James Frank Dobie teamed up with an old rancher/ cattle-man by the name of John Young. Young had stories to tell and Dobie had some idea as how they might be written down. The happy result of this col-laboration was a first-person biography of Young by Dobie entitled *A Vaquero of Brush Country* (1929), from which this story is excerpted. It's the sort of narrative I like most, full of detail and all the how–to stuff of cowboy life on the Texas Panhandle in the golden age of the "Kingdom of Cattle."

★   ★   ★   ★   ★

Jim Hall, a relative of mine, and some of the Duncans owned a con-trolling interest in the Cimarron Cattle Company. Their range was on the Dry Cimarron, in the southeastern corner of Colorado and over into New Mexico and Oklahoma. In the spring of 1878 they claimed a herd of 15,000 cattle on this range and they were anxious to estab-lish a ranch in the Panhandle of Texas. I was offered an opportunity to join in on this new ranch proposition; so I put what small funds I could rake up into the enterprise and took the job of driving a herd of cows to the Plains and locating the ranch.

It must have been along in May when we set out from Refugio. Our herd was made up of 1300 young cows and about 50 bulls, all branded with a newly devised brand, the Spur, made thus: —⊏. That was the year it rained; it rained behind us, it rained ahead of us, and it rained on us.

Every stream we crossed was swimming. The San Antonio River at Strib-bling Crossing in Goliad County was bank full; so was the Coleto. We camped on it, just south of Yorktown; and here while some of the boys were practicing with their six-shooters, Buck Spradlin let his gun go off before it was out of the holster. The bullet entered the fleshy part of his thigh and did not hurt him nearly so badly as it scared him. We swam the Guadalupe River at Gonzales and then followed on up Plum Creek to Lockhart. When we got near the log cabin in which I was born I turned aside to look at it.

Beyond Round Rock, soon to be made famous by the death of Sam Bass, we struck the Western Trail. A few nights later a sudden rain called us all to the herd. At the time I went to bed the sky was so clear and the weather was so promising that I had removed my trousers, thinking to get a few hours of peaceful sleep. I awoke and began dressing in such a hurry that I got my trousers on wrong side in front. Before I could get them changed and my slicker on I was drenching wet. A half dozen times that night I rode into gullies of swimming water. The cattle scattered so that it was noon before we got them together; a count, however, showed that we had not lost a single cow. The worst feature of the rain and the run, to me, was that I had a high fever. I had remained chilled for hours. Some of the boys located a country doctor: he gave me calomel and stayed around camp for three days while I recovered.

The one man in our outfit that I recall most often and most vividly was Sam, the negro cook. He always had a cheerful word or a cheerful song, and he seemed to have an affection for every one of us. When we camped in the vicinity of brush every cowboy before coming in would rope a chunk of wood and snake it up to the chuck wagon. That wood always made Sam grinning happy whether he needed it or not. He was about thirty-five years old, as black as a crow, and weighed around 225 pounds. As he had been raised on a ranch, he was a good rider, and fre-quently one of the boys would get him to "top off" (ride first) a bad horse. One day a cowboy remarked that Sam was too big and strong for a man but not big enough for a horse. At that Sam said *he was a horse* and that he would give a dollar to any man in the outfit who could ride him without spurs. That evening we camped in a sandy place and Sam announced that he was ready to play horse if any man thought he could ride. It was agreed that I should win the first dollar. Sam stripped stark naked, wearing only a bandana around his neck for the rider to hold on to. I really did not have much confidence in my ability to stay on him, for as a boy I had often been thrown by buck negroes who took me on their backs. Nevertheless I pulled off my boots and mounted. Sam started out by jumping straight ahead until he judged I had accommodated myself to that "rhythm"; then he suddenly stopped short and whirled back. I kept straight on, landing on my head. After that every fellow in the crowd had to show off his ability at riding a bucking negro and every one of them tumbled.

When we started out from South Texas Sam had a banjo, but one night someone accidentally stepped on it and demolished it. However, we had chipped in and bought a fiddle at Yorktown, and whenever he got a chance Sam would pick "Green corn, green corn, bring along the demijohn," on this fiddle. Among other selections he had a kind of chant called "Dog" that the boys often called on him to give. The words, evidently not of negro origin, ran thus:

> There was a man who had a dog, a bob-tailed ornery cuss,
> And this here dog got this here man in many an ugly muss.
> The man was on his muscle, and the dog was on his bite;
> To touch that bobtail son-of-a-gun you were sure to start a fight.
> There was a woman who had a cat that fit a fifteen pounds;
> The other cats got up and slid when this here cat came 'round.
> The man and dog came along one day by where this women did dwell;
> The cat he growled fe-ro-cious-ly and made for the dog like—rip.
> The man he cussed and ripped and swore and picked up a big brickbat;
> He swore he'd be damned eternally if he didn't kill that cat.
> The woman she said she'd be darned if he did and picked up a big shotgun;
> She whaled away and shot him in the back with birdshot number one.
> They carried him home on a cellar door and the doctors healed him up;
> He's never since been known to tackle a cat or own a terrier pup.
> Some folks may turn up their nose at this, but I don't give a darn for that,
> For it goes to show that a man may tackle the wrong old Thomas cat.

The most memorial fact of our whole trip of six hundred miles from Refugio county on the coast to the head of Pease River far up on the Plains was Fort Griffin, located in Shackelford County on the west bank of the Clear Fork of the Brazos. It was understood that the Cimarron Cattle Company would have money there for me to pay off hands and buy a three months' stock of provisions for the ranch I was going to establish beyond; but when we arrived, there was no money in the mail. As Fort Griffin was on the edge of the settlements and as there was neither mail nor provisions to be had west of it, nothing remained to do but wait until I could hear from headquarters. In the course of a few days I received the money. Meantime we held our cattle across the river some distance below the town, half of the boys taking turn with the herd while the other half took in the sights.

And in 1878 there were sights in Fort Griffin. Established eleven years before as an outpost against Indians, it became soon after the battle of

Adobe Walls, June 27, 1874, headquarters for thousands of butchers engaged in annihilating the "southern herd" of American bison and also for cowmen and cowboys engaged in establishing ranches on the vast ranges that the slaughter of the buffalo and the attendant subjugation of the Indians were leaving vacant. I had seen Hall's Half Acre in Fort Worth, but here was Hell's Half Hundred Acres. It was beyond all odds the worst hole that I have ever been in. The population at this time was perhaps five thousand people, most of them soldiers, gamblers, cow thieves, horse thieves, murders, wild women, buffalo hunters, altogether the most mongrel and the hardest-looking crew that it was possible to assemble. The fort proper and a big store were up on a hill. The sights were down under the hill in "the Flats," where every house was either a saloon, a gambling den, or a dance hall, generally all three combined. No man who valued his life would go here unarmed or step out alone into the darkness. If about daylight he walked down to the river he might see a man hanging from one of the cottonwood trees with a placard on his back saying, "Horse Thief No. 8"—or whatever the latest number was.[1]

All drinks were two-bits apiece and cigars were the same price. One saloon, the Adobe, popularly called the Bee Hive, had on its front a painted sign representing two hives overhung by branches of flowering honeysuckle and innumerable bees entering and emerging from the hives. Beneath was this verse:

Within this hive we're all alive,
Good whiskey makes us funny;
So if you're dry come up and try
The flavor of our honey.

Everybody seemed to be dry. It was no uncommon sight to see lousy Tonkawa Indians bucks, brutish thugs who called themselves buffalo hunters, and hideously featured wrecks of women all together in the most beastly state of intoxication. The gambling dens ran day and night but were in full blast from midnight on. Keno, poker, monte, chuck-luck, rouge et noir, roulette, faro, casino—every kind of game that the professional gambler might ask for or the tenderfoot be fleeced by was there.

Excepting a comparatively few transient cowboys, some of whom occasionally considered it their duty to shoot out the lights, about the only native or even thoroughly adopted Texans in this town of the Texas frontier were the Tonkawa Indians. Despite the fact that their warriors had given aid to rangers and troops in fighting hostile Indians and despite the fact

---

[1]See West Texas Historical Association *Year Book*, Abilene, Texas, Vol. II, pg. 6.

that the warriors were excellent scouts, the Tonkawas on the whole were the most beggarly, the most degraded, and the most contemptible human beings imaginable. They soon found our camp and hung around it like so many buzzards. Sam threatened to quit cooking unless I detailed a man to help keep them away. They would steal anything, from a dirty dishrag to a sack of flour, that they could lay their hands on.

But the thug element of Fort Griffin was the buffalo hunters—not, generally speaking, the men who had engaged in that business for years and were units in regular skinning crews, but tramp hunters who had drifted out to prey alike on man and beast. They were from Wyoming, from Colorado, from Arkansas and Missouri, from tough Kansas, from everywhere. Some of them had hidden on the Rio Grande until the rangers broke up their gangs there. Many of them were afoot looking to get away and ready to kill a man for a horse or five dollars. There were still some buffaloes scattered over the Plains, but the great slaughter, which reached its climax in 1876 and '77, was over. Estimates of the number of hides brought into Fort Griffin in 1877 vary from 100,000 to 200,000. Before I arrived the price had gone down to sixty cents apiece; wagon trains were carrying them to Fort Worth, but acres of ground were still covered with them.

According to Edgar Rye, a newspaper editor of Fort Griffin and Albany, whose book *The Quirt and Spur* is pretty much a history of Fort Griffin, the traffic in hides at that place between 1875 and 1879 was far greater than the business with ranchers and trail outfits. In the warehouse of one store alone were thirty tons of lead and five tons of powder to supply buffalo hunters.

I talked with cowboys and buffalo hunters who made no bones about charging various bosses with having murdered members of their skinning crews in order to get out of paying them. At that time I had never heard or seen the range ballad called "The Buffalo Hunters," which John A. Lomax in his *Cowboy Songs* has since popularized; but I have no doubt that the song is based on fact. It tells how "a man by the name of Crego" hired the composer of the song to go out on Pease River to "the range of the buffalo." After describing the miseries of the life the skinners led, it concludes thus:

> *The season being over, old Crego he did say*
> *The crowd had been extravagant, was in debt to him that day;*
> *We coaxed him and we begged him and still it was no go—*
> *We left old Crego's bones to bleach on the range of the buffalo.*

The breakup of an industry always leaves men desperate. Many of the buffalo hunters were making for the Indian Territory, the happy hunting grounds for desperadoes; others were making for the Black Hills. Numbers of them were turning into cow thieves. In fact, the majority of the cow thieves that were for some years to depredate upon the ranches of the Plains were recruited from the so-called buffalo hunters. This statement is, I know, at variance with the testimony of some of the old timers; yet it is supported by evidence other than my own. Frank Canton of Oklahoma, for many years inspector for the Texas and Southwestern Cattle Raisers' Association, now dead, has left this testimony: "After the buffalo hunters had killed off all the buffaloes, they went over to the Comanche Agency at Fort Sill and traded their rifles and ammunition to the Indians for ponies. Then they came back to Texas, lay around the government posts for a while, and soon commenced to steal cattle."[2]

I cannot express myself too strongly against the class of men who called themselves buffalo hunters, though again it must be understood that many of the regular skinners were fair men. This opinion has been shared by other observers. Not always were the men who called themselves buffalo hunters truly such, say Root and Connelley.[3] "Scattered here and there over the plains and mountains were bands of desperadoes . . . ostensibly hunting buffalo and other animals for their hides; but really it was plain that their object was to steal stock, rob the express coaches and passengers, and at times murder was resorted to in carrying out their hellish designs." When Mrs. Adair, wife of the John Adair who was to become known all over the West through his partnership with Charles Goodnight, crossed the Plains in 1874, she recorded this impression of the buffalo hunters: "Many of these men are the roughs of the frontier, criminals flying from justice, notorious ruffians and murderers, and the settlers are more afraid of them than of the Indians."[4]

Just before we got ready to leave Fort Griffin three men who were heavily armed and who announced themselves as cattle inspectors came out to the herd and demanded my bill of sale. I showed it to them. Then they inspected the cattle and advised me that I was entitled to a certificate showing that I had a clean herd. They said that their charges for inspection were twenty-five cents per animal and that the certificate for my herd of 1300 cows would therefore cost me $325. I asked the spokesman of the inspectors if that was the penalty for driving a clean herd past Fort Griffin. I also asked for his authority to collect the money. He replied that he did not have to show me papers of authority and that, if I did not pay, the soldiers of the post would take charge of the herd until I produced the money. I told him to bring on the soldiers. At this the men hummed and

[2] *The Cattleman*, Fort Worth, Texas, May, 1923, pg. 23.
[3] *The Overland Stage to California*, Topeka, Kansas, 1901, pp. 99–100.
[4] Adair, Cornelia, *My Diary*, Bath, England, 1918, pp. 96–97.

hawed and consulted; then one of them confided that they would compromise on the payment of one hundred dollars. I knew that they were dead beats. I did not pay a cent and had no trouble getting the herd away.

On the trail again, we were as happy as a bunch of free niggers until we reached the Salt Fork of the Brazos. At the place where we struck it the water was about three hundred yards wide, muddy and ugly. When I rode over to pick out a crossing I found the water hardly deep enough to swim a horse, but waves were rolling on the surface, and hidden bars of quicksand threatened every step. I decided to put the cattle across in small bunches. Out of every bunch we took over, several bogged so that they had to be roped and dragged out. One cowboy's horse bogged and drowned. When the last cow was across we threw the herd into a grassy bend of the river and left them alone while all hands turned to cross the saddle horses and the chuck wagon.

The wagon held what was to be our food supply for three months and we could not afford to take chances on having it turn over. After the remuda was headed right, two cowboys took charge of it while the rest of us tied our ropes on the wagon, so as to help guide and pull it if necessary, and started across. All went well until we reached the opposite bank. Then one of the lead work horses bogged and fell. Before we could get him up, the wagon had settled fast into the mud and quicksand. We all had to get down into the water and scratch the wheels loose. At last, however, we pulled out on dry land, as wet, stiff, and tired as it was possible to be.

"Where are the cattle?" somebody asked.

We had been so busy that we had not thought of them, considering them safe. At the question we all instinctively turned our eyes up and down the north bank. Then somebody uttered some words that would not look well in print. The cattle had all recrossed to the south side and, well scattered out, were quietly grazing. Why they had recrossed the river I do not know. Certainly they had gone "agin nature." Facts are stubborn things.

I never believed in keeping a river between herd and camp. It was too late to try to bring the cattle over again. We simply turned around and took the reumuda and the wagon over to the cattle. By the time we pulled out on the south bank it was dark and rain was falling. We rounded up the herd, but they would not bed down. They walked and milled all night long, never attempting to run but never still. It took all hands to hold them.

Of course the river rose from the rain; but the weather "faired off" next morning, and we were not a bit sorry to mark time for a couple of days while the water went down. We got across without much trouble and went on towards the Wichita. It was bank full, and, knowing that it would soon run down, for we were near the head of it, I decided to lie over a day. While we were there something occurred that fixes the date exactly, July 29, 1878.

Along in the afternoon while the cattle grazed over the prairie and we boys were all sitting in the shade on the bank, some of us half asleep and nobody paying any attention to the sky, we were suddenly startled by a wild yell from Sam. When we looked towards him we saw him coming in a dead run. That Indians were after him no one doubted. In ten seconds every man was on his horse, gun out, running to meet the frightened cook.

"Lawdy, Lawdy, the world's coming to an end. Looky at the sun." This was his greeting.

We looked at the sun. It was passing into eclipse and soon the darkness was such that stars became visible. No newspaper had prepared us for the phenomenon, and Sam was not the only person on the outskirts of civilization to be frightened. We cowboys had sense enough to know what an eclipse was, but I afterwards heard of many frontier folk who had been scared.

We trailed on across Paradise Valley, which was dotted with antelopes. We were bound for somewhere on the upper reaches of Pease River. We struck a rough broken country over which no wagon had ever before rolled; but by digging down banks and pulling with ropes attached to our saddle horns we got the wagon up the steep places. Finally we crossed the last divide between the Gulf of Mexico and Pease River.

The whole world lay before us to choose our range from. All a man had to do at that time to establish his claim in the Panhandle was to strike camp in unappropriated territory and say that he wanted all the territory between certain bounds. His rights were respected. After scouting around several days and getting an idea of the country, I piloted the chuck wagon to a cottonwood motte beside a spring that drained into Pease River. Our journey was at an end. The Spur Ranch was established. Nothing remained to do but locate the cattle and "dig in" for winter.

Less then two years before there had not been a ranch in the Panhandle of Texas. Then in the winter of '76 Charles Goodnight had driven 10,000 head of buffaloes out of the broad and grassy Palo Duro Canyon, trailed in a herd of 1600 cattle, located them along the water, and with line riders to keep back the buffaloes and with the canyon bluffs to keep the cattle in, had founded what was to become one of the most historic ranches of America, the J A Ranch. When I reached the Plains in 1878 Goodnight had already entered into partnership with the moneyed Adair and was buying cattle and staking off land in wholesale quantities. The firm eventually controlled more than a million acres of ground, and J A cattle still graze over more than 300,000 acres of land, though Colonel Goodnight has not for forty years had an interest in the ranch.

About the same time that I located the Spur Ranch, Lee Dyer located on Tule Canyon, which empties into the Palo Duro. A little later he moved east and with Coleman established the Shoe Bar, ⊃ — Ranch, where in '79 I was to have some dealing with him. Our nearest neighbors were Baker and Wiren twenty miles away on the Quitaque. They had about 2000 head of cattle and gave the Lazy F brand, ⊔. With twenty miles between their herd of 2000 cattle and our bunch of 1300 cows it can be seen that the country was not as yet overstocked. Looking on a present day map, I judge that the Spur Ranch was only a few miles north of what is now Roaring Springs in Motley County.

When we turned the cattle loose, scattering them up and down the waterings in small bunches, and had no night-herding to do, we almost felt lost for a few days. The lost feeling, however, did not apply to our appetites, and I think we had about the most luscious eating that I have ever enjoyed. After riding out on the range all day, having eaten nothing since a breakfast of coffee, I got into camp more than once to find Sam grinning and gloating over an oven of buffalo steaks, another oven of roast bear meat, better than pork, a frying pan full of the breast of wild turkey in gravy of flour, water, and grease, and then antelope ribs barbecued on a stick over the coals.

"Boys," Sam would say, "wash her faces and comb yer hairs and spruce up lak ye was goin' to a weddin'. I'se got a reg'lar weddin' feast prepared. It's a weddin' o' dinner and supper. Come 'long, come 'long while she's hot and juicy."

Sometimes Sam would roast a turkey in its feathers. To do this he would dig a pit, build a fire in it, and heat the ground thoroughly; then he would take out the coals. Having removed the entrails from the turkey and salted and peppered it, he would put it in the hole—a "fireless cooker"—in such a way that no dirt could touch the flesh. Next he would cover it with hot earth, then build a fire over the covering. When ten or twenty hours later he lifted the turkey out by its feet, the skin and feathers would scale off by their own weight, and we had a juicy, savory meat so tender that it almost melted at a touch. Turkeys often came right into camp.

The breaks about the foot of the Plains abounded in black bear. One day while I was out riding alone I noticed two old bears and two cubs playing in some tall grass near brush. When they saw me, they disappeared and I supposed they had made for the brush. I had an idea that I might rope one; so, putting spurs to my horse, I ran to the spot where I had seen them vanish. Instead of trying to get away, the bears had lain down in the tall grass and there they were still playing 'possum when my horse plunged among them. As they jumped out, my horse tried to fly straight up. He hit the ground bucking and kept on bucking until the bears were clean out of sight. I never knew which was more scared, the horse or the bears.

All old range men know that the finest plum thickets in the whole cattle country were on Pease and Red rivers. The plums ripen in the fall of the year. Sam often stewed them or made a kind of cobbler out of them. One day while three of the boys were coming in towards camp they struck an unusually fine plum thicket. They got down, ate all they could, and were filling their hats with plums for Sam to cook when all at once they bumped into some Indian squaws that were also picking fruit. The squaws went one way and the boys went the other, and while the boys managed to keep their hats they lost every plum they had gathered.

We were just naturally shy of Indians, squaws or any other kind. No Indians were living in the country, but occasionally bands of them came over from the Indian Territory to hunt or to steal horses. More than one cowboy out alone was picked off and left to rot in the breaks while his horse was ridden back to Fort Sill. The United States officers there consistently refused to allow cowmen to seize their own horses found in possession of the reservation Indians. It was about this time that Lieutenant Colonel Davidson of the United States Army threatened to shoot Captain G. W. Arrington's rangers if they molested some Indian horse thieves. Arrington was not fazed; he was law bringer to the Panhandle, doing there what McNelly and Hall did for the Rio Grande and Nueces country.

One day while riding up a tributary of Pease River that we called Wind River, I saw the tracks of two horses. Mustangs, which were numerous, made tracks like those of any other unshod horses, but we were out two saddle horses that had been seen over in this direction, and I thought that the tracks might have been made by them. They were fresh and were following an old buffalo trail. I could not tell whether they had been made by loose horses or by horses under saddle. I should say here that we were generally rather careful about trailing horsemen, for various riders hiding out and roaming over that country were at the time strictly averse to having anyone approach them, and they had a very effective way of stopping any stranger whom they saw coming too near.

Anyway, I determined to follow the tracks leading out of our range. They were so plain that I struck a gallop. The country was rather rough with spots of brush. As I was coming around one of these clumps of brush, two Indians not fifty feet ahead of me suddenly arose and fired in my direction. I was riding a horse that "could turn on a quarter and give back fifteen cents in change," and right there he turned ends so quickly that I believe he might have given back twenty cents in change. I pulled my gun but I didn't pull on the reins. When I got about a quarter of a mile away up on an open hill I looked back and I could see those two Indians riding in the other direction just about as fast as I had been riding. I never killed an Indian in my life, but I certainly have out-ridden several of them. ·

The Spur cows were not hard to locate, but some of them had a tendency to trail off behind drifting bunches of buffaloes. For several weeks after making camp we kept busy shoving buffaloes out and turning cattle back. According to instructions from headquarters I was to lay claim to a range considerably larger than that necessary to graze the herd of cows, for the Cimarron Cattle Company intended to bring down several thousand cattle from Colorado the next spring. I made a thorough reconnaissance of the country and soon had line riders playing the human fence to the four sides of the Spur claim.

The business of these line riders was to patrol the ranch boundaries, to turn back any cattle that they saw approaching the imaginary line from either side—though there was little likelihood in the present case of cattle's straying into our range, not before a cold norther at least—to follow any outgoing tracks until they found the strays, and to bring them back. Back and forth, back and forth, these line riders must jog their solitary beats, each man to himself. As the constant tendency of cattle in the winter time is to drift south, especially if they have been driven north from their breeding ground, the chief work of the line riders for months to come would be on the southern side of our range. Accordingly, I established a line camp on this side and put two men at it, one to ride east and one to ride west each morning. Each rider after he had reached the end of his beat would back-trail to camp, thus inspecting his line twice daily. The beats were short enough that if necessary the riders could make two round trips daily or linger along any place where the cattle threatened especially to push out.

Meanwhile some of the hands had been detailed to build two dugouts, one at the headquarters camp and one at the line camp. The only tools we had were spades, axes, and a saw; we had neither lumber nor nails. There were in the Old West two general styles of dugouts, each subject to modification and variation, the dugout of the flat plains and the dugout of the broken country. The latter style of dugout reminded one of a cabin that had somehow backed into a hillside; it was a blend of cabin and plains dugout.

Our manner of constructing the dugout at headquarters camp was as follows. We dug an open-topped rectangular hole into the south side of a slope near water. Thus the back wall and a part of each of the two side walls were formed by the ground. The remainder of the two side walls and the front wall were made of logs, chinked with mud. The flat roof butted against the hillside, but a line of mounded earth prevented water from running off the slope on to it. The roof was made first of a layer of logs, next a layer of brush and weeds, and then a layer of dirt well tamped. Such a roof when well settled would turn water—though it might leak tarantulas or even rattlesnakes. At the back end of the room we dug a fireplace and a chimney vent up through the solid wall of dirt. We had no stove pipe to run down through this vent and to stick up on the outside. A blanket did service for the door. If the roof did not leak, the only water that came into a dugout like this was through the chimney hole. A fire made such a room very snug and warm even in the coldest weather. A brush arbor could be built in front of the dugout for use in summer.

About a year after I went to the Panhandle another vaquero and myself were staying in a dugout of this kind that belonged to Lee Dyer over on Little Red River. One morning I got up very early, having to go on a long ride. I made some coffee and then rode off up the hill, leaving my partner still asleep. When I got about a hundred yards away my horse began pitching, and, whirling on me, went plunging down towards the dugout. Before I could stop him he jumped on it, chugging about a barrel of dirt in on the sleeping occupant. In no time the cowboy came out "a-raring and a-snorting," but no worse frightened than I was. I had felt sure that the horse would fall through the roof and kill us all three; however, he lunged upon solid ground before he had damaged himself much or us at all.

The plains dugout was made by digging a pit with a stairway leading to the bottom of it. Then a roof of logs, brush, and dirt was mounded over the open hole. From a distance, such a habitation, except for perhaps a wagon and a horse or two near, looked very much like an enlarged prairie dog hole. Such a dugout required the minimum amount of timber. Fifty years ago it was the typical habitat of squatters in western Kansas. Storm cellars in north Texas, Oklahoma, and Kansas still preserve its architecture.

With the Spur cows located, boundaries of the ranch established, and winter quarters finished, there was not much left to do except routine riding. I discharged all but four hands, appointed one of them, Dick Hudson, as *caporal*, and prepared to go to Trinidad, Colorado, to meet the boss. The letter I had received at Fort Griffin directed me to come to Trinidad as soon as the ranch was established. I was to bring back a herd of cattle from the Dry Cimarron the next spring or summer. The prospects were for an idle winter, and I was well pleased with the idea of spending it in town. I was counting my chickens before they hatched.

Cattle Detective

BY TOM HORN

It's said Tom Horn set down his life's story—from which this sample is excerpted—to hurry the lagging time. That may be so, as the manuscript was written from a Laramie County jail cell in Cheyenne, Wyoming. The year was 1903, and Horn stood convicted of the murder of a fourteen-year-old boy (a thing he denied in court but, allegedly, he'd bragged about around town), had been sentenced to hang, and was awaiting the results of his appeal.

At the time of the killing Horn worked as a stock detective for the Swan Land & Cattle Company. His job was to hunt down rustlers and to act generally as enforcer for the company. More and more this had come to mean ambush and assassination. Horn was known previously to have killed at least four men, and at the time of the trial public opinion ran strongly against him. A great many people had had enough of big monied operations and their hired guns. There was also the age of the victim. The case recieved much attention in the press, almost all of it against Horn. Lurid articles were written purporting to paint a true picture of this cowboy monster. Horn's brisk, truculent autobiography was his response. It's interesting that he doesn't even mention his arrest and trial. What does this mean?

Perhaps he thought the whole business was beneath contempt. He could have defended himself, if only to restate the case he'd made at trial, but he did not. How come? Certainly he was stung by his portrayal in the press, but stung to silence? I believe Horn probably did kill the boy. When Horn set down his story he had no idea that it would ever be published; he was writing for himself—and perhaps a few friends, who would know the truth. Why bother to lie to yourself?

It may or may not be a good idea to hurry along the lagging time—depending on how things turn out in the end. Eventually Horn's appeal was denied, and he was hanged, just a short time after he wrote the words you are about to read. This excerpt is the end of his account.

Immediately following, I've included an article from an 1895 edition of the Philadelphia Times, first unearthed by Dean Krakel, editor of the University of Oklahoma Press edition of *Life of Tom Horn*.

Good or bad, innocent or guilty, he was a cowboy. That's for certain.

★   ★   ★   ★   ★

Early in April of 1887, some of the boys came down from the Pleasant Valley, where there was a big rustler war going on and the rustlers were getting the best of the game. I was tired of the mine and willing to go, and so away we went. Things were in a pretty bad condition. It was war to the knife between cowboys and rustlers, and there was a battle every time the two outfits ran together. A great many men were killed in the war. Old man Blevins and his three sons, three of the Grahams, a Bill Jacobs, Jim Payne, Al Rose, John Tewkesbury, Stolt, Scott, and a man named "Big Jeff" were hung on the Apache and Gila County line. Others were killed, but I do not remember their names now. I was the mediator, and was deputy sheriff under Bucky O'Neil, of Yavapai County, under Commodore Owens, of Apache County, and Glenn Reynolds, of Gila County. I was still a deputy for Reynolds a year later when he was killed by the Apache Kid, in 1888.

After this war in the Pleasant Valley I again went back to my mine and went to work, but it was too slow, and I could not stay at it. I was just getting ready to go to Mexico and was going down to clean out the spring at the mine one evening. I turned my saddle horse loose and let him graze up the cañon. After I got the spring cleaned out, I went up the cañon to find my horse and I saw a moccasin track covering the trail made by the rope my horse was dragging. That meant to go back, but I did not go back. I cut up the side of the mountain and found the trail where my horse had gone out. It ran into the trail of several more horses, and they were all headed south. I went down to the ranch, got another horse and rode over to the Agency, about twenty miles, to get an Indian or two to go with me to see what I could learn about this bunch of Indians.

I got to the Agency about two o'clock in the morning and found that there had been an outbreak and mutiny among Sieber's police. It was like this: Sieber had raised a young Indian he always called "the Kid," and now known as the "Apache Kid." This kid was the son of old Chief Toga-de-chuz, a San Carlos Apache. At a big dance on the Gila at old Toga-de-chuz's camp everybody got drunk and when morning came old Toga was found dead from a knife thrust. An old hunter belonging to another tribe of Indians and called "Rip" was accused of doing the job, but from what Sieber could learn, as he afterwards told me, everybody was too drunk to know how the thing did happen. The wound was given in a very skillful manner and as it split open old Toga's heart it was supposed to be given by one who knew where the heart lay.

Toga and old Rip had had a row over a girl about forty years before (they were both about sixty at this time), and Toga had gotten the best of the row and the girl to boot. Some say that an Indian will forget and forgive the same as a white man. I say no. Here had elapsed forty years between the row and the time old Toga was killed.

Rip had not turned his horse loose in the evening before the killing, so it was supposed he had come there with express intention of killing old Toga.

Anyway the Kid was the oldest son Toga-de-chuz and he must revenge the death of his father. He must, according to all Indian laws and customs, kill old Rip. Sieber knew this and cautioned the Kid about doing anything to old Rip. The Kid never said a word to Sieber as to what he would do. The Kid was first sergeant of the Agency scouts. The Interior Department had given the Agency over to the military and there were no more police, but scouts instead.

Shortly after this killing, Sieber and Captain Pierce, the agent, went up to Camp Apache to see about the distribution of some annuities to the Indians there, and the Kid, as first sergeant of the scouts, was left in charge of the peace of the Agency.

No sooner did Sieber and Captain Pierce get started than the Kid took five of his men and went over on the Aravaipo, where old Rip lived, and shot him. That evened up their account, and the Kid went back to where his band was living up above the Agency. Sieber heard of this and he and Pierce immediately started to San Carlos.

When they got there, they found no one in command of the scouts. Sieber sent word up to the camp where the Kid's people lived to tell the Kid to come down. This he did, escorted by the whole band of bucks.

Sieber, when they drew up in front of his tent, went out and spoke to the Kid and told him to get off his horse, and this the Kid did. Sieber then told him to take the arms of the other four or five men who had government rifles. This also the Kid did. He took their guns and belts and then Sieber told him to take off his own belt and put down his gun and take the other deserters and go to the guardhouse.

Some of the bucks with the Kid (those who were not soldiers) said to the Kid to fight, and in a second they were at it—eleven bucks against Sieber alone. It did not make any particular difference to Sieber about being outnumbered. His rifle was in his tent. He jumped back and got it, and at the first shot he killed one Indian. All the others fired at him as he came to the door of his tent, but only one bullet struck him; that hit him on the shin and shattered his leg all to pieces. He fell, and the Indian ran away.

This was what Sieber told me when I got to the Agency. And then I knew it was the Kid who had my horse and outfit. Soldiers were already on his trail.

From where he had stolen my horse, he and his band crossed over the mountain to the Table Mountain district, and there stole a lot of Bill Atchley's saddle horses. A few miles further on they killed Bill Dihl, then headed on up through the San Pedro country, turned down the Sonoita River, and there they killed Mike Grace; then they were turned back north again by some of the cavalry that was after them.

They struck back north, and Lieutenant Johnson got after them about Pontaw, overtook them in the Rincon Mountains, and had a fight, killing a couple of them, and put all the rest of them afoot. My horse was captured unwounded, and as the soldiers knew him, he was taken to the San Pedro and left there; they sent word to me, and eventually I got him, though he was pretty badly used up.

That was the way the Kid came to break out. He went back to the Reservation, and later on he surrendered. He was tried for desertion, and given a long time by the federal courts, but was pardoned by President Cleveland, after having served a short term.

During the time the Kid and his associates were hiding around on the Reservation, previous to his first arrest, he and his men had killed a freighter, or he may have been only a whisky peddler. Anyway, he was killed twelve miles above San Carlos, on the San Carlos River, by the Kid's outfit, and when the Kid returned to the Agency after he had done his short term and had been pardoned by the President, he was rearrested by the civil authorities of Gila County, Arizona, to be tried for the killing of this man at the Twelve Mile Pole.

This was in the fall of 1888. I was deputy sheriff of Gila County at that time, and as it was a new county, Reynolds was the first sheriff. I was to be the interpreter at the Kid's trial, but on July 4, 1888, I had won the prize at the Globe for tying down a steer, and there was a county rivalry among the cowboys all over the Territory as to who was the quickest man at that business. One Charley Meadows (whose father and brother were before mentioned as being killed by the Cibicus on their raid) was making a big talk that he could beat me tying at the Territorial Fair, at Phoenix. Our boys concluded I must go to the fair and make a trial for the Territorial prize, and take it out Meadows. I had known Meadows for years, and I thought I could beat him, and so did my friends.

The fair came off at the same time as did court in our new county, and since I could not very well be at both places, and, as they said, could not miss the fair, I was not at the trial.

While I was at Phoenix, the trial came off and several of the Indians told about the killing. There were six on trial, and they were all sentenced to the penitentiary at Yuma, Arizona, for life. Reynolds and "Hunky Dory" Holmes started to take them to Yuma. There were the six Indians and a Mexican sent up for one year, for horse stealing. The Indians had their hands coupled together, so that there were three in each of the two bunches.

Where the stage road from Globe to Casa Grande (the railroad station on the Southern Pacific Railroad) crosses the Gila river there is a very steep sand wash, up which the stage road winds. Going up this, Reynolds took his prisoners out and they were all walking behind the stage. The Mexican was handcuffed and inside the stage. Holmes got ahead of Reynolds some little distance. Holmes had three Indians and Reynolds three.

Just as Holmes turned a short bend in the road and got behind a point of rocks and out of sight of Reynolds, at a given signal, each bunch of prisoners turned on their guard and grappled with him. Holmes was soon down and they killed him. The three that had tackled Reynolds were not doing so well, but the ones that had killed Holmes got his rifle and pistol and went to the aid of the ones grappling Reynolds. These three were holding his arms so he could not get his gun. The ones that came up killed him, took his keys, unlocked the cuffs, and they were free.

Gene Livingston was driving the stage, and he looked around the side of the stage to see what the shooting was about. One of the desperadoes took a shot at him, striking him over the eye, and down he came. The Kid and his men then took the stage horses and tried to ride them, but there was only one of the four that they could ride.

The Kid remained an outlaw after that, till he died a couple of years ago of consumption. The Mexican, after the Kid and his men left the stage (they had taken off his handcuffs), struck out for Florence and notified the authorities. The driver was only stunned by the shot over the eye and is a resident and business man of Globe.

Had I not been urged to go to the fair at Phoenix, this would never have happened, as the Kid and his comrades just walked along and put up the job in their own language, which no one there could understand but themselves. Had I not gone to the fair, I would have been with Reynolds and could have understood what they said and it would never have happened. I won the prize roping at the fair, but it was at a very heavy cost.

In the winter I again went home, and in the following spring I went to work on my mine. Worked along pretty steady on it for a year, and in 1890 we sold it to a party of New Yorkers. We got $8,000 for it.

We were negotiating for this sale, and at the same time the Pinkerton National Detective Agency at Denver, Colorado, was writing to me to get me to come to Denver and to go to work for them. I thought it would be a good thing to do, and as soon as all the arrangements for the sale of the mine were made, I came to Denver and was initiated into the mysteries of the Pinkerton institution.

My work for them was not the kind that exactly suited my disposition; too tame for me. There were a good many instructions and a good deal of talk given the operative regarding the things to do and the things that had been done.

James McParland, the superintendent, asked me what I would do if I were put on a train robbery case. I told him if I had a good man with me I could catch up to them.

Well, on the last night of August, that year, at about midnight, a train was robbed on the Denver & Rio Grande Railway, between Cotopaxi and Texas Creek. I was sent out there, and was told that C. W. Shores would be along in a day or so. He came on time and asked me how I was getting on. I told him I had struck the trail, but there were so many men scouring the country that I, myself, was being held up all the time; that I had been arrested twice in two days and taken in to Salida to be identified!

Eventually all the sheriff's posses quit, and then Mr. W. A. Pinkerton and Mr. McParland told Shores and me to go at 'em. We took up the trail where I had left it several days before and we never left it till we got the robbers.

They had crossed the Sangre de Cristo range, come down by the Villa Grove iron mines, and crossed back to the east side of the Sangre de Cristos at Mosca Pass, then on down through the Huerfano Cañon, out by Cucharas, thence down east of Trinidad. They had dropped into Clayton, N.M., and got into a shooting scrape there in a gin mill. They then turned east again toward the "Neutral Strip" and close to Beaver City, then across into the "Pan Handle" by a place in Texas called Ochiltree, the county seat of Ochiltree County. They then headed toward the Indian Territory, and crossed into it below Canadian City. They then swung in on the head of the Washita River in the Territory, and kept down this river for a long distance.

We finally saw that we were getting close to them, as we got in the neighborhood of Paul's Valley. At Washita station we located one of them in the house of a man by the name of Wolfe. The robber's name was Burt Curtis. Shores took this one and came on back to Denver, leaving me to get the other one if ever he came back to Wolfe's.

After several days of waiting on my part, he did come back, and as he came riding up to the house I stepped out and told him someone had come! He was "Peg Leg" Watson, and considered by everyone in Colorado as a very desperate character. I had no trouble with him.

We had an idea that Joe McCoy, also, was in the robbery, but "Peg" said he was not, and gave me information enough so that I located him.

He was wanted very badly by the sheriff of Fremont County, Colorado, for a murder scrape. He and his father had been tried previous to this for murder, had been found guilty, and were remanded to jail to wait sentence, but before Joe was sentenced he had escaped. The old man McCoy got a new trial, and at the new trial was sentenced to eighteen years in the Cañon City, Colorado, penitentiary.

When I captured my man, got to a telegraph station and wired Mr. McParland that I had the notorious "Peg," the superintendent wired back: "Good! Old man McCoy got eighteen years today!" This train had been robbed in order to get money to carry McCoy's case up to the Supreme Court, or rather to pay the attorneys (Macons & Son), who had carried the case up.

Later on I told Mr. McParland that I could locate Joe McCoy, and he communicated with Stewart, the sheriff, who came to Denver and made arrangements for me to go with him and try to get McCoy.

We left Denver on Christmas Eve and went direct to Rifle, from there to Meeker, and on down White River. When we got to where McCoy had been, we learned that he had gone to Ashley, in Utah, for the Christmas festivities. We pushed on over there, reaching the town late at night and could not locate our man. Next morning I learned where he got his meals, and as he went in to get his breakfast, I followed him in and arrested him. He had a big Colt's pistol, but did not shoot me. We took him out by Fort Duchesne, Utah, and caught the D.& R. G. train at Price station.

The judge under whom he had been tried had left the bench when McCoy finally was landed back in jail, and it would have required a new trial before he could be sentenced by another judge; he consented to plead guilty to involuntary manslaughter, and took six years in the Cañon City pen. He was pardoned out in three years, I believe.

Peg Leg Watson and Burt Curtis were tried in the United States court for robbing the United States mails on the highway, and were sentenced for life in the Detroit federal prison. In robbing the train they had first made the fireman break into the mail compartment of the compartment car. They then saw their mistake, and did not even take the amount of a one-cent postage stamp, but went and made the fireman break into the rear compartment, where they found the express matter, and took it. But the authorities proved that it was mail robbery and their sentence was life.

While Pinkerton's is one of the greatest institutions of the kind in existence, I never did like the work, so I left them in 1894.

I then came to Wyoming and went to work for the Swan Land and Cattle Company, since which time everybody else has been more familiar with my life and business than I have been myself.

And I think that since my coming here the yellow journal reporters are better equipped to write my history than am I, myself!

Respectfully,
TOM HORN

"In Arizona and New Mexico, roping contests used to be held as a kind of annual tournament, in August, to the fair, or else as a special entertainment, often comprising, among other features, horse racing, a bull fight, baile and fiesta. Roping contests are generally held in a large field or enclosure—such as the interior of a race course. Inside this compound is built a small corral, in which are confined wild beef cattle, usually three-year-old steers, just rounded up off the range.

"The contest is a time race, to see who can overtake, lasso, throw and tie hard and fast the feet of a steer in the shortest period. The record was made at Phoenix, Arizona, in 1891. The contestants were, Charlie Meadows, Bill McCann, George Iago, Ramon Barca and Tom Horn, all well-known vaqueros of the Mexican-Arizona border. Tom Horn won the contest. Time, 49½ seconds, which I do not think has since been lowered.

"Two parallel lines, about as far apart as the ends of a polo court, were marked by banderoles or guidons. A steer was let out of the corral and driven at a run in a direction at right angles to the lines marked. As the steer crossed the second line, a banderole was dropped, which was the signal for a vaquero to start from the first line, thus giving the beef a running start of 250 yards. The horses used were all large, fleet animals, wonderfully well trained, and swooped for their prey at full speed and by the shortest route, turning without a touch of the rein to follow the steer, often anticipating his turns by a shorter cut. When the vaquero got within fifty yards of his beef the loop of his riata was swinging in a sharp, crisp circle about his right arm, raised high to his right and rear, and when twenty yards closer, it shot forward, hovered for an instant, and then descended above the horns of its victim, which a moment later would land a somersault. Before the beef could recover his surprise or wind he would have a half hitch about his fore legs, a second about his hind legs, and a third found all four a snug little bunch, hard and fast.

"The rope, of course, is not taken from the head; it is all one rope, the slack being successively used. Sometimes the vaqueros used foot-roping instead of head. It requires more skill and is practiced more by the Mexicans, who think it is a good method with large-horned cattle while in herd, where heads are so little separated that a lasso would fall on horns not wanted. In foot-roping the noose is thrown lower and a bit in front of the beef, so that at his next step he will put his foot into the noose before it strikes the ground. If the noose falls too quickly for this, it is jerked sharply upward just as the foot is raised above it.

"I have seen men so skillful at this that they would bet even money on roping an animal on a single throw, naming the foot that they would secure, as right hind, left fore, and so forth. As regards the lash end of the riata, two methods in this contest were also used. In the 'Texas style' the lash of the riata is made hard and fast to the horn of the saddle. The instant the rope 'holds,' a pony who understands his work plants his fore feet forward and checks suddenly, giving the steer a header. His rider dismounts quickly, runs to the beef, which the pony keeps down by holding the rope taut.

"As soon as the vaquero faces the pony and grasps the rope near the beef, the pony moves forward, and with the slack of the rope the beef is secured. While the beef is plunging or wheeling on the rope the pony is careful to keep his head toward the beef, or, as the sailor would say, he goes 'bow on.'

"The Texas method is best adapted to loose ground, where it is much easier on the vaquero, but it is utterly unsuited for mountain work or steep hillsides, as the pony would lose his footing and land up in the bottom of a cañon.

"For such country, the California style is used. Here the lash is not made fast; a few frapping turns are made about the horn, and the rider uses his weight and a checking of the pony to throw the beef. When he dismounts, he carries the lash end forward, keeping it taut, toward the beef, taking up the slack and coils it as he goes, and with it secures the beef. The pony is free after the steer is thrown. It is the more rapid method. Tom Horn used it in the contest won, when he made his record. With it the vaquero has free use of his riata for securing the beef. But it is a hard method, and plainsmen prefer letting Mr. Bronco take the brunt of it.

"Tom Horn is well known all along the border. He served as government guide, packer, scout and as chief of Indian scouts, which latter position he held with Captain Crawford at the time the Mexicans killed him in the Sierra Madre Mountains. He is the hero referred to in the story of 'The Killing of the Captain,' by John Heard, Sr., published some months ago in the Cosmopolitan Magazine."

The Race

BY STEWART EDWARD WHITE

Stewart Edward White was born in 1873 in Grand Rapids, Michigan. After graduating from the University of Michigan he set out adventuring. He worked as prospector and cowboy, and pretty much anything that would make him a few dollars. Eventually his first collection of stories appeared, entitled *The Claim Jumpers* (1901). But his first real success came with the publication of his next book *The Blazed Trail* (1902). This was followed by *Blazed Trail Stories* (1904), in which this story first appeared. All of these tales were said to be based upon White's time as a young man in the Black Hills gold rush.

"The Race" is an adventure tale, a buddy story and a period piece, besides being just a rattling good yarn. The student of the genre may take from it some understanding of the time when the adventure story mixed with the cowboy tale to make our first classic Westerns. That alone is almost enough to allow us to forgive the slightly Jim-Crow treatment of Black Sam the cook, and the decidedly racist protrayal of the Mexican vaqueros.

★　★　★　★　★

This story is most blood-and-thundery, but, then, it is true. It is one of the stories of Alfred; but Alfred is not the hero of it at all—quite another man, not nearly so interesting in himself as Alfred.

At the time, Alfred and this other man, whose name was Tom, were convoying a band of Mexican vaqueros over to the Circle-X outfit. The Circle-X was in the heat of a big round-up, and had run short of men. So Tom and Alfred had gone over to Tucson and picked up the best they could find, which best was enough to bring tears to the eyes of an old-fashioned, straight-riding, swift-roping Texas cowman. The gang was an ugly one: it was sullen, black-browed, sinister. But it, one and all, could throw a rope and cut out stock, which was not only the main thing—it was the whole thing.

Still, the game was not pleasant. Either Alfred or Tom usually rode night-herd on the ponies—merely as a matter of precaution—and they felt just a trifle more shut off by themselves and alone than if they had ridden solitary over the limitless alkali of the Arizona plains. This feeling struck in the deeper because Tom had just entered one of his brooding spells. Tom and Alfred had been chums now for close on two years, so Alfred knew enough to leave him entirely alone until he should recover.

The primary cause of Tom's abstraction was an open-air preacher, and the secondary cause was, of course, a love affair. These two things did not connect themselves consciously in Tom's mind, but they blended subtly to produce a ruminative dissatisfaction.

When Tom was quite young he had fallen in love with a girl back in the Dakota country. Shortly after a military-post had been established near by, and Ann Bingham had ceased to be spoken of by mayors' daughters and officers' wives. Tom, being young, had never quite gotten over it. It was still part of his nature, and went with a certain sort of sunset, or that kind of star-lit evening in which an imperceptible haze dims the brightness of the heavens.

The open-air preacher had chosen as his text the words, "passing the love of woman," and Tom, wandering idly by, had caught the text. Somehow ever since the words had run in his mind. They did not mean anything to him, but merely repeated themselves over and over, just as so many delicious syllables which tickled the ear and rolled succulently under the tongue. For, you see, Tom was only an ordinary battered Arizona cowpuncher, and so, of course, according to the fireside moralists, quite incapable of the higher feelings. But the words reacted to arouse memories of black-eyed Anne, and the memories in turn brought one of his moods.

Tom, and Alfred, and the ponies, and the cook-wagon, and the cook, and the Mexican vaqueros had done the alkali for three days. Underfoot has been an exceedingly irregular plain; overhead an exceedingly bright and trying polished sky; around about an exceedingly monotonous horizon-line and dense clouds of white dust. At the end of the third day everybody was feeling just a bit choked up and tired, and, to crown a series of petty misfortunes, the fire failed to respond to Black Sam's endeavours. This made supper late.

Now at one time in this particular locality Arizona had not been dry and full of alkali. A mighty river, so mighty that in its rolling flood no animal that lives to-day would have had the slightest chance, surged down from the sharp-pointed mountains on the north, pushed fiercely its way through the southern plains, and finally seethed and boiled in eddies of foam out into a southern sea which has long since disappeared. On its banks grew strange, bulbous plants. Across its waters swam uncouth monsters with snake-like necks. Over it alternated storms so savage that they seem to rend the world, and sunshine so hot that it seemed that were it not for the bulbous plants all living things would perish as in an oven.

In the course of time conditions changed, and the change brought the Arizona of to-day. There are now no turbid waters, no bulbous plants, no uncouth beasts, and, above all, no storms. Only the sun and one other thing remain: that other thing is the bed of the ancient stream.

On one side—the concave of the curve—is a long easy slope, so gradual that one hardly realizes where it shades into the river-bottom itself. On the other—the convex of the curve—where the swift waters were turned aside to a new direction, is a high, perpendicular cliff running in an almost unbroken breastwork for a great many miles, and baked as hard as iron in this sunny and almost rainless climate. Occasional showers have here and there started to eat out little transverse gullies, but with a few exceptions have only gone so far as slightly to nick the crest. The exceptions, reaching to the plain, afford steep and perilous ascents to the level above. Anyone who wishes to pass the barrier made by the primeval river must hunt out himself one of these narrow passages.

On the evening in question the cowmen had made camp in the hollow beyond the easy slope. On the rise, sharply silhouetted against the west, Alfred rode wrangler to the little herd of ponies. Still farther westward across the plain was the clay-cliff barriers, looking under the sunset like a narrow black ribbon. In the hollow itself was the camp, giving impression in the background of a scattering of ghostly mules, a half-circle of wagons, ill-defined forms of recumbent vaqueros, and then in the foreground of Sam with his gleaming semicircle of utensils, and his pathetic little pile of fuel which would not be induced to gleam at all.

For, as has been said, Black Sam was having great trouble with his fire. It went out at least six times, and yet each time it hung on in a flickering fashion so long that he had felt encouraged to arrange his utensils and distribute his provisions. Then it had expired, and poor Sam had to begin all over again. The Mexicans smoked yellow-paper cigarettes and watched his off-and-on movements with sullen distrust; they were firmly convinced that he was indulging in some sort of a practical joke. So they hated him fervently and wrapped themselves in their serapes. Tom sat on a wagon-tongue swinging a foot and repeating vaguely to himself in a sing-song inner voice, "passing the love of woman, passing the love of woman," over and over again. His mind was a dull blank of grayness. From time to time he glanced at Sam, but with no impatience: he was used to going without. Sam was to him a matter of utter indifference.

As to the cook himself, he had a perplexed droop in every curve of his rounded shoulders. His kinky gray wool was tousled from perpetual un-decided scratching, and his eyes had something of the dumb sadness of the dog as he rolled them in despair. Life was not a matter of indifference to him. Quite the contrary. The problem of *damp wood* + *matches* = *cooking-fire* was the whole tangle of existence. There was something pitiable in it. Per-haps this was because there is something more pathetic in a comical face grown solemn than in the most melancholy countenance in the world.

At last the moon rose and the fire decided to burn. With the sev-enth attempt to flared energetically; then settled to a steady glow of possi-ble flap-jacks.

But its smoke was bitter, and the evening wind fitful. Bitter smoke on an empty stomach might be appropriately substituted for the last straw of the proverb—when the proverb has to do with hungry Mexicans. Most of the recumbent vaqueros merely cursed a little deeper and drew their serapes closer, but José Guiterrez grunted, threw off his blanket, and ap-proached the fire.

Sam rolled the whites of his eyes up at him for a moment, grinned in a half-perplexed fashion, and turned again to his pots and pans. José, being sulky and childish, wanted to do something to somebody, so he in-solently flicked the end of his long quirt through a mess of choice but still chaotic flap-jacks. The quirt left a narrow streak across the batter. Sam looked up quickly.

"Doan you done do dat!" he said, with indignation.

He looked upon the turkey-like José for a heavy moment, and then turned back to the cooking. In rescuing an unstable coffeepot a mo-ment later, he accidentally jostled against José's leg. José promptly and fiercely kicked the whole outfit into space. The frying-pan crowned a sage-brush; the coffee-pot rolled into a hollow, where it spouted coffee-grounds and water in a diminishing stream; the kettle rolled gently on its side; flap-jacks distributed themselves impartially and moistly; and, worst of all, the fire was drowned out altogether.

Black Sam began stiffly to arise. The next instant he sank back with a gurgle in his throat and a knife thrust in his side.

The murderer stood looking down at his victim. The other Mexi-cans stared. The cowboy jumped up from the tongue of the wagon, drew his weapon from the holster at his side, took deliberate aim, and fired twice. Then he turned and began to run toward Alfred on the hill.

A cowboy cannot run so very rapidly. He carries such a quantity of dunnage below in the shape of high boots, spurs, chaps, and cartridge-belts that his gait is a waddling single-foot. Still, Tom managed to get across the little stony ravine before the Mexicans recovered from their surprise and became disentangled from their ponchos. Then he glanced over his shoulder. He saw that some of the vaqueros were running toward the ar- roya, that some were busily unhobbling the mules, and that one or two had kneeled and were preparing to shoot. At the sight of these last, he began to jump from side to side as he ran. This decreased his speed. Half-way up the hill he was met by Alfred on his way to get in the game, whatever it might prove to be. The little man reached over and grasped Tom's hand. Tom braced his foot against the stirrup, and in an instant was astride behind the saddle. Alfred turned up the hill again, and without a word began applying his quirt vigorously to the wiry shoulders of his horse. At the top of the hill, as they passed the grazing ponies, Tom turned and emptied the re- maining four chambers of his revolver into the herd. Two ponies fell kick- ing; the rest scattered in every direction. Alfred grunted approvingly, for this made pursuit more difficult, and so gained them a little more time.

Now both Alfred and Tom knew well enough that a horse carry- ing two men cannot run away from a horse carrying one man, but they also knew the country, and this knowledge taught them that if they could reach the narrow passage through the old clay bluff, they might be able to escape to Peterson's, which was situated a number of miles beyond. This would be possible, because men climb faster when danger is behind them than when it is in front. Besides, a brisk defence could render even an angry Mexican a little doubtful as to just when he should begin to climb. Accordingly, Alfred urged the pony across the flat plain of the ancient river-bed toward the nearest and only break in the cliff. Fifteen miles below was the regular passage. Otherwise the upper mesa was as impregnable as an ancient fortress. The Mexicans had by this time succeeded in roping some of the scattered animals, and were streaming over the brow of the hill, shouting wildly. Al- fred looked back and grinned. Tom waved his wide sombrero mockingly.

When they approached the ravine, they found the sides almost perpendicular and nearly bare. Its bed was V-shaped, and so cut up with miniature gullies, fantastic turrets and spires, and so undermined by former rains as to be almost impassable. It sloped gently at first, but afterward more rapidly, and near the top was straight up and down for two feet or more. As the men reached it, they threw themselves from the horse and commenced to scramble up, leading the animal by the bridle-rein. From riding against the sunset their eyes were dazzled, so this was not easy. The horse followed gingerly, his nose close to the ground.

It is well known that quick, short rains followed by a burning sun tend to undermine the clay surface of the ground and to leave it with a hard upper shell, beneath which are cavities of various depths. Alfred and Tom as experienced men, should have foreseen this, but they did not. Soon after entering the ravine the horse broke through into one of the underground cavities and fell heavily on his side. When he had scrambled somehow to his feet, he stood feebly panting, his nostrils expanded.

"How is it, Tom?" called Alfred, who was ahead.

"Shoulder out," said Tom briefly.

Alfred turned back without another word, and putting the muzzle of his pistol against the pony's forehead just above the line of the eyes he pulled the trigger. With the body the two men improvised a breastwork across a little hummock. Just as they dropped behind it the Mexicans clattered up, riding bareback. Tom coolly reloaded his pistol.

The Mexicans, too, were dazzled from riding against the glow in the west, and halted a moment in a confused mass at the mouth of the ravine. The two cowboys within rose and shot rapidly. Three Mexicans and two ponies fell. The rest in wild confusion slipped rapidly to the right and left beyond the Americans' line of sight. Three armed with Winchesters made a long detour and dropped quietly into the sagebrush just beyond accurate pistol-range. There they lay concealed, watching. Then utter silence fell.

The rising moon shone full and square into the ravine, illuminating every inch of the ascent. A very poor shot could hardly miss in such a light and with such a background. The two cowmen realized this and settled down more comfortably behind their breastwork. Tom cautiously raised the pony's head with a little chunk of rock, thus making a loophole through which to keep tab on the enemy, after which he rolled on his belly and began whittling in the hard clay, for Tom had the carving habit—like many a younger boy. Alfred carefully extracted a short pipe from beneath his chaparejos, pushed down with his blunt forefinger the charge with which it was already loaded, and struck a match. He poised this for a moment above the bowl of the pipe.

"What's the row anyway!" he inquired, with pardonable curiosity.

"Now, it's jest fifteen mile to th' cut," said Tom, disregarding Alfred's question entirely, "an' of co'se they's goin' to send a posse down thar on th' keen jump. That'll take clost onto three hours in this light. Then they'll jest pot us a lot from on top."

Alfred puffed three times toward the moonlight, and looked as though the thing were sufficiently obvious without wasting so much breath over it.

"We've jest *got* to git out!" concluded Tom, earnestly.

Alfred grunted.

"An' how are we goin' to do it?"

Alfred paused in the act of blowing a cloud.

"Because, if we makes a break, those Greasers jest nat'rally plugs us from behind th' minute we begins to climb."

Alfred condescended to nod. Tom suspended his whittling for a reply.

"Well," said Alfred, taking his pipe from his mouth—Tom contentedly took up whittling again—"there's only one way to do it, and that's to keep them so damn busy in front that they *can't* plug us."

Tom looked perplexed.

"We just got to take our chances on the climbing. Of course, there's bound to be th' risk of accident. But when I give th' word, *you mosey*, and if one of them pots you, it'll be because my six-shooter's empty"

"But you can't expec' t' shoot *an'* climb!" objected Tom.

"Course not," replied Alfred, calmly, "Division of labour: you climb; I shoot."

A light dawned in Tom's eyes, and his shut his jaws with a snap.

"I guess not!" said he, quietly.

"Yo' laigs is longer," Alfred urged, in his gentle voice, "and yo'll get to Peterson's quicker;" and then he looked in Tom's eyes and changed his tone. "All right!" he said, in a business-like manner. "I'll toss you for it."

For reply, Tom fished out an old pack of cards.

"I tell you," he proposed, triumphantly, "I'll turn you fer it. First man that gits a jack in th' hand-out stays."

He began to manipulate the cards, lying cramped on his side, and in doing so dropped two or three. Alfred turned to pick them up. Tom deftly slipped the jack of diamonds to the bottom of the pack. He inserted in the centre those Alfred handed him, and began at once to deal.

"Thar's yore's," he said, laying out the four of clubs, "an' yere's mine," he concluded, producing the jack of diamonds. "Luck's ag'in me early in th' game," was his cheerful comment.

For a minute Alfred was silent, and a decided objection appeared in his eyes. Then his instinct of fair play in the game took the ascendant. He kicked off his chaps in the most business-like manner, unbuckled his six-shooter and gave it to Tom, and perched his hat on the end of his quirt, which he then raised slowly above the pony's side for the purpose of drawing the enemy's fire. He did these things quickly and without heroics, because he was a plainsman. Hardly had the bullets from three Winchesters spatted against the clay before he was up and climbing for dear life.

The Mexicans rushed to the opening from either side, fully expecting to be able either to take wing-shots at close range, or to climb so fast as to close in before the cowboys would have time to make a stand at the top. In this they shut off their most effective fire—that of the three men with the Winchesters-and, instead of getting wing-shots themselves, they received an enthusiastic battering from Tom at the range of six yards.

Even a tenderfoot cannot over-shoot at six yards. What was left of the Mexicans disappeared quicker than they had come, and the three of the Winchesters scuttled back to cover like a spent covey of quail.

Tom then lit Alfred's pipe, and continued his excellent sculpture in the bed of hard clay. He knew nothing more would happen until the posse came. The game had passed out of his hands. It had become a race between a short-legged man on foot and a band of hard riders on the backs of very good horses. Viewing the matter dispassionately, Tom would not have cared to bet on the chances.

As has been stated, Alfred was a small man and his legs were short—and not only short, but unused to exertion of any kind, for Alfred's daylight hours were spent on a horse. At the end of said legs were tight boots with high French heels, which most Easterners would have considered a silly affectation, but which all Westerners knew to be purposeful in the extreme—they kept his feet from slipping forward through the wide stirrups. In other respects, too, Alfred was handicapped. His shoulders were narrow and sloping and his chest was flat. Indoors and back East he would probably have been a consumptive; out here, he was merely short-winded.

So it happened that Alfred lost the race.

The wonder was not that he lost but that he succeeded in finishing at Peterson's at all. He did it somehow, and even made a good effort to ride back with the rescuing party, but fell like a log when he tried to pick up his hat. So someone took off his boots, also, and put him to bed.

As to the rescuing party, it disbanded less than an hour later. Immediately afterward it reorganized into a hunting party—and its game was men. The hunt was a long one, and the game was bagged even unto the last, but that is neither here nor there.

Poor Tom was found stripped to the hide, and hacked to pieces. Mexicans are impulsive, especially after a few of them have been killed. His equipment had been stolen. The naked horse and the naked man, bathed in the light of gray dawn, that was all—except that here and there fluttered bits of paper that had once been a pack of cards. The clay slab was carved deeply—a man can do much of that sort of thing with two hours to waste. Most of the decorative effects were arrows, or hearts, or brands, but in one corner were the words, "passing the love of woman," which was a little impressive after all, even though Tom had not meant them, being, as I said, only an ordinary battered Arizona cow-puncher incapable of the higher feelings.

How do I know he played the jack of diamonds on purpose? Why, I knew Tom, and that's enough.

Dodge

BY WILLIAM MACLEOD RAINE

Place is important in any myth. King Arthur has his Camelot as do the Greek gods their Mount Olympus and their Hades. And speaking of Hades, Dodge City has indeed some pride of place in the story of the Cowboy, and in the myth of the West.

William Macleod Raine was born in London, England in 1871. At age ten his family emigrated to the United States, settling in Arkansas. As he grew up, Raine moved west and eventually established himself as a novelist and chronicler of the cowboy world. He wrote over eighty books in his fifty-odd year career, many of them huge sellers. His novel, *When a Man's a Man,* sold eight hundred thousand copies. And during the first World War the British Government bought half a million copies of his books to be given to the troops. His total number of books in print is close to nineteen million copies.

Though his non-fiction has been much criticized as to its factual accuracy, Raine does offer a consistent, a coherent and colorful, often humorous, take on that mythic American dream-time we call the Old West.

"Dodge" is taken from *Famous Sheriffs and Outlaws*, published in 1929, and is a recognized classic.

★   ★   ★   ★   ★

It was in the days when the new railroad was pushing through the country of the plains Indians that a drunken cowboy got on the train at a way station in Kansas. John Bender, the conductor, asked him for his ticket. He had none, but he pulled out a handful of gold pieces.

"I wantta—g-go to—h-hell," he hiccoughed.

Bender did not hesitate instant. "Get off at Dodge. One dollar, please."

175

Dodge City did not get its name because so many of its citizens were or had been, in the Texas phrase, on the dodge. It came quite respectably way by its cognomen. The town was laid out by A. A. Robinson, chief engineer of the Atchison, Topeka & Santa Fe, and it was called for Colonel Richard I. Dodge, commander of the post at Fort Dodge and one of the founders of the place. It is worth noting this, because it is one of the few respectable facts in the early history of the cowboy capital. Dodge was a wild and uncurried prairie wolf, and it howled every night and all night long. It was gay and young and lawless. Its sense of humor was exaggerated and worked overtime. The crack of the six-shooter punctuated its hilarity ominously. Those who dwelt there were the valiant vanguard of civilization. For good or bad they were strong and forceful, many of them generous and big-hearted in spite of their lurid lives. The town was a hive of energy. One might justly use many adjectives about it, but the word respectable is not among them.

There were three reasons why Dodge won the reputation of being the wildest town the country had ever seen. In 1872 it was the end of the track, the last jumping-off spot into the wilderness, and in the days when transcontinental railroads were building across the desert the temporary terminus was always a gathering place of roughs and scalawags. The payroll was large, and gamblers, gunmen, and thugs gathered for the pickings. This was true of Hays, Abilene, Ogalala, and Kit Carson. It was true of Las Vegas and Albuquerque.

A second reason was that Dodge was the end of the long trail drive from Texas. Every year hundreds of thousands of longhorns were driven up from Texas by cowboys scarcely less wild than the hill steers they herded. The great plains country was being opened, and cattle were needed to stock a thousand ranches as well as to supply the government at Indian reservations. Scores of these trail herds were brought to Dodge for shipment, and after the long, dangerous, drive the punchers were keen to spend their money on such diversions as the town could offer. Out of sheer high spirits they liked to shoot up the town, to buck the tiger, to swagger from saloon to gambling hall, their persons garnished with revolvers, the spurs on their high-heeled boots jingling. In no spirit of malice they wanted it distinctly understood that they owned the town. As one of them once put it, he was born high up on the Guadaloupe, raised on prickly pear, had palled with alligators and quarreled with grizzlies.

Also, Dodge was the heart of the buffalo country. Here the hunters were outfitted for the chase. From here great quantities of hides were shipped back on the new railroad. R. M. Wright, one of the founders of the town and always one of its leading citizens, says that his firm alone shipped two hundred thousand hides in one season. He estimates the number of buffaloes in the country at more than twenty-five million, admitting that many as well informed as he put the figure at four times as many. Many times he and others travelled through the vast herds for days at a time without ever losing sight of them. The killing of buffaloes was easy, because the animals were so stupid. When one was shot they would mill round and round. Tom Nicholson killed 120 in forty minutes; in a little more than a month he slaughtered 2,173 of them. With good luck a man could earn a hundred dollars a day. If he had bad luck he lost his scalp.

The buffalo was to the plains Indian food, fuel, and shelter. As long as there were plenty of buffaloes he was in Paradise. But he saw at once that this slaughter would soon exterminate the supply. He hated the hunter and battled against his encroachments. The buffalo hunter was an intrepid plainsman. He fought Kiowas, Comanches, and the Staked Plain Apaches, as well as the Sioux and the Arapahoe. Famous among these hunters were Kirk Jordan, Charles Rath, Emanuel Dubbs, Jack Bridges, and Curly Walker. Others even better known where the two Buffalo Bills (William Cody and William Mathewson) and Wild Bill.

These three factors then made Dodge: it was the end of the railroad, the terminus of the cattle trail from Texas, the center of the buffalo trade. Together they made "the beautiful bibulous Babylon of the frontier," in the words of the editor of the *Kingsley Graphic*. There was to come a time later when the bibulous Babylon fell on evil days and its main source of income was old bones. They were buffalo-bones, gathered in wagons, and piled beside the track for shipment, hundreds and hundreds of carloads of them, to be used for fertilizer. (I have seen great quantities of such bones as far north as the Canadian Pacific line, corded for shipment to a factory.) It used to be said by way of derision that buffalo bones were legal tender in Dodge.

But that was in the far future. In its early years Dodge rode the wave of prosperity. Hays and Abilene and Ogalala had their day, but Dodge had its day and its night, too. For years it did a tremendous business. The streets were so blocked that one could hardly get through. Hundreds of wagons were parked in them, outfits belonging to freighters, hunters, cattlemen, and the government. Scores of camps surrounded the town in every direction. The yell the cowboy and the weird oath of the bullwhacker and mule skinner were heard in the land. And for a time there was no law nearer than Hays City, itself a burg not given to undue quiet and peace.

Dodge was no sleepy village that could drowse along without peace officers. Bob Wright has set it down that in the first year of its history twenty-five men were killed and twice as many wounded. The elements that made up the town were too diverse for perfect harmony. The freighters did not like the railroad graders. The soldiers at the fort fancied themselves as scrappers. The cowboys and the buffalo hunters did not fraternize a little bit. The result was that Boot Hill began to fill up. Its inhabitants were buried with their boots on and without coffins.

There was another cemetery, for those who died in their beds. The climate was so healthy that it would have been very sparsely occupied those first years if it had not been for the skunks. During the early months Dodge was the city of camps. Every night the fires flamed up from the vicinity of hundreds of wagons. Skunks were numerous. They crawled at night into the warm blankets of the sleepers and bit the rightful owners when they protested. A dozen men died from these bites. It was thought at first that the animals were a special variety, known as the hydrophobia skunk. In later years I have sat around Arizona camp fires and heard this subject discussed heatedly. The Smithsonian Institute, appealed to as referee, decided that there was no such species and that deaths from the bites of skunks were probably due to blood poisoning caused by the foul teeth of the animal.

In any case, the skunks were only one half as venomous as the gunmen, judging by comparative staff statistics. Dodge decided it had to have law in the community. Jack Bridges was appointed first marshal.

Jack was a noted scout and buffalo hunter, the sort of man who would have peace if he had to fight for it. He did his sleeping in the afternoon, since this was a quiet time of the day. Someone shook him out of slumber one day to tell him that cowboys were riding up and down Front Street shooting the windows out of buildings. Jack sallied out, old buffalo gun in hand. The cowboys went whooping down the street across the bridge toward their camp. The old hunter took a long shot at one of them and dropped him. The cowboys buried the young fellow next day.

There was a good deal of excitement in the cow camps. If the boys could not have a little fun without some old donker, an old vinegaroon who couldn't take a joke, filling them full of lead it was a pretty howdy-do. But Dodge stood pat. The coroner's jury voted it justifiable homicide. In future the young Texans were more discreet. In the early days whatever law there was did not interfere with casualties due to personal differences of opinion provided the figure had no unusually sinister aspect.

The first wholesale killing was at Tom Sherman's dance hall. The affair was between soldiers and gamblers. It was started by trooper named Hennessey, who had a reputation as a bad guy and a bully. He was killed, as were several others. The officers at the fort glossed over the matter, perhaps because they felt the soldiers had been to blame.

One of the lawless characters who drifted into Dodge the first year was Billy Brooks. He quickly established a reputation as a killer. My old friend Emanuel Dubbs, a buffalo hunter who "took the hides off'n" many a bison, is authority for the statement that Brooks killed or wounded fifteen men in less than a month after his arrival. Now Emanuel is a preacher (if he is still in the land of the living; I saw him last at Clarendon, Texas, ten years or so ago), but I cannot quite swallow that "fifteen." Still, he had a man for breakfast now and then and on one occasion four.

Brooks, by the way, was assistant marshal. It was the policy of the officials of these wild frontier towns to elect as marshal some conspicuous killer, on the theory that desperadoes would respect his prowess or if they did not would get the worst of the encounter.

Abilene, for instance, chose "Wild Bill" Hickok. Austin had its Ben Thompson. According to Bat Masterson, Thompson was the most danger-ous man with a gun among all the bad men he knew—and Bat knew them all. Ben was an Englishman who struck Texas while still young. He fought as a Confederate under Kirby Smith during the Civil War and under Shelby for Maximilian. Later he was city marshal at Austin. Thompson was the man of the most cool effrontery. On one occasion, during a cattlemen's convention, a banquet was held at the leading hotel. The local congress-man, a friend of Thompson, was not invited. Ben took exception to this and attended in person. By way of pleasantry he shot the plates in front of the diners. Later one of those present made humorous comment. "I always thought Ben was a game man. But what did he do? Did he hold up the whole convention of a thousand cattlemen? No, sir. He waited till he got forty or fifty of us poor fellows alone before he turned loose his wolf."

Of all the bad men and desperadoes was produced by Texas, not one of them, not even John Wesley Hardin himself, was more feared than Ben Thompson. Sheriffs avoided serving warrants of arrest on him. It is re-corded that once, when the county court was in session with a charge against him on the docket, Thompson rode into the room on a mustang. He bowed pleasantly to the judge and the court officials.

"Here I am, gents, and I'll lay all I'm worth that there's no charge against me. Am I right? Speak up, gents. I'm a little deaf."

There was a dead silence until at last the clerk of the court mur-mured, "No charge."

A story is told that on one occasion Ben Thompson met his match in the person of the young English remittance man playing cards with him. The remittance man thought he caught Thompson cheating and dis-creetly said so. Instantly Thompson's .44 covered him. For some unknown reason the gambler gave the lad a chance to retract.

"Take it back—and quick," he said grimly.

Every game in the house was suspended while all eyes turned on the daredevil boy and the hard-faced desperado. The remittance man went white, half rose from his seat, and shoved his head across the table toward the revolver.

"Shoot and be damned. I say you cheat," he cried hoarsely.

Thompson hesitated, laughed, shoved the revolver back into its holster, and ordered the youngster out of the house.

Perhaps the most amazing escape on record is that when Thompson, fired at by Mark Wilson at a distance of ten feet from a double-barreled shotgun loaded with buckshot, whirled instantly, killed him, and instant later shot through the forehead Wilson's friend Mathews, though the latter had ducked behind the bar to get away. The second shot was guesswork plus quick thinking and accurate aim. Ben was killed a little later, in company with his friend King Fisher, and other bad man, at the Palace Theatre. A score of shots were poured into them by a dozen men waiting in ambush. Both men had become so dangerous that their enemies could not afford to let them live.

King Fisher was the humorous gentleman who put up a signboard at the fork of a public road bearing the legend:

THIS IS KING FISHER'S ROAD.
TAKE THE OTHER

It is said that those traveling that way followed his advice. The other road might be a mile or two farther, but they were in no hurry. Another amusing little episode in King Fisher's career is told. He had had some slight difficulty with a certain bald-headed man. Fisher shot him and carelessly gave the reason that he wanted to see whether a bullet would glance from a shiny pate.

El Paso in its wild days chose Dallas Stoudenmire for marshal, and after he had been killed, John Selman. Both of them were noted killers. During Selman's régime John Wesley Hardin came to town. Hardin had twenty-seven notches on his gun and was the worst man killer Texas had ever produced. He was at the bar of a saloon shaking dice when Selman shot him from behind. One year later Deputy United States Marshal George Scarborough killed Selman in a duel. Shortly after this Scarborough was slain in a gunfight by "Kid" Curry, an Arizona bandit.

What was true of these towns was true, too, of Albuquerque and Las Vegas and Tombstone. Each of them chose for peace officers men who were "sudden death" with a gun. Dodge did exactly the same thing. Even a partial list of its successive marshals reads like a fighting roster. In addition to Bridges and Brooks may be named Ed and Bat Masterson, Wyatt Earp, Billy Tilghman, Ben Daniels, Mysterious Dave Mathers, T. C. Nixon, Luke Short, Charlie Bassett, W. H. Harris, and Sughrue brothers, all of them famous as fighters in a day when courage and proficiency with weapons were a matter of course. On one occasion the superintendent of the Santa Fe suggested to the city dads of Dodge that it might be a good thing to employ marshals less notorious. Dodge begged leave to differ. It felt that the best way to "settle the hash" of desperadoes was to pit against them fighting machines more efficient, bad men more deadly than themselves.

The word "bad" does not necessarily imply evil. One who held the epithet was known as one dangerous to oppose. He was unafraid, deadly with a gun, and hard as nails. He might be evil, callous, treacherous, revengeful as an Apache. Dave Mathers fitted this description. He might be a good man, kindly, gentle, never taking more than his fighting chance. This was Billy Tillman to a T.

We are keeping Billy Brooks waiting. But let that go. Let us look first at "Mysterious Dave." Bob Wright has set it down that Mathers had more dead man to his credit than any other man in the West. He slew seven by actual count in one night, in one house, according to Wright. Mathers had a very bad reputation. But his courage could blaze up magnificently. While he was deputy marshal word came that the Henry gang of desperadoes were terrorizing a dance hall. Into that hall walked Dave, beside his chief Tom Carson. Five minutes later out reeled Carson, both arms broken, his body shot through and through, a man with only five minutes to live. When the smoke in the hall cleared away Mathers might have been seen beside two handcuffed prisoners, one of them wounded. In a circle around him were four dead cowpunchers of the Henry outfit.

"Uncle" Billy Tilghman died the other day at Cromwell, Oklahoma, a victim of his own fearlessness. He was shot to death while taking a revolver from a drunken prohibition agent. If he had been like many other bad men he would have shot the fellow down at the first sign of danger. But that was never Tilghman's way. It was his habit to make arrests without drawing a gun. He cleaned up Dodge during the three years while he was marshal. He broke up the Doolin gang, killing Bill Raidler and "Little" Dick in personal duels and capturing Bill Doolin the leader. Bat Masterson said that during Tilghman's term as sheriff of Lincoln County, Oklahoma, he killed, captured, or drove from the country more criminals than any other official that section had ever had. Yet "Uncle" Billy never used a gun except reluctantly. Time and again he gave the criminal the first shot, hoping the man would surrender rather than fight. Of all the old frontier sheriffs none holds a higher place than Billy Tilghman.

After which diversion we return to Billy Brooks, a "gent" of an impatient temperament, not used to waiting, and notably quick on the trigger. Mr. Dubbs records that late one evening in the winter '72–'73 he returned to Dodge with two loads of buffalo meat. He finished his business, ate supper, and started to smoke a postprandial pipe. The sound of a fusillade in an adjoining dance hall interested him since he had been deprived of the pleasures of metropolitan life for some time and had had to depend upon Indians for excitement. (Incidentally, it may be mentioned that they furnished him with a reasonable amount. Not long after this three of his men were caught, spread-eagled, and tortured by Indians. Dubbs escaped after a hair-raising ride and arrived at Adobe Walls in time to take part in the historic defense of that post by a handful of buffalo hunters against many hundred tribesmen.) From the building burst four men. They started across the railroad track to another dance hall, one frequented by Brooks. Dubbs heard the men mention the name of Brooks, coupling it with an oath. Another buffalo hunter named Fred Singer joined Dubbs. They followed the strangers, and just before the four reached the dance hall Singer shouted a warning to the marshal. This annoyed the unknown four, and they promptly exchanged shots with the buffalo hunters. What then took place was startling in the sudden drama of it.

Billy Brooks stood in bold relief in the doorway, a revolver in each hand. He fired so fast that Dubbs says the sounds were like a company discharging weapons. When the smoke cleared Brooks still stood in the same place. Two of the strangers were dead and two mortally wounded. They were brothers. They had come from Hays City to avenge the death of a fifth brother shot down by Brooks some time before.

Mr. Brooks had a fondness for the fair sex. He and Browney, the yardmaster, took a fancy to the same girl. Captain Drew, she was called, and she preferred Browney. Whereupon Brooks naturally shot him in the head. Perversely, to the surprise of everybody, Browney recovered and was soon back at his old job.

Brooks seems to have held no grudge at him from making light of his marksmanship in this manner. At any rate, his next affair was with Kirk Jordan, the buffalo hunter. This was a very different business. Jordan had been in a hundred tight holes. He had fought Indians time and again. Professional killers had no terror for him. He threw down his big buffalo gun on Brooks, and the latter took cover. Barrels of water had been placed along the principal streets for fire protection. These had saved several lives during shooting scrapes. Brooks ducked behind one, and the ball from Jordan's gun plunged into it. The marshal dodged into a store, out of the rear door, and into a livery stable. He was hidden under a bed. Alas! for a large reputation gone glimmering. Mr. Brooks fled to the fort, took the train from the siding, and shook forever the dust of Dodge from his feet. Whither he departed deponent sayeth not.

How do I explain this? I don't. I record a fact. Many gunmen were at one time or another subject to these panics during which the yellow streak showed. Not all of them by any means, but a very considerable percentage. They swaggered boldly, killed recklessly. Then one day some quiet little man with a cold gray eye called the turn on them, after which they oozed out of the surrounding scenery.

Owen P. White gives it on the authority of Charlie Siringo that Bat Masterson sang small when Clay Allison of the Panhandle, he of the well-notched gun, drifted into Dodge and inquired for the city marshal. But the old-timers at Dodge do not bear this out. Bat was at the Adobe Walls fight, one of fourteen men who stood off five hundred bucks of the Cheyenne, Comanche, and Kiowa tribes. He scouted for miles. He was elected sheriff of Ford County, with headquarters at Dodge when only twenty-two years of age. It was a tough assignment, and Bat executed it to the satisfaction of all concerned except the element he cowed.

Personally, I never met Bat until his killing days were past. He was dealing faro at a gambling house in Denver when I, a young reporter, first had the pleasure of looking into his cold blue eyes. It was a notable fact that all the frontier bad man had eyes either gray or blue, often a faded blue, expressionless, hard as jade.

It is only fair to Bat that the old-timers of Dodge do not accept the Siringo point of view about him. Wright said of him that he was absolutely fearless and no trouble hunter. "Bat is a gentleman by instinct, of pleasant matters, good address, and mild until aroused, and then, for God's sake, look out. He is a leader of men, has much natural ability, and good hard common sense. There is nothing low about him. He is high-toned and broad-minded, cool and brave." I give this opinion for what it is worth.

In any case, he was a most efficient sheriff. Dave Rudabaugh, later associated with Billy the Kid in New Mexico, staged a train robbery at Kingsley, Kansas, a territory not in Bat's jurisdiction. However, Bat set out in pursuit with a posse. A near-blizzard was sweeping the country. Bat made for Lovell's cattle camp, on the chance that the bandits would be forced to take shelter there. It was a good guess. Rudabaugh's outfit rode in, stiff and half frozen, and Bat captured the robbers without firing a shot. This was one of many captures Bat made.

He had a deep sense of loyalty to his friends. On two separate occasions he returned to Dodge, after having left the town, to straighten out difficulties for his friends or to avenge them. The first time was when Luke Short, who ran a gambling house in Dodge, had a difficulty with Mayor Webster and his official family. Luke appears to have held the opinion that the cards were stacked against him and that this was a trouble out of which he could not shoot himself. He wired Bat Masterson and Wyatt Earp to come to Dodge. They did, accompanied by another friend or two. The mayor made peace on terms dictated by Short.

Bat's second return to Dodge was caused by a wire from his brother James, who ran a dance hall in partnership with a man named Peacock. Masterson wanted to discharge the bartender, Al Updegraph, a brother-in-law of the other partner. A serious difficulty loomed in the offing. Wherefore James called for help. Bat arrived at eleven one sunny morning, another gunman at heel. At three o'clock he entrained for Tombstone, Arizona, James beside him. The interval had been busy one. On the way up from the station (always known then as the depot), the two men met Peacock and Updegraph. No amenities were exchanged. It was strictly business. Bullets began to sing at once. The men stood across the street from each other and emptied their weapons. Oddly enough, Updegraph was the only one wounded. This little matter attended to, Bat surrendered himself, was fined three dollars for carrying concealed weapons, and released. He ate dinner, disposed of his brother's interest in the saloon, and returned to the station.

Bat Masterson was a friend of Theodore Roosevelt, who was given to admiring men with "guts," such men as Pat Garrett, Ben Daniels, and Billy Tilghman. Mr. Roosevelt offered Masterson a place as United States Marshal of Arizona. The ex-sheriff declined it. "If I took it," he explained, I'd have to kill some fool boy who wanted to get a reputation by killing me." The President then offered Bat a place as Deputy United States Marshal of New York, and this was accepted. From that time Masterson became a citizen of the Empire State. For seventeen years he worked on a newspaper there and died a few years since with a pen in his hand. He was respected by the entire newspaper fraternity.

Owing to the pleasant habit of the cowboys of shooting up the town they were required, when entering the city limits, to hand over their weapons to the marshal. The guns were deposited at Wright & Beverly's Store, in a rack built for the purpose, and receipts given for them. Sometimes a hundred six-shooters would be there at once. These were never returned to their owners unless the cowboys were sober.

To be a marshal of one of these fighting frontier towns was no post to be sought for by a supple politician. The place called for a chilled iron nerve and an uncanny skill with the Colt. Tom Smith, one of the gamest men and best officers who ever wore a star on the frontier, was killed in the performance of his duty. Colonel Breackenridge says that Smith, marshal of Abilene before "Wild Bill," was the gamest man he ever knew. He was a powerful, athletic man who would arrest, himself unarmed, the most desperate characters. He once told Breackenridge that anyone could bring in a dead man but it took a good officer to take lawbreakers while they were alive. In this he differed from Hickok who did not take chances. He brought his men in dead. Nixon, assistant marshal at

Dodge, was murdered by "Mysterious Dave" Mathers, who himself once held the same post. Ed Masterson after displaying conspicuous courage many times, was mortally wounded April 9, 1878, by two desperate men, Jack Wagner and Alf Walker, who were terrorizing Front Street. Bat reached the scene a few minutes later and heard the story. As soon as his brother had died Bat went after the desperadoes, met them, and killed them both. The death of Ed Masterson shocked the town. Civil organizations passed resolutions of respect. During the funeral, which was the largest ever held in Dodge, all business houses were closed. It is not on record that anybody regretted the demise of the marshal's assassins.

Among those who came to Dodge each season to meet the Texas cattle drive were Ben and Bill Thompson, gamblers who ran a faro bank. Previously they had been accustomed to go to Ellsworth, while that point was the terminus of the drive. Here they had ruled with a high hand, killed the sheriff, and made their getaway safely. Bill got into a shooting affray at Ogalala. He was badly wounded and was carried to the hotel. It was announced openly that he would never leave town alive. Ben did not dare go to Ogalala, for his record there outlawed him. He came to Bat Masterson.

Bat knew Bill's nurse and arranged a plan for campaign. A sham battle was staged at the big dance hall, during the excitement of which Bat and the nurse carried the wounded man to the train, got him to a sleeper, and into a bed. Buffalo Bill met them the next day at North Platte. He had relays of teams stationed on the road, and he and Bat guarded the sick man during the long ride bringing him safely to Dodge.

Emanuel Dubbs ran a roadhouse not far from Dodge about this time. He was practising with his six-shooter one day when a splendidly built young six-footer rode up to his place. The stranger watched him as he fired at the tin cans he had put on fence posts. Presently the young fellow suggested he throw a couple of the cans up in the air. Dubbs did so. Out flashed the stranger's revolvers. There was a roar of exploding shots. Dubbs picked up the cans. Four shots had been fired. Two bullets had drilled through each can.

"Better not carry his six-shooter till you learned shoot," Bill Cody suggested, as he put his guns back into their holsters. "You'll be a living temptation to some bad man." Buffalo Bill was on his way back to the North Platte.

Life at Dodge was not all tragic. The six-shooter roared in the land a good deal, but there were very many citizens who went quietly about their business and took no part in the nightlife of the town. It was entirely optional with the individual. The little city had its legitimate theatres as well as its hurdy-gurdy houses and gambling dens. There was the Lady Gay, for instance, a popular vaudeville resort. There were well-attended churches. But Dodge boiled so with exuberant young life, often inflamed by bad liquor, that both theatre and church were likely to be the scenes of unexpected explosions.

A drunken cowboy became annoyed at Eddie Foy. While the comedian was reciting "Kalamazoo in Michigan" the puncher began bombarding the frail walls from the outside with a .45 Colt's revolver. Eddie made a swift strategic retreat. A deputy marshal was standing near the cowpuncher, who was astride a plunging horse. The deputy fired twice. The first shot missed. The second brought the rider down. He was dead before he hit the ground. The deputy apologized later for his marksmanship, but he added by way of explanation, "the bronc sure was sunfishin' plenty."

The killing of Miss Dora Hand, a young actress of much promise, was regretted by everybody in Dodge. A young fellow named Kennedy, the son of a rich cattleman, shot her unintentionally while he was trying to murder James Kelly. He fled. A posse composed of Sheriff Masterson, William Tilghman, Wyatt Earp, and Charles Bassett took the trail. They captured the man after wounding him desperately. He was brought back to Dodge, recovered, and escaped. His pistol arm was useless, but he used the other well enough to slay several other victims before someone made an end of him.

The gay good spirits of Dodge found continual expression in practical jokes. The wilder these were the better pleased was the town. "Mysterious Dave" was the central figure in one. An evangelist was conducting a series of meetings. He made a powerful magnetic appeal, and many were the hard characters who walked the sawdust trail. The preacher set his heart on converting Dave Mathers, the worst of bad men and a notorious scoffer. The meetings prospered. The church grew too small for the crowds and adjourned to a dance hall. Dave became interested. He went to hear Brother Johnson preach. He went a second time and a third. "He certainly preaches like the Watsons and goes for sin all spraddled out," Dave conceded. Brother Johnson grew hopeful. It seemed possible that this brand could be snatched from the burning. He preached directly at Dave, and Dave buried his head in his hands and sobbed. The preacher said he was willing to die if he could convert this one vile sinner. Others of the deacons agreed that they too, would not object to going straight to heaven with the knowledge that Dave had been saved.

"They were right excited an' didn't know straight up," an old-timer explained. "Dave, he looked so whipped his ears flopped. Finally he rose, an' said, 'I've got yore company, friends. Now, while we're all saved I reckon we better start straight for heaven. First off, the preacher; then the deacons; me last.' Then Dave whips out a whoppin' big gun and starts to shootin'. The preacher went right through a window an' took it with him. He was sure in some hurry. The deacons hunted cover. Seemed like they was willin' to postpone taking that through ticket to heaven. After that they never did worry anymore about Dave's soul."

Many rustlers gathered around Dodge in those days. The most notorious of these was a gang of more than thirty under the leadership of Dutch Henry and Tom Owens, two of the most desperate outlaws ever known in Kansas. A posse was organized to run down this gang under the leadership of Dubbs, who had lost some of his stock. Before starting, the posse telephoned Hays City to organize a company to head off the rustlers. Twenty miles west of Hays the posse overtook the rustlers. A bloody battle ensued, during which Owens and several other outlaws were killed and Dutch Henry wounded six times. Several of the posse were also shot. The story has a curious sequel. Many years later, when Emanuel Dubbs was county judge of Wheeler County, Texas, Dutch Henry came to his house and stayed there several days. He was a thoroughly reformed man. Not many years ago Dutch Henry died in Colorado. He was a man with many good qualities. Even in his outlaw days he had many friends among the law-abiding citizens.

After the battle with Henry Owens gang rustlers operated much more quietly, but they did not cease stealing. One night three men were hanged on a cottonwood on Saw Log Creek, ten or twelve miles from Dodge. One of these was a young man of a good family who had drifted into rustling and had been carried away by the excitement of it. Another of the three was the son of Tom Owens. To this day the place is known as Horse Thief Cañon. During its years of prosperity many eminent men visited Dodge including Generals Sherman and Sheridan, President Hayes and General Miles. Its reputation had extended far and wide. It was the wild and woolly cowboy capital of the Southwest, a place to quicken the blood of any man. Nearly all that gay, hard-riding company of cowpunchers, buffalo hunters, bad men, and pioneers have vanished into yesterday's seven thousand years. But certainly Dodge once had its day and its night of glory. No more rip-roaring town ever bucked the tiger.

End of the Trail
(Cowboy Logic and Frolic)

BY EDGAR BEECHER BRONSON

Once he finally reaches the lower trail, with his herd in good order, even the worrying-est trail boss finds himself letting up a little on the men; and they discover themselves unaccountably dreaming of a hot bath, clean duds, a real bed, and a little frolic in the town; mostly this latter. And you know what? Ain't nothin' gonna stand in the way of their little piece of cowboy heaven. No stampede. No flash flood. No nothin' is gonna keep them from their frolic!

Edgar Beecher Bronson (1856–1917) was Nebraska rancher, West Texas cattleman, African big-game hunter, a serious photographer and a darn good writer, though he came to this last fairly late in his life. He published *Reminiscences of a Ranchman* (from which this story is taken) in 1908, and on the strength of its success, published *The Red-Blooded Heroes of the Frontier* and *In Closed Territory* (with nearly 100 illustrations from photos by the author) in 1910. In 1914 he published his final work *The Vanguard*.

★   ★   ★   ★   ★

We were jogging along in the saddle across the divide between the Rawhide and the Niobrara, Concho Curly and I, *en route* from Cheyenne to the ranch to begin the spring calf round-up.

Travelling the lower trail, we had slept out on our saddle-blankets the night before, beside the sodden wreck of a fire in a little cottonwood grove on Rawhide.

While the night there passed was wretched and comfortless to the last degree, for even our slickers were an insufficient protection against the torrents of warm rain that fell upon us hour after hour, the curtain of gray morning mists that hedged us round about was scarce lifted at bidding of the new day's sun, before eyes, ears, and nostrils told us Nature had wrought one of her great miracles while we slept.

All seed life, somnolent so long in whatever earthly cells the winds and rains had assisted to entomb it, had awakened and arisen into a living force; tree vitality, long hibernating invisible, even in sorely wounded, lightning-riven, gray cottonwood torsos, was asserting itself; voices long still, absent God alone knows where, were gladly hailing the return of the spring.

We had lain down in a dull gray dead world, to awaken in a world pulsing with the life and bright with the colour of sprouting seed and re-vivifying sap.

Our eyes had closed on tree trunks gaunt and pale, a veritable spectral wood; on wide stretches of buffalo grass, withered yellow and prone upon the ground, the funereal aspect of the land heightened by the grim outlines of two Sioux warriors lashed on pole platforms for their last resting-place in the branches above our heads, fragments of a faded red blanket pendent and flapping in the wind beneath one body, a blue blanket beneath the other, grisly neighbours who appeared to approach or recede as our fire alternately blazed and flickered—both plainly warriors, for beneath each lay the whitening bones of his favourite war pony, killed by his tribesmen to provide him a mount in the Spirit Land.

It was a voiceless, soundless night before the storm came, bar the soughing of the wind, the weary creaking of bare branches, the feeble murmur of the brook (drunk almost dry by the thirsty land), and the flap-flap of our neighbours' last raiment.

Our eyes opened upon trees crowned with the pale green glory of bursting buds, upon valley and hill slopes verdant as the richest meadow; our ears were greeted with the sweet voices of birds chanting a welcome to the spring, and the rollicking song of a brimful stream, merry over the largess it now bore for man and beast and bird and plant, while the sweet, humid scents of animate, palpitant nature had driven from our nostrils the dry, horrid odours of the dead.

So comes the spring on the plains—in a single night!

Concho Curly was a raw, unlettered, freckled product of a Texas pioneer's cabin isolated in a nook of the west slope of the hills about the head of the Concho River, near where they pitch down to the waterless, arid reaches of the staked plains.

But the miracle of the spring, appealing to the universal love of the mysterious, had set even Curly's untrained brain questioning and philosophising.

After riding an hour or more silent, his chin buried in the loose folds of his neckerchief, Curly sighed deeply and then observed:

"Ol' man, hit shore 'pears to me Ol' Mahster hain't never strained Hisself none serious tryin' to divide up even the good things o' this yere world o' ourn. Looks like He never tried none, an' ef He did, He's shore made a pow'ful pore job!"

"Why, Curley," I asked, "what makes you think so?"

"Some fellers has so dod-blamed much an' some so dod-burned little," he replied. "Why, back whar you-all comes from, thar's oodles o' grass an' fodder an' water the hull year, ain't they, while out here frequent hit's so fur from grass to water th' critters goes hungry to drink an' dry to graze—don't they?"

"Quite true, Curly," I admitted.

"Wall, back thar, then, 'most every feller must be rich, an' have buggies an' ambulances plenty, an' a big gallery round his *jacal*, an' nothin' to do but set on her all day studdyin' what new bunch o' prittys he'll buy for his woman, an' wettin' his whistle frequent with rot-gut to he'p his thinker *select* new kinds o' throat-ticklin' grub to feed his face an' new kinds o' humany quilts an' goose-hair pillers to git to lay on, while out here a hull passle o' fellers is so dod-burned pore they don't even own a name, an' hull families lives 'n' dies 'thout ever gittin' to set in a buggy or to eat anythin' but co'n pone an' sow belly, 'thout no fixin's or dulces to chase them, like th' puddin's an' ice cream you gits to town ef you've got th' spondulix an' are willin' to blow yourse'f reckless.

"On th' level, you cain't make me believe Ol' Mahster had any-thin' to do with th' makin' o' these yere parts out yere—ef He had, He'd a shore give us fellers a squarer deal; 'pears to me like when His job was nigh done an' He was sorta tired an' restin', the boys musta got loose an' throwed this part o' th' country together, kinda careless-like, outen th' leavin's."

And on and on he monologued, plucking an occasional "yes" or "no" from me, till apparently a new line of reflection diverted him and he fell silent to study where it might lead him.

Presently, when I was lolling comfortably in the saddle, half doz-ing, he nudged me in the ribs with the butt of his quirt and remarked:

"Say, ol' man! I reckon I musta been sleep-walkin' an' eatin' loco weed, for I been arguin' plumb wrong.

"Come to think o' hit, while we-all that's pore has to work outra-geous to make a skimp of a livin', you-all that's rich has to work a scan-dalous sight harder to git to keep what you got.

"An' then there's ice! Jest think o' ice! Th' rich has her in th' sum-mer, but d—n me ef th' pore don't get her in th' winter, good an' plenty—makin' hit look like th' good things o' this world is whacked up mighty nigh even, after all, an' that we-all hain't got no roar comin' to us."

Thus happily settled his recent worries, Curly himself dropped into a contented doze, and left me to resume mine.

The season opening promised to be an unusually busy one. It was obvious we were nearing the crest of a three-years' boom. Wild range cattle were selling at higher prices than ever before or since. The Chicago beef-market was correspondingly strong. But there were signs of a reaction that made me anxious to gather and ship my fat beeves soon as possible, before the tide turned.

Every winter two thirds of my herd drifted before the bitter blizzards southeast into the sand hills lying between the sink of Snake Creek and the head of the Blue, a splendid winter range where snow never lay long, and out of which cattle came in the spring in unusually good condition.

Thus, at the end of the spring round-up, I was able to cut fifteen hundred beef steers that, after being grazed under close herd a few weeks on the better-cured, stronger feed on the divide between the Niobrara and Snake Creek, were fit for market, and with them we arrived at our shipping point—Ogallala—July 2, 1882.

Leaving the outfit camped, luckily, on a bench twenty feet above the main valley of the Platte, I rode two miles into town to make shipping arrangements.

A wonderful sight was the Platte Valley about Ogallala in those days, for it was the northern terminus of the great Texas trail of the late '70s and early '80s, where trail-drivers brought their herds to sell and northern ranchmen came to bargain.

That day, far as the eye could see up, down, and across the broad, level valley were cattle by the thousand—thirty or forty thousand at least—a dozen or more separate outfits, grazing in loose, open order so near each other that, at a distance, the valley appeared carpeted with a vast Persian rug of intricate design and infinite variety of colours.

Approached nearer, where individual riders and cattle began to take form, it was a topsy-turvy scene I looked down upon.

The day was unusually, tremendously hot—probably 112° in the shade—so hot the shimmering heat-waves developed a mirage that turned town, herds, and riders upside down—all sprung in an instant to gigantic height, the squat frame houses tall as modern skyscrapers, cattle and riders big as elephants, while here and there deep blue lakes lay placidly over broad expanses that a few moments before were a solid field of variegated, brilliant colours.

Arrived at the Spofford House, the one hotel of the town, I found a familiar bunch of famous Texas cattle kings—Seth Mayberry, Shanghai Pierce, Dillon Fant, Jim Ellison, John Lytle, Dave Hunter, Jess Presnall, etc.—each with a string of long horns for sale.

The one store and the score of saloons, dance-halls, and gambling joints that lined up south of the railway track and formed the only street Ogallala could boast, were packed with wild and woolly, long-haired and bearded, rent and dusty, lusting and thirsty, red-sashed brush-splitters in from the trail outfits for a frolic.

And every now and then a chorus of wild, shrill yells and a fusillade of shots rent the air that would make a tenderfoot think a battle-royal was on.

But there was nothing serious doing, then; it was only cowboy frolic.

The afternoon's fierce heat proved a weather breeder, as some had predicted.

Shortly after supper, but long before sundown, a dense black cloud suddenly rose in the north, swept swiftly above and around us till it filled the whole zenith—an ominous, low-hanging pall that brought upon us in a few minutes the utter darkness of a starless night.

Quite as suddenly as the coming of the cloud, the temperature fell 40° or 50°, and drove us into the hotel.

And we were little more than sheltered behind closed doors before torrents of rain descended, borne on gusts of hurricane force that blew open the north door of the dining-room, picked up a great pin-pool board standing across a biscuit-shooting opening in the partition, swept it across the breadth of the office, narrowly missing Mayberry and Fant, and dashed it to splinters against the opposite wall.

Ten minutes later the violence of rain and downpour slackened, almost stopped.

Shanghai went to the door and looked out, shivered, and shut it with the remark:

"By cripes, fellers! 'pears like Ol' Mahster plumb emptied His tanks that clatter; the hull flat's under water."

"Maybe so He's stackin' us up agin' a swimmin' match," was Fant's cheerful comment.

And within another ten minutes it certainly seemed Fant had called the turn.

A tremendous crash of thunder came, with lightning flashes that illumined the room till our oil lamps looked like fireflies, followed by another tornado-driven downpour it seemed hopeless to expect the house could survive.

And while our ears were still stunned by its first roar, suddenly there came flood waters pouring in over door-sills and through floor cracks, rising at a rate that instantly drove us all to refuge on the second floor of the hotel.

We were certainly in the track, if not the centre, of a waterspout!

But barely were we upstairs before the aerial flood-gates closed, till no more than an ordinary heavy soaking of rain was falling, and the wind slackened sufficiently to permit us to climb out on the roof of the porch and take stock of the situation.

Our case looked grave enough—grave past hope of escape, or even help.

"Fellers," quietly remarked Shanghai, "here's a game where passin' don't go—leastwise till it's cash in an' pass out o' existence. Here's where I'd sell my chance o' seein' to-morrow's sun at a dollar a head, an' agree not to tally more'n about five head. I've been up agin' Yankee charges, where the air was full of lead and the cold steel 'peared to hide all the rest of the scenery; I've laid in a buffalo wallow two days and nights surrounded by Comanches, and been bush-whacked by Kiowas on the Palo Pinto, but never till now has Shanghai been up agin' a game he couldn't figure out a way to beat."

And so, in truth, it looked.

The whole world was afloat, a raging, tossing flood—our world, at least.

To us a universal flood could mean no more.

Far as the eye could see rolled waters.

And the waters were rising all the time, ever rising, higher and higher; not creeping, but rising, leaping up the pillars of the porch!

It seemed only a matter of moments before the hotel must collapse, or be swept from its foundations.

Already the flood beneath us was dotted thick with drifting flotsam—wrecks of houses, fences, stables, sidewalks.

Men, women, and children were afloat upon the wreckage, drifting they knew not where, safe they knew not how long, shrieking for aid no one could lend.

Dumb beasts and fowls drifted by us, their inarticulate terror cries rising shrill above the piping of the wind—cattle bawling, pigs squealing, dogs howling, horses neighing, chickens clucking madly, and even the ducks and geese quacking notes of alarm.

It seemed the end of the world, no less—at least, of our little corner of it.

However the old Spofford House held to her foundations was a mystery, unless she stood without the line of the strongest current.

But hold she stoutly did until, perhaps fifteen minutes after we were driven upstairs, word was passed out to us by watchers within upon the staircase that the rise had stopped—stopped just about half-way between floor and ceiling of the first story.

And right then, just as we were catching our breath to interchange congratulations, a new terror menaced us—a terror even more appalling than the remorseless flood that still held us in its grip.

An inky-black pall of cloud still shut out the stars and shrouded all the earth, but a pall so riven and torn by constantly recurring flashes of sheet-lightning that our entire field of view was lit almost as bright as by a midday sun.

Suddenly, off in the south, over the divide between the Platte and the Republican, an ominous shape uprose like magic from below the horizon—a balloon-shaped cloud of an ashen-gray that, from reflection of the lightning or other cause, had a sort of phosphorescent glow that outlined its form against the inky background and made plain to our eyes, as the hand held before one's face, that we confronted an approaching cyclone.

Nearing us it certainly was at terrific speed, for it grew and grew as we looked till its broad dome stood half up to the zenith, while its narrow tail was lashing viciously about near and often apparently upon the earth.

On it came, head-on for us, for a space of perhaps four minutes—until, I am sure, any onlooker who had a prayer loose about him was not idle.

And perhaps (who knows?) one or another such appeal prevailed, for just as it seemed no earthly power could save us, off eastward it switched and sped swiftly out of our sight.

It was near midnight before the waters began to fall, and morning before the house was free of them.

And when about eight o'clock horses were brought us, we had to wade and swim them about a quarter of a mile to reach the dry uplands.

From the roof of the hotel we could see that even the trail herds were badly scattered and commingled, and it was the general opinion my herd of un-trail-broke wild beef steers were probably running yet, somewhere.

But when I got out to the benchland where I had left them, there they were, not a single one missing. This to my infinite surprise, for usually an ordinary thunderstorm will drift beef herds more or less, if not actually stampede them.

The reason was quickly explained: the storm had descended upon them so suddenly and with such extraordinary violence that they were stunned into immobility.

Apparently they had been directly beneath the very centre of the waterspout, for the boys told me the rain fell in such solid sheets that they nearly smothered, drowned while mounted and sitting their saddles about the trembling, bellowing herd; came down in such torrents they had to hold their hands in shape of an inverted cup above nose and mouth to get their breath!

Miles of the U.P. track were destroyed that laid us up for three days, awaiting repairs.

The first two days the little village was quiet, trail men out bunching and separating their herds, townsmen taking stock of their losses.

But the third day hell popped good and plenty.

Tempers were so fiery and feelings so tindery that it seemed the recent violence of the very elements themselves had got into men's veins and made them bent to destroy and to kill.

All day long street and saloon swarmed with shouting, quarrelling, shooting punchers, owners and peace officers were alike powerless to control.

About noon the town marshal and several deputies made a bold try to quell the turmoil—and then had to mount and ride for their lives, leaving two of Hunter & Evans's men dead in front of The Cowboys' Rest, and a string of wounded along the street.

This incident stilled the worst of the tumult for two or three hours, for many took up pursuit of the marshal, while the rest were for a time content to quietly talk over the virtues of the departed in the intervals between quadrille-sets—for, of course, the dancing went on uninterrupted.

Toward evening, notwithstanding the orgy had again resumed a fast and furious pace, Fant, Mayberry, and myself were tempted to join the crowd in The Cowboys' Rest, tempted by glimpses of a scene caught from our perch on a corner of the depot platform opposite.

"That *is* blamed funny!" remarked Mayberry. "Come along over and let's see her good. We're no more liable to get leaded there than anywhere else."

So over we went.

"The Rest" belied its name sadly, for rest was about the only thing Jim Tucker was not prepared to furnish his wild and woolly patrons.

Who entered there left coin behind—and was lucky if he left no more.

Stepped within the door, a rude pine "bar" on the right invited the thirsty; on the left, noisy "tin horns," whirring wheels, clicking faro "cases," and rattling chips lured the gamblers; while away to the rear of the room stretched a hundred feet or more of dance-hall, on each of whose rough benches sat enthroned a temptress—hard of eye, deep-lined of face, decked with cheap gauds, sad wrecks of the sea of vice here lurching and tossing for a time.

As we entered, Mayberry's foreman met us and whispered to his boss:

"You-all better stan' back a little, colonel, out o' line o' th' door. Ol' one-eyed John Graham, o' th' Hunter outfit, settin' thar in th' corner's layin' fo' th' sheriff—allows 'twas him sot up th' marshal to shell us up this mo'nin'—an' ol' John's shore pizen when he starts."

So back we moved to the rear end of the bar.

The room was packed: a solid line of men and women before the bar, every table the centre of a crowding group of players, the dance-hall floor and benches jam-full of a roistering, noisy throng.

At the moment all were happy and peace reigned.

But there was one obvious source of discord—there were "not enough gals to go round"; not enough, indeed, if those present had been multiplied by ten, a situation certain to stir jealousies and strife among a lot of wild nomads for whom this was the first chance in four months to gaze into a woman's eyes.

To be sure, one resourceful and unselfish puncher—a foreman of one of the trail outfits—was doing *his* best to relieve the prevailing deficiency in feminine dancers, and it was a distant glimpse of his efforts that had brought us over.

Bearing, if not boasting, the proud old Dutch name of Jake De Puyster, this rollicking six-foot-two blond giant had heard Buck Groner growl:

"Hain't had airy show for a dance yet. Nairy heifer's throwed her eye my way 'fore she's been roped and tied in about a second. Reckon it's shoot for one or pull my freight for camp, and I ain't sleepy none."

"You stake you'self out, son, a few minutes, and I'll git you a she-pardner you'll be glad of a chance to dance with and buy prittys for," reassured Jake, and then disappeared.

Ten minutes later he returned, bringing Buck a partner that stopped drinking, dance, and play—the most remarkably clad figure that ever entered even a frontier dance-hall.

Still wearing his usual costume—wide chaps, spurred heels, and belt—having removed nothing but his tall-crowned Mexican sombrero, Jake had mavericked three certain articles of feminine apparel and contrived to get himself into them.

Cocked jauntily over his right eye he wore a bright red toque crowned with a faded wreath of pale blue flowers, from which a bedraggled green feather drooped wearily over his left ear; about his waist wrinkled a broad pink sash, tied in a great double bow-knot set squarely in front, while fastened also about his waist, pendent no more than midway of his long thighs, hung a garment white of colour, filmy of fabric, bifurcated of form, richly ruffled of extremity—so habited came Jake, and, with a broad grin lurking within the mazes of his great bushy beard and monstrous moustache, sidled mincing to his mate and shyly murmured a hint he might have the privilege of the next quadrille.

At first Buck was furious, growled, and swore to kill Jake for the insult, until, infected by the gales of laughter that swept the room, he awkwardly offered his arm and led his weird partner to an unfilled set.

And a sorry hour was this to the other ladies; for, while there were better dancers and prettier, that first quadrille made "Miss De Puyster" the belle of the ball for the rest of the day and night, and not a few serious affrays over disputes for an early chance of a "round" or "square" with her were narrowly avoided.

Just as we reached the rear end of the bar, the fiddles stopped their cruel liberties with the beautiful measures of "*Sobre las Olas*," and Buck led his panting partner up to our group and courteously introduced us thus:

"Miss De Puyster, here's two mighty slick ol' long-horn mossbacks you wants to be pow'ful shy of, for they'd maverick off their own daddy, an' a little short-horn Yankee orfun I wants to ax you to adopt an' try to make a good mother to. Fellers, this yere's Miss De Puyster; she ain't much for pretty, but she's hell for active on th' floor—so dod-burned active I couldn't tell whether she was waltzin' or tryin' to throw me side-holts."

But before we had time to properly make our aknowledgements, a new figure in the dance was called—a figure which, though familiar enough in Ogallala dance-halls, distracted and held the attention of all present for a few minutes.

Later we learned that, early in the day, a local celebrity—Bill Thompson by name, a tin horn by trade, and a desperado by pretence—had proffered some insult to Big Alice, the leading lady of the house, for which Jim Tucker had "called him down good and plenty," but under such circumstances that to resent it then would have been to court a fairer fight than Bill's kind ever willingly took on.

But, remembering he was brother to Ben Thompson, the then most celebrated man-killer in the State of Texas (who himself was to fall to King Fisher's pistol in Jack Harris's San Antonio variety theatre a few years later), brooding Tucker's abuse of him, figuring what Ben would do in like circumstances illumining his view of the situation by frequent resorts to red eye, Bill by evening had rowled himself ready for action.

So it happened that at the very moment Buck finished our introduction to "Miss De Puyster," Bill suddenly stepped within the door of the saloon and took a quick snapshot at Tucker, who was directly across the bar from us and in the act of passing Fant a glass of whisky with his left hand.

The ball cut off three of Tucker's fingers and the tip of the fourth, and, the bar being narrow, spattered us with his blood.

Tucker fell, momentarily, from the shock.

Supposing from Tucker's quick drop he had made an instant kill, Bill stuck his pistol in his waistband and started leisurely out of the door and down the street.

But no sooner was he out of the house than Jim sprang up, seized a sawed-off ten-gauge shotgun, ran to the door, leveled the gun across the stump of his maimed left hand, and emptied into Bill's back at about six paces, a trifle more No. 4 duckshot than his system could assimilate.

Perhaps altogether ten minutes were wasted on this incident and the time taken to tourniquet and tie up Jim's wound and to pack Bill inside and stow him in a corner behind the faro lookout's chair; and then Jim's understudy called, "Pardners fo' th' next dance!" the fiddlers bravely tackled but soon got hopelessly beyond their depth in "The Blue Danube," and dancing and frolic were resumed, with "Miss De Puyster" still the belle of the ball.

The Quest Begins

BY MAX BRAND

A nice slice of Max Brand cowboy story here. You got the cowboy and the boss-man, and the other fellers. You got the horse, and all the cowboy stuff. You got a pretty girl. And Lord, does it move.

Max Brand is a pseudonym for the author Fredrick Faust. This pen name is a sort of double pun. The first name, *Max,* could simply be short for Maximillian—a clue to, or assertion of the author's ethnicity; or it could stand boastfully for maximum—the first, the biggest, the best. Just so, *Brand* suggests the mark of ownership on a head of livestock, but it is also used in the sense of a particular product, a brand name.

Faust considered himself first a poet; indeed, his ambition was to be a quill pen poet, which suggests a good deal, because a quill pen poet must not only write poetry, but must *imagine himself to be* a poet writing poetry. I think he had near total committment, and thereby a lot of access to the life of his own imagination, and that this is exactly how he was able, with such apparent ease, to make stories, create whole worlds about which he knew little or nothing. Though born on the west coast he was by no means what we would call a Westerner for him the wide open spaces held no allure. He was a big-city dweller and lived longest in Chicago, New York and Florence, Italy. He is said to have hated horses.

Faust wrote under a variety of aliases and in nearly every genre: science fiction, historical romance, crime, adventure, fantasy and spy stories (his output totals about 30 million words, which is just astounding) but the Max Brand westerns were, and continue today to be his best known works.

"The Quest Begins" is composed of five consecutive chapters, excerpted from the novel *Trailin'*, and was first published in 1919.

★   ★   ★   ★   ★

"**Y**ou know the old place on the other side of the range?"

"Like a book. I got pet names for all the trees."

"There's a man there I want."

"Logan?"

"No. His name is Bard."

"H-m! Any relation to the old bird that was partners with you back about the year one?"

"I want Anthony Bard brought here," said Drew, entirely overlooking the question.

"Easy. I can make the trip in a buckboard and I'll dump him in the back of it."

"No. He's got to *ride* here, understand?"

"A dead man," said Nash calmly, "ain't much good on a hoss."

"Listen to me," said Drew, his voice lowering to a sort of musical thunder, "if you harm a hair of this lad's head I'll—I'll break you in two with my own hands."

And he made a significant gesture as if he were snapping a twig between his fingers. Nash moistened his lips, then his square, powerful jaw jutted out.

"Which the general idea is me doing baby talk and sort of hypnotizing this Bard feller into coming along?"

"More than that. He's got to be brought here alive, untouched, and placed in that chair tied so that he can't move hand or foot for ten minutes while I talk."

"Nice, quiet day you got planned for me, Mr. Drew."

The grey man considered thoughtfully.

"Now and then you've told me of a girl at Eldara—I think her name is Sally Fortune?"

"Right. She begins where the rest of the calico leaves off."

"H-m! that sounds familiar, somehow. Well, Steve, you've said that if you had a good start you think the girl would marry you."

"I think she *might*."

"She pretty fond of you?"

"She knows that if I can't have her I'm fast enough to keep everyone else away."

"I see. A process of elimination with you as the eliminator. Rather an odd courtship, Steve?"

The cowpuncher grew deadly serious.

"You see, I love her. There ain't no way of bucking out of that. So do nine out of ten of all the boys that've seen her. Which one will she pick?

That's the question we all keep askin', because of all the contrary, freckle-faced devils with the heart of a man an' the smile of a woman, Sally has 'em all beat from the drop of the barrier. One feller has money; another has looks; another has a funny line of talk. But I've got the fastest gun. So Sally sees she's due for a complete outfit of black mournin' if she marries another man while I'm alive; an' that keeps her thinkin'. But if I had the price of a start in the world—why, maybe she'd take a long look at me."

"Would she call one thousand dollars in cash a start in the world—and your job as foreman of my place, with twice the salary you have now?"

Steve Nash wiped his forehead.

He said huskily: "A joke along this line don't bring no laugh from me, governor."

"I mean it, Steve. Get Anthony Bard tied hand and foot into this house so that I can talk to him safely for ten minutes, and you'll have everything I promise. Perhaps more. But that depends."

The blunt-fingered hand of Nash stole across the table.

"If it's a go, shake, Mr. Drew."

A mighty hand fell in his, and under the pressure he set his teeth. Afterward he covertly moved his fingers and sighed with relief to see that no permanent harm had been done.

"Me speakin' personal, Mr. Drew, I'd of give a lot to seen you when you was ridin' the range. This Bard—he'll be here before sunset to-morrow."

"Don't jump to conclusions, Steve. I've an idea that before you count your thousand you'll think that you've been underpaid. That's straight."

"This Bard is something of a man?"

"I can say that without stopping to think."

"Texas?"

"No. He's a tenderfoot, but he can ride a horse as if he was sewed to the skin, and I've an idea that he can do other things up to the same standard. If you can find two or three men who have silent tongues and strong hands, you'd better take them along. I'll pay their wages, and big ones. You can name your price."

But Nash was frowning.

"Now and then I talk to the cards a bit, Mr. Drew, and you'll hear fellers say some pretty rough things about me, but I've never asked for no odds against any man. I'm not going to start now."

"You're a hard man, Steve, but so am I; and hard men are the kind I take to. I know that you're the best foreman who ever rode this range and I know that when you start things you generally finish them. All that I ask is that you bring Bard to me in this house. The way you do it is your own problem. Drunk or drugged, I don't care how, but get him here unharmed. Understand?"

"Mr. Drew, you can start figurin' what you want to say to him now. I'll get him here—safe! And then Sally—"

"If money will buy her you'll have me behind you when you bid."

"When shall I start?"

"Now."

"So-long, then."

He rose and passed hastily from the room, leaning forward from the hips like a man who is making a start in a foot-race.

Straight up the stairs he went to his room, for the foreman lived in the big house of the rancher. There he took a quantity of equipment from a closet and flung it on the bed. Over three selections he lingered long.

The first was the cartridge belt, and he tried over several with conscientious care until he found the one which received the cartridges with the greatest ease. He could flip them out in the night, automatically as a pianist fingers the scale in the dark.

Next he examined lariats painfully, inch by inch, as though he were going out to rope the stanchest steer that ever roamed the range. Already he knew that those ropes were sound and true throughout, but he took no chances now. One of the ropes he discarded because one or two strands in it were, or might be, a trifle frayed. The other he took alternately and whirled with a broad loop, standing in the centre of the room. Of the set one was a little more supple, a little more durable, it seemed. This he selected and coiled swiftly.

Last of all he lingered—and longest—over his revolvers. Six in all, he set them in a row along the bed and without delay threw out two to begin with. Then he fingered the others, tried their weight and balance, slipped cartridges into the cylinders and extracted them again, whirled the cylinders, examined the minutest parts of the actions.

They were all such guns as an expert would have turned over with shining eyes, but finally he threw one aside into the discard; the cylinder revolved just a little too hard. Another was abandoned after much handling of the remaining three because to the delicate touch of Nash it seemed that the weight of the barrel was a gram more than in the other two; but after this selection it seemed that there was no possible choice between the final two.

So he stood in the centre of the room and went through a series of odd gymnastics. Each gun in turn he placed in the holster and then jerked it out, spinning it on the trigger guard around his second finger, while his left hand shot diagonally across his body and "fanned" the hammer. Still he could not make his choice, but he would not abandon the effort. It was an old maxim with him that there is in all the world one gun which is the best of all and with which even a novice can become a "killer."

He tried walking away, whirling as he made his draw, and levelling the gun on the door-knob. Then without moving his hand, he lowered his head and squinted down the sights. In each case the bead was drawn to a centre shot. Last of all he weighed each gun; one seemed a trifle lighter— the merest shade lighter than the other. This he slipped into the holster and carried the rest of his apparatus back to the closet from which he had taken it.

Still the preparation had not ended. Filling his cartridge belt, every cartridge was subject to a rigid inspection. A full half hour was wasted in this manner. Wasted, because he rejected not one of the many he examined. Yet he seemed happier after having made his selection, and went down the stairs, humming softly.

Out to the barn he went, lantern in hand. This time he made no comparison of horses but went directly to an ugly-headed roan, long of leg, vicious of eye, thin-shouldered, and with hips that slanted sharply down. No one with a knowledge of fine horse-flesh could have looked on this brute without aversion. It did not have even size in its favour. A wild, free spirit, perhaps, might be the reason; but the animal stood with hanging head and pendant lower lip. One eye was closed and the other only half opened. A blind affection, then, made him go to this horse first of all.

No, his greeting was to jerk his knee sharply into the ribs of the roan, which answered with a grunt and swung its head around with bared teeth, like an angry dog. "Damn your eyes!" roared the hoarse voice of Steve Nash, "stand still or I'll knock you for a goal!"

The ears of the mustang flattened close to its neck and a devil of hate came up in its eyes, but it stood quiet, while Nash went about at a judicious distance and examined all the vital points. The hoofs were sound, the backbone prominent, but not a high ridge from famine or much hard riding, and the indomitable hate in the eyes of the mustang seemed to please the cowpuncher.

It was a struggle to bridle the beast, which was accomplished only by grinding the points of his knuckles into a tender part of the jowl to make the locked teeth open.

In saddling, the knee came into play again, rapping the ribs of the brute repeatedly before the wind, which swelled out the chest to false proportions, was expelled in a sudden grunt, and the cinch whipped up taut. After that Nash dodged the flying heels, chose his time, and vaulted into the saddle.

The mustang trotted quietly out of the barn. Perhaps he had had his fill of bucking on that treacherous, slippery wooden floor, but once outside he turned loose the full assortment of the cattle-pony's tricks. It was only ten minutes, but while it lasted the cursing of Nash was loud and steady, mixed with the crack of his murderous quirt against the roan's flanks. The bucking ended as quickly as it had begun, and they started at a long canter over the trail.

★　★　★　★　★

Mile after mile of the rough trail fell behind him, and still the pony shambled along at a loose trot or a swinging canter; the steep upgrades it took at a steady jog and where the slopes pitched sharply down, it wound among the rocks with a faultless sureness of foot.

Certainly the choice of Nash was well made. An Eastern horse of blood over a level course could have covered the same distance in half the time, but it would have broken down after ten miles of that hard trail.

Dawn came while they wound over the crest of the range, and with the sun in their faces they took the downgrade. It was well into the morning before Nash reached Logan. He forced from his eye the contempt which all cattlemen feel for sheepherders.

"I s'pose you're here askin' after Bard?" began Logan without the slightest prelude.

"Bard? Who's he?"

Logan considered the other with a sardonic smile.

"Maybe you been ridin' all night jest for fun?"

"If you start usin' your tongue on me, Logan, you'll wear out the snapper on it. I'm on my way to the A Circle Y."

"Listen; I'm all for old man Drew. You know that. Tell me what Bard has on him?"

"Never heard the name before. Did he rustle a couple of your sheep?"

Logan went on patiently: "I knew something was wrong when Drew was here yesterday but I didn't think it was as bad as this."

"What did Drew do yesterday?"

"Came up as usual to potter around the old house, I guess, but when he heard about Bard bein' here he changed his mind sudden and went home."

"That's damn queer. What sort of a lookin' feller is this Bard?"

"I don't suppose you know, eh?" queried Logan ironically. "I don't suppose the old man described him before you started, maybe?"

"Logan, you poor old hornless maverick, d'you think I'm on somebody's trail? Don't you know I've been through with that sort of game for a hell of a while?"

"When rocks turn into ham and eggs I'll trust you, Steve. I'll tell you what I done to Bard, anyway. Yesterday, after he found that Drew had been here and gone he seemed sort of upset; tried to keep it from me, but I'm too much used to judgin' changes of weather to be fooled by any tenderfoot that ever used school English. Then he hinted around about learnin' the way to Eldara, because he knows that town is pretty close to Drew's place, I guess. I told him; sure I did. He should of gone due west, but I sent him south. There *is* a south trail, only it takes about three days to get to Eldara."

"Maybe you think that interests me. It don't."

Logan overlooked this rejoinder, saying: "Is it his scalp you're after?"

"Your ideas are like nest-eggs, Logan, an' you set over 'em like a hen. They look like eggs; they feel like eggs; but they don't never hatch. That's the way with your ideas. They look all right; they sound all right; but they don't mean nothin'. So-long."

But Logan merely chuckled wisely. He had been long on the range.

As Nash turned his pony and trotted off in the direction of the A Circle Y ranch, the sheepherder called after him: "What you say cuts both ways, Steve. This feller Bard looks like a tenderfoot; he sounds like a tenderfoot; but he ain't a tenderfoot."

Felling that this parting shot gave him the honours of the meeting, he turned away whistling with such spirit that one of his dogs, overhearing, stood still and gazed at his master with his head cocked wisely to one side.

His eastern course Nash pursued for a mile or more, and then swung sharp to the south. He was weary, like his horse, and he made no attempt to start a sudden burst of speed. He let the pony go on at the same tireless jog, clinging like a bulldog to the trail.

About midday he sighted a small house cuddled into a hollow of the hills and made toward it. As he dismounted, a tow-headed, spindling boy lounged out of the doorway and stood with his hands shoved carelessly into his little overall pockets.

"Hello, young feller."

"'Lo, stranger."

"What's the chance of bunking here for three or four hours and gettin' a good feed for the hoss?"

"Never better. Gimme the hoss; I'll put him up in the shed. Feed him grain?"

"No, you won't put him up. I'll tend to that."

"Looks like a bad 'un."

"That's it."

"But a sure goer, eh?"

"Yep."

He led the pony to the shed, unsaddled him, and gave him a small feed. The horse first rolled on the dirt floor and then started methodically on his fodder. Having made sure that his mount was not "off his feed," Nash rolled a cigarette and strolled back to the house with the boy.

"Where's the folks?" he asked.

"Ma's sick, a little, and didn't get up to-day. Pa's down to the corral, cussing mad. But I can cook you up some chow."

"All right son. I got a dollar here that'll buy you a pretty good store knife."

The boy flushed so red that by contrast his straw coloured hair seemed positively white.

"Maybe you want to pay me?" he suggested fiercely. "Maybe you think we're squatters that run a hotel?"

Recognizing the true Western breed even in this small edition, Nash grinned.

"Speakin' man to man, son, I didn't think that, but I thought I'd sort of feel my way."

"Which I'll say you're lucky you didn't try to feel your way with pa; not the way he's feelin' now."

In the shack of the house he placed the best chair for Nash and set about frying ham and making coffee. This with crackers, formed the meal. He watched Nash eat for a moment of solemn silence and then the foreman looked up to catch a meditative chuckle from the youngster.

"Let me in on the joke, son."

"Nothin'. I was just thinkin' of pa."

"What's he sore about? Come out short at poker lately?"

"No; he lost a hoss. Ha, ha, ha!"

He explained: "He's lost his only standin' joke, and now the laugh's on pa!"

Nash sipped his coffee and waited. On the mountain desert one does not draw out a narrator with questions.

"There was a feller come along early this mornin' on a lame hoss," the story began. "He was a sure enough tenderfoot—leastways he looked it an' he talked it, but he wasn't."

The familiarity of this description made Steve sit up a trifle straighter.

"Was he a ringer?"

"Maybe. I dunno. Pa meets him at the door and asks him in. What d'you think this feller comes back with?"

The boy paused to remember and then with twinkling eyes he mimicked: "'That's very good of you, sir, but I'll only stop to make a trade with you—this horse and some cash to boot for a durable mount out of your corral. The brute has gone lame, you see.'

"Pa waited and scratched his head while these here words sort of sunk in. Then says very smooth: 'I'll let you take the best hoss I've got, an' I won't ask much cash to boot.'

"I begin wonderin' what pa was drivin' at, but I didn't say nothin'—jest held myself together and waited.

" 'Look over there to the corral,' says pa, and pointed. 'They's a hoss that ought to take you wherever you want to go. It's the best hoss I've ever had.'

"It *was* the best horse pa ever had, too. It was a piebald pinto called Jo, after my cousin Josiah, who's jest a plain bad un and raises hell when there's any excuse. The piebald, he didn't even need an excuse. You see, he's one of them hosses that likes company. When he leaves the corral he likes to have another hoss for a runnin' mate and he was jest as tame as anything. I could ride him; anybody could ride him. But if you took him outside the bars of the corral without company, first thing he done was to see if one of the other hosses was comin' out to join him. When he seen that he was all laid out to make a trip by himself he jest nacherally started in to raise hell. Which Jo can raise more hell for his size than any hoss I ever seen.

"He's what you call an eddicated bucker. He don't fool around with no pauses. He jest starts in and figgers out a situation and then he gets busy slidin' the gent that's on him off'n the saddle. An' he always used to win out. In fact, he was known for it all around these parts. He begun nice and easy, but he worked up like a fiddler playin' a favourite piece, and the end was the rider lyin' on the ground.

"Whenever the boys around here wanted any excitement they used to come over and try their hands with Jo. We used to keep a pile of arnica and stuff like that around to rub them up with and tame down the bruises after Jo laid 'em cold on the ground. There wasn't never anybody could ride that hoss when he was started out alone.

"Well, this tenderfoot, he looks over the hoss in the corral and says: 'That's a pretty fine mount, it seems to me. What do you want to boot?' "

" 'Aw, twenty-five dollars in enough,' says pa.

" 'All right,' says the tenderfoot, 'here's the money.'

"And he counts it out in pa's hand.

"He says: 'What a little beauty! It would be a treat to see him work on a polo field.'

"Pa says: 'It'd be a treat to see this hoss work anywhere.'

"Then he steps on my foot to make me wipe the grin off'n my face.

"Down goes the tenderfoot and takes his saddle and flops it on the piebald pinto, and the piebald was jest as nice as milk. Then he leads him out'n the corral and gets on.

"First the pinto takes a look over his shoulder like he was waiting for one of his pals among the hosses to come along, but he didn't see none. Then the circus started. An' b'lieve me, it was some circus. Jo hadn't had much action for some time, an' he must have used the wait thinkin' up new ways of raisin' hell.

"There ain't enough words in the Bible to describe what he done. Which maybe you sort of gather that he *had* to keep on performin', because the tenderfoot was still in the saddle. He was. An' he never pulled leather. No, sir, he never touched the buckin' strap, but jest sat there with his teeth set and his lips twistin' back—the same smile he had when he got into the saddle. But pretty soon I s'pose Jo had a chance to figure out that it didn't do him no particular harm to be alone.

"The minute he seen that he stopped fightin' and started off at a gallop the way the tenderfoot wanted him to go, which was over there.

"'Damn my eyes!' says pa, an' couldn't do nuthin' but just stand there repeatin' that with variations because with Jo gone there wouldn't be no drawin' card to get the boys around the house no more. But you're lookin' sort of sleepy, stranger?"

"I am," answered Nash.

"Well, if you'd seen that show you wouldn't be thinkin' of sleep. Not for some time."

"Maybe not, but the point is I didn't see it. D'you mind if I turn in on that bunk over there?"

"Help yourself," said the boy. "What time d'you want me to wake you up?"

"Never mind; I wake up automatic. S'long, Bud."

He stretched out on the blankets and was instantly asleep.

★   ★   ★   ★   ★

At the end of three hours he awoke as sharply as though an alarm were clamouring at his ear. There was no elaborate preparation for renewed activities. A single yawn and stretch and he was again on his feet. Since the boy was not in sight he cooked himself an enormous meal, devoured it, and went out to the mustang.

The roan greeted him with a volley from both heels that narrowly missed the head of Nash, but the cowpuncher merely smiled tolerantly.

"Feelin' fit agin, eh, damn your soul?" he said genially, and picking up a bit of board, fallen from the side of the shed, he smote the mustang mightily along the ribs. The mustang, as if it recognized the touch of the master, pricked up one ear and side-stepped. The brief rest had filled it with all the old, vicious energy.

For once more, as soon as they rode clear of the door, there ensued a furious struggle between man and beast. The man won, as always, and the roan, dropping both ears flat against its neck, trotted sullenly out across the hills.

In that monotony of landscape, one mile exactly like the other, no landmarks to guide him, no trail to follow, however faintly worn, it was strange to see the cowpuncher strike out through the vast distances of the mountain-desert with as much confidence as if he were travelling on a paved street in a city. He had not even a compass to direct him but he seemed to know his way as surely as the birds know the untracked paths of the air in the seasons of migration.

Straight on through the afternoon and during the long evening he kept his course at the same unvarying dog-trot until the flush of the sunset faded to a stern grey and the purple hills in the distance turned blue with shadows. Then, catching the glimmer of a light on a hillside, he turned toward it to put up for the night.

In answer to his call a big man with a lantern came to the door and raised his light until it shone on a red, bald head and a portly figure. His welcome was neither hearty nor cold; hospitality is expected in the mountain-desert. So Nash put up his horse in the shed and came back to the house.

The meal was half over, but two girls immediately set a plate heaped with fried potatoes and bacon and flanked by a mighty cup of jet-black coffee on one side and a pile of yellow biscuits on the other. He nodded to them, grunted by way of expressing thanks, and sat down to eat.

Beside the tall father and the rosy-faced mother, the family consisted of the two girls, one of them with her hair twisted severely close to her head, wearing a man's blue cotton shirt with the sleeves rolled up to a pair of brown elbows. Evidently she was the boy of the family and to her fell the duty of performing the innumerable chores of the ranch, for her hands were thick with work and the tips of the fingers blunted. Also she had that calm, self-satisfied eye which belongs to the workingman who knows that he has earned his meal.

Her sister monopolized all the beauty and the grace, not that she was either very pretty or extremely graceful, but she was instinct with the challenge of femininity like a rare scent. It lingered about her, it enveloped her ways; it gave a light to her eyes and made her smile exquisite. Her clothes were not of much finer material than her sister's, but they were cut to fit, and a bow of crimson ribbon at her throat was as effective in that environment as the most costlly orchids on an evening gown.

She was armed in pride this night, talking only to her mother, and then in monosyllables alone. At first it occurred to Steve that his coming had made her self-conscious, but he soon discovered that her pride was directed at the third man at the table. She at least maintained a pretence of eating, but he made not even a sham, sitting miserably, his mouth hard set, his eyes shadowed by a tremendous frown. At length he shoved back his chair with such violence that the table trembled.

"Well," he rumbled, "I guess this lets me out. S'long."

And he strode heavily from the room; a moment later his cursing came back to them as he rode into the night.

"Takes it kind of hard, don't he?" said the father.

And the mother murmured: "Poor Ralph!"

"So you went an' done it?" said the mannish girl to her sister.

"What of it?" snapped the other.

"He's too good for you, that's what of it."

"Girls!" exclaimed the mother anxiously. "Remember we got a guest!"

"Oh," said she of the strong brown arms, "I guess we can't tell him nothin'; I guess he had eyes to be seein' what's happened."

She turned calmly to Steve.

"Lizzie turned down Ralph Boardman—poor feller!"

"Sue!" cried the other girl.

"Well, after you done it, are you ashamed to have it talked about? You make me sore, I'll tell a man!"

"That's enough, Sue," growled the father.

"What's enough?"

"We ain't goin' to have no more show about this. I've had my supper spoiled by it already."

"I say it's a rotten shame," broke out Sue, and she repeated, "Ralph's too good for her. All because of a city dude—a tenderfoot!"

In the extremity of her scorn her voice drawled in a harsh murmur.

"Then take him yourself, if you can get him!" cried Lizzie. "I'm sure I don't want him!"

Their eyes blazed at each other across the table, and Lizzie, having scored an unexpected point, struck again.

"I think you've always had a sort of hankerin' after Ralph—oh, I've seen your eyes rollin' at him."

The other girl coloured hotly through her tan.

"If I was fond of him I wouldn't be ashamed to let him know, you can tell the world that. And I wouldn't keep him trottin' about like a little pet dog till I got tired of him and give him up for the sake of a greenhorn who"—her voice lowered to a spiteful hiss—"kissed you the first time he even seen you!"

In vain Lizzie fought for her control; her lip trembled and her voice shook.

"I hate you, Sue!"

"Sue, ain't you ashamed of yourself?" pleaded the mother.

"No, I ain't! Think of it; here's Ralph been sweet on Liz for two years an' now she gives him the go-by for a skinny, affected dude like that feller that was here. And *he's* forgot you already, Liz, the minute he stopped laughing at you for bein' so easy."

"Ma, are you goin' to let Sue talk like this—right before a stranger?"

"Sue, you shut up!" commanded the father.

"I don't see nobody that can make me," she said, surly as a grown boy. "I can't make any more of a fool out of Liz than that tenderfoot made her!"

"Did he," asked Steve, "ride a piebald mustang?"

"D'you know him?" breathed Lizzie, forgetting the tears of shame which had been gathering in her eyes.

"Nope. Jest heard a little about him along the road."

"What's his name?"

Then she coloured, even before Sue could say spitefully: "Didn't he even have to tell you his name before he kissed you?"

"He did! His name is—Tony!"

"Tony!"—in deep disgust. "Well, he's dark enough to be a dago! Maybe he's a foreign count, or something, Liz, and he'll take you back to live in some castle or other."

But the girl queried, in spite of this badinage: "Do you know his name?"

"His name," said Nash, thinking that it could do no harm to betray as much as this, "is Anthony Bard, I think."

"And you don't know him?"

"All I know is that the feller who used to own that piebald mustang is pretty mad and cusses every time he thinks of him."

"He didn't steal the hoss?"

This with more bated breath than if the question had been: "He didn't kill a man?" for indeed horse-stealing was the greater crime.

Even Nash would not make such an accusation directly, and therefore he fell back on an innuendo almost as deadly.

"I dunno," he said non-committally, and shrugged his shoulders.

With all his soul he was concentrating on the picture of the man who conquered a fighting horse and flirted successfully with a pretty girl the same day; each time riding on swiftly from his conquest. The clues on this trail were surely thick enough, but they were of such a nature that the pleasant mind of Steve grew more and more thoughtful.

★   ★   ★   ★   ★

In fact, so thoughtful had Nash become, that he slept with extraordinary lightness that night and was up at the first hint of day. Sue appeared on the scene just in time to witness the last act of the usual drama of bucking on the part of the roan, before it settled down to the mechanical dog-trot with which it would wear out the ceaseless miles of the mountain-desert all day and far into the night, if need be.

Nash now swung more to the right, cutting across the hills, for he presumed that by this time the tenderfoot must have gotten his bearings and would head straight for Eldara. It was a stiff two-day journey, now, the whole first day's riding having been a worse than useless detour; so the bulldog jaw set harder and harder, and the keen eyes squinted as if to look into the dim future.

Once each day, about noon, when the heat made even the desert and the men of the desert drowsy, he allowed his imagination to roam freely, counting the thousand dollars over and over again, and tasting again the joys of a double salary. Yet even his hardy imagination rarely rose to the height of Sally Fortune. That hour of dreaming, however, made the day of labour almost pleasant.

This time, in the very middle of his dream, he reached the cross-roads saloon and general merchandise store of Flanders; so he banished his visions with a compelling shrug of the shoulders and rode for it at a gallop, a hot dryness growing in his throat at every stride. Quick service he was sure to get, for there were not more than half a dozen cattle-ponies standing in front of the little building with its rickety walls guiltless of paint save for the one great sign inscribed with uncertain letters.

He swung from the saddle, tossed the reins over the head of the mustang, made a stride forward—and then checked himself with a soft curse and reached for his gun.

For the door of the bar dashed open and down the steps rushed a tall man with light yellow moustache, so long that it literally blew on either side over his shoulders as he ran; in either hand he carried a revolver—a two-gun man, fleeing, perhaps, from another murder.

For Nash recognized in him a character notorious through a thousand miles of the range, Sandy Ferguson, nicknamed by the colour of that famous moustache, which was envied and dreaded so far and so wide. It was not fear that made Nash halt, for otherwise he would have finished the motion and whipped out his gun; but at least it was something closely akin to fear.

For that matter, there were unmistakable signs in Sandy himself of what would have been called arrant terror in any other man. His face was so bloodless that the pallor showed even through the leathery tan; one eye stared wildly, the other being sheltered under a clumsy patch which could not quite conceal the ugly bruise beneath. Under his great moustache his lips were as puffed and swollen as the lips of a negro.

Staggering in his haste, he whirled a few paces from the house and turned, his guns levelled. At the same moment the door opened and the perspiring figure of little fat Flanders appeared. Scorn and anger rather than hate or any bloodlust appeared in his face. His right arm, hanging loosely at his side, held a revolver, and he seemed to have the greatest un-concern for the leveled weapons of the gunman.

He made a gesture with that armed hand, and Sandy winced as though a whiplash had flicked him.

"Steady up, damn your eyes!" bellowed Flanders, "and put them guns away. Put 'em up; hear me?"

To the mortal astonishment of Nash, Sandy obeyed, keeping the while a fascinated eye upon the little Dutchman.

"Now climb your hoss and beat it, and if I ever find you in reach again, I'll send my kid out to rope you and give you a hoss-whippin'."

The gun fighter lost no time. A single leap carried him into his saddle and he was off over the sand with a sharp rattle of the beating hoofs.

"Well," breathed Nash, "I'll be hanged."

"Sure you will," suggested Flanders, at once changing his frown for a smile of somewhat professional good nature, as one who greeted an old customer, "sure you will unless you come in an' have a drink on the house. I want something myself to forget what I been doin'. I feel like the dog-catcher."

Steve, deeply meditative, strode into the room.

"Partner," he said gravely to Flanders, "I've always prided myself on having eyes a little better than the next one, but just now I guess I must have been seein' double. Seemed to me that that was Sandy Ferguson that you hot-footed out of that door—or has Sandy got a double?"

"Nope," said the bartender, wiping the last of the perspiration from his forehead, "that's Sandy, all right."

"Then gimme a big drink. I need it."

The bottle spun expertly across the bar, and the glasses tinkled after.

"Funny about him, all right," nodded Flanders, "but then it's hap-pened the same way with others I could tell about. As long as he was winnin'

Sandy was the king of any roost. The minute he lost a fight he wasn't worth so many pounds of salt pork. Take a hoss; a fine hoss is often jest the same. Long as it wins nothin' can touch some of them blooded boys. But let 'em go under the wire second, maybe jest because they's packing twenty pounds too much weight, and they're never any good any more. Any second-rather can lick 'em. I lost five hundred iron boys on a hoss that laid down like that."

"All of which means," suggested Nash, "that Sandy has been licked?"

"Licked? No, he ain't been licked, but he's been plumb annihilated, washed off the map, cleaned out, faded, rubbed into the dirt; if there was some stronger way of puttin' it, I would. Only last night, at that, but now look at him. A girl that never seen a man before could tell that he wasn't any more dangerous now than if he was made of putty; but if the fool keeps packin' them guns he's sure to get into trouble."

He raised his glass.

"So here's to the man that Sandy was and ain't no more."

They drank solemnly.

"Maybe you took the fall out of him yourself, Flanders?"

"Nope. I ain't no fighter, Steve. You know that. The feller that downed Sandy was—a tenderfoot. Yep, a greenhorn."

"Ah-h-h," drawled Nash softly, "I thought so."

"You did?"

"Anyway, let's hear the story. Another drink—on me, Flanders."

"It was like this. Along about evening of yesterday Sandy was in here with a couple of other boys. He was pretty well lighted—the glow was circulatin' promiscuous, in fact—when in comes a feller about your height, Steve, but lighter. Good lookin', thin face, big dark eyes like a girl. He carried the signs of a long ride on him. Well, sir, he walks up to the bar and says: 'Can you make me a very sour lemonade, Mr. Bartender?'

"I grabbed the edge of the bar and hung on tight.

"'A which?' says I.

"'Lemonade, if you please.'

"I rolled an eye at Sandy, who was standin' there with his jaw falling, and then I got busy with lemons and the squeezer, but pretty soon Ferguson walks up to the stranger.

"'Are you English?' he asks.

"I knew by his tone what was comin', so I slid the gun I keep behind the bar closer and got prepared for a lot of damaged crockery.

"'I?' says the tenderfoot. 'Why, no. What makes you ask?'

"'Your damned funny way of talkin',' says Sandy.

"'Oh,' says the greenhorn, nodding as if he was thinkin' this over and discovering a little truth in it. 'I suppose the way I talk is a little unusual.'

"'A little rotten,' says Sandy. 'Did I hear you askin' for a lemonade?'

"'You did.'

"'Would I seem to be askin' too many questions,' says Sandy, terrible polite, 'if I inquires if bar whisky ain't good enough for you?'

"The tenderfoot, he stands there jest as easy as you an' me stand here now, and he laughed.

"He says: 'The bar whisky I've tasted around this country is not very good for any one, unless, perhaps, after a snake has bitten you. Then it works on the principle of poison fight poison, eh?'

"Sandy says after a minute: 'I'm the most quietest, gentle, innercent cowpuncher that ever rode the range, but I'd tell a man that it riles me to hear good bar whisky insulted like this. Look at me! Do I look as if whisky ain't good for a man?'

"'Why,' says the tenderfoot, 'you look sort of funny to me.'

"He said it as easy as if he was passin' the morning with Ferguson, but I seen that it was the last straw with Sandy. He hefted out both guns and trained 'em on the greenhorn.

"I yelled: 'Sandy, for God's sake, don't be killin' a tenderfoot!'

"'If whisky will kill him he's goin' to die,' says Sandy. 'Flanders, pour out a drink of rye for this gent.'

"I did it, though my hand was shaking a lot, and the chap takes the glass and raises it polite, and looks at the colour of it. I thought he was goin' to drink, and starts wipin' the sweat off'n my forehead.

"But this chap, he sets down the glass and smiles over to Sandy.

"'Listen,'" he says, still grinnin', 'in the old days I suppose this would have been a pretty bluff, but it won't work with me now. You want me to drink this glass of very bad whisky, but I'm sure that you don't want it badly enough to shoot me.

"'There are many reasons. In the old days a man shot down another and then rode off on his horse and was forgotten, but in these days the telegraph is faster than any horse that was ever foaled. They'd be sure to get you, sir, though you might dodge them for a while. And I believe that for a crime such as you threaten, they have recently installed a little electric chair which is a perfectly good inducer of sleep—in fact, it is better than a cradle. Taking these things all into consideration, I take it for granted that you are bluffing, my friend, and one of my favourite occupations is calling a bluff. You look dangerous, but I've an idea that you are as yellow as your moustache.'

"Sandy, he sort of swelled up all over like a poisoned dog.

"He says: 'I begin to see your style. You want a clean man-handlin', which suits me uncommon well.'

"With that, he lays down his guns, soft and careful, and puts up his fists, and goes for the other gent.

"He makes his pass, which should have sent the other gent into kingdom come. But it didn't. No, sir, the tenderfoot, he seemed to evaporate. He wasn't there when the fist of Ferguson come along. Ferguson, he checked up short and wheeled around and charged again like a bull. And he missed again. And so they kept on playin' a sort of a game of tag over the place, the stranger jest side-steppin' like a prize-fighter, the prettiest you ever seen, and not developin' when Sandy started on one of his swings.

"At last one of Sandy's fists grazed him on the shoulder and sort of peeved him, it looked like. He ducks under Sandy's next punch, steps in, and wallops Sandy over the eye—that punch didn't travel more'n six inches. But it slammed Sandy down in a corner like he's been shot.

"He was too surprised to be much hurt, though, and drags himself up to his feet, makin' a pass at his pocket at the same time. Then he came again, silent and thinkin' of blood, I s'pose, with a knife in his hand.

"This time the tenderfoot didn't wait. He went in with a sort of hitch step, like a dancer. Ferguson's knife carved the air beside the tenderfoot's head, and then the skinny boy jerked up his right and his left—one, two—into Sandy's mouth. Down he goes again—slumps down as if all the bones in his body was busted—right down on his face. The other feller grabs his shoulder and jerks him over on his back.

"He stands lookin' down at him for a moment, and then he says, sort of thoughtful: 'He isn't badly hurt, but I suppose I shouldn't have hit him twice.'

"Can you beat that, Steve? You can't!

"When Sandy come to he got up to his feet, wobbling—seen his guns—went over and scooped 'em up, with the eye of the tenderfoot on him all the time—scooped 'em up—stood with 'em all poised—and so he backed out through the door. It wasn't any pretty thing to see. The tenderfoot, he turned to the bar again.

"'If you don't mind,' he says, 'I think I'll switch my order and take that whisky instead. I seem to need it.'

"'Son!' says I, 'there ain't nothin' in the house you can't have for the askin'. Try some of this!'

"And I pulled out a bottle of my private stock—you know the stuff; I've had it twenty-five years, and it was ten years old when I got it. That ain't as much of a lie as it sounds.

"He takes a glass of it and sips it, sort of suspicious, like a wolf scentin' the wind for an elk in winter. Then his face lighted up like a lantern had been flashed on it. You'd of thought that he was lookin' his long-lost brother in the eye from the way he smiled at me. He holds the glass up and lets the light come through it, showin' the little traces and bubbles of oil.

"'May I know your name?' he says.

"It made me feel like Rockerbilt, hearin' him say that, in *that* special voice.

"'Me,' says I, 'I'm Flanders.'

"'It's an honour to know you, Mr. Flanders,' he says. 'My name is Anthony Bard.'

"We shook hands, and his grip was three fourths man, I'll tell the world.

"'Good liquor,' says he, 'is like a fine lady. Only a gentleman can appreciate it. I drink to you, sir.'

"So that's how Sandy Ferguson went under the sod. To-day? Well, I couldn't let Ferguson stand in a barroom where a gentleman had been, could I?"

★   ★   ★   ★   ★

Even the stout roan grew weary during the third day, and when they topped the last rise of hills, and looked down to darker shadows in Eldara in the black heart of the hollow, the mustang stood with hanging head, and one ear flopped forward. Cruel indeed had been the pace which Nash maintained, yet they had never been able to overhaul the flying piebald of Anthony Bard.

As they trotted down the slope, Nash looked to his equipment, handled his revolver, felt the strands of the lariat, and resting only his toes in the stirrups, eased all his muscles to make sure that they were uncramped from the long journey. He was fit; there was no doubt of that.

Coming down the main street—for Eldara boasted no fewer than three thoroughfares—the first houses which Nash passed showed no lights. As far as he could see, the blinds were all drawn; not even the glimmer of a candle showed, and the voices which he heard were muffled and low.

He thought of plague or some other disaster which might have overtaken the little village and wiped out nine tenths of the populace in a day. Only such a thing could account for silence in Eldara. There should have been bursts and roars of laughter here and there, and now and then a harsh stream of cursing. There should have been clatter of kitchen tins; there should have been neighing of horses; there should have been the quiver and tingle of children's voices at play in the dusty streets. But there was none of this. The silence was as thick and oppressive as the unbroken dark of the night. Even Butler's saloon was closed!

This, however, was something which he would not believe, no matter what testimony his eyes gave him. He rode up to a shuttered window and kicked it with his heel.

Only the echoes of that racket replied to him from the interior of the place. He swore, somewhat touched with awe, and kicked again.

A faint voice called: "Who's there?"

"Steve Nash. What the devil's happened to Eldara?"

The boards of the shutter stirred, opened, so that the man within could look out.

"Is it Steve, honest?"

"Damn it, Butler, don't you know my voice? What's turned Eldara into a cemetery?"

"Cemetery's right. 'Butch' Conklin and his gang are going to raid the place to-night."

"Butch Conklin?"

And Nash whistled long and low.

"But why the devil don't the boys get together if they know Butch is coming with his gunmen?"

"That's what they've done. Every able-bodied man in town is out in the hills trying to surprise Conklin's gang before they hit town with their guns going."

Butler was a one-legged man, so Nash kept back the question which naturally formed in his mind.

"How do they know Conklin is coming? Who gave the tip?"

"Conklin himself."

"What? Has he been in town?"

"Right. Came in roaring drunk."

"Why'd they let him get away again?"

"Because the sheriff's a bonehead and because our marshal is solid ivory. That's why."

"What happened?"

"Butch came in drunk, as I was saying, which he generally is, but he wasn't giving no trouble at all, and nobody felt particular called on to cross him and ask questions. He was real sociable, in fact, and that's how the mess was started."

"Go on. I don't get your drift."

"Everybody was treatin' Butch like he was the king of the earth and not passin' out any backtalk, all except one tenderfoot——"

But here a stream of tremendous profanity burst from Nash. It rose, it rushed on, it seemed an exhaustless vocabulary built up by long practice on mustangs and cattle.

At length: "Is that damned fool in Eldara?"

"D'you know him?"

"No. Anyway, go on. What happened?"

"I was sayin' that Butch was feelin' pretty sociable. It went all right in the bars. He was in here and didn't do nothin' wrong. Even paid for all the drinks for everybody in the house, which nobody could ask more even from a white man. But then Butch got hungry and went up the street to Sally Fortune's place."

A snarl came from Nash.

"Did they let that swine go in there?"

"Who'd stop him? Would you?"

"I'd try my damnedest."

"Anyway, in he went and got the centre table and called for ten dollars' worth of bacon and eggs—which there hasn't been an egg in Eldara this week. Sally, she told him, not being afraid even of Butch. He got pretty sore at that and said that is was a frame-up and everyone was ag'in' him. But finally he allowed that if she'd sit down to the table and keep him company he'd manage to make out on whatever her cook had ready to eat.

"And Sally done it?" groaned Nash.

"Sure; it was like a dare—and you know Sally. She'd risk her whole place any time for the sake of a bet."

"I know it, but don't rub it in."

"She fetched out a steak and served Butch as if he'd been a king and then sat down beside him and started kiddin' him along, with all the gang of us sittin' or standin' around and laughin' fit to bust, but not loud for fear Butch would get annoyed.

"Then two things come in together and spoiled the prettiest little party that was ever started in Eldara. First was that player piano which Sally got shipped in and paid God-knows-how-much for; the second was this greenhorn I was tellin' you about."

"Go on," said Nash, the little snarl coming back in his voice. "Tell me how the tenderfoot walked up and kicked Butch out of the place."

"Somebody been tellin' you?"

"No; I just been readin' the mind of Eldara."

"It was a nice play, though. This Bard—we found out later that was his name—walks in, takes a table, and not being served none too quick, he walks over and slips a nickel in the slot of the piano. Out she starts with a piece of rippin' ragtime—you know how loud it plays? Butch, he kept on talkin' for a minute, but couldn't hear himself think. Finally he bellers: 'Who turned that damned tin-pan loose?'

"This Bard walks up and bows. He says: 'Sir, I came here to find food, and since I can't get service, I'll take music as a substitute.'

"Them was the words he used, Steve, honest to God. Used them to Butch!

"Well, Conklin was too flabbergasted to budge, and Bard, he leaned over and says to Sally: 'This floor is fairly smooth. Suppose you and I dance till I get a chance to eat?'

"We didn't know whether to laugh or to cheer, but most of us compromised by keeping an eye on Butch's gun.

"Sally says, 'Sure I'll dance,' and gets up.

"'Wait!' hollers Butch; 'are you leavin' me for this wall-eyed galoot?'

"There ain't nothin' Sally loves more'n a fight—we all know that. But this time I guess she took pity on the poor tenderfoot, or maybe she jest didn't want to get her floor all messed up.

"'Keep your hat on, Butch,' she says, 'all I want to do is to give him some motherly advice.'

"'If you're acting that part,' says Bard, calm as you please, 'I've got to tell mother that she's been keeping some pretty bad company.'

"'Some what?' bellers Butch, not believin' his ears.

"And young Bard, he steps around the girl and stands over Butch.

"'Bad company is what I said,' he repeats, 'but maybe I can be convinced.'

"'Easy,' says Butch, and reaches for his gun.

"We all dived for the door, but me being held up on account of my missing leg, I was slow an' couldn't help seein' what happened. Butch was fast, but the young feller was faster. He had Butch by the wrist before the gun came clear—just gave a little twist—and there he stood with the gun in his hand pointin' into Butch's face, and Butch sittin' there like a feller in a trance or wakin' up out of a bad dream.

"Then he gets up, slow and dignified, though he had enough liquor in him to float a ship.

"'I been mobbed,' he says, 'it's easy to see that. I come here peaceful and quiet, and here I been mobbed. But I'm comin' back, boys, and I ain't comin' alone.'

"There was our chance to get him, while he was walking out of that place without a gun, but somehow nobody moved for him. He didn't look none too easy, even without his shootin' irons. Out he goes into the night, and we stood around starin' at each other. Everybody was upset, except Sally and Bard.

"He says: 'Miss Fortune, this is our dance, I think.'

"'Excuse me,' says Sally, 'I almost forgot about it.'

"And they started to dance to the piano, waltzin' around among the tables; the rest of us lit out for home because we knew that Butch would be on his way with his gang before we got very far under cover. But hey, Steve, where you goin'?"

"I'm going to get in on that dance," called Nash, and was gone at a racing gallop down the street.

Aforesaid Bates

BY EUGENE MANLOVE RHODES

It's drought. The cattle are dying, ranches are failing, the community is coming apart; on hand, an avaricious lawyer, a bent deputy and a few others, taking advantage. This is later, more mature Rhodes, and we are glad of it
because it allows us to cotton onto a couple of themes common to his stories.

Bates, the titular hero of the story, is just like all his friends and
neighbors—he's a rancher with a serious problem. With drought, the grazing
is bad, and money must be found to buy feed or the cattle will die. Bates tries
to raise a stake at the card table and instead loses his little all. What is he to
do? What are they all to do? For Rhodes, the guys in the black hats are the
greedy moneymen who prey upon the community. Bates makes his move,
but it is also, in the end, the community that is the hero of the story.

Might this tale be said to be, in one sense, a forerunner to the classic Western movie *High Noon*? I think perhaps. There too, bad men put a
whole community at risk. One man would save the town, but to do this he
must have the help of his neighbors, his girl, etc.

"Aforesaid Bates" first appeared in the *Saturday Evening Post,* August 1923.

★   ★   ★   ★   ★

i

"I wouldn't mind going broke so much," said Dick Mason, "but I
sure hate to see the cattle die, and me not able to do the first
thing to save them." He dipped a finger in spilled beer and
traced circles on the table. In shirt sleeves for the heat, they sat
in the cool dimness of Jake's Place—Mason, Bull Pepper, Blinker Murphy
and Big Jake himself.

"Tough luck," said Murphy. "Losin' 'em fast?"

"Not so many, not yet. But the bulk of 'em are dying by inches.
Dyin' on their feet. The strongest can just get out to grass and back. The

223

others eat brush, wood and all. Hardly any rain last year and no snow last winter. Stock in no shape to stand a spring round up, so the yearlin' steers are all on the range yet. If we'd had rain about the Fourth of July, as we most always do, we might maybe 'a' pulled through, losin' the calf crop. But here it's most August, no rain, no grass—not a steer in shape to sell—and me with a mortgage comin' due right off. Feenish. And I've got a wife and kids now. Other times, when I went broke, it really didn't make no difference. Tham!"

"No, this one's on me," said Jake hastily. "Four beers, Tham."

"We're none of us cattlemen," said Bull Pepper. "And you know us Tripoli fellows never get along too well with your bunch anyway. All the same, we're sorry to see you boys up against it this way."

Lithpin Tham came with the beer. "I gueth all of you won't go under," he said as he slipped the mugs from tray to table. "They thay Charlie Thee ith fixed tho he won't looth many."

"Not him," said Mason sourly. "Charlie See, he had a leased township under fence to fall back on. Good grass, cured on the stem." The door opened and Aforesaid Bates came in, unseen by Mason. "Charlie won't lose much," said Mason. "Why should he? His stuff runs on the open range when every mouthful of grass they took was a mouthful less for ours. Now he turns 'em into his pasture. Grama high as ever it was, cured on the stem. Just like so much good hay. Been nothing to eat it for three years but a few saddle horses. Him and Aforesaid Bates, they're wise birds, they are!"

"What's all this about Aforesaid Bates?" said Bates. "What's the old man been doin' now?" His voice was acid. They turned startled faces toward him.

"You know well enough," said Mason sullenly. "You ran a drift fence across Silver Spring canyon, kept your cattle out on the flat so long as there was a spear of grass, and now you're hogging that saved-up pasture for yourself."

"Well, what are you goin' to do about it?' demanded Bates. He pushed back his hat; his grizzled beard thrust forth in a truculent spike. "Fine specimen you are—backcappin' your own neighbors to town trash!"

"Exception!" cried Bull Pepper sharply, rising to his feet. But Bates ignored him and continued his tirade, with eyes for none but Mason. "Hopper and See and me, we sold out our old stuff last fall. Cut our brands in half, bein' skeery of a drought. And if the rest of you had as much brains as a road lizard, you could have done the same, and not one of you need have lost a cow. But no, you must build up a big brand, you and Hall—hold on to everything. Now the drought hits us and you can't take your medicine. You belly-achin' around because me and Charlie had gumption enough to protect ourselves."

"Say, cool down a little, Andy," said Dick Mason. "You're an old man, and you've been drinking, and I can take a lot from you—but I do wish you'd be reasonable."

"A fat lot I care about what you wish," snarled Bates. "Reasonable! Oh, shucks! Here, three years ago, you was fixed up to the queen's taste— nice likely bunch of cows, good ranch, lots of room, sold your steers for a big price, money in the bank, and what did you do?"

Conjointly with these remarks, Mason tried to rise and Bull Pepper pulled him down. "Don't mind him, Dick—he's half-shot," said Pepper. Simultaneously, different advice reached Mason's other ear. "Beat his fool head off, Mason!" said Murphy. "You lettin' Bates run your business now?" asked Jake.

Meanwhile, Bates answered his own question. "You bought the Rafter N brand, with your steer money as first payment, givin' a mortgage on both brands."

"Now, Andy –"

"Shet up!" said Andy, "I'm talkin'! Brought in six hundred more cattle to eat yourself out—and to eat the rest of us out. Wasn't satisfied with plenty. Couldn't see that dry years was sure to come. To keep reserve grass was half the game. And as if that wasn't enough, next year Harry Hall must follow your lead—and he's mortgaged up to the hilt, too. Both of you got twice as much stock on the range as you got any right to have. Both goin' broke, and serves you right. But instead of blamin' yourselves, as you would if you was halfway decent, you go whimperin' around, blamin' us that cut our stock in two whilst you was a-doublin' yours!"

"You goin' to stand for this?" whispered Murphy. Concurrently, Andrew Jackson Aforesaid Bates raised his voice to a bellow. "Ever since you got married, you been narratin' around that you wasn't no gun man." He unbuckled his pistol belt and sent his gun sliding along the floor. "Old man, says you! Stand up, you skunk, and take it!"

Mason sprung up. They met with a thud of heavy blows, give-and-take. Pepper tried to shove between, expostulating. Murphy and Jake dragged him away. "Let 'em fight it out!" snarled Jake.

There was no science. Neither man tried to guard, duck, sidestep or avoid a blow in any way. They grunted and puffed, surging this way or that, as one or the other reeled back from a lucky hit. Severe punishment; Mason's nose was spurting blood, and Aforesaid's left eye was closed. Just as Mason felt a chair at his legs, a short arm jab clipped his chin; he toppled backward with a crash of splintered chair. He scrambled up and came back with a rush, head down, both arms swinging. A blow caught Bates squarely on the ear; he went down, rolled over, got to his feet undismayed; they stood toe to toe and slugged savagely. The front door opened, someone shouted, a dozen men rushed into the saloon and bore the combatants apart. Words, questions, answers, defiances—Kendricks and Lispenard dragged Mason through the door, protesting. After some persuasion, Mr. Bates also was led away for repairs by Evans and Early, visiting cowmen from Saragossa; and behind them, delighted Tripoli made animated comment; a pleasing tumult which subsided only at a thoughtful suggestion from the House.

"I been expectin' something like this," said Spinal Maginnis, as they lined up to the bar. "Beer for mine, Tham. Them Little World waddies is sure waspy. I'm s'posed to be representing there for the Diamond A, you know. But they wouldn't let me lift a finger. Said their cattle couldn't stand it to be moved one extra foot, and the Diamond A stuff would have to take their chances with the rest. Reckon they're right, at that. Well, it was funny. See and Johnny Hopper and old Aforesaid was walking stifflegged around Hall and Mason. Red Murray, he was swelled up at Hopper, 'cause Turnabout Spring was dryin' up on him, and he'd bought that from Hopper. And all hands sore at Bud Faulkner, on account of his bunch of mares, them broomtails wearing out the range worse than three times the same amount of cattle. They was sure due for a bust-up. This little fuss was only the beginning, I reckon. Well, here's how!"

"I hope they do get to fightin' amongst themselves," growled Murphy, putting down his glass. "Mighty uppity, overbearin' bunch. They've been runnin' it over Tripoli something fierce. Hope they all go broke. Old man Bates, in particular. He's one all-round thoroughbred this-and-that!"

As Murphy brought out the last crushing word, Bull Pepper, standing next to him, hooked his toe behind Murphy's heel and snapped his left arm smartly so that the edge of his open hand struck fair on Murphy's Adam's apple. Murphy went down, gasping. First he clutched at his throat and then he reached for his gun. Pepper pounced down, caught a foot by heel and toe and wrenched violently. Murphy flopped on his face with a yell, his gun exploded harmlessly. Pepper bent the captive leg up at right angles for greater purchase and rolled his victim this way and that. Murphy yelled with pain, dropping his gun. Pepper kicked the gun aside and pounced again. Stooping, he grabbed a twisting handful, right and left, from bulging fullness of flannel shirt at Murphy's hips; and so stooping and straddling over the fallen, lurched onward and upward with one smooth and lusty heave. The shirt peeled over Murphy's head, pinioning his arms. Pepper twisted the tails together beyond the clawing arms, dragged his victim to the discarded gun, and spoke his mind.

"I don't agree with you," he said. He lifted up his eyes from that noisy bundle then for a slow survey of his audience. No one seemed contrary minded. He looked down again at his squirming bundle, shook it vigorously, and stepped upon it with a heavy foot. "Be quiet now, or I'll sqush you!" The bundle became quiet, and Pepper spoke to it in a sedate voice, kindly and explanatory. "Now, brother, it's like this. Bates has never been overly pleasant with me. Barely civil. But I think he's a good man for all that, and not what you said. Be that as it may, it is not a nice thing to be glad because any kind of a man is losing his cattle in a drought. No. Anybody got a string?"

Curses and threats came muffled from the bundle. "Did you hear me?" said Pepper sharply. He swooped down and took up Murphy's guns from the floor. "String is what I want. That silk handkerchief of Tham's will do nicely. Give it to Jake, Tham. You, Jake! You come here! You and Murphy both laid hands on me when I wanted to stop this fight. I'm declarin' myself right now. I don't like to be manhandled by any two men on earth. Step careful, Jake—you're walkin' on eggs! Now, you take two half-hitches around Mr. Murphy's shirt-tails with that handkerchief. Pull 'em tight! Pull 'em tight, I said! Do you maybe want me to bend this gun over your head? That's better. Now, Murphy, get outside and let Tripoli have a look. You and Joe Gandy, you been struttin' around right smart, lately, admirin' yourselves as the local heroes. I don't like it. Peace is what I want—peace and quiet. What's that, Murphy? Shoot me? Not with this gun you won't. This gun is mine."

He laid a large hand to Murphy's back and propelled him through the door.

"You surely aren't tryin' to bust them collar buttons loose, are you? No, no—you wouldn't do that, and me askin' you not to. You go on home, now."

As Pepper turn to cross the plaza, Spinal Maginnis fell in step beside him. "Goin' my way, Mr. Pepper?"

The pacifist stopped short. "I am not," he said with decision. "And I don't know which way you're going, either."

Spinal rubbed his chin, with a meditative eye on the retreating Murphy.

"I don't know that I ever saw a man sacked up before," he said slowly. "Is them tactics your own get-up, or just a habit?"

Mr. Murphy's progress was beginning to excite comment. Men appeared in the deserted plaza, with hard unfeeling laughter. A head peered tentatively from Jake's door. Mr. Pepper frowned. The head disappeared.

The hostility faded from Mr. Pepper's eyes, to be succeeded by an expression of slow puzzlement. He turned to Maginnis and his tones were friendly. "Overlooking any ill-considered peevishness of mine, dear sir and mister—you put your little hand in mine and come along with me."

He led the way to a shaded and solitary bench; he lit a cigarette and surveyed the suddenly populous plaza with a discontented eye; he clasped his knees and contemplated his foot without enthusiasm.

"Well?" said Maginnis at last.

"Not at all," said Pepper. "No, sir. This Dick Mason he's supposed to have brains, ain't he? And the Aforesaid Bates Andy Jackson, he has the name of being an experienced person? Wise old birds, both of 'em?"

"I've heard rumors to that effect," admitted Maginnis.

"Well, they don't act like it," said Pepper. "Tripoli and the cowmen, they've been all crosswise since Heck was a pup. But Mason, he opens up and lays it all before us. Lookin' for sympathy? I don't guess. Then old man Bates gets on the peck like that, exposin' his most secret thoughts to a cold and callous world. It don't make sense. And that fight they pulled off! I've seen school kids do more damage."

"I didn't see the fight," said Maginnis.

"No, you didn't. You and all these here visiting waddies just happened in opportunely—just in time to stop it." Pepper regarded his companion with cold suspicion. "Eddy Early, Lafe and Cole and you, and this man Evans—that's some several old-timers turnin' up in Tripoli—and not one of you been here before in ten years. I tell you, Mr. Spinal Maginnis, Esquire, horsethief and liar—I've been thinkin'!"

"You mustn't do that, feller," said Spinal anxiously. "You'll strain yourself. You plumb alarm me. You don't act nowise like any town man, anyhow. Not to me."

"I was out of town once," admitted Pepper. "Some years ago, that was."

"Curious," said Spinal. "Once a man has put in some few years tryin' to outguess pinto ponies and longhorned steers, he ain't fooled much by the cunnin' devices of his fellow humans. But I'm no sheriff or anything like that—so don't you get uneasy in your mind. On the other hand, if you really insist thinking—Has it got to be a habit with you?"

"Yes. Can't break myself of it. But I won't say a word. Go on with your pranks, whatever they are. But I'm sure sorry for somebody."

"Well, then," said Spinal, "as a favor to me—if them thoughts of yours begin to bother your head, why, when you feel real talkative, just save it up and say it to me, won't you?"

"I'll do that," said Pepper. "You rest easy."

ii

Because the thrusting messa was high and bare, with no overlooking hills or shelter of trees for attacking Apaches, men built a walled town there, shouldering above the green valley; a station and a resting place on the long road to Chihuahua. England fought France in Spain that year, and so these founders gave to their desert stronghold the name of Talavera.

When England and France fought Russia in the Crimea, Talavera dreaded the Apaches no more, and young trees grew on the high mesa, cherished by far-brought water of a brave new ditch. A generation later the mesa was a riot of far-seen greenery; not Talavera now, but Tripoli, for its threefold citizenship: the farmers, the miner folk from the hills, who built homes there as a protest against the glaring desert, and the prosperous gentry from sweltering San Lucas, the county-seat. These last built spaciously; a summer suburb, highest, farthest from the river, latest and up-to-date. Detraction knew this suburb as Lawville.

Where the highest *acequia* curved and clung to enfold the last possible inch of winnings, the wide windows of Yellowhouse peered through the dark luxurious shade of Yellowhouse Yards. The winding *acequia* made here a frontier; one pace beyond, the golden desert held undisputed sway. Generous and gracious, Yellowhouse Yards; but Pickett Boone had not designed them. They had been made his by due process of law. Pickett Boone was the "slickest" lawyer of San Lucas.

"Wildest game ever pulled off in Tripoli," said Joe Gandy. It was the morning after the sacking up of Blinker Murphy. A warmish morning; Gandy was glad for the cool shadows of Yellowhouse Yards.

"Big money?"

"O man! And the way they played it! Dog-everlasting-gone it, Mr. Boone, I watched 'em raise and tilt one pot till I was dizzy—and when it comes to a showdown, Eddie Early had Big and Little Casino, Cole Ralston had Fifteen-Six, Yancey had Pinochle, and old Aforesaid had High, Low, Jack and the game. Yessir; three of 'em stood pat, and bet their fool heads off; and that old mule of a Spinal Maginnis saw it through and raked the pot with just two spindlin' little pair, tens up. I never did see the beat."

Pickett Boone considered leisurely. A film came over his pale eyes. "And they put the boots to Bates?"

"Stuck him from start to finish. They was all winners except him and Spinal. About the first peep o' day, Bates pushes back his chair. 'Thankin' you for your kind attention,' he says, 'This number concludes the evenin's entertainment.' Then he calls for the tab and gives Jake a check for twenty-eight hundred."

"You seem to be bearing up under the loss pretty well," said Boone. He eyed his informant reflectively. "You're chief deputy and willing to be sheriff. But someway you've never made much of a hit with Bates and the Mundo Chico crowd."

Gandy scowled. "After what Bull Pepper's tender heart made him do to Murphy, I dasn't say I'm glad old Bates shot his wad. Bull Pepper here or Bull Pepper there, I'm now declaring myself that I wish I might ha' grabbed a piece of that. I can't see where it helps Tripoli any to have all that good dough carried off to Magdalena and Salamanca and Deming. Jake set in with 'em at first—and set right out again. Lost more than the kitty totted up to all night. They sure was hittin' 'em high."

"Well, what's the matter with Lithpin Tham? I've heard Tham was lucky at cards."

"Some of them visiting brothers must have heard that same thing," said Joe moodily. "Tham sort of hinted he might try a whirl, and them three Salamanca guys just dropped their cards and craned their necks and stared at Tham till it was plumb painful. Tham blushed. Yes, he did. No, sir, them waddies was all set to skin Bates, I reckon, and they wasn't wishful for any help a-tall. They looked real hostile. 'Twasn't any place for a gentleman."

"It is the custom of all banks," said Lawyer Boone reflectively, "to give out no information concerning their clients. But—" His voice trailed to silence.

"I got you," said the deputy. "But a lame man can always get enough wood for a crutch? So you know just about how much Aforesaid had left—is that it?"

"How little," Boone made the correction with tranquility.

"I'm thinking the whole Little World bunch is about due to bust up," said Joe jubilantly.

"He always wanted that Little World country, Pickett Boone did," said Pickett Boone. "Mason's only chance to pay Pickett was to get the Bates to tide him over. Pickett was afraid of that. That's off, after him and Bates beating each other up. To make it sure and safe, Bates blows his roll at poker. Good enough. The banks have loaned money to the cowmen up to the limit, what with the drought and the bottom fallen out of prices. So Mason can't get any more money from any bank. And he can't sell any steers, the shape they're in now. Pickett's got him," said Pickett, with a fine relish. "He'll get Hall too. More than that, he'll get old Bates, himself, if the dry weather holds out."

"But if the drought lasts long enough, don't you stand to lose?" Gandy eyed the money-lender curiously. "As you say yourself, the banks don't think a mortgage on cattle covers the risk when it doesn't rain."

Pickett Boone smiled silkily. "My mortgages cover all risks." Then his lips tightened, his pale eyes were hot with hate, his voice snarled in his throat. "Even if I lose it—I'll break that insolent bunch. Mighty high-headed, they are—but I'll see the lot of 'em cringe yet!"

"They've stuck together, hand-in-glove, till now," said Joe eagerly. "And Mr. Charlie See, with that bunch to back him, he's been cuttin' quite a swath. But they're all crossways and quarrelin' right now—and if the drought keeps up they'll be worse. Once they split," said Joe Gandy, "you and me can get some of our own back."

"Hark!" said Pickett Boone. "Who's coming?"

A clatter of feet, faint and far, then closer, near and clear; a horse's feet, pacing merrily; on the curving driveway Mr. Aforesaid Bates rode under an archway of pecan trees. An ear was swollen, an eye was green and yellow, but Mr. Bates rode jauntily and the uninjured eye was unabashed and benign.

"A fine morning, sir. Get off," said lawyer Boone. "This is an unexpected pleasure."

"The morning is all you claim for it," said Aforesaid Bates, dismounting. "But the pleasure is—all yours. For Andy Bates, it is business that brings him here."

"Say, I'll go," said Gandy.

"Keep your seat, Joe. Stay where you are. Whenever I've got any business that needs hiding I want the neighbors to know all about it. 'It's like this, Mr. Boone, I gave a little party last night and so I thought I might as well come over and sign on the dotted line.'"

"You thought—what?"

"I want to borrow some money of you. I gotta buy hay and corn and what not, hire a mess of hands and try to pull my cattle through."

"Money," said Pickett Boone austerely, "is tight."

"Oh, don't be professional," said Bates. "And you needn't frown. I get you. Why, I never heard of money that wasn't tight."

"Why don't you go to the bank?"

"The bank wouldn't loan me one measly dollar," said Bates, "and well you know it. If it would only rain, now, it would be different. Too risky. That's just like me. Kindhearted. Sparing you the trouble of saying all this, just to save time. Because I've got to get a wiggle."

"If it is too risky for the banks it is too risky for me."

"Whither," said Bates dreamily, "whither are we drifting? Of course it's risky for you. You know it and I know it. What a lot of fool talk! Think I've been vaccinated with a phonograph needle? You've been yearnin' for my ranch since Heck was a pup. That's another thing we both know. I'm betting you don't get it. Halfway House and the brand, I'll bet, against four thousand with interest three years 12 per cent. Call it a mortgage, of course, but it's a bet and you know it. I'm gambling with you."

"The security is hardly sufficient," said Boone icily. "I might consider three thousand for, say, two years. Your cattle may all die."

"Right. Move up one girl. If it doesn't rain," said Aforesaid Bates, with high serenity, "those cattle are not worth one thin dime. And if the cattle go I can't pay. Surest thing you know. But the ranch will be right there—and you'll lend me four thousand on that ranch and your chance on any cattle toughing through, and you'll loan it to me for three years, or not at all. No—and I don't make out any note for five thousand and take four thousand, either. You just save your breath, mister. You'll gamble on my terms, or not at all."

"You assume a most unusual attitude for a would-be borrower," observed the lawyer acidly. His eyes were smoldering.

"Yes, and you are a most mighty unusual will-be lender, too. What do you want me to do? Soft-soap you? Tell you a hard luck story? You've been wanting my scalp, Mister Man. Here's your chance to take it—and you dassent let it pass. I see it in your hard old ugly eye. You want me to borrow this money, you think I can't pay it back, and you think Halfway House is as good as yours, right now. You wouldn't miss the chance for a thousand round hard dollars laid right in your grimy clutch. So all you have to do is offer one more objection—or cough, or raise your eyebrow—and I'm off to sell the ranch to Jastrow. I dare you to wait another minute," said this remarkable borrower, rising. "For I am going—going—"

"Sit down," snapped the lawyer. "I'll make out the mortgage. You are an insolent, bullying, overbearing old man. You'll get your money and I'll get your ranch. Of course, under the circumstances, if you do not keep your day you will hardly expect an extension!"

"Listen to the gypsy's warning," said Mr. Bates earnestly. "You'll never own one square foot of my ranch! Now don't say I didn't tell you. You do all your gloatin' now while the gloatin' is good."

The three rode together to the nearest notary public; the papers were made out and signed; the Aforesaid Bates took his check and departed, whistling. Gandy and Boone paced soberly back to Yellowhouse Yards.

"Mr. Andrew Jackson Aforesaid Bates—the old smart Aleck!" sneered Pickett Boone. "Yah! He's crossed me for ten years and now, by the Lord Harry, I've got him in the bag with Hall and Mason! Patience does it."

Gandy lowered his voice. "We can ease the strain on your patience a little. More ways than one. You know Bates has strung a drift fence across the canyon above Silver Spring? Yes? That's illegal. He's got a right smart of grass in the roughs up there, fenced off so nobody's cattle but his can get to it. If somebody would swear out a complaint, it would be my duty as deputy sheriff to see that fence come down. Then everybody's cattle could get at that fenced grass—"

The lawyer's malicious joy broke out in a startling sound of creaking rusty laughter.

"That would start more trouble, sure! We'll have to make you the next sheriff, Joe. Count on me."

Joe's eyes narrowed. He tapped the lawyer's knee with a strong forefinger: he turned his hand upside down and beckoned with that same finger. "Count *to* me! Cash money, right in my horny hand. Sheriff sounds fine—but you don't have all the say. I've got more ideas, and I need money. Do I get it?"

"If they're good ones."

"They're good and they're cheap. Not too cheap. I name the price. How do I know you'll pay me? Easy. If you don't, I'll tip your game. Sure. That fence now. Uncle Sam's Land Office lets out a roar, old Aforesaid knows it's my duty to take it down. Lovely. D'ye suppose I could make that complaint myself and get away with it? Not much. That old geezer is one salty citizen. And if it comes to his ears that it was you that set up the Land Office—do you see? Oh, you'll pay me a fair price for my brains, Mr. Boone. I'm not losing any sleep about that. We understand each other."

The lawyer peered under drooping lids. "We may safely assume as much," he said gently. "Now those other ideas of yours?"

"What do you think Bates is going to do with that money you lent him? Buy alfalfa with it—cottonseed meal, maybe—that's what. So will the other guys, so far as their money goes—all except Charlie See, with his thirty-six square miles of fenced pasture to fall back on—and Echo Mountain behind that. He doesn't need any hay. Well, you've got plenty money. You go buy up all the alfalfa stacks in the upper end of the valley. You can get it for ten—twelve dollars a ton, if you go about it quietly. Then you soak 'em good. They've got to have it. Farther down the valley, the price will go up to match, once they hear of your antics. Nowhere else to get it, except baled hay shipped in. You know what that costs, and you squeeze 'em accordin'. Same way with work. They'll need teams and teamsters. You run up the price. Them ideas good, hey? Worth good money?"

"They are. You'll get it."

The deputy surveyed his fellow crook with some perplexity. "I swear, I don't see how you do it," he grumbled. "Fifty men here-abouts with more brains in their old boots than you ever had—and they're hustlin' hard to keep alive, while you've got it stacked up in bales."

"I keep money on hand," said the lawyer softly. "Cash money. And when these brainy men need cash money—"

"You needn't finish," said Joe gloomily. "You take advantage of their necessity and pay a thief's price. Funny thing, too. You're on the grab, all right. Money is your god, they say. But you're risking a big loss in your attempt to grab off the Little World range—big risks. And, mister, you're taking long chances when you go up against that Little World bunch—quite aside from money. Get 'em exasperated or annoyed, there isn't one of the lot but is liable to pat you on the head with a post-maul."

The lawyer raised his sullen eyes. "I can pay for my fancies," he said in a small quiet voice. "If it suits my whim to lose money in order to break these birds, I know how to make more. These high-minded gentlemen have been mighty scornful to a certain sly old fox we know of. They owe me for years of insult, spoken and unspoken." He had never looked so much the man as in this sincerity of anger. "Their pride, their brains, their guns!" he cried. "Well, I can buy brains, and I can buy guns, and I'll bring their pride to the dust!"

Gandy threw back his hat and ran his hand through his sandy hair in troubled thought; he eyed his patron with frank and sudden distaste. "My brains, now—they ain't so much. Bates or Charlie See—to go no further—can give me cards and spades. Mason, maybe—I dunno. But I've got just brains enough that you can't hire my gun to go up against that bunch—not even when they're splitting up amongst themselves. You listen to me. Here's a few words that's worth money to hear, and I don't charge you one cent. Listen! *Those . . . birds . . . don't . . . care . . . whether . . . school . . . keeps . . . or . . . not!*—Yessir, my red head is only fair to middlin', but I know that much. Moreover, and in addition thereunto, my dear sir and esteemed employer, those same poor brains enable me to read your mind like coarse print. Yessir. I can and will tell you exactly the very identical thought you now think you think. Bet you money, and leave it to you. You're thinkin' maybe I'll never be sheriff, after all. . . . H'm? . . . No answer. Well, that's goin' to cost you money. That ain't all, either. Just for that, I'm goin' to tell you something I didn't know myself till just now. Oh, you're not the only one who can afford himself luxuries. Listen what I learned." He held his head up and laughed. "That Little World outfit have done me dirt and rubbed it in; and as for me, I am considerable of a rascal." He checked himself and wrinkled his brow in some puzzlement. "A scoundrel, maybe; a sorry rascal at best. But never so sorry as when I help a poisonous old spider like you to rig a snare for them hardshells. So the price of ideas has gone up. Doubled."

"Another idea? You'll get your price—if I use it," said the lawyer in the same small, passionless voice.

"What part of your steer crop do you expect to be in shape to sell?" demanded the vendor of ideas.

"Twenty-five per cent. More, if it should rain soon."

"One in four. Your range is better than theirs and your stock in better shape. And you expect to get, for a yearling steer strong enough to stand shipping?

"Ten dollars. Maybe twelve."

"Here's what you do. There won't be many buyers. You go off somewhere and subsidize you a buyer. Fix him; sell him your bunch, best shape of any around here, for eight dollars or ten. Sell 'em publicly. That will knock the bottom out and put the finishing touches on the Little World people."

"Well, that's splendid," said Boone jubilantly. "That's fine! In reality, I will get my eleven or twelve a head, minus what it costs to fix the buyer."

"Well—not quite," said Gandy. "You really want to figure on paying me enough to keep me contented and happy! What do you care? You can afford to pay for your fancies."

iii

No smoke came from the chimney. Dryford yard was packed and hard, no fresh tracks showed there or in the road from the gate, no answer came to his call. Hens clucked and scratched beneath the apple trees and their broods were plump and vigorous. The door was unlocked. The stove was cold; a thin film of dust spread evenly on shelf and table, chairs and stove.

"Up on the flats, tryin' to save his cows," said Hob. "Thought so. Up against it plenty, cowmen are." Unsaddling, he saw a man on foot coming through the fenced fields to Dryford. Hobby met him at the bars. The newcomer was an ancient Mexican, small and withered and wrinkled, who now doffed a shapeless sombrero with a flourish. *"Buenos dias, caballero!"* he said.

"Buenos dias, senor. My name is Hobby Lull, and I'm a friend of Johnny's."

"Oh, *si, si!* I haf hear El Señor Juan spik of you—oh, manee time. Of Garfiel'—no?"

"That's the place. And where's Johnny? Up on the flat?'

"Oh, *si!* Three months ago. You are to come to my little house, plizz, and I weel tell you, while I mek supper. I am to take care here of for El Señor Johnny, while the young man are gone to help this pipple of Mundo Chico. *Ah, que malo suerte!* Ver' bad luck! for thoss, and they are good pipple—*muy simpatico.* Put the saddle, plizz, and come. Een my house ees milk, eggs, fire, alfalfa for your horse—all theengs. Her is ver' sad—lonlee."

"So Johnny has quit the valley three months ago?" said Hobby on the way.

"Oh, yes! Before that we are to help him cut out the top from all these cottonwoods on the reevir, up beyond the farms. Hees cows they eat the leaf, the little small branch, the mistletoe, the bark. Eet ees not enough. So we are to breeng slow thoss cows with the small calf—oh, veree slow!—and put heem een our pastures, a few here, a few there—and we old ones, we feed them the alfalfa hay from the stack. The pasture, he ees not enough. But eet ees best that they eat not much of these green alfalfa, onlee when eet ees ver' es-short."

"Yes, I know. So as not to bloat them. I noticed a mess of cows and calves in the pastures, as I came in. And up on the flat, are their cattle dying much?"

"Pero no, hombre. Myself, I am old. I do not go—but Zenobio he say no. Some—the old cows, is die—but not so manee. Veree theen, he say, veree poor, but not to die—onlee some."

"I don't understand it," said Hobby. "Drought is a heap worse here than anywhere else. Fifty miles each way, last fall, we had quite some little rain—but not here. Tomorrow, I'll go look see how come."

Tomorrow found Hobby breaking his fast by firelight and well on his way by the first flush of day. He toiled up the deep of the draw and came to the level plain with the sun. Early as he was, another was before him. Far to the south a horseman rode along the rim, heading towards him. Hobby dismounted to wait. This might be Johnny Hopper. But as he drew near Hobby knew the burly chest and bull neck, Pepper of Tripoli, "Bull" Pepper. Garfield was far from Tripoli, but in New Mexico, generally speaking, everyone knew everybody. Hobby sat cross-legged in the sand and looked up; Pepper leaned on the saddlehorn and looked down. "Picnic?"

"Hunting for Hopper, Bates—any of the bunch."

"So'm I. Let's ride. It's going to be a scorcher."

The sun rode high and hot as they came to Halfway House. The plain shimmered white and bare, the grass was gnawed to a stubble of bare roots, the bushes stripped bare; a glare of gray dust was thick about them and billowed heavily under shuffling feet. They rode through a dead and soundless world, the far-off ranges were dwindled and dim, the heat rose quivering in the windless air, and white bones beside the trail told the bitter story of drought.

"Ain't this simply hell?" croaked Pepper. "And where's the cattle? Must be a little grass further out, for I haven't seen one cow yet today. Come to think of it, I didn't see but most might few dead ones either—considerin'."

"That's it, I guess. They've hazed 'em all away from here. Hey, by Jove! Not all of 'em! Look there!" Hobby reined in his horse and pointed. Halfway House lay before them, a splotch of greenery at the south horn of Selden Hill; far beyond and high above, up and up again, a blur of red and white moved on the granite ribs of the mountain. Far and high; but they saw a twinkling of sun on steel, and a thin tapping came steadily to their ears, echoborne from crowning cliffs; tap—tap—tap, steady and small.

"Axes!" said Pepper. "They're chopping something. I know—*sotol!* Heard about it in Arizona. Chopping *sotol* to feed the cattle. C'me on, cowboy—we're goin' to learn something."

There were no cattle in the water pens. They watered their horses, they rode up the Silver Spring trail, steep and hard. Where once the *sotol* bush had made an army here, their lances shining in the sun, a thousand

and ten thousand, the bouldered slope was matted and strewn with the thorn-edged saber-shaped outer leaves of the *sotol*, covering and half-covering those fallen lances.

"Think of that, now! They cleaned off every *sotol* on this hill, like a mowing machine in grass. Fed the fleshy heart to the cows—and chopped off sixteen hundred million outside leaves to get at the hearts." Pepper groaned in sympathy. "Gosh, what a lot of work! They're almost to the top of the mountain, too. If it don't rain pretty quick, they're going to run out of fodder. Here, let's tie our horses and climb up."

"Where I stayed last night," said Hobby, "the old Mexican said the young men were working up here. I see now what they were doing. Reckon there's an axe going in every draw and hill-slope." Turning, twisting, they clambered painfully up the rocky steep and came breathless to the scene of action. The cattle, that once would run on sight, were all too tame now, crowding close upon their sometime enemies in their eagerness for their iron rations; struggling greedily for the last fleshy and succulent leaves. Poor and thin, they were, rough coated, and pot-bellied, but far from feeble; they now regarded the intruders with some impatience, as delaying the proceedings. The axemen were two: Mr. Aforesaid Bates, Mr. Richard Mason. Mr. Bates' ear was still far from normal and the bruise beneath his misused eye was now a sickly green; while Mr. Mason wore a new knob on his jaw, a cut on his chin and a purple bruise across his cheek. Both were in undershirts, and the undershirts were soaked with sweat; both beamed a simple and unaffected welcome to the newcomers.

"Here you are!" said Dick, gaily and extended his axe.

Pepper glowered, his face dark with suspicion. He shook a slow forefinger at them. "Bates, I never was plum crazy about you. There's times when you act just like you was somebody—and I don't like it. All the same, there's something goin' on that ain't noways fittin' and proper. Friend or no friend, I rode out here to wise you up. And now I've got half a mind to ride back without tellin' you. What do you think you're doin', anyhow?"

"Drawing checks," answered Bates. "Checks on the First Bank of Selden Hill." He waved his hand largely. "Mighty good thing we had a deposit here too."

"You know damn well what I mean. What was the idea of pulling that fake fight, huh?"

"Why, Mr. Pepper!" said Mason in a small, shocked voice. "I do hope you didn't think Andy and me was fightin'? Why, that was just our daily dozen. We been tryin' to bring the cattle up by hand since early in May . . . like this. So we felt like we needed exercise—not to get soft, there in town. Must be you've never seen us when we was really fighting."

"Here, I want to say some talk," said Bull firmly. "That's the trouble with you old men, you want the center of the stage all the time. Information is what I want. Where's your cows and calves? There's none here. Where's your mares? We didn't see a track. How's Charlie See making it? Where's Johnny Hopper? Who, why, when, where? The Bates eye, the Mason face—how come? Tell it to me."

"I stepped on my face," said Dick Mason. "The rest is a long story."

"We serve two meals a day," said Bates. "Early as we can and late as we can—dodgin' the sun as much as possible. Cows never get enough, but when their ribs begin to crack we stop chopping. Then they go down to drink in the middle of the day, and come back up for supper. Don't have to drive 'em. Just as far as they can hear an axe they totter to it."

"After this," said Mason, "we're never goin' to work cattle that old-fashioned way again—roundups and all that. When we want to take 'em somewhere, we'll call 'em. Maybe we can just tell 'em where to go. That is," he added, "if it ever rains any more."

"And you're feeding little bunches like this all around the mountain?" said Pepper.

"Correct. We brought up two-three wagonloads of axes and Mexicans and grindstones," said Bates. "We tried to give the cattle to the Mexicans and have them pay us wages, but they wouldn't stand for it. Yessir, all along Selden Hill and Checkerboard, for thirty-five miles, you can behold little pastoral scenes like this, anywhere there's a hillside of *sotol*. They burn the thorns off prickly pears, too, and feed them, as they come to 'em. Them old days of rope and spur is done departed. See and Hopper and Red—them nice young fellows with blistered hands and achin' backs—it was right comical. Tell you while we stir up dinner—and that's after we get those doggies fed. No beef. Not a thing fit to kill. Even the deer are tough and stringy. But you first, Mr. Pepper—you was sayin' you was uneasy in your mind, if any. Spill it."

"You and Hopper bought up a lot of alfalfa down in the valley, didn't you?"

"Yes. That was for all of us. Several stacks."

"Well, Pickett Boone he went snoopin' around and found that out. From Serafino how much you paid. Ten dollars. Cash? No. Written contract or word of mouth? Just a promise. Boone says he'll pay more and pay cash. Twelve dollars! No. Thirteen? Fourteen? No, says Serafino, mighty sorrowful—word of a *caballero*. A trade is a trade. Same way at Zenobio's. But old José Maria fell for it, and Boone bought his hay, over your head, at fourteen. Mateo's too. Isn't that a regular greaser trick?"

"I'd call it a regular Pickett Boone trick, myself. Pickett Boone ought to have his adenoids removed," said Mason, with a trace of acrimony. "He reminds me of a rainy day in a goat shed."

"Well, Boone he's fixin' to bleed you proper. He sends out his strikers right and left, and he's contracted for just about all the hay in this end of the valley—cut and uncut. I'll tell a man! All down in black and white. Pickett Boone, he don't trust no Mexican."

Bates sighed. "That's all right, then. Myself, I think them Mexicans are pretty good *gente*. They sure followed instructions. Kept mum as mice, too."

"What!" said Bull Pepper.

"Yes," said Bates. "To feed what cows and calves we got under fence at Dryford, we really wanted some of that hay. What Boone didn't buy, and a couple of loads we hauled up here to my place. But for all the other ranches except mine, it's a heap easier to haul baled hay from Deming on a level road, than to drag uphill through sand from the valley. So we told the Mexicans what not to say, and how. Made a pool. Mexicans furnished the hay and we furnished Boone. The difference between ten a ton and what Boone pays—close on to four hundred tons, be the same more or less—why, we split it even, half to the Mexicans, half to us."

"Give me that axe," said Pepper.

iv

"The time to take care of cattle durin' a drought," said Aforesaid Bates sagely, "is to begin while it is raining hard."

A curving cliff made shelter of deep shade over Silver Spring. Hobby and Mason washed dishes by the dying fire; Bull Pepper sat petulant on a boulder, and lanced delicately under fresh blisters on his hands; Bates sprawled happily against a bed roll, and smoked a cob pipe; luxurious, tranquil and benign.

"We wasn't quite as forehanded as that," said Bates, "but we done pretty well. First off, Charlie See had his big pasture, knee-high in untouched grass, and everybody cussing him. Cuss words is just little noises in the air. They didn't hurt Charlie none—and the grass was there when needed. Then I built a drift fence across the box and kept everything out of what grass there is in the rough country above here. So I had me a pasture of my own. Plenty rocks and cliffs, some grass and right smart of browse. So far, so good. Then last year it didn't rain much, so See and Hopper and me, we shipped off all our old stuff for what we could get. We even went so far as to name it to the other boys that they might do the same." He paused to knock out his pipe.

"Do you know, boys," said Mason, "that old coot has to bring that up, no matter what he's talking about? Every time. Name it to us? I'll say he did. 'Sell off the old cows and low-grade—keep the young vigorous stuff.'—Lord, how many times I've heard that!"

"And did you sell?" asked Hobby.

"No, I didn't. But Bates, he told us so. He admits it."

"Order having been restored," said Bates, "I will proceed. No snow last winter, no grass this spring. It never rains here from March to July, of course; and along about the middle of April we began to get dubious would it rain in July. So we made a pool. Likewise, we took steps, plenty copious. High time, too. Lots of the old ones was dyin' on us even then."

"Just like he told us they would," said Mason, and winked.

Bates ignored the interruption. "First of all, we rounded up all the broomtailed mares—about four hundred all told. Most of 'em was Bud Faulkner's. but none of us was plumb innocent. We chartered Headlight, sobered him up, give him some certified checks and a couple of Mex boys and headed him for Old Mexico with the mares.

"By then the cow stuff was weak and pitiful. We couldn't have even a shadow of a roundup—but we did what was never seen before in open country. We set up a chuck wagon, a water wagon, one hay wagon and two when needful and a wagon to haul calves in—and by gravy, we worked the whole range with wagons. We had two horses apiece, we fed 'em corn, and we fed hay when we had to; and we moved the cows with calves—takin' along any others that was about to lay 'em down. When we came to a bunch, they'd string out. The strongest would walk off, and then we'd ease what was left to the nearest hospital. We made a pool, you understand. Not mine, yours or his. We took care of the stock that needed it most, strays and all. Why, there was some of Picket Boone's stuff out here, and they got exactly the same lay that ours did—no more, no less.

"We tailed 'em up. I'm leavin' out the pitiful part—the starving, staggering and bawling of 'em, and the question their eyes asked of us. Heartbreakin', them eyes of theirs. I reckon they caught on mighty early that we was doin' our damnedest for 'em, and that we was their one and only chance. A lot of 'em died. It was bad.

"We shoved about two hundred of the strongest cows and calves in the roughs above here, in that pasture I fenced off. They've stripped this end bare as a bone now, and moved up to Hospital Springs. We took the very weakest down to the river. Scattered them out with Johnny's Mexican neighbors. And we had to haul baled hay to feed that bunch to keep 'em alive while we moved 'em. But the great heft of 'em, starving stuff, we threw into Charlie See's pasture. Everybody's, anybody's. Charlie didn't have a head of his own in there, except according to their need."

"That was white of Charlie See—it sure was," said Pepper, staring thoughtfully across the sunburned plain below them. "And he was the most obstreperous of the whole objectionable bunch, too. Hmn! I begin to think you fellows make a strong outfit."

"One for all and all for one—that sort of blitherin' junk," said Mason cheerfully. "Men and brothers, fellow citizens, gentlemen and

boys—you ought to have seen that work. In two months we didn't rope a
cow or trot a horse. We never moved a cow out of a walk, a creeping walk.
We never moved a cow one foot in the wrong direction. We moved 'em
late in the evenin', on into the night, early in the morning; we spoke to
'em politely and we held sunshades over 'em all day. We never slept, and we
ate beans, flies, dust, patent food and salt pork. I ate through four miles of
sidemeat and never struck a shoulder or a ham. And concernin' Charlie
See's pasture-that you was makin' eyes about, Mr. Pepper—I've heard some
loose talk that *if* it rained, and *if* we pulled through, and *if* we was lousy
with money three or four years from now, and if we felt good-natured and
Charlie had been keepin' in his place in the meantime, and we hadn't
changed our minds or got religion, we might do this and that to make it
up to Charlie. But," said Mr. Mason loftily, "I don't take no stock in such,
myself. Talk's cheap."

"And who was the master mind?" asked Hobby. "Who got this
up? You, Uncle Andy?"

"Why, no," said Bates, "I didn't. Charlie See took the lead, naturally, when he threw open his pasture to all hands. We made a pool, I tell
you. Combined all our resources. Them that had brains, they put in brains,
and those that didn't, they put in what they had. Mason had a mess of old
wagons. They come in handy, too. Hopper, he thought of working his
Mexican friends for pasture. Hall, he studied up our little speculation in
hay; Red thought it would be a bright idea to have Bud Faulkner's mares
hie them hence, and Bud, he showed us what an axe would do to *sotol*
bush. I'm comin' to that."

"I had some extra harness, too," said Mason meekly. "Coming
down to facts, the auditor was my idea, too. That's what I said—auditor.
Remember Sam Girdlestone, that was searchin' for oil last year? Well, he
come back visiting, and found us in a fix. We put him to work. He keeps
track of all costs, and credits us with whatever we put in, cash, credit, work,
wagons, or wisdom. We give him a percentage on our losses. He does other
little chores—tails up cows, runs the pump and hunts water, chops up a
few hundred *sotols* between times. But his main job is posting up the account books—at night while we relax. Likely lad, Sam. Aside from that,"
said Mr. Mason, "Andy is a pernicious old liar, and well he know it. Charlie See has got a little sense in his own name—I'll admit that. The rest of us
have just enough brains to keep a stiff upper lip, and that lets us out. Andy
Bates is the man. We may some of us dig up a bolt or two in a pinch—but
old Andy Bates is the man that makes the machine and keeps it oiled.
F'rinstance, Henry Hall broke out into prophecy that Boone wouldn't miss
nary chance to do us dirt on the alfalfa—but it was Aforesaid that rigged
the deadfall accordin'. Bud Faulkner was feeding *sotol*, a head and a half to

a cow and a half, in a day and a half. So Bates gets him a pencil and a tally book, ciphers two-three days till his pencil wore to a stub and announces that if so many *sotol* hearts a day—running in size from a big cabbage head up to a big stove—would keep so many cows alive so many days, then several more *sotol* heads would keep several thousand head till it rained, if any. We saw this, after he explained it to us, and we hired all the Mexicans north of a given point. That's the way it went. You tell 'em, Andy. It's a sad story."

"Cows, calves and stretcher cases attended to," said Bates, "we taken a long look. Way out on the desert west of Turnabout, there's tall grass yet. Tall hay—cured on the stem. It's clear away from all water holes but ours, and too far from ours for any but the ablest. We left them huskies be, right where they was. I'll say they was determined characters. Surreptitious and unbeknownst to them, while they'd gone back to grass, we edged the other cattle easy into the hills and began givin' 'em first aid with *sotol*. June, July and now August most gone—and the sun shinin' in the daytime. Tedious. Only when it would cloud up, it would be a heap worse. Look like it was goin' to rain pitchforks—but nary a drop ever dropped. Gentlemen, it has been plum ree-diculous! We haven't lost many cattle, considerin'. We've kept our stock, we've kept our lips in the position indicated by friend Mason, of Deep Well; and we've kept our sorrows to ourselves."

"Except when desirable to air them?" hinted Pepper. "In Jakes's place, for example? With a purpose, perhaps?"

"Except when desirable. But we've lost most of our calf crop, most of next year's calf crop, our credit is all shot, and what cash we have can't be squandered paying old bills—because we need it to buy what we can't get charged. See? And no one knows how long it will take the *sotol* to make a stand again for 'next time'."

"There ain't going to be no next time," said Mason. "Me and Hall is goin' to keep our cattle sold off, like you said. Or was it you that advised against overstocking? I think you did. We got men chopping *sotol* on every hill and men cooking for 'em in every canyon, and another man sharpening axes on a grindstone, men hauling water to the cooks, men hauling hay to the men who haul water to the cooks, and a man hauling axle grease to the men who haul the hay to the men who haul water to the cooks. Three thousand head we're feedin' *sotol* to. Oh, my back, my back!"

"It seems to me," said Bates, "That I did mention somethin' of the kind. That brings the story to date. That's why I wrote to you, Hobby. You haven't been at Garfield long, your credit's good. We want to ease out all the steers that can put one foot in front of another, and get you to wheedle 'em along to Garfield, gradual, place 'em around amongst the Mexican's pastures, where they'll get a little alfalfa, watch 'em that they don't bloat, buy hay for 'em as needed—on jawbone—and get 'em shaped up for late sales, if any. If the drought breaks, we need all the money we can get. If it stays dry, we need all the money there is. That's the lay. If there should happen to be any steer from a brand that isn't mortgaged, you'll have a claim on him to make you safe. Are you game?"

"You know it," said Hob.

"A very fine scheme," said Bull Pepper approvingly. "But like all best-laid plans, it has a weak point. And I don't see why it shouldn't go a-gley as you, Billy bedam please on that one point."

"Yes?" said Aforesaid encouragingly. "Tell it to us."

"I'm the weak point," said Pepper. "I've thought seriously of shooting Red Murray in the back—some dark night, when I'd be perfectly safe, of course. Charlie See, too—worse'n Red. Most obnoxious young squirt I ever see, Charlie is. Hall and Hopper give me the pip, Faulkner sets my teeth on edge. And as for you two, yourselves—if you will excuse me for being personal?"

"Yes, yes—go on!"

"Even for you old geezers, my knees are not calloused from offering up petitions in your behalf."

"Oh, we know all that," said Aforesaid reassuringly. "But how does the application come in?"

"Tripoli, now," urged Pepper. "You have ill-wishers in Tripoli. But no one comes up here even in good seasons. Tripoli thinks you are chousing each other's cattle, cat-and-dogging all over the shop. Tripoli doesn't know of any of these very interesting steps you have taken—not even that you have driven your mares away. Tripoli doesn't dream that you are in a fair way to pull through if unmolested, or you'd sure be molested a-plenty. Just for sample, if Tripoli storekeepers, or San Lucas storekeepers, where you owed big bills—if they owed big money to one of your ill-wishers, and if they received instructions to demand immediate payment—see? Just begin with that, and then let your fancy lead you where you will. Now that you gentlemen have opened up your souls and showed me the works, what's to hinder me from hiking down and giving the show away?"

"You don't understand," said Bates patiently. "If you had been that kind of a man, we wouldn't have said a word. See?"

"I see," said Pepper. "And you haven't made any mistake, either. If my saddle could talk, I'd burn it. I'll be one to help Lull with your steers—and by the Lord Harry, I'll lend you what money I've got to tide you over."

"Why, that's fine, Bull, and we thank you. Glad to have you plod along with the drive, but we won't need any money. Because," said Bates, "I have already—uh—effected a loan. The best is, I've got three years to pay it in. Boone was very kind."

"You old gray wolf. I sensed it, sort of—and yet I could hardly believe it. I sensed it. You gymnasticked around and made Pickett Boone think you and Mason were on the prod; you went through the motions of goin' broke at poker, so you could trick him into lending you money—virtually extendin' Mason's mortgage. For, of course, that's what you got it for. Dear, oh dear! Ho-ho-ho! I hope to be among those present when they hang you!"

"Had to have that," said Aforesaid modestly. "Mason's mortgage is due directly. We aim to pay Hall's mortgage with our steer money, and when mine falls due, maybe someone will pay that. Lots can happen in three years."

"Give me that axe," said Pepper. "I'm working with the Little World now."

Red-faced and sweating, Andy Bates became aware that someone hailed him from the trail below. He shouldered his axe and zigzagged down the hill.

"That's Joe Gandy," said Bates to Bates. "Gee whiz, I wonder if someone is sueing me already? They have to sue. Can't spare any money now." To the deputy he said, when they met, "Hullo, Joe! What's your will?"

"Sorry Mr. Bates—but it has been reported to the Land Office that you're fencing in government land, and they wrote up for me to investigate. Made me deputy U.S. marshal pro tem. Sorry—but I have to do my duty."

"Yes I know," said Bates, without enthusiasm. "That fence, now? I did build a fence, seems like. Let me see now—what did I do with that fence? Oh yes—I know!" His face brightened, he radiated cheerfulness. "I took it down again. You ride up and see. You'll find a quarter of a mile still standing across the canyon at Silver Spring. That's on my patented land—so be you be damn sure you shut the gate when you go through. Beyond my land, you'll find the fence down, quite a ways anyhow. Wire rolled up and everything. If you find any trees tangled together or rocks piled up, you have my permission to untangle and unpile, if the whim strikes you. Away to your duty with you! I'll wait here till you come back."

With a black look for the old man, Gandy spurred up the trail. It was an hour later when he came back.

"Well?" said Bates, from beneath a stunted cedar.

"The fence is down, as you said—some of it."

"I knew that. What I want to know is, did you shut that gate?"

Gandy's face flamed to the hair-edge. He shook a hand at his tormentor, a threatening index finger extended. "You saved up that grass, turned your cattle in to eat it up, and then took the fence down."

"If such were the case," inquired Bates mildly, "exactly what in the hot hereafter do you propose to do about it? Don't shake your finger at me. I won't have it. Careful, fellow, you'll have a fit if you don't cool off. But you're wrong. Somebody told me that fence was illegal, I remember. So I hot-footed up there and yanked her down. You see," said Bates meekly, "I figured some meddlesome skunk would come snoopin' and pryin' around, and I judged it would be best if I beat him to it. That's one of the best things I do—beating 'em to it."

"You insolent old fool!" bawled Gandy. "Have you got a gun?"

Bates stared. "Why, son," he said beamingly, "I wear my gun only when I go in swimming. No need to stand on ceremony with me—not at any time. Be sure I'm awake, and then go ahead."

Gandy pulled himself together with an effort, breathing hard. "You stubborn fool," he said thickly, "if it wasn't for your old gray beard I'd stomp you right into the ground."

Bates smiled benevolently. "Give up the gun idea, have you? That's good. As to the other proposition, it's like this. I got chores on hand, as you see." He waved his hand at the hillside, where fifty cows awaited his return to resume breakfast. "Feedin' my cows. It would hinder me terrible to be stomped into the ground right now. But I'll tell you what I'll do. Either it will rain or it won't. If it don't rain, my poor corpse will be found somewhere beside a *sotol*, still grasping an axe handle in my—in his—I mean, in its cold dead hands. In that case, all bets is off. But if it ever rains, I'm goin' to heave a long sigh, and a strong sigh altogether. Then I'm goin' to sleep maybe a month. And then I'm goin' down to Tripoli and shave my old gray beard off. When you meet up with me, and I'm wearin' a slick face, you begin stomping that face, right off. Bear it in mind. Be off on your duties, now. I've got no more time to waste on you. Hump yourself, you red-headed son of Satan, or I'll heave this axe at you."

V

Strained, haggard and grim, August burned to a close in a dumb terror of silence. September, with days unchanging, flaming, intolerable desperate: last and irretrievable ruin hovered visible over the forlorn and glaring levels. Twice and again clouds banked black against the hills with lightning flash and thunder, only to melt away and leave the parched land to despair. The equinox was near at hand. With no warning, night came down on misery and morning rose in mist. The mist thickened, stirred to slow vague wheelings, vase and doubtful, at the breath of imperceptible winds; halted, hesitated, drifted; trembled at last to a warm thin rain, silent and still and needle-fine. The mist lifted to low clouds, that fine rain grew to a brisk shower, the shower swelled to a steady downpour; earth and beast and man rejoiced together. Black and low and level, clouds banked from hill to hill, the night fell black and vast, and morning broke in bitter storm. All day it held in windy shrieking uproar, failed through the night to a low driving rain, with gusty splashes and lulls between. Then followed two sunless days and starless night, checkered with shower and slack. The sun-cracked levels soaked and swelled. Runoff started in the hills, dry cañons changed in turn to rivulets, to torrents, to roaring floods, where boulders ground together in a might diapason; and all the air was vibrant with the sound of many waters. The springs were filled and choked, trails were gullied and hillside roads were torn. The fifth day saw blue patches of the sky. But the drought was broken; the brave earth put forth blade and shoot and shaft again.

Dim in the central desert lies a rain-made "lake"—so-called. Its life is but brief weeks or months at best; five years in ten it is not filled at all. Because of that, because it is far from living water, because the deepest well, as yet, has found no water here, the grama grasses are still unruined, untouched save in time of heavy rains. Shallow and small, muddy, insignificant, lonely, unbeautiful; in all the world there is no "lake" so poor—and none more loved. You may guess the reason by the name. It was called *Providencia*—three hundred years ago. Smile if you will. But if the cattle have a name for it, surely their meaning is not different from ours.

The starved life of the Little World still held the old tradition of this lonely lake. Everywhere, in long, slow, plodding strings, converging, they toiled heavily through the famished ranges to their poor land of promise and the lake of their hope.

Pickett Boone's steers were in Tripoli pens. Other small herds were held near by on the mesa, where a swift riot of wild pea-vine had grown since the rains begun. Riders from these herds were in to hear of prices. Steers were in sorry shape buyers were scarce and shy.

John Copeland, steer-buyer, rode out slowly from the pens with Pickett Boone. They halted at a group of conversational cowmen.

"Well, boys, I've sold," said Pickett Boone. He held out his hands palm up, in deprecation. "Ten dollars. Not enough. But what can I do? I can't hold them over—nearly a thousand head."

A murmur of protest ran around the circle of riders. Some were eloquently resentful.

"Sorry, boys," said the buyer. "But we would make more if your stuff shaped so we could pay you fifteen. Your steers are a poor buy at any price. Wait a minute while I settle with Boone." He produced a large flat billbook. "Here's your check, Mr. Boone. Nine thousand, eight hundred dollars. Nine hundred and eighty steers. Correct?"

Boone fingered the check doubtfully. "Why, this is your personal check," he said.

Copeland flipped it over and indicated an endorsement with his thumb. "John Jastrow's signature. You know that—and there's Jastrow, sitting on the fence. 'S all right?"

"Oh, I guess so," said Boone.

"And here's the bill of sale, all made out," said the buyer briskly. "Here's my fountain pen. Sign up and I'll be trading with the others."

A troubled look came to Boone's eyes, but he signed after a moment's hesitation.

"Witnesses," said Copeland. "The line forms on the right. Two of you. Then we'll go over to the other fellows and talk it up together. Thanks. Let's ride."

Boone motioned Copeland to the rear. "Come down as soon as you can," he said in an undertone, "and we'll finish up."

"Huh?" said Copeland blankly.

"Pay me the balance—two dollars a head—and I'll give you my check for five hundred, as we agreed."

"My memory is shockingly poor," said Copeland, and sighed.

Boone turned pale. "Are you going to be a dirty thief and a double-crosser?"

"I wouldn't put it past me," confessed Copeland. "Mine is a low and despicable character. You'd be surprised. But I'm never crooked in the line of my profession. Among gentlemen, I believe, that is called 'the point of honor.' You may have heard of it. If I made any agreement with you— depend upon it, I took the proposition straight to John Jastrow. I never hold out on a client."

"This is a conspiracy!" said Boone. He trembled with rage and fear.

"Prove it," advised the buyer. "Lope up and tell the boys what you framed up. I've got your bill of sale, witnessed. Go tell 'em!"

"They'd shoot me," said Boone, choking on a sob.

"That is what I think," said Copeland unfeelingly, and rode on.

A shout went up as the buyer overtook the cavalcade. "Here come the West Side boys." The newcomers were Mason and Murray, of the Little World, with young Sam Girdlestone attached.

"Hullo, Dick—Where's your herd? And where's the rest of you?"

"Howdy, boys!" said Mason. "Bates and See, they've gone on downtown. We didn't bring any steers. Prices too low.—So we hear."

"Boone sold at ten dollars," said Bill McCall. "I'll starve before I'll take that."

Mason smiled. "We won't sell, either. Not now. We aim to get more than twelve, by holding on a spell."

Boone turned savagely and reined his horse against Mason's. He dared not let these men guess that he had tried to tamper with the price. Stung for a heavy loss, but afraid to seek redress—here was one in his power, on whom he could safely vent his fury. "Your gang may not sell, but you'll sell, right now. Your time's up in a few days, and I'm going to have my money!"

"Well, you needn't shriek about it." Mason's brow was puckered in thought; he held his lower lip doubled between thumb and finger, and remembered, visibly. "That's so, I do owe you something, don't I? A mortgage? Yes, yes. To be sure. Due about October twentieth? . . . Let me see, maybe I can pay you now. Can't afford to sell at such prices."

"I get twelve dollars," declared McCall stoutly, "Or my dogies trudge back home."

"Oh, I'll give you twelve," said the buyer. "Prices have gone up. I just sold that bunch again—them in the pen, for twelve dollars. To Jastrow."

"O-h-h!" A wolf's wail came from Boone's throat.

"How's that?" demanded McCall. "Thought Jastrow bought 'em in the first place?"

"Oh, no. I bought 'em in behalf of a pool."

Mason unrolled a fat wallet. "Here, Mr. Boone, let's see if I've got enough to pay you." He thumbed over checks, counting them. "Here's a lot of assorted checks—Eddy Early, Yancy, Evans—all that poker-playing' bunch. They tot up to twenty-eight hundred all told." He glanced casually at Pickett Boone. That gentleman clung shaking to the saddlehorn, narrowly observed by mystified East Siders. Mason prattled on unheeding, "And old Aforesaid, he gave me a bigish check this morning. Glad you reminded me of it, Mr. Boone."

"You know, Mr. Mason," said Copeland, "You're forgetting your steer money. Here it is. Two dollars a head. Nineteen hundred and sixty dollars. Nice profit. You might better have held out for twelve, Mr. Boone. These Little World people made a pool and brought your steers—and then sold them to Jastrow in ten minutes."

"You come on downtown after a while, Mr. Boone," said Mason. "Bring your little old mortgage and I'll fix you up. Take your time. You're looking poorly."

Sam Girdlestone and Henry Hall were riding down the pleasant street toward supper, when Sam took note of an approaching pedestrian. He had a familiar look, but Sam could not quite place him.

"Who's that, Henry?" said Sam.

Hall reined in, and shouted. "Heavens above! It's Squire Bates, and him shaved slick and clean! Hi, Aforesaid, what's the idea? You gettin' married, or something?" He leaned on the saddlehorn as Bates drew near. "Heavens above, Andy—what in the world has happened to your nose?"

"My nose?" said Bates, puzzled. He glanced down the nose in question, finding it undeniably swollen. He fingered it gingerly. "It does look funny, doesn't it?"

"Look there! What's happened?" cried Sam, in a startled voice. "That man's hurt!"

Bates turned to look. Two men came from the door of Jake's Place, supporting the staggering steps of a third man between them. The third man's arms sprawled and clutched on the escorting shoulders, his knees buckled, his feet dragged, his head drooped down upon his chest, his whole body sagged. Bates held a hand to shield his eyes and peered again. "Why, I do believe it's Joe Gandy!" he declared.

"But what's happened to him, Uncle Andy?" demanded Sam eagerly.

Bates raised clear untroubled eyes to Sam's. "I remember, now," he said. "It was Joe Gandy that hit me on this nose. . . . How it all comes back to me! . . . The Bible says when a man smites you on one cheek to turn the other, so I done that. Then I didn't have any further instructions, so I used my own judgment!"

Twenty Straight on the Prairie

BY EMERSON HOUGH

Emerson Hough was born (1857) and raised in Iowa. After graduating from the Iowa State in 1880, he began a career as an editor and journalist, writing frequently for the outdoor magazines. An avid sportsman and conservationist, he managed the Chicago office of *Field and Stream* for a time, traveled widely, and wrote outdoor adventure stories and features based upon his journeys. He particularly loved the American West, its stories and peoples; and he was to write several, what can only be described as peans, to its mythic heroes and villains. In the late 1890s he began to publish full-length novels. They were immediately and immensely popular. His was a new synthesis of romance and adventure, character, setting and humor. He is generally considered, along with Andy Adams, Owen Wister and Zane Grey, to have first shaped that species of cowboy story we call the Western.

This is a sweet little tale, almost a tenderfoot story, but not quite. We are uncertain exactly when it was written (*North Of 36,* from which it is excerpted, was published two years after his passing) but it is definitely mature work. Even in this short tale we recognize qualities that were to be his signatures.

The story is character driven and evidences a great ear for dialogue and a gentle sense of humor. It is relentlessly optimistic. There's even a pretty girl, though in this story, she remains off stage.

★　★　★　★　★

The great herd, scattered over a mile of grazing ground, by now was well quieted. Wearied by their own exertions, some of the animals were lying down, as though aware that the end of their journey was at hand; the remainder scattered, grazing contentedly. Men were on guard here and there at the edges of the herd; others were at the fire, eating. A sudden excitement arose among the cow hands when word passed that a buyer was on the scene, for so they interpreted the advent of Nabours and his companions. Nabours waved a hand with genuine cowman enthusiasm.

"Look at them!" he exclaimed. "Did you ever see a finer outfit of cows in your borned days, Mr. Pattison?"

The face of the trader remained expressionless, though his eyes were busy as he rode.

"You've got some she-stock in here," said he at length; "some yearlings in too. I should say, too, that you've got several sorts of brands."

"Well, maybe we have," said Nabours. "I'd have a damned sight more if we had not hit so much country where there wasn't no cows coming north. This here herd belongs to a orphant, Mr. Pattison, and in our country they ain't no questions asked about orphants. We put up this herd in our own country. Our road brand is a Fishhook, and when you buy a Fishhook steer you are buying our support of the brand—twenty good men that can shoot. I got to sell these cows straight too."

Pattison reined up, still dubious.

"Let me tell you something. I know beef—that's my trade. You've got maybe three or four hundred of light stuff and shes. They don't pack well. Still, here I am with a good ranch over on the Smoky Hill. It hasn't got a head of stock on it yet.

"I just took in the land and water and trusted to God for the cattle. I know where the real money is, and it isn't in buying lean fours. If I had any way to handle these stockers over on my ranch I'd take your herd straight."

"I can't split no cows," said Jim Nabours. "It's all or none. I got to sell all these cows afore dark. We both allowed that five minutes was plenty."

"Well, it is," said Pattison quietly. "I trade as quick as anybody, and I don't go to the saloon first, as two or three other men have, whom I happen to know, that came on that train. Now I'll tell you what I'll do: If you'll hold out that stuff below the fours I'll give you twenty straight for your fours, right here on the prairie. Five thousand cash down, balance in draft on the First National of Kansas City."

Suddenly Dan McMasters turned to Nabours.

"The herd is sold," said he. "Twenty a head, straight through."

"How do you mean, Dan?"

"I am taking all the she-stuff and stockers for myself. Let Mr. Pattison have the fours."

"But what're you going to do?"

"I am thinking of starting a Northern ranch for myself. It don't take me long to decide either. I believe Mr. Pattison is right. There's where the money is. Besides, I'm leaving Texas before long."

Pattison turned toward him with his quizzical smile, estimating him after his own fashion.

"You bid me up, young man," said he; "but you've sold this herd, yearlings and all, at twenty straight on the prairie.

"Now, we've got plenty time left—two minutes by the watch. I'll give you just a minute and a half to think of me as your partner in my ranch on the Smoky Hill, myself to own half this stuff you've just bought in, you to trail a fresh herd up to us next year and to run this upper ranch for me—all dependent on your investigation of me back East, preferably by telegraph to-night. I've got the land, you've got the cows.

"I'll show you how to get three-four-five cents a pound for beef on the hoof. What do you say?"

McMasters turned his own cool gray eyes upon the other, regarding him with a like smile as their eyes met, and their hands.

"We have traded," said he quietly.

Nabours looked from one to the other, scratching his head.

"Then is my cows sold?" he demanded. "Do we get twenty straight?"

"You heard us," said Pattison. "There is a new company on the new northern range—the PM brand. Mr. McMasters is my partner; you see, I know something about him already. And I want to say to you, sir, you are on the road to more money than you could ever make in Texas. We'll cut this stuff and tally out to-morrow if it pleases you. Come on over to the fire, partner; let's light down."

Each in his mood, Nabours somewhat chastened as he endeavored to figure out how much the five minutes' work had meant to him, they moved to where the giant cart of Buck the cook loomed on the level prairie. Pattison reached into the pocket of his coat and drew out a great package of folded bills, which he tossed on the ground before him as he reached for his coffee cup.

"I think that's five thousand dollars," said he. "I can't carry much cash with me, of course. In town, I'll give you a draft on the First National of Kansas City for fifty-five thousand more if the herd tallies out three thousand head. I am almost ready to take your own tally."

"No," said Jim Nabours, "we haven't tallied out since the last run; I been scared to. If we hadn't had no bad luck down the trail there wouldn't 'a' been money enough in Kansas City to buy all them cows we started with. Do you mean to say to me that you're going to give me sixty thousand dollars for them cows?"

"I certainly am if you don't object too much about it. And I call this a good day's work. I have bought the first northern-trail herd. Besides, I have got a partner and a manager for my ranch, and a line of supply for the ranch, too. Yes, I call it a good five minutes' work.

"You shall have all the time you want to put up your half for these stockers, Mr. McMasters," he added.

"I don't want any time," replied Dan McMasters. "I can raise a little money. You see, I know the history of this herd. I'd almost have been ready to buy it straight through at twenty a head myself."

"I was afraid you would," said Pattison. "But I wanted the cows and a partner too. All right, take your pleasure as to your half of the northern ranch ante. I tell you, I am going to make you more money than either of us ever made in our lives. Lord, this is just the beginning of things! What a fine world it is out here!"

He turned to the others as he went on, tin cup of coffee in hand.

"You see, I am banking on two things that you Texas men didn't know anything about. One is the stockyards at Kansas City. The other is a packing business in Kansas City. There's going to be the market for this range stuff. Meantime I'll have to get some of your boys to drive these fours over to Junction City for me. I'll buy all your ponies except what you need to get back home. My partner and I will need some horses for the PM outfit on the Smoky Hill.

"Oh, I don't blame you for not seeing the game very far ahead up here," he went on. "This is a colder country than you are used to. But if I can hire some of your men to run the herd for us, they can build dugouts in a few days like those you saw in town, and hole up warm and snug for the winter. After a while you'll begin to make hay, but you'll need a whole lot less than you think right now.

"We are going to start the first winter ranch on the heels of the first herd north of thirty-six. I am going to show you that cows will do a heap better when you fatten them north of the edge of winter and north of the tick line.

"Is our five minutes up? I don't like to waste time here. Let's go back to town."

"When do we deliver, then?" asked Nabours.

"You've sold and delivered right now and right here, on the prairie, replied Pattison. "I am hiring all the men that will go in with Mr. McMasters and me; we'd like at least six or eight. Mr. McMasters will come out to help tally to-morrow if that suits you. I never knew a Texas cowman to falsify a count, and I never knew one that didn't go broke trying to pack his own cattle. It takes big men to do big business, and you will have to pardon me if I say it never was in the cards to pack cattle in Texas, by Texas or for Texas. The South needs the North in this thing. It's going to take both the North and the South to make this country out here." He swept a wide arm. "The West! Oh, by golly!"

"Well," sighed Jim Nabours, still unable to credit his sudden good fortune, "my boss is the richest girl in Texas right now, if she was in Texas. I'll have to admit she owes part to a damn Yankee, same as part to us Texans."

He turned earnestly to the Northern trader.

"You've got to see our boss when you get in town," said he. "You'll be glad to see where all your money went to. She shore is prettier than a spotted pup."

"Well, let's ride," laughed Pattison. "We'll have a look at Abilene and the Texas orphan."

"On our way!" said Nabours, and they mounted. Nabours rode off to accost one of his men. "We've sold the herd, Len," said he. "I'll pay off to-morrow in town. All you fellows that wants to hire out to these folks can do it. You split the men to-night, Len, and half of you come to town if you feel like it.

"Oh, yes," he added, turning, as he started off, "I forgot to tell you. I forgot to tell you that Cal Dalhart got killed in town a little while ago. I heard it just when I left. Del Williams done shot him, looks like."

"The hell he did!" remarked Hersey. "Well, it was plain enough the last three months they had it in for each other—both allowing to marry Miss Taisie."

"And now they won't neither of them will," nodded Nabours. "Ain't it hell how men fuss over a woman? Now Del's gone somewheres. Both good cow hands as ever rid. That's the fourth man I've lost since we left home, not mentioning several hundred cows. I'm the onluckiest man in the world.

"Yet," he went on as he joined McMasters and Pattison, addressing the former, "I call this a good day's work. We've brung our brand through, and we've done sold her out. I reckon Mr. Sim Rudabaugh has played in hard luck. He didn't keep us out of Aberlene, now did he?"

"He did his best," replied Dan McMasters. "He got here just a little too late. He came to town on the train just a little while ago. There are two or three of his men here already, maybe more."

Nabours looked at him narrowly, suddenly serious.

"Some of us boys'll be in town to-night," said he.

As they rode by the jumbled heap of the camp-cart goods a very exact observer might have noted that the pair of wide horns carefully cherished by Len Hersey had disappeared since the first passing of the group from town. No one had particularly noticed Len as he rode up near the cart with a stubborn little yearling dogy on his rope; it was thought the cook had requisitioned beef. But now, as the party turned to leave the herd, the keen eye of Pattison caught sight of an astonishing creature, scarce larger than a calf, but bearing so enormous a spread of horns as would have graced any immemorial steer of the Rio Grande.

"My Lord!" he exclaimed. "What on earth is that? Is that the way cattle grow down in your country?"

"Yes, sir," replied Len gravely, still holding the animal on his reata. "He's a nice little yearling. Give him time, an' he'll raise right smart o'horn. O'course, he's still young. Texas, she sort of runs to horn, in some spots, special seems like."

"Spots? Spots? What spots?" demanded Pattison. "Where'd that critter come from?"

"He come from our range, sir," replied Len. "He range over with a bunch near the Laguna Del Sol. They all watered in there, at the Laguna. Near's we could tell there must be something in the water in the Laguna sort of makes the cows in there run to horn, like."

"Well, I should say so! But still, you can't make me believe that any steer less than four could ever grow horns like that."

"Oh, yes, they kin." Rejoined this artless child of the range. "My pap used to drive down to Rockport, on the coast—I've helped drive south, to ship cows on the Plant steamers. I reckon they was going to Cuby. We had to rope every steer and throw him down and take a ax and chop off his horns, they was so wide. That was to give more room on the boats. Some steers didn't like to have their horns chopped off thataway. Well, here we got plenty of room for horns anyhow." He swept an arm over the field of waving grass reaching on to the blue horizon. "Give me three years more on this dogy and I promise you he'll have horns.

"Speaking of horns, Jim," he resumed; "once when we were driving in a coast drive we turned in a lot of dogies, of course claimin' a cow was a cow, an' nache'l, four years old even if it was only a yearling. Well, the damn Yankee who was buying our cows he kicked on so many dogies. Of course, none of us fellers'd ever heard of a thing like that; a buyer allus taken the run o' the delivery, head for head. Says he, 'I ain't buyin' yearlin's, I'm buyin' fours.'

"Well, we driv in another dogy right then, on of them Lagunies, an' he had horns big as this one here. The damn little fool he put on more airs than any Uvalde mossy horn about his headworks. It was just like he said, 'Look at me! I done riz these her horns in one year, where it taken you maybe a hunderd.' Cows was their pride, mister, same as us. Uh-huh.

"But do you believe me? That damn Yankee wouldn't take my word that the horns of them Lagunies gets their growth early sometimes. I says, 'Mister, I'll bet you a hundred dollars that's a four.' 'Well, maybe it is,' says he. He scratch his haid. But he couldn't git over it. When we come to load in at the boat he says, 'Well I be damned ef that ain't the littlest cow I ever seen fer a four.' I was sort o'hot by then, and I says, 'Boss, you're right—that ain't a four, it's a yearlin'.'

"Well, then he swung around the other way. Says he, 'It kain't noways be a yearlin', not with them horns. I bought too many cows not to know that much. It don't stand to reason that no yearlin' can raise no horns more'n five foot acrost.' You see, mister, that yearlin' was carryin' horns about like this one—one of our Lagunies. O'course, I don't say that all Texas cows has horns like that as yearlin's; you can see that fer yore own self right here. Only way we could convince that gentleman was to show him."

"Well, that may all be," said Pattison, nettled, "Anyhow, I always take my own judgment in cattle, ages and all. I've known buyers who couldn't tell long twos from threes. I've studied cattle.

"I never did much," said Len Hersey; "I never had time. But my folks couldn't never break me of gamblin'—monte, you know. Sometimes I win a shirt, and then agin I'd lose one. Right now"—he looked ruefully at his elbow—"I'd like fer to win one. I'll gamble that critter's a yearlin', now. I'd hate to take a man's money on a cinch; but ef you, now, was feelin you'd like to peel off a couple of hundred against my hawse an' saddle, an' what's left of my shirt, why, I'd hate to rob you—I'd bet that that's a year-lin'. I was goin' to kill it fer beef. We don't eat the horns, mister, but them Lagunies is special tender on account of that something in the water around there."

"You fool Texans deserve to be trimmed," said Pattison; "a boy like you putting your judgment up against that of one of the oldest buyers that ever saw Kansas City."

"I know it—I know I'm foolish," nodded Len Hersey, "I was borned thataway. I allus hatter be bettin' on monte er somethin'. Still I'll bet thataway on this here yearlin' ef you insist. Does you?"

"I certainly do, just to teach you a lesson. Here, Mr. Nabours"—he pulled out his roll of bills once more—"take this couple hundred, against this man's horse and saddle. You be the judge. He bets that's a yearling. That suit you?" He turned to Len Hersey, who still was holding the mooted animal on his reata.

"Yes, all right," humbly replied that youth.

"Throw him, Len," commanded Nabours; "then we'll all look him over and decide." He was as solemn as his man.

Len sunk a spur and with a leap his pony crossed in front of the quarry, swept its feet from under it. It was thrown with such violence that one of its horns was knocked off and lay entirely free on the grass. Jim Nabours, dismounting, gravely held up the remaining horn, easily detach-able from the normal stubby yearling growth on the dogy's head. He looked at Pattison dubiously, none too sure how he would take this range jest. But the Northern man was a sportsman. He broke into a roar of laughter, which for hours he renewed whenever the thought again came to his mind.

"Give him his money, Nabours," said he. "He's won it fair and I've had a lesson, and when your boys come to town the treat's on me. Keep those horns for me," he added. "If I don't sell old Mitch or young Phil Armour at Kansas City with those horns I'll eat them both!" Again he went off into gusty laughter, in which all could join.

"Sho, now." said Len Hersey. "Now look at that! He must of got his horns jarred loose, like, in some night run in the timber. I've knowed that to happen."

"Len," commanded Nabours, "I don't want no more of this damned foolishness. Here's ten dollars, and that's enough to buy you a shirt, and I want to see you do it. He'll only play the rest at monte or faro or something," turning to Pattison.

"No, give it all to him." The latter rejoined. "It's his. Let him play it. I've done as much myself when I was younger. And monte's a cinch compared to buying and packing and shipping cattle to the East."

They turned and rode toward town, young in the youth of the open range, where to-morrow did not yet loom.

Hopalong Nurses a Grouch

BY CLARENCE E. MULFORD

When I was a kid, growing up in the late '50s and early '60s, there were three cowboy kings: Roy Rogers, Gene Autry, and Hopalong Cassidy. I knew them from TV, and spent many rainy weekend afternoons watching their old movies. My personal favorite was Roy; I didn't care for Gene. And Hopalong I liked okay, but there was something staid about him, something middle-aged; in the person of actor Bill Boyd, his hair was white, which was a thing not necessarily to be held against him, but odd. He didn't drink or swear or gamble; that was alright with me, I didn't do those things either—then. He did his talking in a quiet, earnest voice, and was always reasonable, even respectful to the villains he was soon to thrash or gun down. He was always neat and clean—not much of a recommendation to a nine-year-old boy. But he did dress all in black, and the trimmings (hat, gun belt, boots) were fancy, and I loved that. Imagine my surprise when I read my first Hopalong Cassidy story, and set this book Hoppy beside the movie Hoppy. The original Hoppy is nearly the complete opposite of the movie character. Clarence E. Mulford's Hoppy is a bow-legged down-at-heels saddle-tramp, an ornery, bad-tempered, hot-headed young galloot. He smokes, drinks, gambles, swears, shoots up the place, and then drinks some more. His clothes are filthy and he smells like a horse. He's a misanthrope and a bully, and you can't help loving him.

Clarence E. Mulford published his first Hopalong Cassidy story in *Outing Magazine* in 1905. In 1907 he published the first of the Hoppy novels: *Bar 20,* following this in 1910 with *Hopalong Cassidy,* then in 1911 with *Bar 20 Days,* from which this story is excerpted.

So, please introduce yourself to the real Hopalong Cassidy. And if you've already had the pleasure, just say howdy to an old friend. But, if he's got even a little of that wild look in his eye, best save your piece for later.

★　★　★　★　★

After the excitement incident to the affair at Powers' shack had died down and the Bar-20 outfit worked over its range in the old, placid way, there began to be heard low mutterings, and an air of peevish discontent began to be manifested in various childish ways. And it was all caused by the fact that Hopalong Cassidy had a grouch, and a big one. It was two months old and growing worse daily, and the signs threatened contagion. His foreman, tired and sick of the snarling, fidgety, petulant atmosphere that Hopalong had created on the ranch, and driven to desperation, eagerly sought some chance to get rid of the "sore-thumb" temporarily and give him an opportunity to shed his generous mantle of the blues. And at last it came.

No one knew the cause for Hoppy's unusual state of mind, although there were many conjectures, and they covered the field rather thoroughly; but they did not strike on the cause. Even Red Connors, now well over all ill effects of the wounds acquired in the old ranch house, was forced to guess; and when Red had to do that about anything concerning Hopalong he was well warranted in believing the matter to be very serious.

Johnny Nelson made no secret of his opinion and derived from it a great amount of satisfaction, which he admitted with a grin to his foreman.

"Buck," he said, "Hoppy told me he went broke playing poker over in Grant with Dave Wilkes and them two Lawrence boys, an' that shore explains it all. He's got pack sores from carrying his unholy licking. It was due to come for him, an' Dave Wilkes is just the boy to deliver it. That's the whole trouble, an' I know it, an' I'm damned glad they trimmed him. But he ain't got no right of making us miserable because he lost a few measly dollars."

"Yo're wrong, son; dead, dead wrong," Buck replied. "He takes his beatings with a grin, an' money never did bother him. No poker game that ever was played could leave a welt on him like the one we all mourn, an' cuss. He's been doing something that he don't want us to know—made a fool of hisself some way, most likely, an' feels so ashamed that he's sore. I've knowed him too long an' well to believe that gambling had anything to do with it. But this little trip he's taking will fix him up all right, an' I couldn't 'a' picked a better man—or one that I'd rather get rid of just now."

"Well, lemme tell you it's blamed lucky for him that you picked him to go," rejoined Johnny, who thought more of the woeful absentee than he did of his own skin. "I was going to lick him, shore, if it went on much longer. Me an' Red an' Billy was going to beat him up good till he forgot his dead injuries an' took more interest in his friends."

Buck laughed heartily. "Well, the three of you might 'a' done it if you worked hard an' didn't get careless, but I have my doubts. Now look here—you've been hanging around the bunk house too blamed much lately. Henceforth an' hereafter you've got to earn your grub. Get out on that west line an' hustle."

"You know I've had a toothache!" snorted Johnny with a show of indignation, his face as sober as that of a judge.

"An' you'll have a stomach ache from lack of grub if you don't earn yore right to eat purty soon," retorted Buck. "You ain't had a toothache in yore whole life, an' you don't know what one is. G'wan, now, or I'll give you a backache that'll ache!"

"Huh! Devil of a way to treat a sick man!" Johnny retorted, but he departed exultantly, whistling with much noise and no music. But he was sorry for one thing: he sincerely regretted that he had not been present when Hopalong met his Waterloo. It would have been pleasing to look upon.

While the outfit blessed the proposed lease of range that took him out of their small circle for a time, Hopalong rode farther and farther into the northwest, frequently lost in abstraction which, judging by its effect upon him, must have been caused by something serious. He had not heard from Dave Wilkes about that individual's good horse which had been loaned to Ben Ferris, of Winchester. Did Dave think he had been killed or was still pursuing the man whose neck-kerchief had aroused such animosity in Hopalong's heart? Or had the horse actually been returned? The animal was a good one, a successful contender in all distances from one to five miles, and had earned its owner and backers much money—and Hopalong had parted with it as easily as he would have borrowed five dollars from Red. The story, as he had often reflected since, was as old as lying—a broken-legged horse, a wife dying forty miles away, and a horse all saddled which needed only to be mounted and ridden.

These thoughts kept him company for a day and when he dismounted before Stevenson's "Hotel" in Hoyt's Corners he summed up his feelings for the enlightenment of his horse.

"Damn it, bronc! I'd give ten dollars right now to know if I was a jackass or not," he growled. "But he was an awful slick talker if he lied. An' I've got to go up an' face Dave Wilkes to find out about it!"

Mr. Cassidy was not known by sight to the citizens of Hoyt's Corners, however well versed they might be in his numerous exploits of wisdom and folly. Therefore the habitues of Stevenson's Hotel did not recognize him in the gloomy and morose individual who dropped his saddle on the floor with a crash and stamped over to the three-legged table at dusk and surlily demanded shelter for the night.

"Gimme a bed an' something to eat," he demanded, eyeing the three men seated with their chairs tilted against the wall. "Do I get 'em?" he asked, impatiently.

"You do," replied a one-eyed man, lazily arising and approaching him. "One dollar, now."

"An' take the rocks outen that bed—I want to sleep."

"A dollar per for every rock you find," grinned Stevenson, pleasantly. "There ain't no rocks in my beds," he added.

"Some folks likes to be rocked to sleep," facetiously remarked one of the pair by the wall, laughing contentedly at his own pun. He bore all the ear-marks of being regarded as the wit of the locality—every hamlet has one; I have seen some myself.

"Hee, hee, hee! Yo're a droll feller, Charley," chuckled Old John Ferris, rubbing his ear with unconcealed delight. "That's a good un."

"One drink, now," growled Hopalong, mimicking the proprietor, and glaring savagely at the "droll feller" and his companion. "An' mind that it's a good one," he admonished the host.

"It's better," smiled Stevenson, whereat Old John crossed his legs and chuckled again. Stevenson winked.

"Riding long?" he asked.

"Since I started."

"Going fur?"

"Till I stop."

"Where do you belong?" Stevenson's pique was urging him against the ethics of the range, which forbade personal questions.

Hopalong looked at him with a light in his eye that told the host he had gone too far. "Under my sombrero!" he snapped.

"Hee, hee, hee!" chortled Old John, rubbing his ear again and nudging Charley. "He ain't no fool, hey?"

"Why, I don't know, John; he won't tell," replied Charley.

Hopalong wheeled and glared at him, and Charley, smiling uneasily, made an appeal: "Ain't mad, are you?"

"Not yet," and Hopalong turned to the bar again, took up his liquor and tossed it off. Considering a moment he shoved the glass back again, while Old John tongued his lips in anticipation of a treat. "It is good—fill it again."

The third was even better and by the time the fourth and fifth had joined their predecessors Hopalong began to feel a little more cheerful. But even the liquor and an exceptionally well-cooked supper could not separate him from his persistent and set grouch. And of liquor he had already taken more than his limit. He had always boasted, with truth, that he had never been drunk, although there had been two occasions when he was not far from it. That was one doubtful luxury which he could not afford for the reason that there were men who would have been glad to see him, if only for a few seconds, when liquor had dulled his brain and slowed his speed of hand. He could never tell when and where he might meet one of these.

He dropped into a chair by a card table and, baffling all attempts to engage him in conversation, reviewed his troubles in a mumbled soliloquy, the liquor gradually making him careless. But of all the jumbled words his companions' diligent ears heard they recognized and retained only the bare term "Winchester"; and their conjectures were limited only by their imaginations.

Hopalong stirred and looked up, shaking off the hand which had aroused him. "Better go to bed, stranger," the proprietor was saying. "You an' me are the last two up. It's after twelve, an' you look tired and sleepy."

"Said his wife was sick," muttered the puncher. "Oh, what you saying?"

"You'll find a bed better'n this table, stranger—it's after twelve an' I want to close up an' get some sleep. I'm tired myself."

"Oh, that all? Shore I'll go to bed—like to see anybody stop me! Ain't no rocks in it, hey?"

"Nary a rock," laughingly reassured the host, picking up Hopalong's saddle and leading the way to a small room off the "office," his guest stumbling after him and growling about the rocks that lived in Winchester. When Stevenson had dropped the saddle by the window and departed, Hopalong sat on the edge of the bed to close his eyes for just a moment before tackling the labor of removing his clothes. A crash and a jar awakened him and he found himself on the floor with his back to the bed. He was hot and his head ached, and his back was skinned a little—and how hot and stuffy and choking the room had become! He thought he had blown out the light, but it still burned, and three-quarters of the chimney was thickly covered with soot. He was stifling and could not endure it any longer. After three attempts he put out the light, stumbled against his saddle and, opening the window, leaned out to breathe the pure air. As his lungs filled he chuckled wisely and, picking up the saddle, managed to get it and himself through the window and on the ground without serious mishap. He would ride for an hour, give the room time to freshen and cool off, and come back feeling much better. Not a star could be seen as he groped his way unsteadily towards the rear of the building, where he vaguely remembered having seen the corral as he rode up.

"Huh! Said he lived in Winchester an' his name was Bill—no, Ben Ferris," he muttered, stumbling towards a noise he knew was made by a horse rubbing against the corral fence. Then his feet got tangled up in the cinch of his saddle, which he had kicked before him, and after great labor he arose, muttering savagely, and continued on his wobbly way. "Goo' Lord, it's darker'n cats in—oof!" he grunted, recoiling from forcible contact with the fence he sought. Growling words unholy he felt his way along it and finally his arm slipped through an opening and he bumped his head solidly against the top bar of the gate. As he righted himself his hand struck the nose of a horse and closed mechanically over it. Cow-ponies look alike in the dark and he grinned jubilantly as he complimented himself upon finding his own so unerringly.

"Anything is easy, when you know how. Can't fool me, ol' cayuse," he beamed, fumbling at the bars with his free hand and getting them down with a fool's luck. "You can't do it—I got you firs', las', an' always; an' I got you good. Yessir, I got you good. Quit that rearing, you ol' fool! Stan' still, can't you?" The pony sidled as the saddle hit its back and evoked profane abuse from the indignant puncher as he risked his balance in picking it up to try again, this time successfully. He began to fasten the girth, and then paused in wonder and thought deeply, for the pin in the buckle would slide to no hole but the first. "Huh! Getting fat, ain't you, piebald?" he demanded with withering sarcasm. "You blow yoreself up any more'n I'll bust you wide open!" heaving up with all his might on the free end of the strap, one knee pushing against the animal's side. The "fat" disappeared and Hopalong laughed. "Been learnin' new tricks, ain't you? Got smart since you been travellin', hey?" He fumbled with the bars again and got two of them back in place and then, throwing himself across the saddle as the horse started forward as hard as it could go, slipped off, but managed to save himself by hopping along the ground. As soon as he had secured the grip he wished he mounted with the ease of habit and felt for the reins. "G'wan now, an' easy—it's plumb dark an' my head's bustin'."

When he saddled his mount at the corral he was not aware that two of the three remaining horses had taken advantage of their opportunity and had walked out and made off in the darkness before he replaced the bars, and he was too drunk to care if he had known it.

The night air felt so good that it moved him to song, but it was not long before the words faltered more and more and soon ceased altogether and a subdued snore rasped from him. He awakened from time to time, but only for a moment, for he was tired and sleepy.

His mount very quickly learned that something was wrong and that it was being given its head. As long as it could go where it pleased it could do nothing better than head for home, and it quickened its pace towards Winchester. Some time after daylight it pricked up its ears and broke into a canter, which soon developed signs of irritation in its rider. Finally Hopalong opened his heavy eyes and looked around for his bearings. Not knowing where he was and too tired and miserable to give much thought to a matter of such slight importance, he glanced around for a place to finish his sleep. A tree some distance ahead of him looked inviting and towards it he rode. Habit made him picket the horse before he lay down and as he fell asleep he had vague recollections of handling a strange picket rope some time recently. The horse slowly turned and stared at the already snoring figure, glanced over the landscape, back to the queerest man it had ever met, and then fell to grazing in quiet content. A slinking coyote topped a rise a short distance away and stopped instantly, regarding the sleeping man with grave curiosity and strong suspicion. Deciding that there was nothing good to eat in that vicinity and that the man was carrying out a fell plot for the death of coyotes, it backed away out of sight and loped on to other hunting grounds.

★ ★ ★ ★ ★

Stevenson, having started the fire for breakfast, took a pail and departed towards the spring; but he got no farther than the corral gate, where he dropped the pail and stared. There was only one horse in the enclosure where the night before there had been four. He wasted no time in surmises, but wheeled and dashed back towards the hotel, and his vigorous shouts brought Old John to the door, sleepy and peevish. Old John's mouth dropped open as he beheld his habitually indolent host marking off long distances on the sand with each falling foot.

"What's got inter you?" demanded Old John.

"Our broncs are gone! Our broncs are gone!" yelled Stevenson, shoving Old John roughly to one side as he dashed through the doorway and on into the room he had assigned to the sullen and bibulous stranger. "I knowed it! I knowed it!" he wailed, popping out again as if on springs. "He's gone, an' he's took our broncs with him, the measly, low-down dog! I knowed he wasn't no good! I could see it in his eye; an' he wasn't drunk, not by a darn sight. Go out an' see for yoreself if they ain't gone!" he snapped in reply to Old John's look. "Go on out, while I throw some cold grub on the table—won't have no time this morning to do no cooking. He's got five hours' start on us, an' it'll take some right smart riding to get him before dark; but we'll do it, an' hang him, too!"

"What's all this here rumpus?" demanded a sleepy voice from upstairs. "Who's hanged?" and Charley entered the room, very much interested. His interest increased remarkably when the calamity was made known and he lost no time in joining Old John in the corral to verify the news.

Old John waved his hands over the scene and carefully explained what he had read in the tracks, to his companion's great irritation, for Charley's keen eyes and good training had already told him all there was to learn; and his reading did not exactly agree with that of his companion.

"Charley, he's gone and took our cayuses; an' that's the very way he came—'round the corner of the hotel. He got all tangled up an' fell over there, an' here he bumped inter the palisade, an' dropped his saddle. When he opened the bars he took my roan gelding because it was the best an' fastest, an' then he let out the others to mix us up on the tracks. See how he went? Had to hop four times on one foot afore he could get inter the saddle. An' that proves he was sober, for no drunk could hop four times like that without falling down an' being drug to death. An' he left his own critter behind because he knowed it wasn't no good. It's all as plain as the nose on your face, Charley," and Old John proudly rubbed his ear. "Hee, hee, hee! You can't fool Old John, even if he is getting old. No, sir, b' gum."

Charley had just returned from inside the corral, where he had looked at the brand on the far side of the one horse left, and he waited impatiently for his companion to cease talking. He took quick advantage of the first pause Old John made and spoke crisply.

"I don't care what corner he came 'round, or what he bumped inter; an' any fool can see that. An' if he left that cayuse behind because he thought it wasn't no good, he was drunk. That's a Bar-20 cayuse, an' no hoss-thief ever worked for that ranch. He left it behind because he stole it; that's why. An' he didn't let them others out because he wanted to mix us up, neither. How'd he know if we couldn't tell the tracks of our own animals? He did that to make us lose time; that's what he did it for. An' he couldn't tell what bronc he took last night—it was too dark. He must 'a' struck a match an' seen where that Bar-20 cayuse was an' then took the first one nearest that wasn't it. An' now you tell me how the devil he knowed yourn was the fastest, which it ain't," he finished, sarcastically, gloating over a chance to rub it into the man he had always regarded as a windy old nuisance.

"Well, mebby what you said is—"

"Mebby nothing!" snapped Charley. "If he wanted to mix the tracks would he 'a' hopped like that so we couldn't help telling what cayuse he rode? He knowed we'd pick his trail quick, an' he knowed that every minute counted; that's why he hopped—why, yore roan was going like the wind afore he got in the saddle. If you don't believe it, look at them toe-prints!"

"H'm; reckon yo're right, Charley. My eyes ain't nigh as good as they once was. But I heard him say something 'bout Winchester," replied Old John, glad to change the subject. "Bet he's going over there, too. He won't get through that town on no critter wearing my brand. Everybody knows that roan, an'—"

"Quit guessing!" snapped Charley, beginning to lose some of the tattered remnant of his respect for old age. "He's a whole lot likely to head for a town on a stolen cayuse, now ain't he! But we don't care where he's heading; we'll foller the trail."

"Grub pile!" shouted Stevenson, and the two made haste to obey.

"Charley, gimme a chaw of yore tobacker," and Old John, biting off a generous chunk, quietly slipped it into his pocket, there to lay until after he had eaten his breakfast.

All talk was tabled while the three men gulped down a cold and uninviting meal. Ten minutes later they had finished and separated to find horses and spread the news; in fifteen more they had them and were riding along the plain trail at top speed, with three other men close at their heels. Three hundred yards from the corral they pounded out of an arroyo, and Charley, who was leading, stood up in his stirrups and looked keenly ahead. Another trail joined the one they were following and ran with and on top of it. This, he reasoned, had been made by one of the strays and would turn away soon. He kept his eyes looking well ahead and soon saw that he was right in his surmise, and without checking the speed of his horse in the slightest degree he went ahead on the trail of the smaller hoof-prints. In a moment Old John spurred forward and gained his side and began to argue hot-headedly.

"Hey! Charley!" he cried. "Why are you follering this track?" he demanded.

"Because it's his; that's why."

"Well, here, wait a minute!" and Old John was getting red from excitement. "How do you know it is? Mebby he took the other!"

"He started out on the cayuse that made these little tracks," retorted Charley, "an' I don't see no reason to think he swapped animules. Don't you know the prints of yore own cayuse?"

"Lawd, no!" answered Old John. "Why, I don't hardly ride the same cayuse the second day, straight hand-running. I tell you we ought to foller that other trail. He's just cute enough to play some trick on us."

"Well, you better do that for us," Charley replied, hoping against hope that the old man would chase off on the other and give his companions a rest.

"He ain't got sand enough to tackle a thing like that single-handed," laughed Jed White, winking to the others.

Old John wheeled. "Ain't, hey! I am going to do that same thing an' prove that you are a pack of fools. I'm too old to be fooled by a common trick like that. An' I don't need no help—I'll ketch him all by myself, an' hang him, too!" And he wheeled to follow the other trail, angry and outraged. "Young fools," he muttered. "Why, I was fighting all round these parts afore any of 'em knowed the difference between day an' night!"

"Hard-headed old fool," remarked Charley, frowning, as he led the way again.

"He's gittin' old an' childish," excused Stevenson. "They say warn't nobody in these parts could hold a candle to him in his prime."

Hopalong muttered and stirred and opened his eyes to gaze blankly into those of one of the men who were tugging at his hands, and as he stared he started his stupefied brain sluggishly to work in an endeavor to explain the unusual experience. There were five men around him and the two who hauled at his hands stepped back and kicked him. A look of pained indignation slowly spread over his countenance as he realized beyond doubt that they were really kicking him, and with sturdy vigor. He considered a moment and then decided that such treatment was most unwarranted and outrageous and, further more, that he must defend himself and chastise the perpetrators.

"Hey!" he snorted, "what do you reckon yo're doing, anyhow? If you want to do any kicking, why kick each other, an' I'll help you! But I'll lick the whole bunch of you if you don't quit mauling me. Ain't you got no manners? Don't you know anything? Come 'round waking a feller up an' man-handling—"

"Get up!" snapped Stevenson, angrily.

"Why, ain't I seen you before? Somewhere? Sometime?" queried Hopalong, his brow wrinkling from intense concentration of thought. "I ain't dreaming; I've seen a one-eyed coyote som'ers, lately, ain't I?" he appealed, anxiously, to the others.

"Get up!" ordered Charley, shortly.

"An' I've seen you, too. Funny, all right."

"You've seen me, all right," retorted Stevenson. "Get up, damn you! Get up!"

"Why, I can't—my han's are tied!" exclaimed Hopalong in great wonder, pausing in his exertions to cogitate deeply upon this most remarkable phenomenon. "Tied up! Now what the devil do you think—"

"Use yore feet, you thief!" rejoined Stevenson roughly, stepping forward and delivering another kick. "Use yore feet!" he reiterated.

"Thief! Me a thief! Shore I'll use my feet, you yaller dog!" yelled the prostrate man, and his boot heel sank into the stomach of the offending Mr. Stevenson with sickening force and laudable precision. He drew it back slowly, as if debating shoving it farther. "Call me a thief, hey! Come poking 'round kicking honest punchers an' calling 'em names! Anybody want the other boot?" he inquired with grave solicitation.

Stevenson sat down forcibly and rocked to and fro, doubled up and gasping for breath, and Hopalong squinted at him and grinned with happiness. "Hear him sing! Reg'lar ol' brass band. Sounds like a cow pulling its hoofs outen the mud. Called me a thief, he did, just now. An' I won't let nobody kick me an' call me names. He's a liar, just a plan, squaw's dog liar, he—"

Two men grabbed him and raised him up, holding him tightly, and they were not over careful to handle him gently, which he naturally resented. Charley stepped in front of him to go to the aid of Stevenson and caught the other boot in his groin, dropping as if he had been shot. The man on the prisoner's left emitted a yell and loosed his hold to sympathize with a bruised shinbone, and his companion promptly knocked the bound and still intoxicated man down. Bill Thomas swore and eyed the prostrate figure with resentment and regret. "Hate to hit a man who can fight like that when he's loaded an' tied. I'm glad, all the same, that he ain't sober an' loose."

"An' you ain't going to hit him no more!" snapped Jed White, reddening with anger. "I'm ready to hang him, 'cause that's what he deserves, an' what we're here for, but I'm damned if I'll stand for any more mauling. I don't blame him for fighting, an' they didn't have no right to kick him in the beginning."

"Didn't kick him in the beginning," grinned Bill. "Kicked him in the ending. Anyhow," he continued seriously, "I didn't hit him hard—didn't have to. Just let him go an' shoved him quick."

"I'm just naturally going to clean house," muttered the prisoner, sitting up and glaring around. "Untie my han's an' gimme a gun or a club or anything, an' watch yoreselves get licked. Called me a thief! What you you fellers, then?—sticking me up an' busting me for a few measly dollars. Why didn't you take my money an' lemme sleep 'stead of waking me up an' kicking me? I wouldn't 'a' cared then."

"Come on, now; get up. We ain't through with you yet, not by a whole lot," growled Bill, helping him to his feet and steadying him. "I'm plumb glad you kicked 'em; it was coming to 'em."

"No, you ain't; you can't fool me," gravely assured Hopalong. "Yo're lying, an' you know it. What you going to do now? Ain't I got money enough? Wish I had an even break with you fellers! Wish my outfit was here!"

Stevenson, on his feet again, walked painfully up and shook his fist at the captive, from the side. "You'll find out what we want of you, you damned hoss-thief!" he cried. "We're going to tie you to that there limb so yore feet'll swing above the grass, that's what we're going to do."

Bill and Jed had their hands full for a moment and as they finally mastered the puncher, Charley came up with a rope. "Hurry up—no use dragging it out this way. I want to get back to the ranch some time before next week."

"Why I ain't no hoss-thief, you liar!" Hopalong yelled. "My name's Hopalong Cassidy of the Bar-20, an' when I tell my friends about what you've gone an' done they'll make you hard to find! You gimme any kind of a chance an' I'll do it all by myself, sick as I am, you yaller dogs!"

"Is that yore cayuse?" demanded Charley, pointing.

Hopalong squinted towards the animal indicated. "Which one?"

"There's only one there, you fool!"

"That so?" replied Hopalong, surprised. "Well, I never seen it afore. My cayuse is—is—where the devil is it" he asked, looking around anxiously.

"How'd you get that one, then, if it ain't yours?"

"Never had it—'t ain't mine, nohow," replied Hopalong, with strong conviction. "Mine was a hoss."

"You stole that cayuse last night outen Stevenson's corral," continued Charley, merely as a matter of form. Charley believed that a man had the right to be heard before he died—it wouldn't change the result and so could not do any harm.

"Did I? Why—" his forehead became furrowed again, but the events of the night before were vague in his memory and he only stumbled in his soliloquy. "But I wouldn't swap my cayuse for that spavined, saddle-galled, ring-boned bone-yard! Why, it interferes, an' it's got the heaves something awful!" he finished triumphantly, as if an appeal to common sense would clinch things. But he made no headway against them, for the rope went around his neck almost before he had finished talking and a flurry of exitement ensued. When the dust settled he was on his back again and the rope was being tossed over the limb.

The crowd had been too busily occupied to notice anything away from the scene of their strife and were greatly surprised when they heard a hail and saw a stranger sliding to a stand not twenty feet from them. "What's this?" demanded the newcomer, angrily.

Charley's gun glinted as it swung up and the stranger swore again. "What you doing?" he shouted. "Take that gun off'n me or I'll blow you apart!"

"Mind yore business an' sit still!" Charley snapped. "You ain't in no position to blow anything apart. We've got a hoss-thief an' we're shore going to hang him regardless."

"An' if there's any trouble about it we can hang two as well as we can one," suggested Stevenson, placidly. "You sit tight an' mind yore own affairs, stranger," he warned.

Hopalong turned his head slowly. "He's a liar, stranger; just a plain, squaw's dog of a liar. An' I'll be much obliged if you'll lick hell outen 'em an' let—why hullo, hoss-thief!" he shouted, at once recognizing the other.

It was the man he had met in the gospel tent, the man he had chased for a horse-thief and then swapped mounts with. "Stole any more cayuses?" he asked, grinning, believing that everything was all right now. "Did you take that cayuse back to Grant?" he finished.

"Han's up!" roared Stevenson, also covering the stranger. "So yo're another one of 'em, hey? We're in luck to-day. Watch him, boys, till I get his gun. If he moves, drop him quick."

"You damned fool!" cried Ferris, white with rage. "He ain't no thief, an' neither am I! My name's Ben Ferris an' I live in Winchester. Why, that man you've is Hopalong Cassidy—Cassidy, of the Bar-20!"

"Sit still—you can talk later, mebby," replied Stevenson, warily approaching him. "Watch him, boys!"

"Hold on!" shouted Ferris, murder in his eyes. "Don't you try that on me! I'll get one of you before I go; I'll shore get one! You can listen a minute, an' I can't get away."

"All right; talk quick."

Ferris pleaded as hard as he knew how and called attention to the condition of the prisoner. "If he did take the wrong cayuse he was too blind drunk to know it! Can't you see he was!" he cried.

"Yep; through yet?" asked Stevenson, quietly.

"No! I ain't started yet!" Ferris yelled. "He did me a good turn once, one that I can't never repay, an' I'm going to stop this murder or go with him. If I go I'll take one of you with me, an' my friends an' outfit'll get the rest."

"Wait till Old John gets here," suggested Jed to Charley. "He ought to know this feller."

"For the Lord's sake!" snorted Charley. "He won't show up for a week. Did you hear that, fellers?" he laughed, turning to the others.

"He knows me all right; an' he'd like to see me hung," replied the stranger. "I won't give up my guns, an' you won't lynch Hopalong Cassidy while I can pull a trigger. That's flat!" He began to talk feverishly to gain time and his eyes lighted suddenly. Seeing that Jed White was wavering, Stevenson ordered them to go on with the work they had come to perform, and he watched Ferris as a cat watches a mouse, knowing that he would be the first man hit if the stranger got a chance to shoot. But Ferris stood up very slowly in his stirrups so as not to alarm the five with any quick movement, and shouted at the top of his voice, grabbing off his sombrero and waving it frantically. A faint cheer reached his ears and made the lynchers turn quickly and look behind them. Nine men were tearing towards them at a dead gallop and had already begun to forsake their bunched-up formation in favor of an extended line. They were due to arrive in a very few minutes and caused Mr. Ferris' heart to overflow with joy.

Cowboy Dave

BY FRANK V. WEBSTER

The name Frank V. Webster was a pseudonym, not for one author but for several; St. George Rathbone, Weldon J. Cobb, J. W. Lincoln, to name just three no one's ever heard of. It is unclear who exactly wrote *Cowboy Dave*. This is fitting, you will see that our hero, young Dave, has a problem with his paternity also.

The Webster books were all productions of the Stratemeyer Syndicate, founded by Edward Stratemeyer in 1905. A ghostwriter himself for a number of Horatio Alger, Jr. novels, (*Cowboy Dave* has many similarities, and the Webster books were often compared with the Algers.) Stratemeyer soon cottened that the real money in this kind of book was in holding the copyright. And since his was a mind able to devise many more stories than he possibly had time to write, he employed a stable of ghostwriters. It was their job to execute the stories according to his outline. Each novel ran about 60,000 words, for this the author recieved a flat fee. They were published in inexpensive editions, frequently in series, and they were very popular.

Cowboy Dave, from which this selection was excerpted, was first published in 1915.

★   ★   ★   ★   ★

 "**H**i! Yi! Yip!"

"Woo-o-o-o! Wah! Zut!"

"Here we come!"

What was coming seemed to be a thunderous cloud of dust, from the midst of which came strange, shrill sounds, punctuated with sharp cries, that did not appear to be altogether human.

The dust-cloud grew thicker, the thunder sounded louder, and the yells were shriller.

From one of a group of dull, red buildings a sun-bronzed man stepped forth.

He shaded his eyes with a brown, powerful hand, gazed for an instant toward the approaching cloud of animated and vociferous dust and, turning to a smiling Chinese who stood near, with a pot in his hand, remarked in a slow, musical drawl:

"Well Hop Loy, here they are, rip-roarin' an' snortin' from th' round-up!"

"Alle samee hungly, too," observed the Celestial with unctious blandness.

"You can sure make a point of that Hop Loy," went on the other. "Hungry is their middle name just now, and you'd better begin t' rustle th' grub, or I wouldn't give an empty forty-five for your pig-tail."

"Oi la!" fairly screamed the Chinese, as, with a quick gesture toward his long queue, he scuttled toward the cook house, which stood in the midst of the other low ranch buildings. "Glub leady alle samee light now!" Hop Loy cried over his shoulder.

"It better be!" ominously observed Pocus Pete, foreman of the Bar U ranch, one of the best-outfitted in the Rolling River section. "It better be! Those boys mean business, or I miss my guess," the foreman went on. "Hard work a-plenty, I reckon. Wonder how they made out?" he went on musingly as he started back toward the bunk house, whence he had come with a saddle strap to which he was attaching a new buckle. "If things don't take a turn for th' better soon, there won't any of us make out," and, with a gloomy shake of his head, Pocus Pete, to give him the name he commonly went by, tossed the strap inside the bunk house, and went on toward the main building, where, by virtue of his position as head of the cowboys, he had his own cot.

Meanwhile the crowd of yelling, hard-riding, sand dust-stirring punchers, came on faster than ever.

"Hi! Yi! Yip!"

"Here we come!"

"Keep th' pot a-bilin'! We've got our appetites with us!"

"That's what!"

Some one fired his big revolver in the air, and in another moment there was an echo of many shots, the sharp crack of the forty-fives mingling with the thunder of hoofs, the yells, and the clatter of stirrup leathers.

"The boys coming back, Pete?" asked an elderly man, who came to the door of the main living room of the principal ranch house.

"Yes, Mr. Carson, they're comin' back, an' it don't need a movin' picture operator an' telegraphic despatch t' tell it, either."

"No, Pete. They seem to be in good spirits, too."

"Yes, they generally are when they get back from round-up. I want to hear how they made out, though, an' what th' prospects are."

"So do I, Pete," and there was an anxious note in the voice of Mr. Randolph Carson, owner of the Bar U ranch. Matters had not been going well with him, of late.

With final yells, and an increase in the quantity of dust tossed up as the cowboys pulled their horses back on their haunches, the range-riding outfit of the ranch came to rest, not far away from the stable. The horses, with heaving sides and distended nostrils that showed a deep red, hung their heads from weariness. They had been ridden hard, but not unmercifully, and they would soon recover. The cowboys themselves tipped back their big hats from their foreheads, which showed curiously white in contrast to their bronzed faces, and beat the dust from their trousers. A few of them wore sheepskin chaps.

One after another the punchers slung their legs across the saddle horns, tossed the reins over the heads of their steeds, as an intimation that the horses were not to stray, and then slid to the ground, walking with that peculiarly awkward gait that always marks one who has spent much of his life in the saddle.

"Grub ready, Hop Loy?" demanded one lanky specimen, as he used his blue neck kerchief to remove some of the dust and sweat from his brown face.

"It better be!" added another, significantly; while still another said, quietly:

"My gal has been askin' me for a long, long time to get her a Chinaman's pig-tail, an' I'm shore goin' t' get one now if I don't have my grub right plenty, an' soon!"

"Now you're talkin'!" cried a fourth, with emphasis.

There was no need of saying anything further. The Celestial had stuck his head out of the cook house to hear these ominous words of warning, and now, with a howl of anguish, he drew it inside again, wrapping his queue around his neck. Then followed a frantic rattling of pots and pans.

"You shore did get him goin', Tubby!" exclaimed a tall, lanky cowboy, to a short and squatty member of the tribe.

"Well, I aimed to Skinny," was the calm reply. "I am some hungry."

The last of the cowboys to alight was a manly youth, who might have been in the neighborhood of eighteen or nineteen years of age. He was tall and slight, with a frank and pleasing countenance, and his blue eyes looked at you fearlessly from under dark brows, setting off in contrast his sunburned face. Had any one observed him as he rode up with the other cowboys, it would have been noticed that, though he was the youngest, he was one of the best riders.

He advanced from among the others, pausing to pet his horse which stuck out a wet muzzle for what was evidently an expected caress. Then the young man walked forward, with more of an air of grace than characterized his companions. Evidently, though used to a horse, he was not so saddle-bound as were his mates.

As he walked up to the ranch house he was met by Mr. Carson and Pocus Pete, both of whom looked at him rather eagerly and anxiously.

"Well, son," began the ranch owner, "how did you make out?"

"Pretty fair, Dad," was the answer. "There were more cattle than you led us to expect, and there were more strays than we calculated on. In fact we didn't get near all of them."

"Is that so, Dave?" asked Pocus Pete, quickly. "Whereabouts do you reckon them strays is hidin'?"

"The indications are they're up Forked Branch way. That's where we got some, and we saw more away up the valley, but we didn't have time to go for them, as we had a little trouble; and Tubby and the others thought we'd better come on, and go back for the strays to-morrow."

"Trouble, Dave?" asked Mr. Carson, looking up suddenly.

"Well, not much, though it might have been. We saw some men we took to be rustlers heading for our bunch of cattle, but they rode off when we started for them. Some of the boys wanted to follow but it looked as though it might storm, and Tubby said we'd better move the bunch while we could, and look after the rustlers and strays later."

"Yes, I guess that was best," the ranch owner agreed. "But where were these rustlers from, Dave?"

"Hard to say, Dad. Looked to be Mexicans."

"I reckon that'd be about right," came from Pocus Pete. "We'll have to be on th' watch, Mr. Carson."

"I expect so, Pete. Things aren't going so well that I can afford to lose any cattle. But about these strays, Dave. Do you think we'd better get right after them?"

"I should say so, Dad."

"Think there are many of them?"

"Not more than two of us could drive in. I'll go to-morrow with one of the men. I know just about where to look for them."

"All right, Dave. If you're not too much done out I'd like to have you take a hand."

"Done out, Dad! Don't you think I'm making a pretty good cowpuncher?"

"That's what he is, Mr. Carson, for a fact!" broke in Pete, with admiration. "I'd stake Cowboy Dave ag'in' any man you've got ridin' range to-day. That's what I would!"

"Thanks, Pete," said the youth, with a warm smile.

"Well, that's the truth, Dave. You took to this business like a duck takes to water, though the land knows there ain't any too much water in these parts for ducks."

"Yes, we could use more, especially at this season," Mr. Carson admitted. "Rolling River must be getting pretty dry; isn't it, Dave?"

"I've seen it wetter, Dad. And there's hardly any water in Forked Branch. I don't see how the stray cattle get enough to drink."

"It is queer they'd be off up that way," observed Pete. "But that might account for it," he went on, as though communing with himself.

"Account for what?" asked Dave, as he sat down in a chair on the porch.

"Th' rustlers. If they were up Forked Branch way they'd stand between th' strays and th' cattle comin' down where they could get plenty of water in Rolling River. That's worth lookin' into. I'll ride up that way with you to-morrow, Dave, an' help drive in them cattle."

"Will you, Pete? That will be fine!" the young cowboy exclaimed. Evidently there was a strong feeling of affection between the two. Dave looked to Mr. Carson for confirmation.

"Very well," the ranch owner said, "you and Pete may go, Dave. But don't take any chances with the rustlers if you encounter them."

"We're not likely to," said Pocus Pete, significantly.

From the distant cook house came the appetizing odor of food and Dave sniffed the air eagerly.

"Hungry?" asked Mr. Carson.

"That's what I am, Dad!"

"Well, eat heartily, get a good rest, and tomorrow you can try your hand at driving strays."

Evening settled down over the Bar U ranch; a calm, quiet evening, in spite of the earlier signs of a storm. In the far west a faint intermittent light showed where the elements were raging, but it was so far off that not even the faintest rumble of thunder came over Rolling River, a stream about a mile distant, on the banks of which were now quartered the cattle which the cowboys had recently rounded up for shipment.

The only sounds that came with distinctness were the occasional barking and baying of a dog, as he saw the rising moon, and the dull shuffle of the shifting cattle, which were being guarded by several cowboys who were night-riding.

Very early the next morning Dave Carson and Pocus Pete, astride their favorite horses, and carrying with them a substantial lunch, set off after the strays which had been dimly observed the day before up Forked Branch way.

This was one of the tributaries of Rolling River, the valley of which was at one time one of the most fertile sections of the larges of our Western cattle states. The tributary divided into two parts, or branches, shortly above its junction with Rolling River. Hence its name. Forked Branch came down from amid a series of low foot-hills, forming the northern boundary of Mr. Randolph Carson's ranch.

"We sure have one fine day for ridin'," observed Pocus Pete, as he urged his pony up alongside Dave's.

"That's right," agreed the youth.

For several miles they rode on, speaking but seldom, for a cowboy soon learns the trick of silence—it is so often forced on him.

As they turned aside to take a trail that led to Forked Branch, Dave, who was riding a little ahead, drew rein. Instinctively Pocus Pete did the same, and then Dave, pointing to the front, asked:

"Is that a man or a cow?"

★　　★　　★　　★　　★

Pocus Pete shaded his eyes with his hand and gazed long and earnestly in the direction indicated by Dave Carson. The two cow-ponies, evidently glad of the little rest, nosed about the sun-baked earth for some choice morsel of grass.

"It might be either—or both," Peter finally said.

"Either or both?" repeated Dave. "How can that be?"

"Don't you see two specks there, Dave? Look ag'in."

Dave looked. His eyes were younger and perhaps, therefore, sharper than were those of the foreman of Bar U ranch, but Dave lacked the training that long years on the range had given the other.

"Yes, I do see two," the youth finally said, "But I can't tell which is which."

"I'm not altogether sure myself," Pete said, quietly and modestly. "We'll ride a little nearer," he suggested, "an' then we can tell for sure. I guess we're on th' track of some strays all right."

"Some strays, Pete? You mean our strays; don't you?" questioned Dave.

"Well, some of 'em 'll be, probably," was the quiet answer. "But you've got t' remember, Dave, that there's a point of land belongin' t' Centre O ranch that comes up here along the Forked Branch trail. It may be some of Molick's strays."

"That's so. I didn't think of that, Pete. There's more to this business than appears at first sight."

"Yes, Dave; but you're comin' on first-rate. I was a leetle opposed to th' Old Man sendin' you East to study, for fear it would knock out your natural instincts. But when you picked up that man as soon as you did," and he waved his hand toward the distant specks, "when you did that, I know you've not been spoiled, an' that there's hope for you."

"That's good, Pete!" and Dave laughed.

"Yes, I didn't agree with th' Old Man at first," the foreman went on, "but I see he didn't make any mistake."

Mr. Carson was the "Old Man" referred to, but it was not at all a term of disrespect as applied to the ranch owner. It was perfectly natural to Pete to use that term, and Dave did not resent it.

"Yes, I'm glad Dad did send me East," the young man went on, as they continued on their way up the trail. "I was mighty lonesome at first, and I felt—well, cramped, Pete. That's the only way to express it."

"I know how you felt, Dave. There wasn't room to breathe in th' city."

"That's the way I felt. Out here it—it's different."

He straightened up in the saddle, and drew in deep breaths of the pure air of the plains; an air so pure and thin, so free from mists, that the very distances were deceiving, and one would have been positive that the distant foot-hills were but half an hour's ride away, whereas the better part of a day must be spent in reaching them.

"Yes, this is livin'—that's what it is," agreed Pocus Pete. "You can make them out a little better now, Dave," and he nodded his head in the direction of the two distant specks. They were much larger now.

"It's a chap on a horse, and he's going in the same direction we are," Dave said, after a moment's observation.

"That's right. And it ain't every cowpuncher on Bar U who could have told that."

"I can see two—three—why, there are half a dozen cattle up there, Pete."

"Yes, an' probably more. I reckon some of th' Centre O outfit has strayed, same as ours. That's probably one of Molick's men after his brand," Pete went on.

The Bar U ranch (so called because the cattle from it were branded with a large U with a straight mark across the middle) adjoined, on the north, the range of Jason Molick, whose cattle were marked with a

large O in the centre of which was a single dot, and his brand consequently, was known as Centre O.

"Maybe that's Len," suggested Dave, naming a son of the adjoining
ranch owner.

"It may be. I'd just as soon it wouldn't be, though. Len doesn't always know how to keep a civil tongue in his head.

"That's right, Pete. I haven't much use for Len myself."

"You an' he had some little fracas; didn't you?"

"Oh, yes, more than once."

"An' you tanned him good and proper, too; didn't you Dave?"
asked the foreman with a low chuckle.

"Yes, I did." Dave did not seem at all proud of his achievement.
"But that was some time ago," he added. "I haven't seen Len lately."

"Well, you haven't missed an awful lot," said Pete, dryly.

The two rode on in silence again, gradually coming nearer and
nearer to the specks which had so enlarged themselves, by reason of the
closing up of the intervening distance, until they could be easily distinguished as a number of cattle and one lone rider. The latter seemed to be
making his way toward the animals.

"Is he driving them ahead of him?" asked Dave, after a long and
silent observation.

"That's the way it looks," said Pocus Pete. "It's Len Molick all
right," he added, after another shading of his eyes with his hand.

"Are you sure?" Dave asked.

"Positive. No one around here rides a horse in that sloppy way
but him."

"Then he must have found some of his father's strays, and is taking
them to the ranch."

"I'm not so sure of that," Pete said.

"Not so sure of what?"

"That the cattle are all his strays. I wouldn't be a bit surprised but
what some of our had got mixed up with 'em. Things like that have been
known to happen you know."

"Do you think—" began Dave.

"I'm not goin' to take any chances thinkin'," Pete said significantly. "I'm going to make sure."

"Look here, Dave," he went on, spurring his pony up alongside of
the young cowboy's. "My horse is good and fresh an' Len's doesn't seem to
be in such good condition. Probably he's been abusin' it as he's done before. Now I can take this side trail, slip around through the bottom lands,
an' get ahead of him."

"But it's a hard climb up around the mesa, Pete."

"I know it. But I can manage it. Then you come on up behind Len, casual like. If he has any of our cattle—by mistake," said Pete, significantly, "we'll be in a position to correct his error. Nothin' like correctin' errors right off the reel, Dave. We'll have him between two fires, so to speak."

"All right, Pete. I'll ride up behind him, as I'm doing now, and you'll head him off; is that it?"

"That's it. You guessed it first crack out of th' box. If nothin's wrong, why we're all right; we're up this way to look after our strays. And if somethin' is wrong, why we'll be in a position to correct it—that's all."

"I see." There was a smile on Dave's face as his cowboy partner, with a wave of his hand, turned his horse into a different trail, speeding the hardy little pony up so as to get ahead of Len Molick.

Dave rode slowly on, busy with many thought, some of which had to do with the youth before him. Len Molick was about Dave's own age, that is apparently, for, strange as it may seem, Dave was not certain of the exact number of years that had passed over his head.

It was evident that he was about eighteen or nineteen. He had recently felt a growing need of a razor, and the hair on his face was becoming wiry. But once, when he asked Randolph Carson, about a birthday, the ranch owner had returned an evasive answer.

"I don't know exactly when your birthday does come, Dave," he had said. "Your mother, before she—before she died, kept track of that. In fact I sometimes forget when my own is. I think yours is in May or June, but for the life of me I can't say just which month. It doesn't make a lot of difference, anyhow."

"No, Dad, not especially. But just how old am I?"

"Well, Dave, there you've got me again. I think it's around eighteen. But your mother kept track of that, too. I never had the time. Put it down at eighteen, going on nineteen, and let it go at that. Now say, about that last bunch of cattle we shipped—"

Thus the ranchman would turn the subject. Not that Dave gave the matter much thought, only now, somehow or other, the question seemed to recur with increased force.

"Funny I don't know just when my birthday is," he mused. "But then lots of the cowboys forget theirs."

The trail was smooth at this point, and Dave soon found himself close to Len, who was driving ahead of him a number of cattle. With a start of surprise Dave saw two which bore the Bar U brand.

"Hello, Len," he called.

Len Molick turned with a start. Either he had not heard Dave approach, or he had pretended ignorance.

"Well, what do you want?" demanded the surly bully.

"Oh, out after strays, as you are," said Dave, coolly. "Guess your cattle and ours have struck up an acquaintance," he added, with assumed cheerfulness.

"What do you mean?"

"I mean they're traveling along together just as if they belonged to the same outfit."

"Huh! I can't help it, can I, if your cows tag along with our strays?" demanded Len with a sneer.

"That's what I'm here for—to help prevent it," Dave went on, and his voice was a trifle sharp. "The Bar U ranch can't afford to lose any strays these days," he resumed. "The Carson outfit needs all it can get, and, as representative of the Carson interests I'll just cut out those strays of ours, Len, and head them the other way."

"Huh! What right have you got to do it?"

"What right? Why my father sent me to gather up our strays. I saw some of them up here yesterday."

"Your father?" The sneer in Len's voice was unmistakable.

"Yes, of course," said Dave, wondering what was the matter with Len. "My father, Randolph Carson."

"He isn't your father!" burst out Len in angry tones. "And you aren't his son! You're a nameless picked-up nobody, that's what you are! A nobody! You haven't even a name!"

And with this taunt on his lips Len spurred his horse away from Dave's.

★　★　★　★　★

Something seemed to strike Dave Carson a blow in the face. It was as though he had suddenly plunged into cold water, and, for the moment, he could not get his breath. The sneering words of Len Molick rang in his ears:

"You're a nameless, picked-up nobody!"

Having uttered those cruel words, Len was riding on, driving before him some of his father's stray cattle, as well as some belonging to the Bar U ranch. The last act angered Dave, and anger, at that moment, was just what was needed to arouse him from the lethargy in which he found himself. It also served, in a measure, to clear away some of the unpleasant feeling caused by the taunt.

"Hold on there a minute, Len Molick!" called Dave, sharply.

Len never turned his head, and gave no sign of hearing.

A dull red spot glowed in each of Dave's tanned cheeks. With a quick intaking of his breath he lightly touched the spurs to his horse—lightly, for that was all the intelligent beast needed. Dave passed his taunting enemy on the rush, and planting himself directly in front of him on the trail, drew rein so sharply that his steed reared. The cows, scattered by the sudden rush, ambled awkwardly on a little distance, and then stopped to graze.

"What do you mean by getting in my way?" growled Len.

"I mean to have you stop and answer a few questions," was the calm retort.

"If it's about these cattle I tell you I'm not trying to drive off any of yours," said Len, in whining tones. He knew the severe penalty attached to this in a cow country, and Dave was sufficiently formidable, as he sat easily on his horse facing the bully, to make Len a little more respectful.

"I'm not going to ask you about these cattle—at least not right away," Dave went on. "This is about another matter. You said something just now that needs explaining."

"I say a good many things," Len admitted, and again there sounded in his voice a sneer. "I don't have to explain to you everything I say; do I?"

"You do when it concerns me," and Dave put his horse directly across the trail, which, at this point narrowed and ran between two low ranges of hills. "You said something about me just now—you called me a nameless, picked-up nobody!"

Dave could not help wincing as he repeated the slur.

"Well, what if I did?" demanded the bully.

"I want to know what you mean. You insinuated that Mr. Carson was not my father."

"He isn't!"

"Why do you say that, and how do you know?" Dave asked. In spite of his dislike of Len, and the knowledge that the bully was not noted for truth-telling, Dave could not repress a cold chill of fear that seemed to clutch his heart.

"I say that because it's so, and how I know it is none of your affair," retorted Len.

"Oh yes, it is my affair, too!" Dave exclaimed. He was fast regaining control of himself. "It is very much my affair. I demand an explanation. How do you know Mr. Carson isn't my father?"

"Well, I know all right. He picked you up somewhere. He doesn't know what your name is himself. He just let you use his, and he called you Dave. You're a nobody I tell you!"

Dave spurred his horse until it was close beside that of Len's. Then leaning over in the saddle, until his face was very near to that of the bully's, and with blazing eyes looking directly into the shrinking ones of the other rancher's son, Dave said slowly, but with great emphasis:

"Who—told—you?"

There was menace in his tone and attitude, and Len shrank back.

"Oh, don't be afraid!" Dave laughed mirthlessly. "I'm not going to strike you—not now."

"You—you'd better not," Len muttered.

"I want you first to answer my questions," Dave went on. "After that I'll see what happens. It's according to how much truth there is in what you have said."

"Oh, it's true all right," sneered the bully.

"Then I demand to know who told you!"

Dave's hand shot out and grasped the bridle of the other's horse, and Len's plan of flight was frustrated.

"Let me go!" he whiningly demanded.

"Not until you tell me who said I am a nobody—that Mr. Carson is not my father," Dave said, firmly.

"I—I—" began the shrinking Len, when the sound of another horseman approaching caused both lads to turn slightly in their saddles. Dave half expected to see Pocus Pete, but he beheld the not very edifying countenance of Whitey Wasson, a tow-headed cowpuncher belonging to the Centre O outfit. Whitey and Len were reported to be cronies, and companions in more than one not altogether pleasant incident.

"Oh, here you are; eh; Len?" began Whitey. "And I see you've got the strays."

"Yes, I've got 'em," said Len, shortly.

"Any trouble?" went on Whitey, with a quick glance at Dave. The position of the two lads—Dave with his hand grasping Len's bridle—was too significant to be overlooked.

"Trouble?" began Len. "Well, he—he—"

"He made a certain statement concerning me," Dave said, quietly, looking from Len to Whitey, "and I asked him the source of his information. That is all."

"What did he say?"

"He said I was a nameless, picked-up nobody, and that Mr. Carson was not my father. I asked him how he knew, and he said some one told him that."

"So he did!" exclaimed Len.

"Then I demand to know who it was!" cried Dave.

For a moment there was silence, and then Whitey Wasson, with a chuckle said:

"I told Len myself!"

"You did?" cried Dave.

"Yes, he did! Now maybe you won't be so smart!" sneered Len. "Let go my horse!" he cried, roughly, as he swung the animal to one side. But no force was needed; as Dave's nerveless hand fell away from the bridle. He seemed shocked—stunned again.

"You—you—how do you know?" he demanded fiercely, raising his sinking head, and looking straight at Whitey.

"Oh, I know well enough. Lots of the cowboys do. It isn't so much of a secret as you think. If you don't believe me ask your father—no, he ain't your father—but ask the Old Man himself. Just ask him what your name is, and where you came from, and see what he says."

Whitey was sneering now, and he chuckled as he looked at Len. Dave's face paled beneath his tan, and he did not answer.

A nameless, picked-up nobody! How the words stung! And he had considered himself, proudly considered himself, the son of one of the best-liked, best-known and most upright cattle raisers of the Rolling River country. Now who was he?

"Come on, Len," said Whitey. "If you've got the strays we'll drive them back. Been out long enough as 'tis."

He wheeled his horse, Len doing the same, and they started after the straying cattle.

"Hold on there, if you please," came in a drawling voice. "Jest cut out them Bar U steers before you mosey off any farther, Whitey," and riding around a little hillock came Pocus Pete.

"Um!" grunted Whitey.

"Guess you'll be needin' a pair of specs, won't you, Whitey?" went on the Bar U foreman, without a glance at Len or Dave. "A Centre O brand an' a Bar U looks mighty alike to a feller with poor eyes, I reckon," and he smiled meaningly.

"Oh, we can't help it, if some of the Randolph cattle get mixed up with our strays," said Len.

"Who's talkin' to you?" demanded Pocus Pete, with such fierceness that the bully shrank back.

"Now you cut out what strays belong to you, an' let ours alone, Mr. Wasson," went on Pocus Pete with exaggerated politeness. "Dave an' I can take care of our own I reckon. An' move quick, too!" he added menacingly.

Whitey did not answer, but he and Len busied themselves in getting together their own strays. Pocus Pete and Dave, with a little effort, managed to collect their own bunch, and soon the two parties were moving off in opposite directions. Dave sat silent on his horse. Pete glanced at him from time to time, but said nothing. Finally, however, as they dismounted to eat their lunch, Pete could not help asking:

"Have any trouble with them, Dave?"

"Trouble? Oh, no."

Dave relapsed into silence, and Pete shook his head in puzzled fashion. Something had happened, but what, he could not guess.

In unwonted silence Dave and Pete rode back to the Bar U ranch, reaching it at dusk with the bunch of strays. They were turned in with the other cattle and then Dave, turning his horse into the corral, walked heavily to the ranch house. All the life seemed to have gone from him.

"Well, son, did you get the bunch?" asked Mr. Carson as he greeted the youth.

"Yes—I did," was the low answer. Mr. Carson glanced keenly at the lad, and something he saw in his face caused the ranch owner to start.

"Was there any trouble?" he asked. It was the same question Pocus Pete had propounded.

"Well, Len Molick and Whitey Wasson had some of our cattle in with theirs."

"They did?"

"Yes, but Pete and I easily cut 'em out. But—Oh, Dad!" The words burst from Dave's lips before he thought. "Am I your son?" he blurted out. "Len and Whitey said I was a picked-up nobody! Am I? Am I not your son?"

He held out his hands appealingly.

A great and sudden change came over Mr. Carson. He seemed to grow older and more sorrowful. A sigh came from him.

Gently he placed on arm over the youth's drooping shoulders.

"Dave," he said gently. "I hoped this secret would never come out—that you would never know. But, since it has, I must tell you the truth. I love you as if you were my own son, but you are not a relative of mine."

The words seemed to cut Dave like a knife.

"Then if I am not your son, who am I?" Dave asked in a husky voice.

The ticking of the clock on the mantle could be plainly, yes, loudly heard, as Mr. Carson slowly answered in a low voice:

"Dave, I don't know!"

How I Became a Cowboy

BY FRANK HARRIS

Frank Harris (James Thomas Harris) was born in Ireland in 1856 and emigrated to America in 1871. His early life is shrouded in doubt, but if you are to believe his three-volume, admittedly unreliable autobiography, *My Life and Loves*, he worked first in New York with pick and shovel, as a sandhog, digging the foundations for the Brooklyn Bridge. Later, according to *My Reminiscences as a Cowboy* (from which this story is excerpted) he moved to Chicago where he found work in a hotel. There he managed to save a little money and so impressed two "cattle kings" that they invited him to come in as a partner in their business. "That," claims Harris, "was how I wandered into the land of dime novels and gunplay in the early seventies."

Frank Harris is best known as a journalist and a man of letters, a friend to great artists (George Bernard Shaw and Oscar Wilde, to name just a couple.) But Frank Harris was also a prodigious liar, who often reinvented his life in his reminiscences and autobiographical writings. So there may be very little truth in his cowboy tales. But this statement *is* true, and may be said to express the sentiment of this anthology. Near his life's end, Harris sat upon his balcony in Nice, gazing out over the blue Mediterranean sea, and wrote these words: "Kings and cowboys I have known, and the cowboys stand out above the rest. I am six thousand miles from them at this moment and fifty-six years in time, but they seem nearer to me than this morning's newspaper." Couldn't have said it better.

★　★　★　★　★

Chicago in the early seventies was a city of 350,000 inhabitants. Life there pleased me, but did not impress me greatly. The city was brisk and busy, the houses fine, I thought, and the great lake boundless like the sea; but my reading had taught me to expect all this and more.

Yet my life in Chicago was destined to be the turning point of my existence! I learned to invest the money, most of my salary of $150 a month, knowing I should need it one day, and the day came sooner than I thought.

One day in August, as acting manager of the Fremont Hotel, I received a Spanish family named Vidal. Señor Vidal was like a French Officer of middle height, trim figure; he was very dark with gray mustache waving up at the ends. His wife, motherly but stout, had large dark eyes and small features; a cousin, a man of about thirty, was rather tall with sharp imperious ways. At first I did not notice the girl who was talking to her Indian maid. I understood at once that the Vidals were rich and gave them the best rooms. "All communicating—except yours," I added, turning to the young man, "it is on the other side of the corridor, but large and quiet." A shrug and a contemptuous nod were all I got for my pains from him.

As I handed the keys to the bell boy, the girl appeared in a black mantilla. "Any letters for us?" she asked quietly. For a minute I stood dumfounded, enthralled. Then, "I'll see," I replied, and went to the rack, but only to give myself a countenance. I knew there were none.

"None, I'm sorry to say," I half-apologized watching the girl as she moved away.

"What's the matter with me?" I said to myself angrily. "She's nothing wonderful, this Miss Vidal; pretty, yes, and dark with fine dark eyes, but nothing extraordinary." But it would not do; I was shaken in a new way and would not admit it even to myself. In fact the shock was so great that my head took sides against heart and temperament at once, as if alarmed.

Next day I found out that the Vidals were on their way to their hacienda near Chihuahua in Northern Mexico. They meant to rest in Chicago for three or four days because Señora Vidal had heart trouble. I discovered besides that Señor Arriga was either courting his cousin or betrothed to her.

In a thousand little ways I took occasion to commend myself to the Vidals. The beauty of the girl grew on me extraordinarily: yet it was the pride and reserve in her face that fascinated me more even that her great dark eyes or her fine features and splendid coloring.

It is to be presumed that the girl saw how it was with me and was gratified. She betrayed herself in no way, but she was always eager to go downstairs to the lounge and missed no opportunity of making some inquiry at the desk.

One little talk I got with my goddess: one morning she came to the office to ask about reserving a Pullman drawing-room for El Paso. I undertook at once to see to everything, and when the dainty little lady added in her funny accent: "We have so many baggage, twenty-six bits," I said as earnestly as if my life depended on it:

"Please trust me. I shall see to everything. I only wish," I added, "I could do more for you."

"That's kind," said the coquette, "very kind," looking full at me. Emboldened by despair at her approaching departure I added: "I'm so sorry you're going. I shall never forget you, never."

Taken aback by my directness, the girl laughed saucily: "*Never* means a week, I suppose!"

"You will see," I went on hurriedly as if driven, as indeed I was. "If I thought I should not see you again, and soon, I should not wish to live."

"Hush, hush," she said gravely. "You are too young to take vows and I must not listen." But seeing my sad face, she added: "You have been very kind. I shall remember my stay in Chicago with pleasure." She stretched out her hand. I took it and held it, treasuring every touch.

Her look and the warmth of her fingers I garnered up in my heart as purest treasure.

As soon as she had gone and the radiance with her, I cudgeled my brains to find some pretext for another talk. "She goes to-morrow," hammered in my brain and my heartache choked me, almost preventing my thinking. Suddenly the idea of flowers came to me. I'd buy a lot. No; every one would notice them and talk. A few would be better. How many? I thought and thought.

When they came into the lounge next day ready to start, I handed her three splendid red rosebuds, prettily tied up with maidenhair fern.

"How kind!" she exclaimed, coloring. "And how pretty," she added, looking at the roses. "Just three?"

"One for your hair," I said with love's cunning, "one for your eyes and one for your heart."

"Will you remember?" I added in a low voice intensely.

She nodded and then looked up sparkling. "As long—as ze flowers last," she laughed, and was back with her mother.

I saw them into the omnibus and got kind words from all the party, even from my rival, Señor Arriga, but cherished most her look and word as she went out of the door.

Holding it open for her, I murmured as she passed, for the others were within hearing: "I shall come soon."

The girl stopped at once, pretending to look at the tag on a trunk the partner was carrying. "El Paso is far away," she sighed, "and the hacienda ten leagues further on. When shall we arrive—when?" she added, glancing up at me.

"When" was the significant word to me for many a month; her eyes had filled it with meaning.

I've told of this meeting with Miss Vidal at length because it marked an epoch in my life; it was the first time that love had cast her glamour over me making beauty superlative, intoxicating. The passion rendered it easier for me to resist ordinary temptation, for it taught me there was a whole gorgeous world in Love's kingdom that I had never imagined, much less explored.

At the back of my mind was the fixed resolve to get to Chihuahua somehow or other in the near future and meet my charmer again and that resolve in due course shaped my life anew.

Some time later that year, three strangers came to the hotel, all cattlemen I was told, but of a new sort. Two of them, Reece and Ford, I was to know well.

Harrel Ford, the "Boss" as he was called, was a Westerner from near Leavenworth, Kansas, who owned, it was said, half a dozen ranches and twenty thousand head of cattle; he had just brought four thousand head into the stock yards to be sold. Reece was his partner. Reece, I soon found out, was an Englishman, a lover of books and so became interesting to me at once.

All three, however, were remarkably quiet and discreet and nothing would have been known about them had they not been attended by a Mexican servant whom every one knew as Bob. Bob was at least as taciturn as his masters when sober, but living in the hotel with nothing to do, the other servants got after him and soon discovered that his weak point was a love of strong drink. When he had got outside half a bottle of Bourbon, Bob would brag to beat the band and had stories innumerable at command which gained in the telling from the curious broken jargon he used for American. He was as small as a dime and as cattle-wise as a cow's mother.

Harrel Ford's quiet resolution made an impression on me from the beginning. In appearance he was like any of a dozen tall, thin lantern-jawed Westerners whom I had met; the hawk-like features, sallow skin and careless slangy speech were common, but behind his careless manner were hard, keen, grey eyes and a suggestion of immutable decision—a bad antagonist to bargain or fight with.

Reece, whom I was to know best, was a very different kind of man than either Bob or Ford. He was younger, though even quieter than Ford, rather tall, dark and handsome; a little dandyish in dress and talked like the Englishman he was. Though Reece was a partner, Bob, the Mexican, always called Ford "the Boss." I found out the reason later.

Ford never rode in Chicago; indeed, appeared to be more interested in the stock markets than the stock yards, but Reece, in the daytime,
was always in cord breeches and high brown boots, and took my fancy by
always riding everywhere. Ford seemed to accept my little kindnesses as
usual, but Reece was of richer and more generous blood. He asked me one
day to come for a ride, adding that Bob, the Mexican servant, would get me
a mount; I confessed I had no breeches, but Reece showed me how to put
straps on my ordinary trousers. And the same afternoon he took me out for
a ride and then together we paid a visit to the stock yards, where to my surprise I found that Ford and Reece had still over two thousand head of cattle and nearly two hundred horses which they had driven up on the long
trail from New Mexico to Kansas City and thence by train to Chicago.

I found they were all going down again in the spring and the profits were big. Cows could be bought for a dollar a head, "most everywhere
near the Rio Grande," and they fetched from twenty to thirty dollars each
in Chicago. The profits were enormous but the risks were huge.

"I'd like to go down with you," I confessed, but Reece at once
warned me about the risks. Indians took nearly one herd out of every two
and a good many cowboys lost their lives on the trail. As 5,000 cattle con-
stituted a herd the loss was heavy.

"What do you do if the Indians get your herd?" I asked.

"Go back and get another," replied Reece carelessly, and then
added, seeing that I had made up my mind, "but you must see Ford, he's
the chief in this business and I shouldn't like to go against him." So he dismissed the matter from his kindly, careless mind.

Fortunately for me, I made up to Bob before I tackled Ford. I had
learned a little Spanish grammar in my spare time and knew a few sen-
tences by heart: I shot off a *"buenos dias, Señor,"* one morning at Bob and
was answered with a volubility that surprised and overwhelmed me. I had
to explain that I was only just learning, a beginner.

"I understan'," replied Bob with grim contempt, "all American
man. He asks '*si habla Español*' and den dat's all he know."

But he found that I knew more than that and meant to know
much more and soon we were talking half-Spanish, half-English, and Bob
taught me a good deal more than the proper pronunciation of the new
tongue.

In one of our talks I told him I thought of going with Ford and
Reece into the Southwest.

"Reece good man," said Bob, "at once—*Caballero*—*muy bueno*; but
Ford hard, hard as nail: you talk with me, learn ride. . .then speak with
Boss."

So I resolved to bide my time and wait. But one day Ford spoke to me. He began by saying: "You want to go down on the trail, Reece tells me. I'm not going down after this next summer. Why don't you take my place and go in partnership with Reece? It would only cost you six or seven thousand dollars."

"I haven't got so much"—I confessed naïvely—"though I could have by next spring. I have only a couple of thousand dollars saved or at most three thousand."

"Come in for what you have got," said the Boss. "I only took a hand to help Reece. If he's willing to let you in for a quarter for three thousand I'll sell you so much of my mortgage. Then you and I'll have a quarter each against Reece's half and perhaps you will be able to teach him to save and be careful. He's too easy, too generous, too Southern—that's what's the matter with him."

I accepted the offer in principle and when the opportunity offered, talked it over with Reece. Reece, it appeared, had taken a great fancy to me, perhaps because I deferred to him and admired him openly. Without any purpose he had begun teaching me to ride and finding me an apt pupil he took a liking to me as we all do to those we help and can mold.

Half unconsciously, too, I had copied Reece in dress, imitated his seat on horseback, modeled myself outwardly at least on him, and this flattered him and increased his liking for me. It must be remembered that I was only seventeen at that time and he was a man of 35. But the hero-worship had an even deeper effect on me. We all grow by imitating our heroes and even when we no longer copy them, something of them remains in us.

At length, on one of our afternoon rides together, it was settled by Reece and myself practically as the Boss had proposed.

Then and not till then did I approach the hotel proprietor; I offered to give up my place before the winter began if he would give me a month's salary as bonus. The chief agreed to my proposal on condition that I shouldn't work for any other hotel in Chicago, and we shook hands on the first of September.

A few days later my new friends—the Boss, Reece, Dell and Bob—and I took train for St. Louis, and from St. Louis to Kansas City, at that time a jumping-off place, so to speak. Here we packed our town clothes carefully away in bags for wagon transport, and then, like school boys released, pulled on chaps, flannel shirts and high boots, buckled on cartridge belts and revolvers, slung rifles along our saddles and started off in true cowboy style to ride the two or three hundred miles to Eureka, Kansas, where the partners had a ranch.

The Boss had left a wagon and half a dozen horses in a stable just outside Kansas City in charge of a colored man named Paul. Charlie Bates, a Kansan, had stayed with Paul on what he called "grub wages." By Reece's advice I picked a young mare out of the bunch for my own use and gave the Boss twenty dollars for her. I hadn't had Moll for an hour when I realized that I had made a good bargain.

★   ★   ★   ★   ★

That first ride into the Southwest was of the essence of romance: it was a plunge a thousand miles into the unknown; it was like an old border foray, with enough strangeness to interest and enough danger to warm the blood. One's comrades were all new, too, and had to be learned.

With the intensified resolution given to me by my success in Chicago, I set myself to master riding, the chief art of the cowboy. At once, I realized my life would often depend on it, because being near-sighted, I'd never be a good shot. For the first days I suffered tortures; my hips were all raw, but after washing, or rather frying them well with salt water and whiskey every night, I soon got hard and suffered no further inconvenience. I was more than repaid for all my troubles and pains by Reece's approval. Before the week was over, Reece remarked one evening: "If you persevere you'll ride this summer as well as Bob."

"What can he do that I can't do?" I asked Reece.

"Oh," said Reece, "ask him and you will soon see!"

So the next time we met I asked Bob. He looked at me with a little grin and then said: "Drop something on the ground, a handkerchief or a coin or anything you like." So I dropped a dollar. Immediately Bob shouted, tore away on his horse fifty or sixty yards, swung round and came past me at full gallop.

As he neared the dollar he caught the horse's mane in his left hand, swung down and picked up the dollar and swung back again into place without any apparent exertion. I realized at once that it was an extraordinary feat and set myself forthwith to learn it.

If I say it took me at least a fortnight, working every day for two or three hours, my readers may be surprised. But let them try it and they will find out it takes some doing.

Bob was a little man, five feet four in height, weighing perhaps one hundred and twenty-five pounds; he was weather-beaten and dried up so that he looked like leather; but he was very active and strong in spite of the fact that he must have been fifty years of age. From his appearance it would have been impossible to say what age he was; but he had fought with Santa Anna all through the Mexican War, so he could hardly be less than fifty, though his little brown eyes were just as bright and quick as they had been when he was sixteen, and his seat in the saddle just as firm and his wrist just as supple-strong.

The life was enchanting. Our three wagons, each drawn by a pair of good horses, could make their thirty miles a day. Although one man was always detailed to hunt for the pot, very often he would be accompanied by half a dozen, who would race down buffalo and kill perhaps three or four cows or calves with revolvers. In the heat of the day the cowboys would play cards for wages to come or shoot one against the other, or simply skylark about. We took seventy to a hundred ponies for the dozen cowboys, and each man broke three or four of these to his own special requirements.

Every now and then one came across a broncho with some particular and peculiar vice. And these were often the most admired and the best cared for of the whole herd for a very simple reason. It was the custom whenever one gang of cowboys met another immediately to trade a broncho and, of course, the most vicious animal was always the one to be swapped. The trading was conducted in the slow Yankee fashion. The spokesman of gang A would try to get the representative of gang B to give some money to boot:

"I guess my hoss is wuth two o' yourn; look at 'im."

"Looks ain't nuthen: I'll bet you five dollars my hoss'll run (gallop) faster'n yourn."

If it was found impossible to get money to boot, half a dozen curious bets would be made, for none of the bets were allowed to suggest the horse's special trick. Finally the bets were agreed to: everything was settled and the two bronchos were solemnly put forward. Then came the heart of the fun.

One of the A gang mounted the horse of the B gang and proceeded to show his paces. Commonly he found a practiced and extraordinary buckjumper; but aided by a Mexican saddle it was possible to sit the worst bucker, provided the broncho could not buck himself out of his saddle, which, however, occasionally happened. After this trial one of the B gang would mount the horse which the A gang had offered. The broncho itself and money, too, changed hands on the result of this contest. Usually the broncho had some impish or devilish trick.

I remember mounting one which seemed to have no fault of any kind. Fortunately for me I was riding on an English saddle, which is like a racing pad in front. The broncho walked, trotted, loped and galloped to perfection. I began to think that the other gang didn't understand the game, and I turned and cantered carelessly back to the crowd. Suddenly, without warning, the beast tucked its forelegs under it and I went rolling over and over like a shot rabbit. I got up half dazed and bleeding from nose and mouth amid yells of laughter from both gangs.

"Quiet to ride, ain't he? Pity he put his foot in that prairie dog's hole,"—and another roar of laughter.

The broncho we usually traded was a very good-looking black mare which had been ruined by rough handling when broken in. She would walk or trot or gallop for two or three minutes and then would stand stock still—a confirmed jibber. Nothing could make her move. And at last the rider had to dismount and pack his own saddle and bridle back to the starting point.

We had another horse which was certain to win the game, or at least to draw it, but she was seldom put forward, for we used her for races on account of her speed and bottom, and a broncho which was swapped was sometimes subjected to a good deal of ill treatment. Blue Dick, as this mare was called, was a fleabitten gray, fifteen and a half hands and pure bred, if it is possible to judge breeding from form and pace and courage.

She had been bought cheap because she had broken up a trap in Kansas City and savaged the groom. After a long time we cured her of every vice save one. When ridden by some one she didn't know she used to stretch her head out again and again till she got the reins a little loose: then she would turn round as quick as a snake, get your toe in her mouth and bit like a fiend. The pain was so horrible—excruciating—I have seen a strong man fall from her back fainting with agony.

It was usually arranged that the crowd which won gained both horses; if the result was a draw, each gang took possession again of its own steed.

I tell these stories just to give an idea of the life. The days spent on the trail were, for the first year, at least, of time-consuming interest. Riding tempered the great heat and made the climate absolutely delightful.

The plains varied from 700 to 1,500 feet above sea level; but that was not sufficient to account for the dry lightness of the atmosphere, which exhilarated one like champagne. Shielded on one side by 1,500 miles of plains and on the other by the Rocky Mountains this vast track of country was completely protected from the rain. So dry was the atmosphere that when we killed a buffalo the carcass would dry up to dust without putrefying, and this gave us better jerked meat than was to be found anywhere else in the world, better even than the biltong of South Africa. All you had to do was to take, say, the loin of a buffalo, though the rump was generally used, cut it into strips, sprinkle a little salt on it, and hang it over lines from one wagon to another, or even throw it on the top of the wagon, and leave it there for a day or two, then turn it and leave it another couple of days, and you had beef which looked like strips of mahogany, yet which ate like the best beef slightly salted; for these hard, wood-like strips got soft in the mouth at once.

Another peculiarity of this dry atmosphere on the great plains was that the short buffalo grass used to dry up and cure itself on the ground, becoming, in fact, hay, without the trouble of cutting and stacking.

It was often said thirty years ago that buffalo meat was praised only by Westerners because they were pretty hungry when they ate it. At the time I thought this a reasonable explanation, but on the trail I found it to be simply silly. Buffalo meat, even when one is not hungry, is the best meat I've ever eaten; as much superior to ordinary beef as grouse is superior to the barn-fed fowl, for not only has it greater tenderness and greater juiciness, but also the game flavor: it was, I decided—the first time I ate it as the hundredth—the best food in the world.

Yet unfortunately the buffalo has been wiped out, and his place given to ordinary domestic cattle. He was indeed an easy prey for several reasons: the bulls were just as savage as the African bull buffalo, but the African bull can retreat into forest, or, worse still, into the heavy thorn bush which he alone can pass through without difficulty; he has therefore an immense advantage over the man hunting him. But a herd of buffalo out on the plains had no protection and could be ridden down and shot, from ten or twelve yards distance, almost as easily as cattle. Moreover, the hunters soon found a peculiarity of the buffalo which placed him at their mercy. Near any salt lick, where the buffaloes were wont to congregate at early morning, it was only necessary to conceal one's self in a neighboring hollow and shoot straight. So long as the hunter kept out of sight, buffalo after buffalo could be killed. At every shot the uninjured buffaloes would lift their head and look about; but seeing nothing, would again begin to wallow and roll about as if there was no danger to be feared. One morning a hunter killed a herd of thirty-five at such a lick merely for their hides. The hides, untanned, were worth always about five dollars apiece, and each of them weighed some forty pounds. They were too thick and stiff to make good pelts; the hides of the calves and young cows made the best robes.

★　　★　　★　　★　　★

Before going down to buy cattle in New Mexico in the Spring, we spent the winter months on Reece's Ranch. I shall never forget the coming to the Ranch. We did not even stop at the little village of Eureka, but left the trail and rode a bee-line across the prairie for home. After nearly ten miles of hard riding we came to a bridge over a little creek that was perhaps fifteen yards wide and three feet deep, and then Ford and Reece began to race up a long slope. I followed hard on their heels, when suddenly on the very ridge of the slope in front I saw the ranch. It was simply a large one-story frame building lifted about three feet from the ground; all the winds of heaven blew underneath it, and the fowls and dogs used this as a shady resting place.

There was a room in which the Boss, Reece and I slept on bunks, and behind a dining room; across the passage from the chief room there was a great room where all the men slept, and behind it the kitchen ruled over by Peggy, an Indian. He was called Peggy on the theory that cooking was woman's work. There was hardly any furniture in the place; the boys slept on buffalo rugs thrown on bunks round the walls. There was no ornament except pictures from the illustrated papers pasted on the walls. Here and there rifles were hung, and shotguns, revolvers and bowie-knives, a perfect arsenal of modern weapons.

In one corner of the sitting room was a big easy chair, always claimed by any one who was not well, and buffalo rugs were everywhere in heaps.

About three hundred yards from the house was a great stable which Reece had had built of stone. It would hold a hundred horses, had twenty loose boxes for the best horses and immense hay lofts above and enormous corn bins and harness rooms at the side. It was infinitely warmer in winter and cooler in summer and altogether more comfortable than the wooden shanty where the masters lived.

Not a moment of the day on the ranch hung heavy on my hands. The breaking-in of the colts palled a little till an incident took place which taught me that if I had an excellent seat in the saddle I had still a good deal to learn about horses.

An unbroken black mare was brought out one morning, saddled and bridled, and I jumped on her back. Instead of bucking or kicking the animal simply stood stock still as if carved in stone. I played with the bridle and coaxed her; the black took absolutely no notice. One of the men passing by gave her a sharp cut across the hind-quarters with a quirt and an encouraging shout. The mare did not even turn her head or seek to brush the pain away with a switch of her tail. She seemed hypnotized with fear.

The boys began soon to chaff me; but I had sense enough to take no notice, and the noise brought Reece out to see what was the matter. I felt that in sitting still I had Reece's approval, so I smiled at the boys and paid no attention to Charlie, whose chaff was the loudest. At length Reece said:

"Why don't you get on Charlie and show the tenderfoot how to ride?"

"I'd soon make her go," said Charlie, glad to show off; but after ten minutes of useless efforts he altered his tune.

"No one can make that mare stir except Bob," he said viciously as he dismounted. Without a word Reece went over the mare, handled her, pulled her ears gently once or twice, then got on her back, and the mare walked away at once.

"How did you do it?" I asked running alongside.

"Search me," answered Reece laughing, "I don't know."

"How did you get such power?" I persisted.

"When I was young," said Reece, "I used to break-in all our colts and a lot of them were thoroughbreds with any amount of spirit—that taught me. Breakin'-in's the best practice in the world."

"Has Bob got your power?" I asked jealously. Reece nodded his handsome head.

"Really?" I exclaimed.

"Bob knows more about cattle," Reece summed up dispassionately, "than any one I ever saw. He's not so good with horses. For instance, his seat now ain't so good as yours; but he knows all animals, I guess, and what he don't know about steers and bulls ain't worth considering. He's a wonder! You should take Bob as a teacher," he added smiling.

"I was right, wasn't I?" I asked eager for a little praise, "to sit the mare without beating her?"

"Sure, sure!" replied Reece. "She was frightened with all the novel experience. What would you have done if they put a bit in your mouth all of a sudden? To punish her could only make her worse; that's why I came out. These Western men believe too much in brute force—like all young people," he added, as if thinking aloud.

From that moment I resolved to make a friend of Bob and so get the heart of his mystery sooner or later. Meanwhile I went on with my breaking-in persistently morning after morning and soon realized that half the bad temper of horses being pure fear, gentleness and patience were infinitely more effective than whip or spur or rough usage.

One day we were riding in the prairie when we sighted a "coyote" or prairie wolf. It had begun to get warm, and the coyote loped along in front of us apparently unconcerned, as if he knew we had no chance of catching him. A quarter of an hour's riding showed us that we had no chance and just as this impression became dominant, the wolf stopped and turned round to look at his pursuers. A young fellow named Capper, from Wyoming, had got his rifle out at the first halt and now stopped, took a snapshot at the coyote, and as luck would have it, broke his leg, though the coyote must have been six or seven hundred yards away.

"A good shot," cried Reece, pulling his horse to a standstill, "what did you sight for?"

"Seven hundred yards," said the youth casually, "this Winchester is real good," he added modestly. Somehow or other his manner pleased me.

After waiting for the majority of the men who had ridden on eagerly to enjoy the catching of the wounded coyote, we all set off homeward, and a very tired, excited crew sat down to dinner on the ranch that day: Charlie, of course, the loudest of the bunch. He kept on praising Capper's shot till even I saw purpose in it, and at last he came out flat-footed with the conclusion:—

"Joe Capper's the best shot in this camp," but nobody seemed to pay much attention to him till he said: "I'd like to bet a month's pay on Joe against any of us."

Bob took him up

"I cover your fifty dollars," he squeaked, "Bent's a better shot." Bent, to my astonishment, didn't say a word, in fact, was about the first to leave the table and go about his business. But the money was staked in the Boss' hands and the match fixed for the next Sunday at six in the morning.

The test was a true Western one, and is usually reserved for winter when the snow is on the ground. A turkey was buried, leaving only neck and head above the ground. Perhaps because it was so closely caged, the bird's head was not still for a second. The constantly moving mark, I thought, brought an element of chance into the contest. Capper was there with his Winchester, surrounded by Charlie and others, laughing and joking.

Bent, on the other hand, stood by himself making careful preparation. To my astonishment, he drew the cartridge of his Winchester and refilled it, measuring the powder most carefully in a little steel measure before pouring it into the shell.

"One would think," I remarked, "that good shooting depended on a single grain of powder."

"That's it," said Bent quietly, "that's the fact." I stared at the man.

The men were to shoot alternatively at three turkeys. The shooting line was drawn at first one hundred yards from the turkey, then two and at least three hundred yards. Capper knelt down, fired quickly and missed. His second shot killed the turkey. Another bird was put into the next hole and again he killed it. Charlie was jubilant.

"Go in and beat that if you can," he cried jeeringly to Bent. Another turkey was in position, and Bent knelt down. He aimed, as it seemed to me, an interminable time and then fired. Before the smoke cleared away showing the turkey was killed, Bent had risen as if in no doubt of the result, opened his rifle and cleaned the barrel out with an oiled rag. By that time another turkey was ready, and he knelt and again killed the bird.

"Good, good," I cried almost beside myself with admiration of the man's uncanny skill. "But why do you take so long to aim?".

"There's a little wind," Bent replied simply; "I wait till it's still."

Again quietly he killed his bird and won a hearty cheer from the boys. Charlie insisted that Capper should have another shot, the first shot should not have counted, and so forth. In silence Capper knelt down. This time I noticed he also took a long time to aim—and killed his bird.

Going back to the ranch I stuck close to Bent. I wanted to know how he had learned his markmanship. Was it merely long practice?

"An' the rifle," Bent corrected, "fine shootin' all in the gun. Capper, I guess, is as good a shot as I am or anybody else, if he'd take care and load properly and use his brains. He missed the first time through not taking thought of the wind."

"Do you mean," I questioned, "that anybody could be a first-rate shot?"

"I reckon so," Bent replied, "anybody with good eyes. Anybody," he went on, "can learn to hold straight." Bent's matter-of-fact simplicity and carefulness made a great impression on me. I felt sorry: I could never become a good shot with my poor eyes.

★   ★   ★   ★   ★

Of course, little by little I got to know every one on the ranch and got to know, too, a good deal of the life that lay before me.

It was in March, I think, the buffalo grass just sprouting, when we resolved to start for the Rio Grande. Reece was to be our boss, Ford not going down, and the men all got $40 a month and a commission on the profits if we succeeded in bringing cattle up to Chicago.

The first days on the trail were not especially exciting. Every one was up about four o'clock, well before daybreak. The first man to awake would throw some buffalo chips (dry dung) on the fire; Peggy, the Indian cook, would soon swing a kettle on it and make the coffee, while some of us went down to the creek and washed our hands and faces, or even had a bath. Then we came fresh and eager to the hot coffee and hot biscuits, with a grill of buffalo steaks and fat bacon.

The air, even in early Spring and before sunrise, was warm, like fresh milk. Suddenly the curtain of the night would be drawn back, opal tints would climb up the eastern heaven, and these would change to mother-of-pearl, and break into streams of rose and crimson; in a moment the sun would show above the horizon, and at once it was day. After breakfast we would wash up and put things away in one of the wagons; Bent and the negroes would generally climb into a wagon and go to sleep again: the wagons would then be harnessed and commence their journey southward, while the rest of us would mount our bronchos and go on in front, detaching two of our number to drive the rest of the horses. In one respect these bronchos were something like Texan cattle—they all followed a leader and were therefore very easy to drive; bar anything unusual, one had simply to ride behind them, and an occasional flick of the whip or even a shout would keep them moving.

Five or six of us used to be perpetually riding together on young, fresh horses, summer day after summer day. Of course, there was all manner of skylarking and playing about. Some one would have mounted a new horse and want to prove it; immediately a bet would be made, and we would have a race to decide whether the new beast could gallop or not. If he turned out very fast, I would generally be sent off to get Shiloh or Blue Dick out of the herd and see how he would shape beside the fastest we had got. Shiloh was a thoroughbred horse, bought by Reece in Kentucky; as a three-year-old he had done a half-mile in forty-nine seconds, and over a mile was almost as fast as a Derby winner—was certainly as fast as good plating form. He could beat Blue Dick in a sprint or a scurry, but stretch the course from two miles to ten and Blue Dick would beat him a long way. I used to think that if you cantered Blue Dick for half a mile or so before you made her gallop, you could gallop until you were tired without tiring her.

I remember one occasion when I had to test her: we had camped about sixteen miles from Albuquerque, New Mexico. The men had been skylarking about with a prairie rattlesnake, trying to lift it on little twigs of sagebrush and throw it at each other. The prairie rattlesnake is very small, three feet or so in length, and thin as a whip-lash, whereas the forest rattlesnake is five or six feet long and as thick as a girl's arm; but the prairie rattlesnake, though small, is just as venomous and ten times as quick and bad-tempered as his larger brother. The play ended, therefore, as might have been expected: the rattlesnake stung one of the men, a half-Indian, half-Greaser.

As one of the lightest of the party, I was immediately called and told by Reece, our chief, to round up Blue Dick and ride into Albuquerque and bring out a bottle of whisky, for it appeared that our small barrel had been allowed to get quite empty, and the poisoned man could only have a glass or so. I put a racing pad on Blue Dick's back and started with the boss's last words in my ears, "Don't spare the horse; Indian Pete is in a bad way." Pete was a silent, sulky creature, but the need was imminent, and though I was filled with anxiety about the mare I was to ride, I intended to do my best. I trotted the two hundred or three hundred yards to the creek and took her through the ford quite quietly. On the opposite bank I let her begin to canter, and I cantered for the next mile or so, till she had got quite dry and warm, and then I began to answer her craving for speed and let her go faster into a sort of hand-gallop. I kept at this for about half an hour, and then loosed her out: in an incredibly short time I found myself on the outskirts of the town. I drew Blue Dick together for the last mile and let her go as hard as she could lay legs to ground. I pulled up at the first saloon in the main street, threw myself from her back, hitched her to the post, rushed in and got a bottle of whisky, stuffed it in my pocket, and buckling my belt round it so as to keep it safe, rushed out, threw myself on Blue Dick's back, and was again racing down the street within two minutes, I should think, from the time I drew rein. Now, I said to myself, I must find out what Blue Dick can do. The heat was tremendous; it must have been quite ninety in the shade, perhaps a hundred and thirty-five in the sun; but the air was light, and though the mare was in a reek of sweat, she was breathing as easily as when she started. Gradually the fear of being late grew upon me, and I let her race as she would: the mare herself seemed to realize that speed was needed, for she settled down to her long stretching gallop, which I always compared to the gallop of a wolf, so tireless it seemed, and long and easy. Mile after mile swept past, and at last I saw the rise in the prairie which was the edge of the creek, and the few, mingy cottonwood trees that showed me I was almost home. Again and again I had strained forward to look at the mare; there seemed no sign of distress in her; and then a sort of exultation in her tireless strength came to me, and wild joy that she was uninjured, and I shook her together with a shout, lifting her in her stride at the same time. At once she got hold of the bit, and before I could do anything had bolted with me at lightning speed. Down to the creek over the steep bank with a plunge into the water; across, up the opposite bank, and away like a mad thing. I had overshot the wagons by a hundred yards before I could pull her up. There were a dozen hands to take the whisky bottle, which was fortunately whole. I threw myself off the mare and gave her to the care of Mexican Bob, to walk about; but almost at once any anxiety I had about Blue Dick vanished, for she set herself to munch some buffalo grass, and I saw that the long, hard gallop had done her no harm.

Strange to say, the whisky didn't cure the Indian; he could not keep it on his stomach. He didn't even seem to try: from the first he believed that he was done for; he said, "I'm a dead 'un," wrapped himself in his blanket and wanted to be left alone. When I saw him he was in a comatose state, and it was impossible to rouse him. We poured some whisky down his throat, but it was thrown up again immediately: a couple of hours later he was dead.

That same night we buried him under one of the dwarf cottonwood trees near the bank of the creek, and there he probably sleeps quietly enough till this day. Our grief was not deep; none of us knew him well; he was not companionable; he simply disappeared—swept out of sight, like wreckage on a stream.

★   ★   ★   ★   ★

I shall never forget my comrades: especially Wild Bill, Bent and Charlie— all dead already a long time ago, heroes of a tragic Odyssey.

When I went down on the trail the first time, Wild Bill (Hickok was his real surname) attracted my interest immediately. He was very good look- ing; about 6 feet in height with broad shoulders in spite of his light waist; the features of his face excellent, long straight nose; heavy mustache, dark and long and fine eyes, now gray, now blue—an extremely good-looking man. He had been made City Marshal of one of the new towns springing up, Wi- chita or Fort Dodge (I forget the precise place). Within a week of his elec- tion he had been called to a saloon where there was a row, and had settled it by shooting three of the most quarrelsome. Coming out of the saloon, Bill met a man who made an incautious gesture; quick as a flash he drew and shot—a popular railway boss. Peace—never much esteemed by cowboys and railway hands—seemed dear at the price: a vigilance committee was formed, and next morning two hundred armed men surrounded the Marshal's house to drive him out of the country or kill him. Suddenly the door opened and Bill appeared on the porch, a revolver in each hand.

"What do you 'uns want?"

"Get out! Who killed old Bourbon? Git."

The voices were hardly raised; but there was deadly menace in the quiet tones.

"I want my salary before I go."

"You'll get no salary," said one man in front, meditatively. "I'd go quick if I were you; 'taint healthy for you here."

"That's so; that's so"—a score of voices.

"All right," replied Hickok, quietly, "all right. I s'pose I kin git somethin' to eat first"; and he moved to the door and entered the house.

He had not been fired at partly because it would have been awk- ward for the first man who raised his hand, and partly because his careless hardihood pleased the crowd. The boys dispersed, but Hickok had to find work some distance away, his methods were too brusque to be popular. And so he took a turn with us on the trail as a cowboy at sixty dollars a month and grub.

It was understood that he would only go with us as far as San Anton, where he was said to have friends. He was not a real cowboy, but a friend of Reece.

Wild Bill was such a peculiar product of the border that he deserves a careful study. He deserves study, too, for the same reason that a
mountain tells you more of a country than a piece of plain. He was a freak
if you will, but a freak only possible in Western America after the great
Civil War. On getting to know him well through months of intimacy, it
became clear to me that he was a product of the war—a characteristic
product of a desperate struggle.

With the curiosity of a boy in a strange country, who in spite of
himself was impressed by the sort of unwilling respect which every one
showed to Bill Hickok, I attached myself to him and plied him with questions. If ever a man was unwilling to talk about himself, incapable of any
conscious self-painting, inarticulate in a peculiar degree, it was this man.
Shaw's fighters, and Conan Doyle's, and, of course, Shakespeare's have all
the glib tongue of trained talkers; but the real fighting men are sometimes
wholly inarticulate. Again and again I tried to get out of Hickok how he
became so great a revolver shot, the deadest shot in all the Winning of the
West. At one time I found out that he always had "a sort of liking for it"; at
another, that he practised a great deal as a boy: and again that his father was
a "mighty good shot," that "everybody round us thought a lot of it." Mere
hints for the picture, but the picture came one day when I chanced to ask
him to tell me about his first row, the first time he killed a man. For some
reason or other his guard of secretiveness seemed to break down before
this direct assault, or perhaps what I took for secretiveness was merely con-
stitutional silence or reticence bred of slow speech. The reader must judge,
but in any case, this is what I gathered bit by bit from him.

Bill Hickok had been brought up in Missouri, near Pleasant Hill.
Just before the war he was a boy of eighteen or nineteen, his father was a
Yankee and Abolitionist, and they lived in the very hottest center of a slave
State when feeling ran at its highest. The father seems to have been a sort
of John Brown, with perhaps less piety but more pugnacity, who spoke his
mind against slavery in season and out of season, and was willing at any
time to put his life on the block. "Why the old man didn't get killed," Wild
Bill said, "I don't know: he was always shootin' off his mouth even when
he hadn't no need to."

"Didn't he bring you up strictly," I asked, and seeing that he did
not understand, I added, "religiously?"

"I should smile," Bill answered. "He was always taking me to the
old Methodist Chapel, and he used to pray so loud I was clean ashamed of
him. The only thing he ever showed me was how to swing an ax and use a
revolver. I could shoot better than the old man from the start," he added.

"But how did you get into your first row?" I asked.

"Well," he said, "it was just before the war and I was kind o' sore. None of the boys about that I used to go to school with would speak to me. They used to shout 'Abolitionist!' after me. So I got mad, and when the girls tossed their heads too and wouldn't look at me, I sort of took it that I *would* be an Abolitionist, though I didn't care nuthin' about the slaves; I always thought niggers should be made to work for white folks anyway. But being forced into defendin' them I did a good job of it and soon the country proved mighty unpleasant for me, so I got out of town. I found work in Pleasant Hill and as I never talked much I got on pretty well. But they were red hot Southerners, all of them, and I was kind o' marked as a black Abolitionist on account of my father. They even tried to tar and feather the old man one night, but some of them got hurt. He got shot twice, but he was very tough—sort of wiry—and he warn't in bed more'n a week."

Again I came back to the subject. "But how about your first row?" I asked, and after numberless attempts I got him to confess it.

It seems as a sort of outcast, Bill had taken to gambling at Pleasant Hill, and used perpetually to haunt a gambling saloon. He felt he was not wanted and was not liked, but sometimes in the heat of the game the ill-feeling used tbe forgotten, just as at other times it became more pronounced.

The spice of danger tempted the reckless spirit of the youth. "Sometimes I was rich and could enjoy myself," he explained, "and that was great as I hadn't had much fun in my life. Sometimes I lost all and it was hell. But even then I was better off than on the farm. I always did like cussin' better than preachin', and a handout at cards seemed to me then better than preachin' any day.

"I had got a gold watch that I froze on to. I had won it fair and square, but one night I had no money and I asked Ned Tomlin, the son of the banker (I knew him at school) to lend me fifty dollars on the watch: I wanted to play. He didn't seem to want to; was mighty cool in fact: told me I didn't ought to play there anyway. I said nuthin', but I laid it up for him, and at last he gave me the money. I soon lost it all; one always does lose borrowed money, and I have noticed one generally loses when one wants most to win—a sort of contrary spirit in the damned pips. About that time there was a great fuss about Abe Lincoln's election, and all slave-owners got spoutin' round and raisin' hell. I got a letter tellin' me I had better get out: Pleasant Hill warn't no place for Abolitionists. I paid no attention. Then I got a letter from Tomlin tellin' me I had better pay back the fifty dollars and take my watch: he had no use for it. I just paid no attention.

"One night I was up in the gamblin' saloon and they began talkin' about watches, and one of 'em up and said Ned Tomlin was going to carry my watch across the square at Pleasant Hill and auction it off as an Abolitionist's watch who did not pay his debts. I saw it was up to me, so I asked when Tomlin was goin' to do this. It was a Wednesday I remember, and they said, 'Saturday at twelve o'clock, when all the farmers would be in town.' That made me mad, and I just up and said, 'If dead men can carry watches across a public square, Tomlin may carry my watch,' an' I went off to bed.

"On the Saturday morning I got my horse and hitched it up fifty yards down Fremont Street, so as to give me a chance if the crowd did turn on me, as I sort of expected they might. I knew in any case I would have to leave Pleasant Hill: I had felt for sometime it was getting rather warm. On the mornin' I went into the square, and sure enough about twelve o'clock Tomlin left the Planter's House and came down with a hull crowd about him; he had a revolver in his right hand, my watch in his left, and I went out to meet him. I was willin' to give him a chance, so when we got pretty near together I called out pleasant-like:

" 'I guess you have got my watch, Ned, and I want it.' He said: 'I want my fifty dollars. I never did see an Abolitionist that would pay what he owed,' and he kind o' lifted his hand. I drew at once and fired, and as he dropped it came to me that I would have my watch, so I ran in and grabbed it and crowded it in my pocket and turned to go; but they just leapt me. I must have shot the first one, because he let go, and then I started to run as hard as I could lick for Fremont Street, where my broncho was hitched. As I went, everybody seemed to run and have a shot at me; they must have been excited, for none of 'em hit me till I got to the pony and loosed him and threw myself into the saddle; then I got it in the shoulder—bored me right through. And as I went down the street lickety split I got it again in the left leg—poor shootin' eh?"

"But did Tomlin shoot at you?" I asked.

"I guess so," was the reply.

"Why didn't he hit you?"

"The fellow who gits there fust is generally safe," was the answer.

"And afterwards," I asked, "what did you do?"

"I went off to St. Louis, and from there I wrote to my father, and I got the first letter from the old man I ever read. He told me I had witnessed for the faith, and he was proud of me, and he had put a mortgage on the farm because he saw he would not need it long, and he sent me the five hundred dollars he had raised. I had a good time in St. Louis on it and won nearly five thousand. While I was playin' round, the war broke out, and then I heard my father had been killed—they got him at last. I joined the Northern Army and was made a scout. That is how it began: that's all there's to it . . ."

Every one spoke of Wild Bill as being a dead shot, but I had no idea how good he was till on the trail.

We had all been skylarking, and some one proposed to shoot for money. A piece of paper was plastered up on one of the fence posts, perhaps four inches wide by five long. We stood about 40 yards away from the post and paid a dollar for a shot; whoever hit the paper got five dollars; but there were a great many more misses than hits.

Suddenly some one proposed to ride past the paper and see if he could hit it from the galloping horse. We had missed twenty times, every one had missed, when I suddenly saw Wild Bill passing on his horse. I ran over to him and asked him if he would try. None of us had been able to ride past and hit the mark.

"How often do you want hits?" asked Bill.

"Three or four times, if it would be possible," was my answer, "please do it."

He smiled, rode away a few yards and then turned round and came at full speed past the post, perhaps thirty yards away. As he came he whipped out two revolvers and fired right and left, two shots from each and then went on and disappeared. When we got to the paper we found four bullets in it; they could be covered by the palm of one's hand. Such markmanship put an end to the game. We all realized that such skill was beyond our hoping. He was the surest shot, as the kids say, since a horse-pistol was raised from a Colt.

Lonesome Dove

BY LARRY MCMURTRY

Stop for a moment and conjure up your ideal cowboy. What's he like? In this remarkable story, our stereotypical image of the Cowboy as a young man, is turned a little on its ear. Augustus McCrae and Captain Call are both old-hands. Neither of them is the strong silent type either: positively garrulous, in fact. It helps of course, that in them Larry McMurtry has created two of the most beloved characters in American literature.

Out on the trail, as you push your cattle north, a kind of isolation sets in. Your attention is so fixed on the care of the herd, the landscapes you must traverse, and company of your fellows, that a man can lose track of how the rest of the world has changed. In that case, it may be a good idea to get yourself back to some place you once knew well, and take stock.

This excerpt is taken from Larry McMurtry's masterly, 1986 Pulitzer-prize winning novel *Lonesome Dove*.

★   ★   ★   ★   ★

"Well, if we wasn't doomed to begin with, we're doomed now," Augustus said, watching Bolivar ride away. He enjoyed every opportunity for pronouncing doom, and the loss of a cook was a good one.

"I expect we'll poison ourselves before we get much farther, with no regular cook," he said. "I just hope Jasper gets poisoned first."

"I never liked that old man's cooking anyway," Jasper said.

"You'll remember it fondly, once you're poisoned," Augustus said.

Call felt depressed by the morning's events. He did not particularly lament the loss of the wagon—an old wired-together wreck at best—but he did lament the loss of Bol. Once he formed a unit of men he didn't like to lose one of them, for any reason. Someone would have to assume extra work, which seldom sat well with whoever had to do it. Bolivar had been with them ten years and it was trying to lose him suddenly, although Call had not really expected him to come when he first announced the trip. Bolivar was a Mexican. If he didn't miss his family, he'd miss his country, as the Irishman did. Every night now, Allen O'Brien sang his homesick songs to the cattle. It soothed the cattle but not the men—the songs were too sorrowful.

Augustus noticed Call standing off to one side, looking blue. Once in a while Call would fall into blue spells—times when he seemed almost paralyzed by doubts he never voiced. The blue spells never came at a time of real crisis. Call thrived on crisis. They were brought on by little accidents, like the wagon breaking.

"Maybe Lippy can cook," Augustus suggested, to see if that would register with Call.

Lippy had found an old piece of sacking and was wiping the mud off his head. "No, I never learned to cook, I just learned to eat," Lippy said.

Call got on his horse, hoping to shake off the low feeling that had settled over him. After all, nobody was hurt, the herd was moving well, and Bol was no great loss. But the low feeling stayed. It was as if he had lead in his legs.

"You might try to load that gear on them mules," he said to Pea.

"Maybe we can make a two-wheel cart," Pea said. "There ain't much wrong with the front of the wagon. It's the back end that's busted up."

"Dern, Pea, you're a genius for figuring that out," Augustus said.

"I guess I'll go into San Antonio," Call said. "Maybe I can hire a cook and buy a new wagon.

"Fine, I'll join you," Augustus said.

"Why?" Call asked.

"To help judge the new chef," Augustus said. "You'd eat a fried stove lid if you was hungry. I'm interested in the finer points of cooking, myself. I'd like to give the man a tryout before we hire him."

"I don't see why. He won't have nothing much tenderer than a stove lid to cook around this outfit anyway," Jasper said. He had been very disappointed in the level of the grub.

"Just don't get nobody who cooks snakes," he warned. "If I have to eat any more snakes I'm apt to give notice."

"That's an idle threat, Jasper," Augustus said. "You wouldn't know where to go if you was to quit. For one thing, you'd be skeert to cross a river."

"You ought to let him be about that," Call said, when they had ridden out of earshot. Jasper's fear of water was nothing to joke about. Call had seen grown men get so scared of crossing rivers that it was practically necessary to knock them out at every crossing—and a shaky man was apt to panic and spook the herd. Under normal circumstances, Jasper Fant was a good hand, and there was nothing to be gained by riding him about his fear of water.

On the way to San Antonio they passed two settlements—nothing more than a church house and a few little stores, but settlements anyway, and not ten miles apart.

"Now look at that," Augustus said. "The dern people are making towns everywhere. It's our fault, you know."

"It ain't our fault and it ain't our business, either," Call said. "People can do what they want."

"Why, naturally, since we chased out the Indians and hung all the good bandits," Augustus said. "Does it ever occur to you that everything we done was probably a mistake? Just look at it from a nature standpoint. If you've got enough snakes around the place you won't be overrun with rats or varmints. The way I see it, the Indians and the bandits have the same job to do. Leave 'em be and you won't constantly be having to ride around these dern settlements."

"You don't have to ride around them," Call said. "What harm to they do?"

"If I'd have wanted civilization I'd have stayed in Tennessee and wrote poetry for a living," Augustus said. "Me and you done our work too well. We killed off most of the people that made this country interesting to begin with."

Call didn't answer. It was one of Gus's favorite themes, and if given a chance he would expound on it for hours. Of course it was nonsense. Nobody in their right mind would want the Indians back, or the bandits either. Whether Gus had ever been in his right mind was an open question.

"Call, you ought to have married and had six or eight kids," Augustus remarked. If he couldn't get anywhere with one subject he liked to move on to another. Call's spirits hadn't improved much. When he was low it was hard to get him to talk.

"I can't imagine why you think so," Call said. "I wonder what's become of Jake?"

"Why, Jake's moseying along—starved for a card game, probably," Augustus said.

"He ought to leave that girl and throw in with us," Call said.

"You ain't listening," Augustus said. "I was trying to explain why you ought to marry. If you had a passel of kids, then you'd always have a troop to boss when you felt like bossing. It would occupy your brain and you wouldn't get gloomy as often."

"I doubt that marriage could be worse than having to listen to you," Call said, "but that ain't much of a testimonial for it."

They reached San Antonio late in the day, passing near one of the old missions. A Mexican boy in a brown shirt was bringing in a small herd of goats.

"Maybe we ought to take a few goats to Montana," Augustus said. "Goats can be melodious, more so than your cattle. They could accompany the Irishman and we'd have more of a singsong."

"I'll settle for more of a wagon," Call said.

Fortunately they were able to buy one almost at once from a big livery stable north of the river. It was necessary to buy two more mules to pull the wagon back to the herd. Fortunately the mules were cheap, twenty dollars a head, and the big German who ran the livery stable threw in the harness.

Augustus volunteered to drive the wagon back to the herd on condition he could have a drink and a meal first. He hadn't been to San Antonio in years and he marveled at the new establishments that had sprung up.

"Why, this place'll catch New Orleans if it don't stop growing," he said. "If we'd put in a barbershop ten years ago we'd be rich now."

There was a big saloon on the main street that they'd frequented a lot in their rangering days. It was called the Buckhorn, because of the owner's penchant for using deer horns for coat and hat racks. His name was Willie Montgomery, and he had been a big crony of Augustus's at one time. Call suspected him of being a card sharp, but if so he was a careful card sharp.

"I guess Willie will be so glad to see us he'll offer us a free dinner, at least," Augustus said, as they trotted over to the saloon. "Maybe a free whore, too, if he's prospering."

But when they strode in, there was no sign of Willie or anyone they recognized. A young bartender with slick hair and a string tie gave them a look when they stepped to the bar, but seemed as if he could scarcely be troubled to serve them. He was wiping out glasses with a little white towel and setting each one carefully on a shelf. The saloon was mostly empty, just a few cardplayers at a table in the back.

Augustus was not one to stand patiently and be ignored by a bartender. "I'd like a shot of whiskey and so would my companion, if it ain't too much trouble," he said.

The bartender didn't look around until he had finished polishing the glass he had in his hand.

"I guess it ain't, old-timer," he said. "Rye, or what will it be?"

"Rye will do, provided it gets here quick," Augustus said, straining to be polite.

The young bartender didn't alter his pace, but he did provide two glasses and walked slowly back to get a bottle of whiskey.

"You dern cowboys ought to broom yourselves off before you walk in here," he said with an insolent look. "We can get all the sand we need without the customers bringing it to us. That'll be two dollars."

Augustus pitched a ten-dollar gold piece on the bar and as the young man took it, suddenly reached out, grabbed his head and smashed his face into the bar, before the young man could even react. Then he quickly drew his big Colt, and when the bartender raised his head, his broken nose gushing blood onto his white shirtfront, he found himself looking right into the barrel of a very big gun.

"Besides the liquor, I think we'll require a little respect," he said. "I'm Captain McCrae and this is Captain Call. If you care to turn around, you can see our pictures when we was younger. Among the things we don't put up with is dawdling service. I'm surprised Willie would hire a surly young idler like you."

The cardplayers were watching the proceedings with interest, but the young bartender was too surprised at having suddenly had his nose broken to say anything at all. He held his towel to his nose, which was still pouring blood. Augustus calmly walked around the bar and got the picture he had referred to, which was propped up by the mirror with three or four others of the same vintage. He laid the picture on the bar, took the glass the young bartender had just polished, slinging it lazily into the air back in the general direction of the cardplayers, and then the roar of the big Colt filled the saloon.

Call glanced around in time to see the glass shatter. Augustus had always been a wonderful pistol shot—it was pleasing to see he still was. All of the cardplayers scurried for cover except a fat man in a big hat. Looking more closely, Call remembered him—his name was Ned Tym, and he was a seasoned gambler, too seasoned to be disturbed by a little flying glass. When it stopped flying, Ned Tym coolly took his hat off and blew the glass from the brim.

"Well, the Texas Rangers is back in town," he said. "Hello, Gus. Next time I see a circus I'll ask them if they need a trick shot."

"Why, Ned, is that you?" Augustus said. "My old eyes are failing. If I'd recognized you I'd have shot your hat off and saved a glass. Where do you keep your extra aces these days?"

Before Ned Tym could answer, a man in a black coat came running down the stairs at the back of the saloon. He wasn't much older than the bartender.

"What's going on here, Ned?" the man asked, prudently stopping by the card table. Augustus still held the big pistol in his hand.

"Oh, nothing, John," Ned said. "Captain McCrae and Captain Call happened in and Captain McCrae gave us a little demonstration with his pistol, that's all."

"It ain't all," the bartender said, in a loud voice. "The old son of a bitch broke my nose."

With a movement so graceful it seemed almost gentle, Augustus reached across the bar and rapped the bartender above the ear with his gun barrel. A tap was enough. The bartender slid out of sight and was seen no more.

"Why'd you do that?" the man in the black coat asked. He was angry, but, even more, he seemed surprised. Call glanced at him and judged him no threat—he sipped his whiskey and left the theatrics to Augustus.

"I'm surprised you have to ask why I did that," Augustus said, holstering his gun. "You heard the name he called me. If that's city ways, they don't appeal to me. Besides, he was a dawdling bartender and deserved a lick. Do you own this place, or what's your gripe?"

"I own it," the man said. "I don't allow shooting in it, either."

"What became of Wee Willie Montgomery?" Augustus asked. "you didn't have to whack the bartender just to get a glass of whiskey when he owned it."

"Willie's woman run off," Ned Tym informed them. "He decided to chase her, so he sold the place to Johnny here."

"Well, I can't say that I think he made a good choice," Augustus said, turning back to the bar. "Probably chose bad in the woman department too. Maybe if he's lucky she'll get plumb away."

"No, they're living up in Fort Worth," Ned said. "Willie was determined not to lose her."

Call was looking at the picture Augustus had fetched from behind the bar. It was of himself and Gus and Jake Spoon, taken years before. Jack was grinning and had a pearl-handled pistol stuck in his belt, whereas he and Gus looked solemn. It had been taken in the year they chased Kicking Wolf and his band all the way to the Canadian, killing over twenty of them. Kicking Wolf had raided down the Brazos, messing up several families of settlers and scaring people in the little settlements. Driving them back to the Canadian had made the Rangers heroes for a time, though Call had known it was hollow praise. Kicking Wolf hadn't been taken or killed, and there was nothing to keep him on the Canadian for long. But for a few weeks, everywhere they went there was some photographer with his box, wanting to take their picture. One had cornered them in the Buckhorn and made them stand stiffly while he got his shot.

The young man in the black coat went over behind the bar and looked at the fallen bartender.

"Why did you have to break his nose," he asked.

"He'll thank me someday," Augustus said. "It will make him more appealing to the ladies. He looked too much like a long-tailed rat, as it was. With no better manners than he had, I expect he was in for a lonely life."

"Well, I won't have this!" the young man said loudly. "I don't know why you old cowboys think you can just walk in and do what you please. What's that picture doing on the bar?"

"Why, it's just a picture of us boys, back in the days when they wanted to make us senators," Augustus said. "Willie kept it on the mirror there so when we happened in we could see how handsome we used to look."

"I'm a notion to call the sheriff and have the two of you arrested," the young man said. "Shooting in my bar is a crime, and I don't care what you done twenty years ago. You can get out of here and be quick about it or you'll end up spending your night in jail." He got angrier as he spoke.

"Oh, now, John, I wouldn't threaten these gentlemen if I was you," Ned Tym said, appalled at what he was hearing. "This is Captain Call and Captain McCrae."

"Well, what's that to me?" the man said, whirling on Ned. "I never heard of them and I won't have these old cowboys coming in here and making this kind of mess."

"They ain't old cowboys," Ned said. "They're Texas Rangers. You've heard of them. You've just forgot."

"I don't know why I would have," the man said. "I just lived here two years, miserable ones at that. I don't necessarily keep up with every old-timer who ever shot at an Indian. It's mostly tall tales anyway, just old men bragging on themselves."

"John, you don't know what you're talking about," Ned said, growing more alarmed. "Captain Call and Captain McCrae would be the last ones to brag."

"Well, that's your opinion," John said. "They look like braggarts to me."

Call was beginning to feel annoyed, for the young man was giving them unmannerly looks and talking to them as if they were trash; but then it was partly Gus's fault. The fact that the bartender had been a little slow and insolent hadn't necessarily been a reason to break his nose. Gus was touchy about such things though. He enjoyed having been a famous Texas Ranger and was often put out if he didn't receive all the praise he thought he had coming.

Gus held the picture out so the young man could see it.

"You have to admit that's us," he said. "Why would you keep our picture propped up behind your bar and then expect us to stand there and be treated like spit when we walk in?"

"Oh, well, I never even noticed them dern pictures," John said. "I ought to have thrown all that old junk out, but I never got around to it. Just drink your drink and skedaddle or be ready to go to jail. Here comes the sheriff now."

Sure enough, in about a minute, Tobe Walker stepped into the bar. He was a heavyset man with a walrus mustache who looked older than his years. Call was amused to see him, for what the angry young man didn't know was that Tobe had been in their Ranger troop for four years, just before they quit. He had only been sixteen then, but he made a good Ranger. Tobe had looked up to both of them as if they were gods, and was an unlikely man to arrest them. His eyes widened when he saw them.

"Why, can it be?" he asked. "Captain Call?"

"Well, Tobe," Call said, shaking his hand.

Augustus, too, was highly amused by the turn of events.

"'I god, Tobe," he said, "I guess it's your duty to handcuff us and march us off to jail."

"Why would I do that?" Tobe asked. "There's times when I think I ought to jail myself, but I don't know why I'd want to jail you two."

"Because you're hired to keep the peace and these old soaks have been disturbing it," John said. The fact that Tobe obviously recognized them only made him more testy.

Tobe became immediately frosty. "What's that you say, John?" he asked.

"I guess you heard me, sheriff, unless you're deaf," John said. "These men came in here and broke my bartender's nose. Then one of them shot off a gun for no reason. Then they pistol-whipped the bartender. I offered them a chance to leave, but since they haven't, I'm a notion to file charges and let the law take its course."

He said his little say so pompously that it struck the three of them as funny. Augustus laughed out loud, Call and Tobe smiled, and even Ned Tym chimed in with a chuckle.

"Son, you've misjudged our reputation," Augustus said. "We was the law around here when you was still sucking a teat. So many people think we saved them from the Indians that if you was to bring charges against us, and any of the boys that rangered with us got wind of it, they'd probably hang *you*. Anyway, whacking a surly bartender ain't much of a crime."

"John, I'd advise you to stop your name-calling," Tobe said. "You're acting too hot. You'd best just apologize and bring me a whiskey."

"I'll be damned if I'll do either one," John said, and without another word stepped over the fallen bartender and went back upstairs.

"What's he got, a whore up there?" Augustus asked hopefully. He was beginning to feel restive and would have liked some female company.

"Yes, John keeps a *señorita*," Tobe said. "I guess you'll have to excuse him. He's from Mobile and I've heard it said people in those parts are hotheaded."

"Well, it ain't a local prerogative," Augustus said. "We've got hotheads in our crew, and ain't none of them from Mobile, Alabama."

They got a whiskey bottle, sat down at a table and chatted for a while, talking of old times. Tobe inquired after Jake, and they carefully refrained from mentioning that he was on the run from the law. While they were talking, the bartender got up and staggered out the back way. His nose had stopped bleeding but his shirt was drenched in blood.

"Hell, he looks like he's been butchered," Tobe said cheerfully.

Ned Tym and his friends soon resumed their card game, but the other players' nerves were shaken and Ned soon drained them of money.

Tobe Walker looked wistful when they told him they were taking a herd to Montana. "If I hadn't married, I bet I'd go with you," he said. "I imagine there's some fair pastures up there. Being a lawman these days is mostly a matter of collaring drunks, and it does get tiresome."

When they left, he went off dutifully to make his rounds. Augustus hitched the new mules to the new wagon. The streets of San Antonio were silent and empty as they left. The moon was high and a couple of stray goats nosed around the walls of the old Alamo, hoping to find a blade of grass. When they had first come to Texas in the Forties people had talked of nothing but Travis and his gallant losing battle, but the battle had mostly been forgotten and the building neglected.

"Well, Call, I guess they forgot us, like they forgot the Alamo," Augustus said.

"Why wouldn't they?" Call asked. "We ain't been around."

"That ain't the reason—the reason is we didn't die," Augustus said. "Now Travis lost his fight, and he'll get in the history books when someone writes up this place. If a thousand Comanches had cornered us in some gully and wiped us out, like the Sioux just done Custer, they'd write songs about us for a hundred years."

It struck Call as a foolish remark. "I doubt there was ever a thousand Comanches in one bunch," he said. "If there had been they would have taken Washington, D.C."

But the more Augustus thought about the insults they had been offered in the bar—a bar where once they had been hailed as heroes—the more it bothered him.

"I ought to have given that young pup from Mobile a rap or two," he said.

"He was just scared," Call said. "I'm sure Tobe will lecture him next time he sees him."

"It ain't the pint, Woodrow," Augustus said. "You never do get the pint."

"Well, what is it, dern it?" Call asked.

"We'll be the Indians, if we last another twenty years," Augustus said. "The way this place is settling up it'll be nothing but churches and dry-goods stores before you know it. Next thing you know they'll have to round up us old rowdies and stick us on a reservation to keep us from scaring the ladies."

"I'd say that's unlikely," Call said.

"It's dern likely," Augustus said. "If I can find a squaw I like, I'm apt to marry her. The thing is, if I'm going to be treated like an Indian, I might as well act like one. I think we spent our best years fighting on the wrong side."

Call didn't want to argue with nonsense like that. They were nearly to the edge of town, passing a few adobe hovels where the poorer Mexicans lived. In one of them a baby cried. Call was relieved to be leaving. With Gus on the prod, anything could happen. In the country, if he got mad and shot something, it would probably be a snake, not a rude bartender.

"We didn't fight on the wrong side," Call said. "What's a miracle is that you stayed on the right side of the law for as long as you have. Jake's too cowardly to be much of an outlaw, but you ain't."

"I may be one yet," Augustus said. "It'd be better than ending up like Tobe Walker, roping drunks for a living. Why, the man nearly cried when we left, he wanted to come so bad. Tobe used to be quick, and look at him now, fat as a gopher."

"It's true he's put on weight, but then Tobe was always chunky built," Call said. On that one, though, he suspected Gus was right. Tobe had looked at them sadly when they mounted to ride away.

The Last Running

BY JOHN GRAVES

The slaughtering of the last of the great buffalo herds was not merely the senseless act of vandalism it is often portrayed. There was method to it, and reason. With the buffalo gone, the native peoples were without a main prop of their culture, to say nothing of their subsistence. They would have no choice but to remove to reservations. Then again, the grasses and the water was wanted for the cattle, and cattle was king in those days.

In this story it is years later and an old cowboy sits on the porch of his ranch house ruminating on the days gone by and the life he has led. Within his view, in a paddock he has specially constructed, are fourteen buffalo, the last of their kind thereabouts. One day a band of Comanches turns up and demand, as their right, one of the bison.

This is a wonderful story of the end of the old west; bittersweet but bright and hard as a West Texas noonday sun.

★   ★   ★   ★   ★

They called him Pajarito, in literal trader-Spanish interpretation of his surname, or more often Tom Tejano, since he had been there in those early fighting days before the Texans had flooded up onto the plains in such numbers that it became no longer practical to hate them with specificity.

After the first interview, when he had climbed down from the bed where an aching liver held him and had gone out onto the porch to salute them, only to curse in outrage and clump back into the house when he heard what they wanted, the nine of them sat like grackles about the broad gray-painted steps and talked, in Comanche, about Tom Texan the Little Bird and the antique times before wire fences had partitioned the prairies. At least, old Juan the cook said that was what they were talking about.

Mostly it was the old men who talked, three of them, one so decrepit that he had had to make the trip from Oklahoma in a lopsided carryall drawn by a piebald mare, with an odd long bundle sticking out the back, the rest riding alongside on ponies. Of the other six, two were middle-aged and four were young.

Their clothes ran a disastrous gamut from buckskin to faded calico and blue serge, but under dirty Stetsons they wore their hair long and braided, plains style. Waiting, sucking Durham cigarettes and speaking Comanche, they sat about the steps and under the cottonwoods in the yard and ignored those of us who drifted near to watch them, except the one or two whom they considered to have a right to their attention. Twice a day for two days they built fires and broiled unsymmetrical chunks of the fat calf which, from his bed, furiously, Tom Bird had ordered killed for them. At night—it was early autumn—they rolled up in blankets about the old carryall and slept on the ground.

"They show any signs of leaving?" Tom Bird asked me when I went into his room toward evening of the second day.

I said, "No, sir. They told Juan they thought you could spare one easily enough, since all of them and the land too used to be theirs."

"They didn't used to be nobody's!" he shouted.

"They've eaten half that animal since they got here," I said. "I never saw anybody that could eat meat like that, and nothing but meat."

"No, nor ever saw anything else worth seeing," he said, his somber gray eyes brooding. He was one of the real ones, and none of them are left now. That was in the twenties; he was my great-uncle, and at sixteen he had run away from his father's farm in Mississippi to work his way to the brawling acquisitive Texas frontier. At the age of eighty-five he possessed— more or less by accident, since cattle rather than land had always meant wealth to him—a medium-large ranch in the canyon country where the Cap Rock falls away to rolling prairies, south of the Texas Panhandle. He had buried two wives and had had no children and lived there surrounded by people who worked for him. When I had showed up there, three years before the Comanches' visit, he had merely grunted at me on the porch, staring sharply at my frail physique, and had gone right on arguing with his manager about rock salt in the pastures. But a month later, maybe when he decided I was going to pick up weight and live, we had abruptly become friends. He was given to quick gruff judgments and to painful retractions.

He said in his room that afternoon, "God damn it. I'll see them in hell before they get one, deeper than you can drop an anvil."

"You want me to tell them that?"

"Hell, yes," he said. "No. Listen, have you talked any with that old one? Starlight, they call him."

I said that neither Starlight nor the others had even glanced at any of us.

Tom Bird said, "You tell him you're kin to me. He knows a lot, that one."

"What do you want me to say about the buffalo?"

"Nothing," he said and narrowed his eyes as a jab of pain shot through him from that rebellious organ which was speaking loudly now of long-gone years of drinking at plains mudholes and Kansas saloons. He grunted. "Not a damn thing," he said. "I already told them."

Starlight paid no attention at all when I first spoke to him. I had picked up a poor grade of Spanish from old Juan in three years but was timid about using it, and to my English he showed a weathered and not even disdainful profile.

I stated my kinship to Tom Bird and said that Tom Bird had told me to speak to him.

Starlight stared at the fourteen pampered bison grazing in their double-fenced pasture near the house, where my great-uncle could watch them from his chair in the evenings. He had bred them from seed stock given him in the nineties by Charles Goodnight, and the only time one of them had ever been killed and eaten was when the governor of the state and a historical society had driven out to give the old man some sort of citation. When the Comanches under Starlight had arrived, they had walked down to the pasture fence and had looked at the buffalo for perhaps two hours, hardly speaking, studying the cows and the one calf and the emasculated males and the two bulls—old Shakespeare, who had killed a horse once and had put innumerable men up mesquite trees and over fences, and his lecherous though rarely productive son, John Milton.

Then they had said, matter-of-factly, that they wanted one of the animals.

Starlight's old-man smell was mixed with something wild, perhaps wood smoke. His braids were a soiled white. One of the young men glanced at me after I had spoken and said something to him in Comanche. Turning then, the old Indian looked at me down his swollen nose. His face was hexagonal and broad, but sunken where teeth were gone. He spoke.

The young man said in English with an exact accent, "He wants to know what's wrong with old Tom Bird, not to talk to friends."

All of them were watching me, the young ones with more affability than the others. I said Tom Bird was sick in the liver, and patted my own.

Starlight said in Spanish, "Is he dying?"

I answered in Spanish that I didn't think so but that it was painful.

He snorted much like Tom Bird himself and turned to look again at the buffalo in the pasture. The conversation appeared to have ended, but not knowing how to leave I sat there on the top step beside the old Comanche, the rest of them ranged below us and eyeing me with what I felt to be humor. I took out cigarettes and offered them to the young man, who accepted the package and passed it along, and when it got back to me it was nearly empty. I got the impression that this gave them amusement, too, though no one had smiled. We all sat blowing smoke into the crisp evening air.

Then, it seemed, some ritual biding time had passed. Old Starlight began to talk again. He gazed at the buffalo in the pasture under the fading light and spoke steadily in bad Spanish with occasional phrases of worse English. The young Indian who had translated for me in the beginning lit a small stick fire below the steps. From time to time one of the other old men would obtrude a question or a correction, and they would drop into the angry Comanche gutturals, and the young man, whose name was John Oak Tree, would tell me what they were saying.

The story went on for an hour or so; when Starlight stopped talking they trooped down to the carryall and got their blankets and rolled up in them on the ground. In the morning I let my work in the ranch office wait and sat down again with the Comanches on the steps, and Starlight talked again. The talk was for me, since I was Tom Bird's kinsman. Starlight did not tell the story as I tell it here. Parts I had to fill in later in conversation with Tom Bird, or even from books. But this was the story.

★　★　★　★　★

Without knowing his exact age, he knew that he was younger than Tom Bird, about the age of dead Quanah Parker, under whom he had more than once fought. He had come to warrior's age during the big fight the white men had had among themselves over the black men. Born a Penateka or Honey Eater while the subtribal divisions still had meaning, he remembered the surly exodus from the Brazos reservation to Oklahoma in 1859, the expulsion by law of the Comanches from all of Texas.

But white laws had not meant much for another ten years or so. It was a time of blood and confusion, a good time to be a Comanche and fight the most lost of all causes. The whites at the Oklahoma agencies were Northern and not only tolerated but sometimes egged on and armed the parties striking down across the Red, with the full moon, at the line of settlements established by the abominated and tenacious Texans. In those days, Starlight said, Comanches held Texans to be another breed of white men, and even after they were told that peace had smiled again among whites, they did not consider this to apply to that race which had swarmed over the best of their grass and timber.

In the beginning, the raids had ritual formality and purpose; an individual party would go south either to make war, or to steal horses, or to drive off cattle for trading to the New Mexican *comancheros* at plains rendezvous, or maybe just reminiscently to run deer and buffalo over the old grounds. But the distinctions dimmed. In conservative old age Starlight believed that the Comanches' ultimate destruction was rooted in the loss of the old disciplines. That and smallpox and syphilis and whiskey. And Mackenzie's soldiers. All those things ran in an apocalyptic pack, like wolves in winter.

They had gone horse raiding down into the Brazos country, a dozen of them, all young and all good riders and fighters. They captured thirty horses here and there in the perfect stealth that pride demanded, without clashes, and were headed back north up the Keechi Valley near Palo Pinto when a Texan with a yellow beard caught them in his corral at dawn and killed two of them with a shotgun. They shot the Texan with arrows; Starlight himself peeled off the yellow scalp. Then, with a casualness bred of long cruelty on both sides, they killed his wife and two children in the log house. She did not scream as white women were said to do, but until a hatchet cleaved her skull kept shouting, "Git out! Git, git, git."

And collecting five more horses there, they continued the trek toward the Territory, driving at night and resting at known secret spots during the days.

The leader was a son of old Iron Shirt, Pohebits Quasho, bullet-dead on the Canadian despite his Spanish coat of mail, handed down from the old haughty days. Iron Shirt's son said that it was bad to have killed the woman and the children, but Starlight, who with others laughed at him, believed even afterward that it would have been the same if they had let the woman live.

What was certain was that the Texans followed, a big party with men among them who could cut trail as cleanly as Indians. They followed quietly, riding hard and resting little, and on the third evening, when the Comanches were gathering their herd and readying themselves to leave a broad enclosed creek valley where they had spent the day, their sentry on a hill yelled and was dead, and the lean horsemen with the wide hats were pouring down the hillside shouting the long shout that belonged to them.

When it happened, Starlight was riding near the upper end of the valley with the leader. The only weapons with them were their knives and Starlight's lance, with whose butt he had been poking the rumps of the restive stolen horses as they hazed them toward camp below. As they watched, the twenty or more Texans overrode the camp, and in the shooting and confusion the two Comanches heard the end of their five companions who had been there afoot.

"I knew this," the leader said.

"You knew it," Starlight answered him bitterly. "You should have been the sentry, Know-much."

Of the other two horse gatherers, who had been working the lower valley, they could see nothing, but a group of the Texans rode away from the camp in that direction, yelling and firing. Then others broke toward Starlight and the leader a half mile above.

"We can run around them to the plain below," the son of Iron Shirt said. "Up this creek is bad."

Starlight did not know the country up the creek, but he knew what he felt, and feeling for a Comanche was conviction. He turned his pony upstream and spurred it.

"Ragh!" he called to the leader in farewell. "You're dirty luck!" And he was right, for he never saw the son of Iron Shirt again. Or the other two horse gatherers either.

But the son of Iron Shirt had been right, too, because ten minutes later Starlight was forcing his pony among big fallen boulders in a root tangle of small steep canyons, each of which carried a trickle to the stream below. There was no way even to lead a horse up their walls; he had the feeling that any one of them would bring him to a blind place.

Behind him shod hoofs rang; he whipped the pony on, but a big Texan on a bay horse swept fast around a turn in the canyon, jumping the boulders, and with a long lucky shot from a pistol broke Starlight's pony's leg. The Comanche fell with the pony but lit cat-bouncing and turned, and as the Texan came down waited crouched with the lance. The Texan had one of the pistols that shot six times, rare then in that country. Bearing down, he fired three times, missing each shot, and then when it was the moment Starlight feinted forward and watched the Texan lurch aside from the long bright blade, and while he was off balance, Starlight drove it into the Texan's belly until it came out the back. The blade snapped as the big man's weight came onto it, falling.

Starlight sought the pistol for a moment but not finding it ran to the canyon wall and began climbing. He was halfway up the fifty feet of its crumbling face when the other Texan rode around the turn and stopped, and from his unquiet horse, too hastily, fired a rifle shot that blew Starlight's left eye full of powdered sandstone.

He was among swallows' nests. Their molded mud crunched under his hands; the birds flew in long loops, chittering about his head. Climbing, he felt the Texan's absorbed reloading behind and below him as the horse moved closer, and when he knew with certainty that it was time, looked around to see the long caplock rifle rising again . . .Watched still climbing, and guessing at the instant, wrenched himself hard to the right, seizing the roots of a cedar that grew almost at the top of the cliff.

The bullet smashed through his upper left arm, and he hung only by his right, but with the long wiry strength of trick horsemanship he swung himself up and onto the overhanging turf of the cliff's top. A round rock the size of a buffalo's head lay there. Almost without pausing he tugged it loose from the earth and rolled it back over the cliff. It came close. The Texan grabbed the saddle as his horse reared, and dropped his rifle. They looked at each other. Clutching a blood-greasy, hanging arm, the Comanche stared down at a big nose and a pair of angry gray eyes, and the young Texan stared back.

Wheeling, Starlight set off trotting across the hills. That night before hiding himself he climbed a low tree and quavered for hours like a screech owl, but no one answered. A month later, an infected skeleton, he walked into the Penateka encampment at Fort Sill, the only one of twelve to return.

That had been his first meeting with Tom Bird.

★ ★ ★ ★ ★

When telling of the fights, Starlight stood up and gestured in proud physical representation of what he and others had done. He did not give it as a story with a point; it was the recountal of his acquaintance with a man. In the bug-flecked light of a bulb above the house's screen door the old Indian should have looked absurd—hipshot, ugly, in a greasy black hat and a greasy dark suit with a gold chain across its vest, the dirty braids flying as he creaked through the motions of long-unmeaningful violence.

But I did not feel like smiling. I looked at the younger Indians expecting perhaps to find amusement among them, or boredom, or cynicism. It was not there. They were listening, most of them probably not even understanding the Spanish but knowing the stories, to an ancient man who belonged to a time when their race had been literally terrible.

In the morning Starlight told of the second time. It had been after the end of the white men's war; he was a war chief with bull horns on his head. Thirty well-armed warriors rode behind him when he stopped a trail herd in the Territory for tribute. Although the cowmen were only eight, their leader, a man with a black mustache, said that four whoa-haws were too many. He would give maybe two.

"Four," Starlight said. "Texan."

It was an arraignment, and the white man heard it as such. Looking at the thirty Comanches, he said that he and his people were not Texans but Kansas men returning home with bought cattle.

"Four whoa-haws," Starlight said.

The white man made a sullen sign with his hand and spoke to his men, who went to cut out the steers. Starlight watched jealously to make certain they were not culls, and when three of his young men had them and were driving them away, he rode up face to face with the white leader, unfooled even though the mustache was new.

"Tejano," he said. "Stink sonabitch." And reached over and twisted Tom Bird's big nose, hard, enjoying the rage barely held in the gray eyes. He patted his scarred left biceps and saw that the white man knew him, too, and reached over to twist the nose again, Tom Bird too prudent to stop him and too proud to duck his head aside.

"Tobacco, Texan," Starlight said.

Close to snarling, Tom Bird took out a plug. After sampling and examining it and picking a bit of lint from its surface, Starlight tucked it into his waistband. Then he turned his horse and, followed by his thirty warriors, rode away.

In those days revenge had still existed.

He had been, too, with Quanah Parker when the half-white chief had made a separate peace with Tom Bird—Tom Tejano the Pajarito now, looming big on the high plains—as with a government, on the old Bird range up along the Canadian. There had been nearly two hundred with Quanah on a hunt in prohibited territory, and they found few buffalo and many cattle. After the peace with Tom Bird they had not eaten any more wing-branded beef, except later when the Oklahoma agency bought Bird steers to distribute among them.

They had clasped hands there in Quanah's presence, knowing each other well, and in the cowman's tolerant grin and the pressure of his hard fingers Starlight had read more clearly the rout of his people than he had read it anywhere else before.

"Yah, Big-nose," he said, returning the grip and the smile. Tom Bird rode along with them hunting for ten days and led them to a wide valley twenty miles long that the hide hunters had not yet found, and they showed him there how their fathers had run the buffalo in the long good years before the white men. November it had been, with frosted mornings and yellow bright days; their women had followed them to dress the skins and dry the meat. It was the last of the rich hunting years.

After that whenever Tom Bird passed through Oklahoma he would seek out the Indian who had once pulled his nose and would sometimes bring presents.

But Starlight had killed nine white men while the fighting had lasted.

* * * * *

Dressed, Tom Bird came out onto the porch at eleven o'clock, and I knew from the smooth curve of his cheek that the liver had quit hurting. He was affable and shook all their hands again.

"We'll have a big dinner at noon," he told Starlight in the same flowing pidgin Spanish the old Comanche himself used. "Juan's making it especially for my Comanche friends, to send them on their trip full and happy."

Still unfooled, Starlight exhumed the main topic.

"No!" Tom Bird said.

"You have little courtesy," Starlight said. "You had more once."

Tom Bird said, "There were more of you then. Armed."

Starlight's eyes squinted in mirth which his mouth did not let itself reflect. Absently, Tom Bird dug out his Days O' Work and bit a chew, then waved the plug apologetically and offered it to the Comanche. Starlight took it and with three remaining front teeth haggled off a chunk, and pretended to put it into his vest pocket.

They both started laughing, phlegmy, hard-earned, old men's laughter, and for the first time—never having seen Tom Bird out-argued before—I knew that it was going to work out.

Tom Bird said, "Son of a coyote, you . . . I've got four fat *castrados*, and you can have your pick. They're good meat, and I'll eat some of it with you."

Starlight waggled his head mulishly. "Those, no," he said. "The big bull."

Tom Bird stared, started to speak, closed his mouth, threw the returned plug of tobacco down on the porch, and clumped back into the house. The Indians all sat down again. One of the other older men reached over and picked up the plug, had a chew, and stuck it into his denim jacket. Immobility settled.

"Liberty," Starlight said out of nowhere, in Spanish. "They speak much of liberty. Not one of you has ever seen liberty, or smelled it. Liberty was grass, and wind, and a horse, and meat to hunt, and no wire."

From beyond the dark screen door Tom Bird said, "The little bull."

Starlight without looking around shook his head. Tom Bird opened the door so hard that it battered back against the house wall, loosening flakes of paint. He stopped above the old Indian and stood there on bowed legs, looking down. "You rusty old bastard!" he shouted in English. "I ain't got but the two, and the big one's the only good one. And he wouldn't eat worth a damn."

Starlight turned his head and eyed him.

"All right," Tom Bird said, slumping. "All right."

"Thank you, Pajarito," Starlight said.

"Jimmy," the old man said to me in a washed-out voice, "go tell the boys to shoot Shakespeare and hang him up down by the washhouse."

"No," John Oak Tree said.

"What the hell you mean, no?" Tom Bird said, turning to him with enraged pleasure. "That's the one he wants. What you think he's been hollering about for two whole days?"

"Not dead," John Oak Tree said. "My grandfather wants him alive."

"Now ain't that sweet?" the old man said. "Ain't that just beautiful? And I can go around paying for busted fences from here to Oklahoma and maybe to the God damn Arctic Circle, all so a crazy old murdering Comanche can have him a pet bull buffalo."

Starlight spoke in Spanish, having understood most of the English. "Tom Tejano, listen," he said.

"What?"

"Listen," Starlight said. "We're going to kill him, Tom Tejano. We."

"My butt!" said Tom Bird, and sat down.

★   ★   ★   ★   ★

In the afternoon, after the fried chicken and the rice and mashed beans and the tamales and the blistering chili, after the courteous belching and the smoking on the porch, everyone on the ranch who could leave his work was standing in the yard under the cottonwoods as the nine Comanches brought their horses up from the lot, where they had been eating oats for two days, and tied them outside the picket fence, saddled.

After hitching Starlight's mare to the carryall, without paying any attention to their audience they began to strip down, methodically rolling their shed clothes into bundles with hats on top and putting them on the back of the carryall. Starlight reeled painfully among them, pointing a dried-up forefinger and giving orders. When they had finished, all of them but he wore only trousers and shoes or moccasins, with here and there scraps of the old bone and claw and hide and feather paraphernalia. John Oak Tree had slipped off the high-heeled boots he wore and replaced them with tennis sneakers.

A hundred yards away, gargling a bellow from time to time, old Shakespeare stood jammed into a chute where the hands had choused him. Between bellows, his small hating eye peered toward us from beneath a grayed board; there was not much doubt about how *he* felt.

The Indians took the long, blanketed bundle from the carryall and unrolled it.

"For God's sake!" a cowboy said beside me, a man named Abe Reynolds who had worked a good bit with the little buffalo herd. "For God's sake, this is nineteen damn twenty-three?"

I chuckled. Old Tom Bird turned his gray eyes on us and glared, and we shut up. The bundle held short bows, and quivers of arrows, and long, feather-hung, newly reshafted buffalo lances daubed with red and black. Some took bows and others lances, and among the bowmen were the two old men younger than Starlight, who under dry skins still had ridged segmented muscles.

"Those?" I said in protest, forgetting Tom Bird. "Those two couldn't. . ."

"Because they never killed one," he said without looking around. "Because old as they are, they ain't old enough to have hunted the animal that for two whole centuries was the main thing their people ate, and wore, and made tents and ropes and saddles and every other damn thing they had out of. You close your mouth, boy, and watch."

Starlight made John Oak Tree put on a ribboned medal of some kind. Then they sat the restless ponies in a shifting line, motley still but somehow, now, with the feel of that old terribleness coming off of them like a smell, and Starlight walked down the line of them and found them good and turned to raise his hand at Tom Bird.

Tom Bird yelled.

The man at the chute pulled the bars and jumped for the fence, and eight mounted Indians lashed their ponies into a hard run toward the lumpy blackness that had emerged and was standing there swaying its head, bawling-furious.

Starlight screeched. But they were out of his control now and swept in too eagerly, not giving Shakespeare time to decide to run. When the Indian on the fastest pony, one of the middle-aged men, came down on him shooting what looked like a steady jet of arrows from beside the pony's neck, the bull squared at him. The Indian reined aside, but not enough. The big head came up under the pony's belly, and for a moment horse and rider paused reared against the horns and went pin-wheeling backward into the middle of the on-rushing others.

"Them idiots!" Abe Reynolds said. "Them plumb idiots!"

One swarming pile then, one mass with sharp projecting heads and limbs and weapons, all of them yelling and pounding and hacking and stabbing, and when old Shakespeare shot out from under the pile, shrugging them helter-skelter aside, he made a run for the house. Behind him they came yipping, leaving a gut-ripped dead horse on the ground beside the chute and another running riderless toward the northeast. One of the downed hunters sat on the ground against the chute as though indifferently. The other—one of the two oldsters—was hopping about on his left leg with an arrow through the calf of his right.

But I was scrambling for the high porch with the spectators, those who weren't grabbing for limbs, though Tom Bird stood his ground cursing as Shakespeare smashed through the white picket fence like dry sunflower stalks and whirled to make another stand under the cottonwoods. Some of the Indians jumped the fence and others poured through the hole he had made, all howling until it seemed there could be no breath left in them. For a moment, planted, Shakespeare stood with arrows bristling brightly from his hump and his loins and took someone's lance in his shoulder. Then he gave up that stand, too, and whisked out another eight feet of fence as he leveled into a long run down the dirt road past the corrals.

They rode him close, poking and shooting.

And finally, when it was all far enough down the road to have the perspective of a picture, John Oak Tree swung out leftward and running parallel to the others pulled ahead and abruptly slanted in with the long bubbling shriek, loud and cutting above all the other noise, that you can call rebel yell or cowboy holler or whatever you want, but which deadly exultant men on horseback have likely shrieked since the Assyrians and long, long before. Shakespeare ran desperately free from the sharp-pointed furor behind him, and John Oak Tree took his dun pony in a line converging sharply with the bull's course, and was there, and jammed the lance's blade certainly just behind the ribs and pointing forward, and the bull skidded to his knees, coughed, and rolled onto his side.

"You call that fair?" Abe Reynolds said sourly.

Nobody had. It was not fair. Fair did not seem to have much to do with what it was.

Starlight's carryall was headed for the clump of horsemen down the road, but the rest of us were held to the yard by the erect stability of Tom Bird's back as he stood in one of the gaps in his picket fence. Beside the chute, Starlight picked up the two thrown Indians and the saddle from the dead horse, the old hunter disarrowed and bleeding now, and drove on to where the rest sat on their ponies around Shakespeare's carcass.

Getting down, he spoke to John Oak Tree. The young Indian dismounted and handed his lance to Starlight, who hopped around for a time with one foot in the stirrup and got up onto the dun pony and brought it back toward the house at a run, the lance held high. Against his greasy vest the big gold watch chain bounced, and his coattails flew, but his old legs were locked snugly around the pony's barrel. He ran it straight at Tom Bird where he stood in the fence gap, and pulled it cruelly onto its hocks three yards away, and held out the lance butt first.

"I carried it when I pulled your nose," he said. "The iron, anyhow."

Tom Bird took it.

"We were there, Tom Tejano," Starlight said.

"Yes," my great-uncle said. "Yes, we were there."

The old Comanche turned the pony and ran it back to the little group of his people and gave it to John Oak Tree, who helped him get back into the carryall. Someone had caught the loose pony. For a few moments all of them sat, frozen, looking down at the arrow-quilled black bulk that had been Shakespeare.

Then, leaving it there, they rode off down the road toward Oklahoma, past the fences of barbed steel that would flank them all the way.

A cowhand, surveying the deadly debris along the route of their run, said dryly, "A neat bunch of scutters, be damn if they ain't."

I was standing beside old Tom Bird, and he was crying. He felt my eyes and turned, the bloody lance upright in his hand, paying no heed to the tears running down the sides of his big nose and into his mustache.

"Damn you, boy," he said. "Damn you for not ever getting to know anything worth knowing. Damn me, too. We had a world, once."

Permissions Acknowledgments

Chapter 42 of *Lonesome Dove* by Larry McMurtry. Copyright © 1985 by Simon and Schuster. Reprinted with permission of author.

"Establishing a Ranch on the Plains" by John D. Young and James Frank Dobie. From *A Vaquero of the Brush Country: The Life and Times of John D. Young.* Copyright © 1929, 1957, 1998 by John D. Young and J. Frank Dobie.

"The Genesis of Pecos Bill," "The Adventures of Pecos Bill," and "The Exodus of Pecos Bill," by Moody C. Boatright. From *Tall Tales from Texas* (Dallas: Southwest Press, 1934). Reprinted as *Tall Tales from Texas Cow Camps.* Copyright © 1982 by Southern Methodist University.

The Last Running by John Graves. Copyright © 1959 by Atlantic Monthly Press. Copyright © 1974, 1990 by John Graves. Reprinted with permission of author.

"Sugar" by Tom McGuane. From *Some Horses.* Copyright © 1999 by The Lyons Press.

CPSIA information can be obtained
at www.ICGtesting.com
Printed in the USA
LVOW03s1921121217
559534LV00012B/1302/P

9 781592 289042